DARK SPACE UNIVERSE
THE ENEMY WITHIN

(1st Edition)

by Jasper T. Scott

www.JasperTscott.com

@JasperTscott

TABLE OF CONTENTS

ACKNOWLEDGMENTS

There are so many people to thank when it comes to writing and publishing a book. As always I have to say thank you to my wife for the support she provides at home. And then there's my editing team—a big thanks goes out to my editor, Aaron Sikes, and to my volunteer editor, Dave Cantrell (who really should get paid for all the work he puts in on my books). I'd also like to say a special thanks to Karol Ross for spending countless hours reading and commenting on my work. She saved me from more than a few overused phrases.

Finally, I'd like to thanks to all of my advance readers. I always cringe when I send out a rough draft of my work, because I know there's hundreds of typos and unclear passages, but these readers faithfully help me to find them, and somehow, they still have nice things to say about the book when they're finished reading! My sincere thanks go out to each of these brave individuals: Bruce A. Thobois, Chase Hanes, Claude Chavis, Daniel Eloff, Davis Shellabarger, Gary Matthews, George Dixon, Gregg Cordell, Harry Huyler, Ian F. Jedlica, John Nash, Karl Keip, Marten Ekema, Mary Kastle, Michael Madsen, Peter Hughes, and Rafael Gutierrez. Thank you, all of you!

To those who dare,
And to those who dream.
To everyone who's stronger than they seem.

"Believe in me / I know you've waited for so long / Believe in me / Sometimes the weak become the strong."

—STAIND, Believe

PREVIOUSLY IN DARK SPACE UNIVERSE

SPOILER ALERT: If you haven't read Dark Space Universe (Book 1), you may prefer to purchase and read it from Amazon, as the below synopsis covers the events of that book.

Etherus, the god and ruler of humanity, warned the three hundred million non-believers aboard *Astralis* of the dangers lurking beyond the Red Line, but he allowed them to leave his kingdom and seek the true nature of the universe by traveling to the cosmic horizon.

Tyra Forster, captain of the *Inquisitor,* along with Lucien Ortane and a crew of trained explorers, known as Paragons, blazed a path for *Astralis,* but they soon ran into the Faros, a hostile race of alien slavers. The Faros relentlessly chased them across multiple star systems until the *Inquisitor* became separated from *Astralis.*

Captain Forster and her crew spent the next eight years in stasis while their robotic navigator, Pandora, took them to the cosmic horizon and a rendezvous with *Astralis.* Soon after reaching that rendezvous, they learned that Pandora was actually a spy for the Faros, and an alien fleet arrived to enslave them all.

During the ensuing battle, the crew of the *Inquisitor* was forced to abandon ship and flee from *Astralis* in shuttles. All of the shuttles were intercepted or destroyed, except for Lucien's, which was badly damaged, but he managed to set down in a Faro colony with three of his fellow crew.

There the Faros' leader, Abaddon, nearly killed them, but a runaway Faro slave named Oorgurak helped them escape to Freedom Station, a haven for former Faro slaves-turned-pirates, known as Marauders.

Lucien and his surviving crew mates are certain that *Astralis* must have been captured by the Faro fleet. They are now looking for a Marauder captain who will help them find and rescue their people, but little do they know, the Faros' agenda isn't as simple as it seems, and the people of *Astralis* are in far greater danger than they think....

CHAPTER 1

Freedom Station

Garek stood in front of a broad viewport, watching alien ships glide in and out of Freedom station's hangar. It was a cavernous space with berths for starships lining the walls and ceiling. A fuzzy blue shield held the atmosphere in, and a dozen different species of aliens bustled around on the deck—ground crew for the various starships in the hangar.

Garek eyed the nearest ship: a smaller vessel, shaped like a winged-insect. He wondered how he could get aboard without being noticed.

He turned to look at the double-wide doors leading out into the hangar. Warnings lined those doors in an alien language. He could understand them thanks to the U-shaped translator band that the green-skinned Faro, *Oorgurak,* had given to him and the others. The warnings read:

CAUTION. NO GRAVITY BEYOND THIS POINT.

No problem there, Garek thought. He was already wearing mag boots. He went back to gazing at the insect-ship. Getting aboard wasn't his only problem. After that, he'd need to figure out how to fly it. What kind of security systems would it have? Would some of the crew still be on board?

Despair clawed at Garek's resolve. His plan to go back and find *Astralis* and rescue his daughter from the Faros was looking more and more desperate. He didn't even know the coordinates to the *Inquisitor's* brief rendezvous with *Astralis.*

A heavy hand landed on his shoulder, and Garek flinched away, already rounding on his would-be assailant. He had his stun pistol out and aimed at the being's head before his eyes even registered who it was.

"Hey, hold your fire! I just want to talk," Lucien said. Standing beside him was Brak, the Gor, and the kid's girlfriend, Addy.

Garek's aim didn't waver. "You're not going to talk me out of this."

Lucien glanced over his shoulder, as if checking to make sure no one else was there with them. He turned back and nodded to the viewport and the hangar beyond. "Those are alien ships out there. What do you think you're going to do? Even if you can sneak on board one of them, and it just happens to be empty, how do you think you're going to pilot it?"

Garek shrugged. "Won't be the first time I've flown an alien ship. They're all the same. Controls for thrust, pitch, and yaw. It's not like I'm planning to take it into combat."

"You might not have a choice. You think *Astralis* is

going to be mysteriously abandoned with your daughter there waiting for you? Besides, you don't even know where *Astralis* is! The only one who knew the coordinates of the rendezvous was Pandora, and Brak left her in pieces on the *Inquisitor's* bridge."

Garek felt a muscle jerk in his cheek. "Why don't you mind your own damn business and let me worry about rescuing my daughter?"

Lucien placed a hand on his shoulder once more. Garek glared at that hand.

"I'm sorry, Garek."

"So that's it, we're just giving up?"

"I never said that. Just because we can't go running back to *Astralis* doesn't mean we can't find and rescue our people. We know that the Faros are slavers, and three hundred million slaves aren't going to disappear without a trace. There'll be slave markets to sell them. We find those markets, and we find our people."

"And how do you propose we do that?"

"We join a Marauder crew as Oorgurak suggested, learn about the universe from them, and get our bearings. Hopefully by the time we figure out where to look for our people, we'll have enough money to pay one of these Marauder captains to take us there."

Garek scowled. Lucien's plan wasn't as immediately satisfying as his, but it was far more realistic. "Fine," he said, gesturing to the dark corridor he'd come down just a few minutes ago. "Lead the way."

* * *

Freedom Station

They followed Lucien through Freedom Station, walking down dirty, discolored corridors with flickering glow panels. Lucien was looking for the alien who had brought them here—Oorgurak. It made sense to offer their services to him first, if for no better reason than because he was the only Marauder captain they knew. It also didn't hurt that Oorgurak was some kind of Faro super soldier, one of the so-called *Elementals*.

"What are you looking for?" Addy asked.

Lucien shook his head. "Our green-skinned Faro friend. He might be willing to let us sign-on with his ship."

"He was a prisoner until recently. What makes you think he even has a ship?" Addy asked.

"When we were in the mess hall together he mentioned he has a crew, so he must have a ship."

Garek snorted. "So you're just going to wander the station aimlessly until you bump into him?"

Lucien stopped walking and turned to face the scarred veteran. "You have a better idea?"

"Matter of fact I do." Garek turned to the nearest alien passerby and tapped him on the shoulder. "Hey, do you know—"

The alien rounded on him with a shrill, echoing scream. White tentacles writhed around the being's head like snakes, each of them with a mouth and fangs. The being's face was a wrinkly, sunken horror of red quills with dozens of glinting silver eyes nestled between them. The tentacles lunged and snapped their jaws bare inches from Garek's nose, each of them screaming in his face before retreating.

After a few seconds, the tentacles retreated and relaxed to dangle around the alien's shoulders like hair, but two fat tentacles remained erect. They gave an echoing scream that Lucien's translator band interpreted as: "Do not touch us."

With that, the alien turned and stalked off on two bony white legs.

"Maybe don't try that again..." Addy whispered.

Even Brak looked shocked.

"What in the netherworld..." Garek muttered.

"Netherworld is right," Lucien added. A flicker of movement caught his eye, and he turned to see an alien melting out of the shadows of an alcove beside them. It was a gray-skinned humanoid. He was short with huge slanting, lidless black eyes, and an over-sized head.

It spoke in a warbling stutter: "You are lucky. Scarpathians have been known to kill for less."

Lucien frowned. "Who are you?"

"I am Ka'ta'wa."

"Katawa?" Lucien asked.

The alien inclined its over-sized head to them. "Yes."

A bulky black shape moved into Lucien's peripheral vision and he turned to see a lumbering black monster approaching them, walking on four legs as thick as tree trunks. It had a mouth full of protruding teeth, and a single, giant orange eye, striated with red veins in the center of its horned forehead.

A small hairless red creature rode on its back.

"Get out the way!" the little red being chirped at them in an amplified voice. "*It* is hungry!"

Katawa glanced at the approaching aliens, and then back to Lucien. "Follow me."

"Why?" Garek demanded while keeping half an eye on the lumbering monster headed their way.

"To talk about rescuing your people," Katawa replied, and then turned to walk down a narrow corridor that branched off from the one where they were standing.

Lucien watched the alien go. The corridor Katawa had chosen was lit by a solitary glow panel that flickered on and off, periodically casting both the little alien and its surroundings into utter darkness.

"I don't like the look of this," Addy said.

"Neither do I," Lucien said, shaking his head.

Garek wordlessly followed the gray alien.

"Garek, wait! It could be a trap," Addy said.

Brak hissed. "If it is a trap, the gray one will be sorry for springing it," the Gor said before starting down the corridor after Katawa and Garek.

Lucien cast one more glance at the lumbering one-eyed beast heading toward him. It licked its lips with a fat purple tongue, and splattered the deck with shiny gobs of drool.

"You crazy, you!" the little red alien screamed from atop its mount. "*It* will swallow you whole!"

Lucien grabbed Addy's hand and pulled her into the narrow corridor after Garek. "Trap or not, we'll stand a better chance against the one small gray alien than that monster."

They turned to watch as the beast reached the spot where they had been standing. It pawed the deck angrily, its claws shrieking against the scuffed metal. Then it lifted its giant head and sniffed the air in great snorts. After just a second, it turned to face them. The monster's orange eye flicked up and down, then side to side, as if measuring the adjoining corridor to see if it would fit.

"Let's go..." Lucien urged, tugging on Addy's hand to pull her deeper into the corridor.

She nodded absently.

The monster lunged at them. Its jaws snapped right in front of Addy's face, blasting them with its fetid breath. Lucien reflectively yanked Addy away from the beast.

The red little humanoid laughed and slapped his mount. "I told you! Crazy, you!"

Lucien pulled Addy along, hurrying to catch up with Garek and Brak. They were with the gray alien, standing outside a door. The corridor plunged into darkness, and Lucien slowed his pace. He groped the walls for support. The light snapped back on just as Lucien's eyes were beginning to adjust. He squinted through the glare to see that Garek and Brak were gone, as was the gray alien.

CHAPTER 2

Freedom Station

Lucien and Addy ran to the door where they'd last seen Garek and Brak. The light in the corridor flickered off just as they reached the door, plunging everything into darkness once more. Lucien activated the headlamps on his helmet just in time to see the door slide open and Katawa appear. The alien's big black eyes squinted up into the light radiating from Lucien's headlamps. After a moment's hesitation, Katawa pulled him into the room with surprising strength, and Addy followed.

The room was small, with low ceilings and appropriately small furniture—a low bed/sofa, and equally low table and chairs with a tiny kitchen along the adjacent wall. Brak stood in one corner by the bed, his chin almost touching his chest because of the low ceiling. Garek stood beside him with arms crossed, his helmet brushing the ceiling.

The door slid shut behind them and the gray alien went to sit at his table. He gestured to the chairs around him.

"Please, sit."

Seeing that there was nowhere to hide an ambush, Lucien relaxed somewhat and pulled out a small chair to sit awkwardly beside the alien. His knees were forced up to his chest by the chair's stubby legs. It was like attending a child's tea party. Addy sat down beside him, while Brak sat on the other side of Katawa and turned his chair so he could stretch his legs out behind the table. He rolled his giant shoulders, working the kinks out of his neck from standing under such a low ceiling. Garek came and stood beside the table, his arms still crossed.

"What's this about?" Lucien asked, nodding to Katawa.

"You said you wanted to talk about rescuing our people," Garek added. "How do you even know they need rescuing?"

Katawa blinked his huge eyes at them. "I overheard you talking in the mess hall."

Lucien began nodding slowly. Not long ago they'd been talking with Oorgurak about rescuing their people over a meal in the station's mess hall. They'd asked Oorgurak for help, and Oorgurak had asked them what they had to offer in exchange. When it became apparent that they had nothing to offer, Oorgurak had lost all interest in the topic.

The Marauders were pirates and mercenaries, all ex-slaves of the Farosien Empire with no greater ambition than their own survival and continued freedom. Asking them to pick a fight with their old masters for free was offensive to them. But for some reason, this particular Marauder was offering to help. Lucien had a feeling it wasn't out of the kindness of his heart.

"What do you want in exchange for helping us rescue our people?" he asked.

"You help me go home."

"Where's home?" Lucien asked.

"Etheria."

Lucien blinked and shook his head. "You're from Etheria?"

Katawa nodded.

That didn't fit for a number of reasons. Lucien had been to Etheria, and he'd only ever met Etherians living there. If these gray aliens inhabited the same galaxy as the Etherians, why hadn't he seen them before? Furthermore, what was someone from Etheria doing this far outside the Red Line? Etherus had forbidden travel beyond that line for as long as anyone could remember. *Astralis* had only been allowed to cross it at their own risk, and soon after they'd done so, they'd found out why: it was a political boundary between the Etherian and Farosien Empires, and anyone who crossed it was fair game for Abaddon.

"Let's say I believe you," Lucien said. "How are we supposed to help you get home? We don't even have a ship. And since you need our help, I suspect you don't have one, either."

"I do have a ship."

Lucien felt his eyes narrowing. "Then we're back to why."

"I need your help to find the lost fleet."

Addy leaned forward with sudden interest, her brow

furrowed and green eyes sharp. "What lost fleet?"

"The one the Etherians sent to negotiate with Abaddon."

Lucien slowly shook his head. "You're saying the Etherians took a whole fleet past the Red Line? When was that? I've never heard about it."

"More than ten thousand years ago."

Lucien sat back with a frown. "Then they must have returned home by now."

Katawa shook his head. "The crew was executed by Abaddon. Before they died they sent their fleet away to keep Abaddon from finding it."

"And it's been lost ever since?" Addy asked.

Again, the alien inclined his head. "Yes."

"How do you know all of this?" Lucien asked.

"Because I was one of the crew."

Lucien blinked. "So you're over ten thousand years old?"

The alien shook his head. "I am over five hundred thousand years old."

"And you came from Etheria ten thousand years ago," Lucien said, still not buying the story.

Katawa inclined his head in another shallow nod.

"You've been out here all this time?" Addy asked. "Why didn't you go home?"

"I do not know the way."

"But this lost Etherian fleet has the location programmed into their nav computers," Lucien suggested.

"Yes."

"You're from Etheria and you don't know where it is?" Lucien asked. "How's that possible?"

"We could not risk allowing the location to fall into enemy hands. We were made to forget the way before we left. Our ships were programmed to return there automatically."

"This is a waste of time," Garek said. "By now the Faros have found that fleet and re-purposed it for themselves."

Katawa shook his head. "If they had found it, they would have developed the same technologies by now."

"You're saying that Farosien tech is inferior to Etherian tech?" Garek asked.

Katawa looked up at him, blinking his huge eyes. "You did not know this?"

"The Etherians are very secretive," Lucien explained. "But it's reassuring to hear that someone might be capable of defeating the Faros."

"So the question is, if they can, why don't they?" Addy said. "Why allow the Farosiens to exist? Why not just destroy them and set all of the slaves free?"

Lucien felt his brow tense into a knot. "That's a good question." He nodded to Katawa. "You lived in Etheria. Why don't they attack the Faros?"

Katawa shook his oversized head. "I do not know. I have also wondered this."

Addy frowned. "You said it's been ten thousand years. In all of that time they never sent anyone to rescue you? You're one of them!"

"Perhaps they do not wish to lose another fleet."

Addy snorted and shook her head.

"Let's say we agree to help you," Lucien said. "How can we help you find this missing fleet, and how does finding the fleet help *us?*"

"You can be made to look like Faros. I cannot. You will be able to move freely through the empire."

"So you want to paint us blue and shave off all our hair," Garek said. "Then what? We go around randomly asking the Faros if they've seen a derelict fleet? If that's your strategy, it's no wonder you haven't been able to find anything in ten thousand years."

"You didn't answer my second question," Lucien pointed out. "How does finding this fleet help us?"

"You wish to fight a war against Abaddon. You will need ships for that. If you find the fleet, you can keep the vessels."

Garek appeared to perk up with this suggestion. "How many ships were in the fleet?"

"More than a thousand, all heavily armed."

Garek whistled. "When Etherus sends an envoy, he doesn't mess around."

"Where do we start looking?" Lucien asked.

"First you must be disguised. Then we will take my ship to follow the trail."

"There's a trail?" Addy asked.

"Yes. I have kept notes from my searching."

Lucien nodded along with that and turned to Addy. "What do you think?"

"It's a risky plan. What if someone discovers we're not actually Faros? We won't sound like them when we talk."

"That's a good point," Lucien replied. The translator bands they wore didn't replace their native language or their accents; the technology simply allowed them to understand what was said in other languages.

"Your minds can be programmed to speak their

language. I have a device for this."

Lucien's brow furrowed. "Will it teach us their accents, too?"

The gray alien inclined his head. "Yes."

"Sounds like you've been planning this for a long time," Garek said.

"I had hoped to convince Oorgurak and the other green skins, but they do not believe the fleet can be found."

Garek grunted. "Maybe because the Etherians flew it into a black hole. Why leave it drifting somewhere for the Faros to find? And how could Abaddon kill the entire crew without destroying their ships? You expect me to believe they left more than a thousand warships unattended while they went to negotiate with a hostile alien race?"

"They were not unattended. My people were at the helm."

"And they stole away with the fleet when negotiations broke down," Addy said, nodding.

"Yes. We hid the fleet and erased our memories of its location."

"Why?" Garek demanded. "Why not use it to go home?"

"We learned things about Etherus that made us want to stay here. The fleet was to be our insurance that our people would not become slaves. Only one of us knew its location. If we were enslaved, he was to keep the fleet's location a secret. If, however, we were made citizens of the Farosien Empire, its location would be revealed."

"Why not simply keep the ships and use them to defend yourselves?" Addy asked. "You could have formed your own empire out here."

"A thousand ships would never have been enough to defend us."

"And yet we're supposed to risk our lives finding them so we can use them to fight a war against the Faros?" Garek asked.

"Defending a colony is different from hiding in the shadows and striking targets of opportunity."

Lucien turned to Addy. "I'm willing to risk it if you are."

Addy nodded. "What have we got to lose?"

"Just our lives," Lucien said.

"It's worth the risk. Can you imagine all the worlds we're going to see? If we look and sound like Faros, they won't even try to attack us! We'll be able to come and go as we please."

Lucien looked to Brak next. Enigmatic as ever, the Gor hadn't said a thing in all this time. "What do you think, buddy?"

"I think they cannot make *me* look like a Faro."

That was a good point. Humans and Faros looked very much alike, but Gors were completely different, from their skull-shaped faces to their giant feet and over-sized, muscular frames. "What about Brak?" Lucien asked.

"He will be a shadow."

"A what?" Lucien asked.

"You mean he'll be *like* a shadow?" Addy suggested.

Katawa shook his head. "Shadows are Faro slaves. They appear as shadows. Their garments hide their features to make them less noticeable and more aesthetically pleasing to the Faros."

Lucien remembered the shadowy beings that they'd

seen when they first met the Faros and Abaddon. Brak had killed a few of them on the landing pad before running away on his impulsive quest to free Faro slaves.

"I will also be a shadow," Katawa said.

Lucien waited for Brak's reaction. After a moment, Brak bared his dagger-sharp black teeth in a grin. "I agree with this plan."

"Garek?" Lucien asked.

The scarred veteran hesitated. "We should talk about this."

"We are talking."

In private. Garek's voice echoed inside Lucien's head, spoken via their augmented reality contacts (ARCs) rather than aloud.

What's wrong? Lucien asked. *I thought you wanted to rescue your daughter?*

I do, but I don't trust this guy.

What does he have to gain by lying to us? Lucien countered. *If he's a spy for Abaddon, there are less convoluted ways to capture us. In fact, if he is a spy, why not simply call in the Faros' fleet and capture all of the Marauders on Freedom Station? Why lure us away with this story?*

I don't know. He might not be a spy, but he has an agenda that he's not telling us about.

You can't possibly know that, Lucien replied.

"Well?" Addy asked, growing impatient with the awkward silence.

"Majority rules," Lucien decided, nodding to Garek. "You can either join us or not."

Garek frowned, but said nothing.

Lucien turned to Katawa. "When do we start?"

"Right now." The gray alien said as he rose from the table. "Follow me."

CHAPTER 3

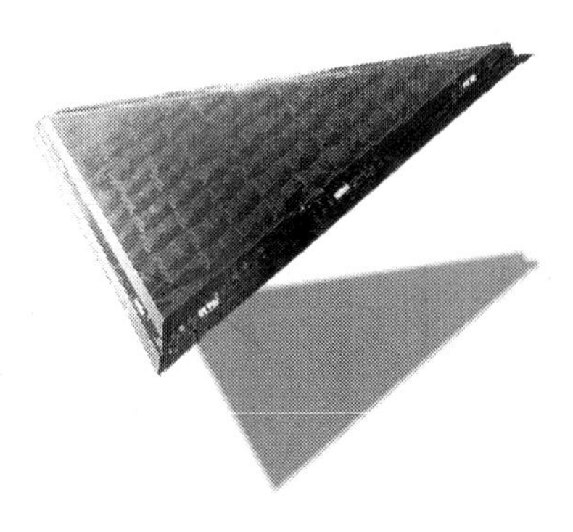

Astralis

SEVEN DAYS UNTIL THE FAROS ATTACK...

Chief of Security Lucien Ortane sat in the front of an unmarked hover car, eating a burger and watching the back door of a night club in Sub-District Two of *Astralis.* Brak sat beside him eating his own kind of burger—all meat, no bun, and so raw it was practically dripping.

"Don't get blood on the seats," Lucien mumbled around a mouthful.

Brak grunted and stuffed the rest of the raw burger into his mouth.

Lucien shook what was left of his meal at the rear entrance. "I don't get it. My source said the deal was going down here. Tonight." They'd parked in the shadows of an alley that ran crosswise to the one looping around the night club. The club was located in a particularly seedy part of Sub-District Two, and *night club* was a misnomer. The Crack of Dawn was a strip club, pure and simple, but more than that, it was a front for the Coretti Brothers' black market arms dealing and money laundering.

The whole neighborhood was run by the Corettis, and the police in Sub-District Two knew better than to go patrolling around here. The only cops found in this neighborhood were dead ones, hence why no one from Lucien's department had volunteered for this mission. Unfortunately, since Sub-District Two wasn't technically part of Fallside's jurisdiction, the mission was volunteer only. Lucien could have passed on his tip to the chief of security for Sub-District Two and let their department handle it, but he wasn't convinced that would amount to anything. He strongly suspected the chief and/or several of his deputies and detectives were on the Coretti brothers' payroll.

"Look," Brak pointed. The back door of the club opened and six sketchy-looking characters poured out—including one Joseph Coretti, eldest of the three Coretti brothers. Lucien would have recognized him anywhere: medium height and build, skinny and pale to the point of looking sickly, with gaunt cheeks and blue-black hair slicked back from his forehead. He had a square jaw and silver eyes that shone in the dark like two pearls. A *glow* stick dangled out the side of his mouth, glowing blue-white all along its length and glowing orange from the lit end.

Lucien could have pulled him up on charges for drug possession right there, but there was that little problem of not having jurisdiction. Not to mention, simple possession charges wouldn't keep Joe Coretti locked up for long.

Two of the goons with Joe were pushing a large black case on a hover cart between them. Something was off about the taller of the two, but Lucien couldn't quite tell what it was... short dark hair, dark eyes, blank, generic face... it wasn't his appearance. Something else. He stood too straight. His movements were too precise, like a machine. But he looked human. An android maybe? Androids were illegal. That might be another thing to pin on Coretti. No way to prove it without a warrant, though.

Lucien watched as the rigid man and his more-human looking counterpart pushed the case to the front of the group and waited there. Joe blew out a stream of smoke and glanced up at a flickering street light.

"Ten to one there's weapons in that case," Lucien said.

Brak nodded. "Want me to get a better look?"

Lucien glanced at his partner. The Gor was a unique asset on stakeouts thanks to his innate cloaking abilities. "Not yet. Let's wait and see who shows up."

They didn't have to wait long. A long black hover van with tinted windows came screaming down the alley, flying low to the ground.

"Hello..." Lucien whispered. The car stopped right in front of Coretti's gang and four tall men in black suits jumped out.

Joe nodded to the case on the hover cart and his men popped it open, but the four men in suits blocked Lucien's view of the contents.

"All right, now you can go," Lucien said, nodding to Brak.

The Gor nodded back and the air shimmered around him as he cloaked himself. The door slid open, and he slipped out. Lucien watched him go, then went back to watching the group of gangsters in the alley. The four who'd arrived in the van were gesturing wildly to the case, as if it wasn't what they'd ordered. Coretti's goons began posturing in turn, and soon everyone had drawn their sidearms and was pointing them at each other's heads.

"Go on, start shooting," Lucien mumbled. "Save me the trouble of booking you all later."

Technically none of them would die thanks to cloning and the technology for transfer of consciousness, but resurrection wasn't a given right when it came to criminals. Murderers, for example, were almost never brought back—a kind of passive death penalty.

Unfortunately, none of the gangsters opened fire. Joe held up his hands and said something that cooled everyone's tempers. They all holstered their weapons, and the four black-suited men shut the case and loaded it into the back of their van. Lucien frowned, wishing he could hear what had been said between them. He hadn't brought any listening gear because he had Brak, but he hadn't anticipated this deal going down so fast.

Before the men in suits could leave the scene, Lucien saw the telltale shimmer of a cloaking shield deactivate, and a naked gray monster appeared, standing to one side of the gangsters.

"Brak, you dumb skriff!" Lucien gritted out.

All eyes turned to the naked Gor, and weapons flew out of their holsters once more.

Lucien waved open the door on his side of the hover car and ran out with his own sidearm drawn. "Fallside PD!" he yelled, flashing his holographic badge in their eyes as he ran. "Drop your weapons and put your hands in the air!"

Joe Coretti smirked around the butt of his glow stick as Lucien skidded to a stop beside Brak.

"Well, well. Aren't you a little far from home, Chief?"

"What's in the case, Coretti?"

"You got a warrant? Oh, wait—" Coretti broke off, shaking his head. "—not your jurisdiction. I almost forgot."

"It won't matter who's jurisdiction this is when I submit the recordings I just took of this deal going down. I've got you on at least three different charges here."

"You sure about that?" Joe asked. "You just asked me what's in the case, so I'm betting you've got nothing."

"Hand over the case and we'll see about that."

The men in black suits traded glances with each other, but said nothing.

"Or what?" Coretti smiled smugly and blew a cloud of fragrant smoke in Lucien's direction.

Lucien frowned. He had no authority here, and Joe knew it. The whole purpose of tonight's stakeout had been to get enough evidence for a warrant, not to bring Coretti in prematurely without any hard evidence to make a conviction stick. *What was Brak thinking?*

"We'll be back," Lucien said, and grabbed Brak's forearm, dragging him back toward their hover car.

"Sure you will," Joe said. "In the meantime—" He made a shooing gesture with both hands, and gold rings glinted in the dim, flickering light of the alley.

Lucien walked backward all the way to the car, not taking eyes off any of them for a second. Once they were back inside, the black van raced away and Joe Coretti returned to his club, waving a vulgar sign at them as he left.

When they were all gone, Lucien shot a scowl at Brak. "What the frek were you thinking?"

Brak bared his black teeth and hissed. "They were about to leave. I had to get their attention."

"Why?"

"I think I recognize one of them. I need to see his face to be sure."

"And?"

"It is who I think. Judge Cleever's son."

Lucien blinked. "Are you sure?"

"Yes."

Lucien played back the visual log from his ARCs and ran the faces of the men in black suits through *Astralis's* database. Sure enough, one of them was a match for Titarus Cleever, only child and son of High Court Judge Exolia Cleever. Lucien checked Titarus's record and found a long list of bookings for misdemeanor crimes.

"Looks like this kid has a habit of getting into trouble," Lucien said. "No convictions, though. Mommy's probably always there to bail him out. Nice work, Brak. With this lead, our investigation is really going to open up. If Cleever is dismissing cases to keep her son out of jail, it might explain why we've had so much trouble getting charges against the Corettis to stick."

Brak nodded.

Then Lucien spotted something at the bottom of Titarus's record. "Wait—that can't be right."

"What cannot be right?" Brak asked.

"It says here Titarus was charged with murder six months ago—*posthumously.* He died in a shootout between two rival gangs before he could be arrested. Apparently he murdered his own step-father and another high court judge sentenced him to remain dead." Lucien turned to Brak. "That couldn't have been Titarus we saw. It's just some look-alike." To confirm that, Lucien checked the facial recognition score. "Facial match was only eighty percent."

Brak hissed. "It is dark. A perfect match requires better lighting."

"Or the right person," Lucien replied. "Unless someone's found a way to bring the dead back to life without going through the Res. Center, I'd say we just hit a dead end." Lucien blew out a breath and checked the time on his ARCs—it was ten PM. "We spent six hours sitting here—for nothing! Did you even get a look at what was in the case?"

"No."

Lucien rubbed tired eyes and shook his head. "Great."

"This is not for nothing. The patient hunter always catches his prey. We need more time if we are to catch Coretti."

Lucien glanced at Brak with bleary eyes. "What *I* need is a vacation."

Brak hissed and looked away. "You would not make a good hunter."

"Good thing I prefer my meat grown in a vat."

Brak gave no reply to that, and Lucien ordered the car's driver program to take them home.

After a few minutes of racing down the dark alleys and streets of *Astralis's* sub levels, they emerged on the surface and flew up to five hundred meters, out over the frozen landscape of Winterside—trees laden with snow, rooftops white, ski hills lit up with spotlights and hover lifts carrying late night skiers back up, while others raced down: an endless loop on repeat.

Lucien shivered at the sight of all that snow, thanking his luck that he and Tyra could afford a place in the more desirable, and *warmer*, city of Fallside.

They crossed the fuzzy blue shield wall between Winterside and Fallside. At night all the colors of the latter city's ever-changing trees were cloaked in shadows, but here and there streetlights revealed bright pools of red and gold. Lucien directed the car to drop Brak off at his apartment first.

After that, the car flew on toward his home, a mansion clinging to the side of Hubble Mountain in the center of *Astralis's* ground level. Lucien's thoughts turned to his family while he waited to arrive. He'd left Tyra at home with the girls on one of her rare days off. Not that it mattered. She'd brought her work home with her, so it wasn't as though they were going to spend any quality time together.

He scowled, nursing old grievances. As the councilor of Fallside, Tyra didn't get a lot of time off, but what time she did get, she never seemed to spend with her family. Maybe a vacation *would* be a good idea, Lucien thought as the car hovered in for a landing on his driveway. He resolved to mention the idea to Tyra... a beachside resort in Summerside, perhaps...

CHAPTER 4

Astralis

FOUR HOURS UNTIL THE FAROS ATTACK...

Sand gleamed gold in the sun. Generated waves swished up the beach, tickling children's toes and making them squeal with delight. An artificial sun beamed down from the artificial sky. Lucien shaded his eyes with one hand and peered up at the distant floor of Level One, faded blue from all of the air in between. Five kilometers of atmosphere blanketed the ground level of *Astralis,* providing enough room for clouds to form, for the illusion to look almost as real as it felt. Lucien's eyelids fluttered shut against the warmth of the fusion-powered sun. *Fusion-powered.* That clicked, and Lucien smiled. *Astralis's* sun was the same as any other in that respect, just a lot smaller.

He sighed, allowing the warmth to melt some of the ice

around his heart. His ears pricked with girlish laughter. It belonged to his one-year-old and five-year-old daughters, Theola and Atara. His eyes cracked open and he squinted up at Level One once more, imagining for a moment that all those glinting viewports were stars he could travel to—but he couldn't actually travel anywhere. It was hard to feel trapped aboard a spaceship with thousands of decks and millions of square kilometers of space, and yet he did.

"Contemplating the unknown again, Lucien?" his wife asked.

His gaze came down for a landing, catching diamonds off the water as it fell. He checked that his children were both fine—they were making sandcastles at the water's edge—and then he turned to his wife.

Tyra lay on a purple beach towel beside him, sunbathing in the intermittent shade of a tall palm tree from ancient Earth. A light breeze blew, bringing the smell of sand, flower blossoms, and salt water to Lucien's nostrils. Palm fronds skittered, and black blades of shade flickered over his wife's flawless skin.

Lucien remembered when the top of that tree had barely come up to his shoulder. That was over eight years ago, right after he'd awoken on *Astralis* to the unsettling news that he'd just *died.* Death wasn't permanent, but memory loss was. Lucien had no recollection of anything that had happened in the first month after coming aboard *Astralis*.

Apparently he'd been assigned to *Astralis's* expeditionary forces along with all the other ex-Paragons. They'd served together aboard Tyra's galleon, the *Inquisitor*, going out to explore nearby systems for sentient life. But something had gone wrong, and they'd never returned.

Instead, a hostile race of aliens had joined *Astralis* at the rendezvous, and they'd barely escaped the subsequent battle. Ever since then the expeditionary forces had been grounded, and *Astralis* had taken care to avoid contact with any other aliens. Their mission was cosmological—to determine the nature of the universe, not to meet all of it's inhabitants.

"Hello?" Tyra propped herself up on her elbows and frowned at him. "Are you ignoring me?"

Lucien flashed an apologetic smile. "Sorry. I'm just remembering. Or trying to."

"I see..."

"Doesn't it ever bother you?" He asked. "Not knowing what happened to us out there?"

Tyra shook her head. "You can't dwell on that. You'll drive yourself crazy."

Lucien nodded slowly, and his gaze slipped away from his wife, out to the hemmed-in ocean and the archipelago of sandy, palm-studded islands. Each of them was dotted with quaint little huts and villages, as well as a handful of modern mansions scattered between. This was Summerside, a tropical island paradise. Fuzzy blue shield walls ran from the soaring, balcony-lined sides of the wedge-shaped ship to its center, segregating each of the ship's four climate zones and cities from each other.

Lucien gazed out over the water to Hubble Mountain at the center of *Astralis*. More than one hundred kilometers distant, he could just barely see the faded blue outline of the mountain and the inverted glass pyramid at its peak, glinting in the sun. The Academy of Science. Directly below that, in the mountain itself, were the government offices where his wife and all the other councilors worked. For most people, the

Academy was symbolic of *Astralis.* The inverted pyramid was the symbol on its flag, the symbol that evoked patriotism in the hearts of its people, but to Lucien it was the hateful symbol of his wife's neglect. Even here, at a resort in the farthest corner of the ship, the Academy's shadow still loomed over them. *Out of mind, but never out of sight,* Lucien thought.

Tyra was a councilor and a workaholic, one of the elected rulers on *Astralis* who got to have a say in where they went and how they got there. Meanwhile, he was an ex-Paragon in Etheria's army, now the chief of security for Fallside. He was an explorer with nothing to explore, trapped in a giant metal box.

It had grated on Lucien's spirits over the past eight years to be whisked through the universe at high speed, getting to see all of the alien planets along the way, cataloged in tantalizing detail by astronomers at the Academy, but never being allowed to set foot on any of them.

That was a Paragon's job: to explore—not to baby-sit a bunch of scientists as they flew right by all of the sights on their way to the edge of the universe.

Now, finally, they'd arrived at that edge—only to find that there were a whole lot more stars and galaxies to explore beyond the old cosmic horizon. Just more of the same for another thirty billion light years. And after that...

A vast stretch of emptiness: *The Black.* Tyra had bent his ear about the implications for months following the discovery.

"Do you realize what this means!" Tyra had been all but hyperventilating at the time.

"No." Lucien was busy feeding Theola. His wife's dinner was a block of ice at the other end of the dining table. She hadn't even noticed it sitting there yet. She was three hours late.

"We've just disproved the *cosmological principle."*

"The what?" Lucien asked.

"It means the universe isn't all the same everywhere! It has this big empty stretch, and we have no idea what could have caused that! It might be filled with dark matter, or dark energy, or both! Or maybe it's some kind of ripple in the fabric of space-time—some kind of mountain or a cliff. It might even be a real *physical* edge, and when something reaches it, it just pops out of existence, or disintegrates."

Theola smacked her bowl of chunky green goop and flipped it into Lucien's lap. He scowled at the mess, and his one-year-old daughter giggled. He flashed her a long-suffering smile, and she smiled winningly back with all six of her half-in-half-out baby teeth. Theola was late to eating solid foods. Something to do with a sensory integration disorder. This was his latest attempt to get her to eat something other than milk. Buttery smooth purees were all she would tolerate, and barely at that.

"Well, I can't blame you this time, Theebs," Lucien said, his nose wrinkling at the smell of the mess in his lap. "I wouldn't eat it either."

"Da-da! Blubalidee! Blub-blub... blub..." Theola replied, blowing bubbles with her saliva, and then popping her thumb in her mouth for a good suck.

"Are you even listening to me, Lucien?" Tyra demanded.

Theola craned her neck to look up at her mother, and

Lucien followed her gaze to give his wife an exasperated look. "I might have listened, if you'd been home three hours ago, when I called you and you said you were *on your way.*"

"With this news, can you blame me? I got caught up. Chief Ellis needed me to—"

Lucien held up a hand to stop her. "Save it. That's the third time this week. Why did you bother having kids if you weren't going to be around to raise them? You're barely here to tuck them in at night!" Atara was alone in her room, playing with her toys.

Tyra's eyes narrowed at him. "That's not fair. You know I have a demanding job. It's what allows us to live here—" she gestured to their surroundings. High ceilings. Real hardwood floors. Crystal chandeliers. Expensive furniture. Their mansion clung to the base of Hubble Mountain, overlooking Planck lake in the picturesque city of *Fallside*. It had a fantastic view from nearly all of its floor-to-ceiling windows. "You think all of this comes without sacrifice?" Tyra went on, nodding to herself as if he'd just answered *yes*. "Maybe that's because it's not your responsibility to pay for it. Your income barely covers our energy bill! Everything else is on me—my shoulders, *my* sweat—while you get to spend the whole day patrolling paradise."

Lucien blinked at her, speechless. He looked away, out the bay window at the end of the dining table. He gazed down on the kaleidoscope of yellows, reds, and golds around Planck Lake: the ever-changing leaves of *Fallside*. The scientists who'd engineered *Astralis* had used stasis fields to freeze the trees that way. Each of them was a living sculpture, a middle finger to nature. The mighty hubris of science had reared its head all over *Astralis,* and the message was clear: *We are the gods here.*

"You've got nothing to say to that, because you know I'm right. You're happy to enjoy the luxuries afforded by my job, but not to endure the sacrifices."

Lucien looked away from the window. "All of this isn't worth a *newton* if we don't have the time to enjoy it."

At that, Tyra frowned and her gaze slipped away from his, fleeing out the window. This was the only problem in their marriage—the only thing they needed to fix but somehow never could. It was as though they were caught in a stasis field like the trees in Fallside: their lives looked beautiful on the outside, but on the inside everything was frozen and stuck.

On the bad days, after putting the kids to bed, Lucien would sit in their echoing great room with a book and a glass of whiskey for company. He'd watch the electric fireplace crackle, sipping his drink, his eyes glazed, his holo-reader open to the same page of the same book that he'd been pretending to read for the past month. On days like that, he wondered if he should just take the kids and leave. Maybe that would get his wife to sit up and take notice. Or maybe she'd come home as usual, a few hours before midnight, re-heat her cold dinner, and flop into bed, not even noticing her family's absence, just as she never seemed to notice their presence.

Lucien winced at those memories. All he wanted was for his wife to *show up*—to be there, to laugh at his jokes while he did the dishes, to clink glasses with him after dark and kiss by the light of an artificial moon.

Lucien wondered if he should finally talk to Tyra about all of this, to let her know just how bad it had gotten....

The sound of waves swishing and children laughing brought him back and reminded him why they were here. *No,* he decided, flexing his fingers through the hot sand and nodding to the hateful, inverted glass pyramid at the top of Hubble Mountain. He'd wait until the end of their vacation, until Tyra had a chance to finally spend some time with her family and see what she was missing.

"Chief Councilor Ellis!" Tyra said brightly. "What's so urgent?"

Lucien's blood boiled at the sound of his wife answering a comms call on their vacation. He turned to her, his skin feeling hot and tight, like an over-inflated balloon just about to explode.

Tyra's blue eyes were rainbow-colored in the light of her ARCs. She was smiling at Ellis like he'd just saved her from the dullest moment of her life.

That's it... Lucien thought, his teeth clenching.

Tyra sat up suddenly. "That's impossible...! No, of course, I'll catch the first shuttle back. I'd love to say a few words.... Give me one hour." Tyra nodded. "See you soon."

The colored light left Tyra's gaze as the transmission ended and her ARCs returned to their usual transparency. She turned to him with a broad grin. "You're never going to believe this!"

Lucien met her enthusiasm with a scowl. "I thought we agreed to unplug. Shut off our ARCs and spend some time as a family for a change."

"I did, but I have to leave a way to contact me in case of an emergency."

"It's always an emergency."

"This is different."

"Save it, Tyra," Lucien said, shaking his head.

She reached for his hand and squeezed until the bones in his fingers ground together. "They've found us."

Lucien's brow furrowed. "Who has?"

"Us—you, me, the rest of the crew. The *Inquisitor* made it! Somehow they *made it* all the way here without us. They spent the past eight years catching up with us."

Lucien blinked in shock, the news finally settling in. "You're telling me we never died?"

Tyra shook her head and a grin sprang to her lips. "We're on our way to meet them right now. The judiciary will probably rule that we have to integrate our memories and put the extra clones in stasis. Who knows what we'll learn? You and I might even be married twice!"

Or divorced twice, Lucien thought, but didn't say. He flashed her a tight smile. "So you're going back to work."

"Just for a day or two, until we bring the *Inquisitor* on board."

Lucien looked away, his jaw set, his mind churning with conflicting thoughts.

"You can come with me," Tyra said. "You're going to have to meet yourself at some point."

"Sure. Why not."

"You don't sound excited."

He wasn't excited, but maybe he should be. Tyra had said they'd have to integrate their memories, consolidate two lives into one. The injection of a fresh perspective might be just what they needed. "You're right," he said. "We should be there to welcome them home—but we're extending our vacation by however many days this takes."

Tyra nodded, a smile tugging at the corners of her mouth once more. "Agreed."

Lucien's gaze drifted to their girls again just in time to see Theola go stomping through Atara's sandcastle, flattening it in an instant. Atara screamed and smacked her sister's thigh in revenge. Theola fell down and burst into tears.

Lucien sighed. "I'll get the girls," he said, already on his way down the beach. He scooped up Theola and grabbed Atara's hand, chiding her for smacking her sister.

"But Dad, she—"

"It doesn't matter," he replied. "We have to go, anyway."

And upon hearing that, Atara started crying, too.

CHAPTER 5

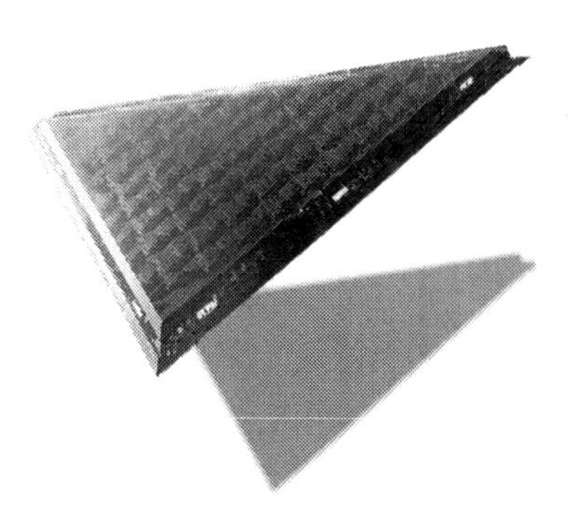

Astralis

TEN MINUTES UNTIL THE FAROS ATTACK...

Tyra Ortane stood to one side of the comms station in the operations room of *Astralis.* She watched with a conspiratorial smile as Chief Councilor Ellis stepped to the fore. He was wearing his ceremonial white council robes, as was she.

Tyra balanced on the balls of her feet, ready to jump into view as soon as Ellis introduced her. It took all of her will not to fidget while she waited for the *Inquisitor* to respond to their hail. The galleon had arrived at the rendezvous less than a minute ago, but the seconds were passing like hours.

She couldn't wait to find out what her clone had seen and done. Although, technically, the Tyra she was about to speak with was the original and *she* was the clone. Meeting herself was going to be like stepping into a time machine, since as Chief Councilor Ellis had just informed her, the crew of the *Inquisitor* had spent the past eight years in stasis while their navigator bot took them to the cosmic horizon. It made sense, of course: there was no way that a galleon could support its crew for eight years otherwise.

What that meant was that both of their copies—*originals*—aboard the galleon were still technically twenty-two years old. There were probably many more new developments in their lives here on *Astralis* than there were in their lives aboard the *Inquisitor.*

Despite that, one question remained: what had happened eight years ago to bring that alien fleet bearing down on *Astralis?* And who were those aliens? What did they want? Why had they been so hostile? *Astralis* hadn't run into them again since that time, but they had deliberately kept a low profile.

A tone sounded from the comms and a 3D hologram sprang to life on the viewscreen directly behind the comms station, revealing the bridge of a star galleon. Tyra saw herself sitting in the captain's chair at the center of the galleon's bridge. Sitting beside her was none other than her husband, Lucien.

Tyra grinned and waited for her introduction. If nothing else, Lucien's proximity to her on the bridge suggested that the sparks had already begun to fly between them.

"I am Chief Councilor Ellis. On behalf of *Astralis,* welcome back, Captain Forster. We have much to discuss. Please land your galleon in hangar bay forty-seven. Meanwhile, I have someone here who's eager to speak with you—councilor?" Ellis turned to her and nodded, to which Tyra stepped into view of the holocorder.

"It's... you," Lucien said, glancing at the identical copy of her sitting in the captain's chair beside him, and then back.

Tyra fought to contain a giddy smile while the copy of her on the screen stared at her in wide-eyed disbelief.

"I'm a *councilor?" Captain Tyra* asked.

Tyra inclined her head to herself. "We stopped sending out expeditions after yours almost got us all killed."

The captain nodded slowly, acknowledging the wisdom in that. By now she and her crew would know better than anyone about the dangers of exploring.

Tyra's gaze flicked between Lucien and the captain, wondering if their relationship was strictly professional.

"What is it?" Lucien asked. "You keep looking at me like there's something you want to say."

"It's just a shock for me to see us in this context."

"Us?" the captain echoed.

Tyra hesitated. "I suppose you're going to find out before you integrate your memories, anyway, so there's no reason I can't tell you."

"Find out what?" Lucien demanded.

"We're married, Lucien. With two kids. Atara and Theola."

"You're *what?"* a woman that Tyra didn't recognize demanded as she stood up from the comms station on the *Inquisitor's* bridge. Tyra recognized the woman's jealousy in an instant, and her smile vanished as she eyed this *other woman* with a reciprocal flash of her own jealousy. This woman and Lucien were obviously some kind of couple.

The captain held up a hand to forestall further

revelations. "Councilor, perhaps you'd better wait to tell us more. You've all been living our lives without us for the past eight years while we've been in stasis. I'm sure a lot has happened that will seem strange to us."

"Of course... you're right. I shouldn't have said anything," Tyra replied, sweeping her reaction under the carpet of a smile. "I apologize. It will be easier to understand everything that's happened after you integrate, and our memories become *your* memories, too."

"Agreed," the captain said.

Tyra inclined her head to them. "See you soon, Captain. *Astralis* out."

As the transmission ended, Tyra felt the ache spreading in her chest, and a knot tightened in her throat, making it hard to breathe.

So much for destiny. Given the choice between that other woman and me, Lucien chose her. Did that mean their marriage was a sham? Were they together by convenience or by accident? Tyra's logical brain took over, rationalizing the situation: no one was really destined to be together. The idea of two souls somehow reaching across time and space to be together was a childish notion for untrained, and uneducated minds. *Romance is two parts chemistry, and one part opportunity.* A simple equation of attraction plus availability.

Tyra had been so lost in her thoughts that she hadn't even noticed that Ellis had disappeared without a word. She turned in a circle, scanning the operations center for him. There was an urgent bustle of activity, and a sudden hush in the room. Ellis was leaning over the sensor operator's station, his mouth agape.

"It's not possible," he breathed, his voice a strangled

whisper. "Double check those sensor profiles!"

"I've already triple-checked them, sir. There's no mistake. They're exactly the same type of ships we encountered eight years ago."

"They followed us for *eight years?*" Councilor Ellis demanded. "Who in the netherworld are these people?"

A split second later the room's speakers crackled with, "Red alert! Action stations, action stations! This is not a drill. We are under attack by a hostile alien fleet. Repeat, red alert! This is not a drill!"

A battle klaxon roared in their ears, and Councilor Ellis turned to her in horror.

Tyra gazed blankly back, her mind racing. *My children... I have to get my children!*

The intercom crackled once more: "Attention all citizens, this is Admiral Stavos, we are under attack by a hostile alien fleet. If you find yourself near the outer hull, please proceed along emergency evacuation routes to the nearest shelter as calmly and quickly as possible. Keep all emergency lanes and corridors clear for Marines and repair crews. Violators will be stunned without warning. I repeat, we are under attack, please proceed along emergency evacuation routes as calmly and quickly as possible. This is not a drill."

It took a physical effort for Tyra to stop herself from running out the doors of the operations room to go find her family.

Chief Councilor Ellis crossed over to her and grabbed her arm, shaking her lightly to get her attention. Her eyes darted from the exit to look at him. Lucien was with the kids. He would know what to do. Her job as councilor of Fallside was to coordinate the evacuation efforts and emergency response teams in her city.

"We need to go!" Ellis yelled to be heard over the ship's blaring klaxons.

Tyra nodded. "Lead the way!"

CHAPTER 6

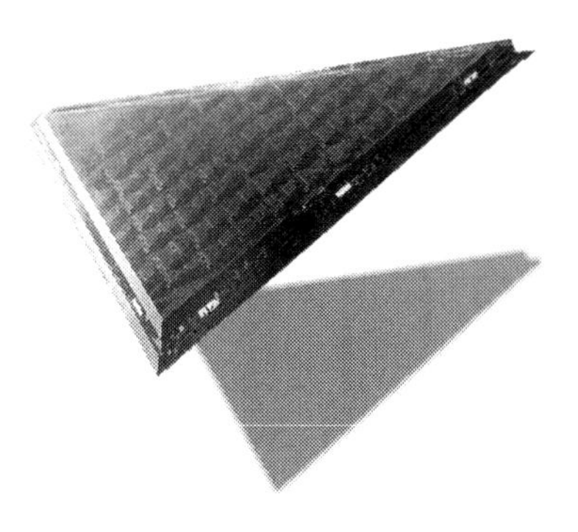

Astralis

Lucien was at home, eating lunch at the breakfast table with his daughters when the red alert came. For the first few seconds he was too shocked to move; he just sat there listening to Admiral Stavos' subsequent call for the evacuation of the ship's outermost compartments. When both announcements were over, all was silent, but for the distant screaming of *Astralis's* civil defense sirens.

"Aliens are attacking us?" Atara asked with all the seriousness of a child who suddenly didn't sound like one.

Theola's baby blues flicked to her sister, and then back to him. She was sitting in her high chair, sucking her thumb.

"Dad?" Atara pressed. "What are we supposed to do?"

He was busy asking himself the same thing. His job as the chief of security in Fallside was to help coordinate the evacuation from the ship's outer compartments to its shelters, and to keep the population from losing their heads in the crisis. But his job as a father was to keep his children safe, and he couldn't just leave them at home alone. First things first, he had to get his children to the nearest shelter. They'd have their own provisions for childcare, which would free him up to do his job.

An incoming message trilled inside Lucien's head, conveyed directly to his brain by his augmented reality implant. A priority comms icon flashed on his ARCs. He mentally answered it.

Deputy Laos's gaunt face appeared in the top right of his field of view. He looked stricken. "Chief! We need you back at the station. It's chaos out there. We have looters all across the ship, and reports of shots being fired in four different hangar bays."

"What?" Lucien shook his head. "Why the hangar bays?"

"People are trying to steal ships and escape. Last one who tried that was a *councilor,* if you can believe that. We're taking him into custody as we speak."

Lucien blinked in shock. "No, I can't believe that. He should be setting an example for everyone else right now, not abandoning ship."

"Yeah, well..." Laos trailed off. "Just get back here, Chief. We need you. People are scared."

Lucien nodded. If people were trying to flee the ship, and a *councilor* was leading the charge with a gun, things had to be *really* bad out there. What weren't *Astralis's* leaders telling them? "I'll be there as soon as I can get my kids to the nearest shelter."

"The nearest shelter to your location is in Hubble

Mountain, Chief—number twelve."

Lucien nodded. "Thanks, Laos. See you soon." He ended the transmission and turned to Atara. "Let's go, sweetheart."

"Where?"

Lucien lifted Theola out of her chair. She gave him an oblivious smile, and he smiled tightly back.

"We're going to the shelter. You'll be safe there."

"Is mommy going to be there?" Atara asked.

"No."

She grabbed his hand and squeezed. "But you will be, right?"

Lucien grimaced and went down on his haunches beside Theola. "I will be there, but first I have to take care of a few things."

"What things?"

"I have to make sure nobody gets hurt right now. They're scared and they're doing stupid things. Daddy's job is to keep them safe."

"But I'm scared, too!" Atara said, with tears springing to her eyes.

Theola picked up on the mood of their discussion, and she made a frowny face, just about to burst into tears herself.

Lucien flashed a silly grin at his one-year-old and began bouncing her on his hip. Theola's frowny face vanished and she was smiling again. Turning back to Atara, Lucien adopted a more serious look and reached out with his free hand to wipe the tears from Atara's cheeks with his thumb. Her long black hair, bright red lips, and delicate, feminine features were all the spitting image of her mother. "I need you to be a big girl now, Atara. Can you do that for Daddy?"

Atara gave no reply; her lips quivered like rose petals in the wind. "You're strong, Atara. Just like your mother."

She shook her head. "I'm not like her. I'm like you."

Lucien frowned. He didn't have time to address that. "Like me, then. Daddy's job is to protect the people in Fallside. Your job is to protect your sister. Do you think you can do that?"

Atara nodded, and wiped away the rest of her tears with the back of her hand.

Lucien flashed her a grim smile and kissed her on the cheek. "I knew I could count on you." He got up from his haunches and pulled Atara along to the garage. He was halfway there before Atara suddenly stopped walking, and their arms pulled taut like a tow-rope.

"What about Theola's things?" Atara asked.

Lucien blinked. He'd completely forgotten about the diaper bag. "Can you go get that for me, honey? I need to get her bottles ready."

Atara nodded and took off at a run. Ten minutes later they were all seated in the back of the family's hover car. "Take us to us to Emergency Shelter Twelve as fast as possible." Lucien said, speaking to the car's driver program.

"Right away, Mr. Ortane. Please buckle up to avoid any accidental injuries," the car replied.

Lucien hurried to buckle his seat's four-point harness. Atara did likewise, while the garage door finished opening. Theola was already buckled in her car seat and sucking away on her thumb.

Before the garage door had even finished sliding up, the car raced out of the garage and up into a sunny blue sky. It was a deceptively beautiful day, not a cloud in sight—*except for the alien invasion bearing down on us,* Lucien thought, as he gazed worriedly up at the faint glinting lights from the viewports in the floor of Level One. He half expected to see that sky shatter and cave in on them, only to get sucked back out in a gust of depressurizing atmosphere. He winced at the thought. If that actually happened, millions of people were going to die.

The car tilted suddenly to one side, banking sharply on its way back around to Hubble Mountain. Blue sky slid up and the rippled blue surface of Planck Lake took its place as the car went side-on with the ground. Lucien instinctively reached for the nearest safety rail, but when he didn't feel the anticipated tug of gravity, he let go and reached for Atara's hand instead. The G-forces from that turn had been all but eliminated by the car's inertial management system.

"Are we going to die?" Atara asked, while gazing out the window at the water and trees sweeping by below.

Lucien could still hear the muted howling of civil defense sirens. "No, honey, we're going to be just fine. This will all be over soon." He gave Atara's hand a reassuring squeeze.

"You promise?" Atara asked, her eyes wide and fraught with terror.

Lucien would have said or done anything to make her feel safe again, but a little voice whispered, warning him not to make promises he couldn't keep. He pushed those doubts down and nodded convincingly. "I promise, Atara."

She nodded back, having bought the lie.

CHAPTER 7

Astralis

"Let's go, let's go! Double time!" Footsteps ricocheted down the corridor like bullets, Marine bots mostly, with their immobile expressions and glowing holoreceptor eyes.

The enemy was landing troop ships on *Astralis's* relatively defenseless upper hull. It wouldn't be long before they cut a way in. The battle was not going well.

Garek grimaced between gasps for air. He'd gone soft. Then again, it had never been easy keeping up with machines.

His squad arrived at the end of their assigned corridor and the bots found cover positions behind bulkheads, crouching and leaning out to aim their weapons at the doors where the enemy was expected to come through.

Garek was a sergeant, which supposedly meant this particular horde of metal was his to command, but they didn't seem to need commanding. Each of them was faster, stronger, and tougher than him. They weren't made of hollow exosuit shells with soft, meaty centers. Bots were all shell, no meat.

The circular sensor display in the top left of Garek's HUD flashed in warning as red dots began pouring in just ahead of their position, on the other side of the bulkhead doors. "Get ready!" he snapped over the comms.

His squad replied with a flurry of acknowledging comm clicks. Their aim never wavered. Their guns never trembled. Not like his arms, which were already growing tired from aiming the cannons in his suit gauntlets.

We're not ready for this, Garek thought. He wasn't the only one who'd gotten soft during the past eight years of insular bliss. It wasn't unusual to see navy officers warming stools in *Astralis's* bars at four o'clock in the afternoon—or even three.

For the first time, Garek understood the wisdom of automating all the lower echelons in the military. Bots weren't prone to the attrition of easy living.

A molten orange circle appeared near the base of the doors; the sharp, shimmering tip of some kind of blade protruded from that spot. A molten line raced across the doors until it drew a full circle. Then came a *bang* as something hit the doors from the other side. The doors bulged inward, moving on hinges of liquid metal. A crack appeared, and Garek saw movement on the other side. *Bang!*

The doors fell, revealing a smoke-filled corridor beyond. "Open fire!" Garek yelled, even as his arms jackhammered with golden streams of thudding cannon fire. Red HUD shading marked enemy targets through the smoke. His squad fired with ruthless precision, their bullets splashing against red-shaded targets.

The enemy came walking through amidst a noisy hail of shrapnel. Garek kept expecting to see one of them fall, muscles spasming in agony, but as the smoke cleared, Garek saw no bodies—only erect, bipedal aliens, and they wore no armor. Instead, each of them wore antiquated black robes, and pristine blue skin showed where sleeves, lapels, and hems ended. Glowing eyes pricked through the smoke, casting about curiously, as if bored with the noisy tirade of cannons.

"AP cannons having no effect," one of the bots reported on the command channel. "Switching to explosive rounds."

Garek's squad stopped firing, a momentary pause while they switched out regular magazines for explosive ones. Garek's ears rang with the echoes of gunfire as he hurried to do the same, all the while wondering: *why are they just standing there? And why don't they have any weapons?*

As one, the aliens raised their hands, palms out, as if to say: *stop, don't shoot!*

Garek blinked in shock. Maybe they'd got it all wrong. Maybe these aliens weren't hostile. *Maybe they came in peace. Maybe we were the ones who fired the first shots eight years ago.*

"Weapons hold!" Garek ordered, a split second before his squad would have opened fire. Garek stood up and stepped out of cover. He held his hands up, palms out, like he saw the aliens doing, and switched his comms to external speaker mode. "We don't want to fight you," he said. "This is a peaceful vessel on a peaceful mission of exploration." He didn't expect the aliens to understand him, but he hoped they'd be able to infer something from his tone of voice.

One of the blue-skinned aliens turned to him. This one wore gray robes rather than black. It had glowing, ice-blue eyes, and wore some kind of luminous gold crown on its head, while the others flaunted hairless blue scalps. The one with the crown made a gesture to his fellows, and they lowered their palms. Then it stepped to the fore.

"Hello, Garek," it said.

Garek flinched. "You know my name?" And on the heels of that: "You're speaking Versal! How..." He shook his head, uncomprehending. "Who are you?"

"My name is Lucien," the alien said.

Garek's eyebrows shot up as that name clicked into place. Lucien Ortane was the chief of security in Fallside. What was an alien doing with his name? In his experience most alien names were an un-pronounceable series of clicks, chirps, and growls.

"As for who I am, I am the God and ruler of this universe," the alien went on. "And *we* are Faros. We met once before, but you don't remember that meeting."

The *Inquisitor.* That explained how this being knew him. Garek worked some moisture into his suddenly dry mouth and shook his head. "You should be speaking to our leaders. I can escort you to an audience with them if you like," Garek suggested.

"I am already speaking with them."

Garek blinked. Confusion swirled. "I'm not a lead—"

"Not you. Not here. I am in many places. Your leaders have agreed to a surrender." The Faro's blue eyes brightened, and a smile curved his lips. "Your people are now slaves of the Farosien Empire."

Garek's blood turned to ice. "What do you mean slaves?"

The alien didn't have a chance to reply. There came a

tell-tale flash of dazzling white light that left them both momentarily blind and groping in a sea of white cotton. *Astralis* had just jumped away. The surrender must have been a ploy to escape.

When Garek finished blinking the spots from his eyes, he saw that the alien's smile was broader than ever. He looked delighted. "So you have some fight in you after all. Good!"

"Weapons free!" Garek yelled.

His squad opened fire with a roar of explosive rounds. The corridor turned white again, but this time from the constant flurry of explosions. Amidst the bursts of light and glowing shrapnel, the blue aliens stood their ground, shielded from the onslaught by unseen means. Slowly, they drew shimmering swords from scabbards on their backs, and they started toward Garek's squad. The crown-wearing alien reached the first bot and casually sliced it in half with his sword. The pieces clattered as they fell. Those swords were shimmering for a reason. The blades had to be razor-shielded—sheathed in microscopically-sharp energy shields.

Garek's guts twisted into a knot as he imagined being sliced in half just like that bot. "Fall back!" he yelled over the squad's comm channel. He turned and ran as fast as he dared in the confines of the ship's corridors. His feet slammed the deck like thunder. With his suit's augmented strength, Garek was able to put a lot of distance between him and the invading aliens in just a few seconds. He breathed out a shaky sigh as he neared the end of the corridor.

They wouldn't be able to touch him with their swords now, and it didn't look like the aliens had any ranged weapons. No sooner had he finished that thought than a flash of movement raced into and out of Garek's peripheral vision with an accompanying *thup-thup-thup* of robes slapping bare skin, like a flag flying high in a stiff wind.

The crown-wearing alien now stood blocking the way at the end of the corridor. Garek stumbled as he tried to slow down, but he was moving too fast. With his exosuit's augmented strength he'd already hit 45 kph.

The Faro gave a gaping grin, and a black tongue flicked over black lips. He thrust out his shimmering sword a split second before Garek collided with him. The sword went through him, armor and all, with a searing heat. The alien stumbled back a few steps with his momentum, but he pushed back with impossible strength, and managed to remain standing. The Faro's blazing blue eyes were wide and gleeful.

Garek coughed, splattering the inside of his helmet with a crimson ink-blot. He could feel his blood boiling where it touched the alien sword; he heard it sizzling as smoke rose from his belly. Garek gaped, breathless, at the blue-skinned monster before him, the one who called himself by a human name and spoke their language as if it were his own.

Darkness swelled, and Garek's head swam. The Faro pulled him close, until those glowing blue eyes were all he could see, and then the alien whispered into the audio-pickup in the chin of Garek's helmet.

"Don't worry, I'll take good care of your daughter."

Garek's eyes flew wide, and he raged against the encroaching darkness. He grabbed the Faro's neck in both of his hands and squeezed with all of the strength he had left. The alien sneered and flexed his neck against the assault, battling with Garek's hands, trying to break his grip. Then something popped and snapped. Garek felt bones grind together beneath his fingers, and the alien's head sagged at an odd angle, blue eyes suddenly dim and fading. Garek let go and stumbled away, taking the alien's shimmering, sizzling sword with him in his belly. He coughed up another crimson ink-blot. Unable to see, he reached for his helmet with numb hands and twisted it off. Stumbling in a dizzy circle and fighting to remain standing, Garek batted clumsily at the hilt of the sword protruding from his torso. After several tries, he managed to grab the sword and pull it free. Blood bubbled lazily from a broad slit in his suit, and Garek collapsed to his knees, eyes wide and blinking. His mind raged against his body, urging it to stand and fight, but his muscles didn't so much as twitch.

Garek blinked, watching the last bot in his squad fall in half a dozen pieces as three swords flashed through it at the same time. Then the blue-skinned aliens stalked toward him. It was all he could do to remain conscious and watch as they came for him. Those aliens hoisted him to his feet, pulling him up as if he weighed nothing at all, then they turned and held him facing their fallen leader, the one whose neck Garek had snapped. The alien lay on the deck with that haughty grin frozen on its lips, blue eyes bright and staring at the ceiling.

Garek blinked and heaved a shuddering gasp. Those eyes had been dim a moment ago. As he watched, the impossible happened. The dead rose to life. The alien's broken neck once again held its grinning head high, and those glowing blue eyes swept to Garek.

The dead alien spoke: "You cannot kill me." It held out a strangely glowing hand to its fallen sword, and the blade snapped into its palm. The dormant weapon shimmered to life with a barely audible *hum* of energy.

Garek blinked, wondering what he'd just seen. Some kind of grav gun? But there was no device in the alien's hand—just as he hadn't seen any kind of shield emitter lurking beneath the alien's robes. It was as if they weren't really flesh and blood, but some kind of living technology.

The alien leader stalked toward him. With a derisive twist of its lips, the one who called himself Lucien—*light-bringer*—ran him through, over and over again. The shimmering blade flashed in and out of Garek's torso with a searing heat, and his mouth opened in a soundless scream.

Just as he felt his life slipping away, the alien held up a glowing palm to his face and blinded him with pure, radiant light. *Light-bringer,* he thought, as the light swept him into a blinding sea. For a frozen heartbeat, Garek saw the mind of his enemy laid bare; it unfolded before him in a landscape of thoughts, memories, and plans as old as time. He wanted to scream out a warning to any who would listen, but it was over before he could: the light faded, taking this strange new world with it, and he was left to flail in the dark.

Alien whispers skittered around him, followed by hissing laughter. Somehow Garek knew that alien had seen into him, just as he had seen into it. It had been to the landscape of *his* mind and found something there, some vital weakness in *Astralis* that would be their undoing.

Garek battled the darkness, every ounce of his being clawing for purchase, fingernails cracking as they held to a shadowy cliff over a gaping abyss. He tried thinking the thoughts that would activate his comms and allow him to send the others a warning, but he couldn't tell if it worked, and he no longer had the strength to hold on. He lost his grip and fell into the abyss. The darkness was so absolute that not even time could escape. This was death: falling forever in a frozen instant between all that was, and all that wasn't, into a place so empty that not even energy could exist.

CHAPTER 8

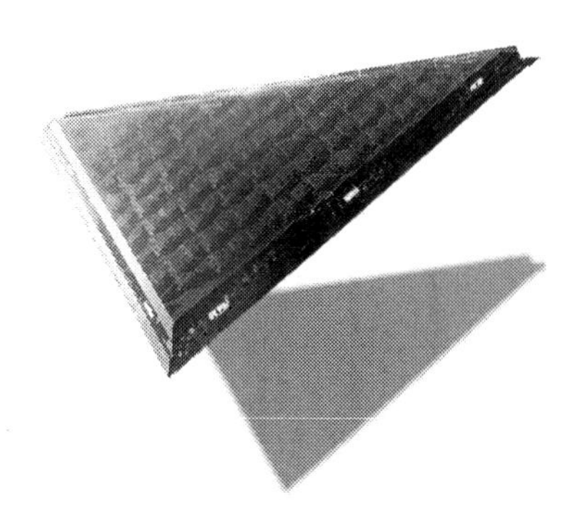

Astralis

Astralis jumped. Tyra stood blinking spots from her eyes as the afterglow from the jump faded. Confusion warred with tenuous hope in her brain. The last thing she'd heard from the battle was that they were overrun and the enemy was boarding them. How had they gone from that to being able to jump away?

Tyra stared at the holomap of Fallside in her office, where she and the heads of various departments and emergency response units had gathered to oversee the evacuation of Fallside's outer sections. Her responsibility didn't extend to directing the defense of her city, but she could clearly see the green dots that marked the locations where squads of Marines had been deployed, and the red and green *X*s, that indicated where enemy soldiers and friendly Marines had fallen. There were only a handful of red *X*s for fallen enemies, but plenty of green.

"We jumped? What's happening, Madam Councilor?" Fallside's Chancellor of Education sidled up to her, his high brow furrowed with concern.

Tyra shook her head. "I know as much as you do, Chancellor." Turning away from the others in the room, Tyra walked over to a window overlooking Fallside and used her ARCs to mentally place a call to Chief Councilor Ellis. He answered after just a brief delay.

"This had better be important."

"What's happening?" Tyra demanded.

Ellis sighed. "Your curiosity can wait, Mrs. Ortane."

She pressed on, "We jumped away?"

"Yes."

"How?"

"At the risk of repeating my—"

"Never mind. I'm joining you on the bridge."

"You don't have clearance!"

"Then grant me clearance! If I'm supposed to keep Fallside safe, I need to know what I'm up against. Where are we now? Were we followed? How many hostiles do we have on board? What's the nature and disposition of the enemy forces?"

"None of that is any of your concern, Councilor. Rest assured Admiral Stavos and General Graves are doing everything they can to keep us safe."

Tyra didn't reply, but Ellis must have heard her panting over the comms.

"Did you hear me, Councilor?"

"I heard you," she said as she reached the nearest elevator.

"Why are you out of breath?"

"See you soon," she said, and ended the comms. She punched in *-500* on the keypad and the elevator dropped swiftly through Hubble Mountain, down past two hundred and fifty meters of dirt, and past more than a kilometer of decks on its way to the command level.

Tyra's AR implant trilled with an incoming call from Ellis, and a corresponding comms icon flashed in the top right corner of her field of view. She muted the sound and ignored the flashing icon.

Leaving the familiar comforts of the surface behind on her way down into the labyrinthine depths of the ship's sub-levels, Tyra felt more cut off from her children than ever, but she'd already checked in with Lucien, and both Atara and Theola were safely hidden away in Hubble Mountain Shelter Twelve.

Besides, the only way she could know how much danger they were really in was by going down to the bridge and demanding answers, so it wasn't like she was abandoning them. Not really.

The elevator reached sub level five hundred, and the door slid open. Tyra jogged out into a no-frills corridor that sported low ceilings with exposed conduits and naked, scuffed metal walls.

She pulled up a map on her ARCs to locate the bridge and followed the guide prompts to get there: *take next left down Corridor C. Make right at junction four. Await scans at Security Checkpoint Delta.*

Tyra must have jogged past a dozen squads of Marine bots with their human sergeants trailing safely behind before one of those sergeants thought to ask where she was going.

"On my way to the bridge to see Admiral Stavos and General Graves," she said, between gasps for air.

"I'll escort you there," the sergeant said.

"Thank you... Sergeant Ikes," Tyra replied, looking his name up on her ARCs. She thanked her luck that he'd asked where she was going. This sergeant was probably her best bet to actually get into the bridge. Sergeant Ikes led the way there, striking a brisk pace that made her feel like she needed to jog to keep up. The sergeant's squad of bots clanked along behind her, their metal feet striking the deck in perfect synchrony.

When they arrived at the bridge, a pair of guard bots scanned her and the sergeant with flickering blue fans of light while the sergeant's squad fanned out to wait on either side of the doors.

As soon as the scans were complete, the doors parted to reveal a vast chamber with several tiers of catwalks and control stations. The far wall soared with four-story-high viewscreens and unparalleled starry vistas.

Sergeant Ikes led Tyra straight up to a holo table in the center of the deck where they'd emerged. Familiar faces leaned over that table, aglow in the azure light of holo imagery.

The sergeant fetched up short in front of a broad-shouldered, barrel-chested man in a Marine's gleaming black exosuit. His helmet was missing, revealing dark hair, clipped peach-fuzz short, and the collar of a Marine's uniform, sporting the four silver stars of a general's insignia.

"Sergeant Ikes reporting, General," he said, saluting crisply.

The general straightened from leaning over the table and returned his salute; then his eyes flicked to Tyra and he looked her up and down with one dark eyebrow raised.

"I have Madam Councilor Ortane here from Fallside to see you, sir," Sergeant Ikes explained.

"I didn't request to see any councilors," he barked gruffly, and Sergeant Ikes faltered visibly. The sergeant glanced uncertainly at Tyra, and she smiled sympathetically back.

"My fault," she said. "I led Sergeant Ikes to believe I had been summoned here."

Graves snorted. "I see. In that case, you can leave."

"This way, ma'am..." Ikes said, taking her by the arm to lead her back the way they'd come.

Tyra jerked her arm free and stood her ground. "Hold on! I have tens of millions of people trampling each other on their way to get to shelters that were only built to hold a few hundred thousand. If I'm expected to calm all those people down and bring order, I need to know what's going on."

General Graves ground his teeth. "I don't have time for this. Councilor Ellis—"

Chief Councilor Ellis looked up from the holo table with a tight smile. "I'll deal with her, General." Ellis came and took her aside. "I told you not to come here," he chided in his most patient voice, the one he reserved for detractors at political rallies.

Tyra rounded on him with arms crossed over her chest. "I'll go just as soon as you answer my questions."

Ellis's eyes narrowed. "What do you want to know?"

"How did we get away? We were surrounded. They must have had quantum jamming fields engaged. They did the last time."

"We jumped through their jamming field."

Horror sliced through Tyra at that. "I thought jumping through a magnetic field could cause a jump failure... what do you call it?"

A new voice joined the discussion: "Scattering. The chances were high, but we didn't have a choice."

Tyra turned to see Admiral Stavos come striding up to them. He stopped a few feet away, a picture of calm and obsessive neatness. His short white hair—a fashionable color for a man with his rank and position—was perfectly combed and gelled into submission, and his matching Van Dyke beard was trimmed to a regulation length. His uniform was neatly pressed and a spotless white with gold buttons and medals gleaming brightly, as if they'd just been polished. The five golden stars of his rank insignia glittered on his collar, winking at Tyra from the shadows under his chin.

"How high were the chances?" Tyra pressed.

"Forty-seven percent. Not odds I'd want to play again with three hundred and fifty million lives hanging in the balance."

Tyra nodded woodenly. The admiral had just tossed a coin to determine their survival. No wonder he'd waited until they'd already been boarded to jump out. He'd probably been hoping to find some other way to escape. Any other way.

"Where are we now?" she asked.

Ellis shrugged. "Does it matter? Somewhere."

Tyra chambered a deadly look, twin barrels glaring at him. "Did the enemy fleet follow us?"

"Not yet," Admiral Stavos replied. "But we still have hundreds of alien troops on board, and we're having difficulty eliminating them. We're jamming all outbound comms to make sure they can't transmit a signal to their fleet, but they might still find a way to do that if they can disable our jammers."

"*Hundreds* of alien troops? That's *it?* You're telling me a few hundred aliens are overwhelming our defenses?"

"I'm afraid so," Stavos replied.

Tyra was shocked. They had over a million Marine bots on *Astralis,* plus thousands of human sergeants and security forces. It was absurd to think a few hundred of *anything* could overwhelm all of them.

Ellis nodded. "Now you know why the general is in such a bad mood. They have us falling back faster than we can retreat."

"How is that possible?" Tyra asked.

"Our weapons appear to be ineffectual against their personal shields," Admiral Stavos put in. "At the risk of damaging our own ship, we're bringing heavier firepower to bear."

"What do they want? Have they made contact with us? Any demands?"

"Unfortunately, they have," Ellis said. "Their leader is aboard... several dozen clones of him, anyway." Tyra's eyes widened at that. "They all speak Versal fluently."

"Versal?" The shocks just kept coming. Tyra shook her head, struggling to process the implications of that. "What were his—*their*—demands?"

"First he introduced himself and explained who they are," Ellis said. "Apparently they're a race of humanoids called the Faros, and they claim to have been created by Etherus alongside the Etherians. They were to be Etheria's army, but they instigated a rebellion, which led to the Great War. After which, as you know, Etherus put some of the rebel

Etherians in human bodies to give them a taste of freedom. The part that's news to us is that Etherus exiled all the Faros beyond the Red Line."

"So that arbitrary line that Etherus told everyone not to cross is a *political* boundary?"

Ellis nodded. "Part of a treaty that the Faros signed with Etherus before humans even existed. It divides the Farosien Empire from the Etherian Empire."

Tyra scowled. "Etherus might have mentioned that before we left."

"He might have mentioned a lot of things," Ellis replied. "Anyway, their leader calls himself Lucien, and he—"

Tyra held up a hand to stop Ellis there. "Lucien? You mean like my *Lucien?*"

"I know. I thought that was strange, too. Might be a coincidence, but we're going to have to look into it. Anyway, the alien Lucien seems to know a lot about us. He claims to have met our people aboard the *Inquisitor* eight years ago, and apparently he killed several of them personally, or one of his clones did, anyway."

Tyra gaped at Ellis. "Did he say why? Did they provoke him somehow?"

"They refused to submit to slavery. The very same offense we are busy committing now. Admiral Stavos pretended to surrender and then jumped through their jamming field without warning, despite the high risk of scattering."

Admiral Stavos nodded along with that. "Lady luck is definitely with us. Let's hope it stays that way."

A female lieutenant rushed up to the admiral, breathless, her golden eyes wide and flickering with images from her ARCs. "Admiral, we have a problem!" she said.

He turned and nodded for her to continue. "Yes?"

"Reactors sixteen, seventeen, and eighteen are all registering unusual activity."

"Define unusual, Lieutenant Ruso."

"Radiation spikes well outside normal bounds. Power output is erratic. If it continues like this, there'll be a containment failure and they'll all go critical."

"So shut them down. We have hundreds of reactors. We can live without three of them."

"I tried, sir. They're not responding."

"Then send teams to shut them down manually!"

"I would, sir, but two of those reactors are behind enemy lines."

The admiral's expression froze somewhere between horror and dawning realization. "Clever little kakards... How long do we have before those reactors blow?"

"Ten, maybe twenty minutes."

"At least those sections are evacuated. If we're lucky the blue-skins will blow themselves up and save us the trouble."

"Hopefully, sir, but one of the affected reactors is behind *our* lines. The operators on site say the manual overrides aren't working."

Admiral Stavos ran a hand through his beard. "They don't have access to that one, so they must be hacking our control systems."

"That's what I thought, but it might also be a physical data probe traveling through the coolant pipes or electrical conduits. Whatever the case, the effects are spreading from one reactor to another, and fast... I think we're going to have to shut down all of our other reactors preemptively until we can find the source of the problem."

Admiral Stavos shook his head. "If we do that, the whole ship will be running on fumes. Gravity, life support, lights, jamming fields—all of that will be running on reserve power, and when reserves start to run dry, systems will fail all over the ship—including the comms jammers that are keeping the enemy from calling in their fleet."

"Yes, sir, but if we don't shut everything down now, the enemy is going to keep turning our reactors into bombs, one after another, until *Astralis* rips itself apart."

Tyra couldn't believe what she was hearing. "How could something like this happen?"

"Shut them down," Admiral Stavos growled.

"Yes, sir," Lieutenant Ruso replied, already turning to leave.

"And find the problem before we run out of power! I want every available man and bot on the job."

"Aye, sir," she said, and took off at a run.

Admiral Stavos turned back to Tyra and Ellis. "Excuse me, councilors."

"Wait—" Tyra said. "How long do we have before power starts to fail?"

"That depends. We're going to have to ration it, so some systems are going to go down immediately. Gravity sucks the most power, so I'm going to have to kill that first."

Tyra blinked in shock and shook her head. "You *can't*. There's millions of people on the surface level! Our water reservoirs are there. You kill the gravity, and there'll be nothing to hold them in place. The tiniest shift in our momentum will send trillions of gallons floating free, bulldozing homes, uprooting trees, and drowning everyone in their path."

"I have no intention of maneuvering the ship while gravity is offline, so Newton's first law should save us—*an object in motion stays in motion unless acted on by an unbalanced force.*"

"You're assuming that an unbalanced force needs to come from the engines, but we're talking about a complex system of forces, including *weather* forces that are constantly engaged all over *Astralis*. One rain drop, falling at the moment that you turn off the gravity, will sail on until it hits the surface of a lake, and when it does, it will knock a dozen more raindrops free and send them flying back up into the sky."

The admiral's lips quirked into a grim smile. "So find an umbrella."

"You're missing the point, Admiral. You can't predict what the effects of this will be. There's too many variables, too many tiny fluctuations."

Stavos leveled an accusing finger at her. "No, *you're* missing the point, Councilor. You think I don't understand chaos theory? I was schooled in science by the Academy, the same as you. The difference is, I also studied war, and war is all about minimizing casualties.

"There are three hundred million people living in *Astralis*, and over ninety percent of them live either above or below the surface. To them, turning off the gravity will only be a minor nuisance, and I can protect them by doing so. As for the other ten percent who live under boundless skies—yes, their homes might be bulldozed, or they might temporarily lose their lives in the chaos, but when it's all over, the other ninety percent will still be around to resurrect them. My way, everybody lives—your way, everybody dies. I think that makes the choice obvious, don't you?"

Tyra had nothing to say to that. All she could think about was a tidal wave the size of Planck Lake crashing into Hubble Mountain, cracking it open, and drowning her children.

Admiral Stavos turned and stalked away, heading for the comms control station. Ellis followed him there, and Tyra listened in horror as the two of them delivered a dire warning to everyone on board, saying they had just five minutes to secure themselves and their belongings as best they could.

Before they'd even finished speaking, Tyra placed a call to her husband.

"Tyra? I—"

"Lucien! Get back to the shelter! They're going to turn off the gravity. Find the girls and keep them safe!"

"I know. I'm already on my way," Lucien replied, sounding out of breath. "I'll let you know when I get there. You'd better find someplace safe, too."

Tyra nodded. "I will. I love you."

"Love you, too," he replied.

CHAPTER 9

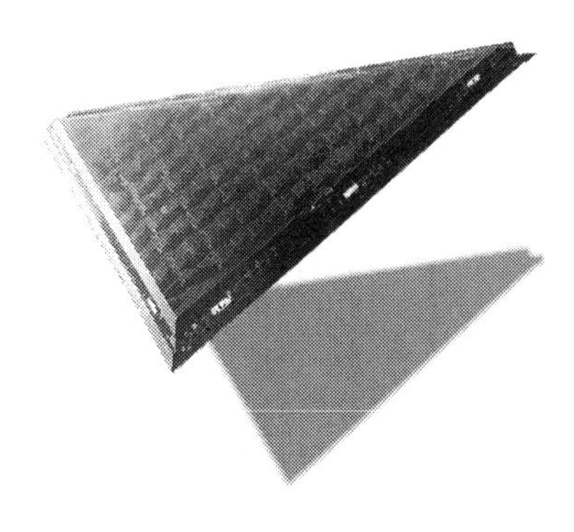

Astralis

As the patrol car raced out of the station, Lucien glanced at his old partner, Brak, sitting in the back beside him. Before he'd been promoted to chief of security, they'd worked together every day, but now they only did so occasionally, whenever Lucien could find an excuse to leave the station and go out on patrol.

"Thanks for coming with me, buddy," Lucien said. Brak's presence made this look more like official police business, and less like the chief of security for Fallside abandoning his duty in the middle of a crisis.

"It is nothing to mention," Brak growled, and bared his dagger-sharp black teeth in a fearsome grimace that was probably meant to be a brotherly smile.

They'd been friends forever, since long before *Astralis* had left New Earth, and the Etherian Empire, since before they could even count to ten. Well, at least before Lucien could; Gors grew up a lot faster than humans. Their relationship had oscillated from Lucien acting like the big brother, to Brak doing so, and back again until their respective levels of maturity had more or less equalized and they'd graduated together as Paragons and peers.

Soon after that, Lucien had decided to join *Astralis's* mission to the cosmic horizon. Brak had followed him with the plan to change his mind, but when that plan failed, the Gor had decided to join *Astralis's* mission, too, supposedly for the adventure, but Lucien suspected otherwise. Brak had fallen back into their old pattern. He was being the big brother again.

Lucien glanced at the timer on his ARCs, counting down until gravity switched off all over *Astralis.*

Thirty seconds until the picturesque surface level became a nightmare. There were fail-safes in place to prevent gravity from ever failing. It was supposed to be impossible. More than ninety percent of the ship's reactors would have to go offline before the gravity did, and even then it would have remained at a fraction of normal strength.

But this wasn't some kind of unforeseen systems failure. Chief Councilor Ellis and Admiral Stavos were shutting off the ship's gravity intentionally—*pre-emptively,* they said. *Before something worse happens.*

It was hard to imagine something worse. What they were about to do was unconscionable. Lucien gazed fixedly out the side window of the hover, watching the scenery roll by beneath them...

Then the timer hit zero, and the hover bucked under them. Lucien's guts twisted, but didn't surge up into his throat as he'd expected. The hover's grav lifts were now an unbalanced force, sending it rocketing up and pushing him down into his seat.

The driver program detected the problem and negated their vertical thrust, but they sailed on with their momentum until Lucien heard the dorsal maneuvering jets firing to push them back down. The contents of Lucien's stomach surged, and his seat restraints dug into his shoulders, holding him down. Acid burned in the back of his throat and he grimaced with distaste.

"We are experiencing a gravity malfunction. Please make sure your seat buckles are securely fastened," the driver program said.

Unused seat belts floated up to eye level with Lucien before the buckles reached the end of their slack and bounced back down. Simultaneously, thousands of individual strands of his hair went through the same vertical whiplash effect.

But outside nothing appeared to be happening. *Astralis* wasn't in motion like his hover was, at least not *changing* motion, so there was nothing to knock anything loose from its initial state of rest relative to the rest of the ship.

Lake water stayed in lake beds. Trees remained rooted. Parked hover cars still sat on their landing pads.

Lucien breathed a sigh of relief.

Then a sudden flash of light dazzled his eyes, and he winced against the glare. Had *Astralis* just jumped again? But no, that couldn't be. They couldn't jump out while running on reserve power...

A titanic *boom,* rumbled through the sky, stealing his attention.

Thunder? Lucien wondered, as he peered up at the

cloudless blue sky over Fallside. As he watched, the sky shivered; then it caved in, and fire gushed out between tumbling chunks of molten orange metal. The debris fell like meteors, each the size of a house or building. A gaping black hole appeared in the clear blue sky. Smoke swirled inside that opening, and molten debris plummeted.

The shock wave hit next. A blast of heat knocked the hover sideways, and Lucien's seat restraints dug into his chest and shoulders with terrifying force. Alarms screamed in the cockpit, and the driver program issued a banal warning: "We are experiencing turbulence, please make sure your seat buckles are securely fastened."

"What is happening?" Brak shook his skull-shaped head, his gaunt cheeks slack and black teeth bared in a quizzical sneer.

Wind roared, buffeting their hover car with stifling heat. Lucien blinked as rivers of sweat ran into his eyes. *Wake up.* He thought. This couldn't be real.

Just as the force of the shock wave was abating, the hover lurched upward again, pinning them in their seats. So much for zero-G, Lucien thought. He had yet to experience more than a moment of it.

"Driver, what's going on?" Lucien demanded. "Why are we ascending?"

"We are experiencing turbulence, please do not be alarmed."

Lucien scowled at the unhelpful answer, and turned to look out the side window of the hover, hoping he'd be able to see for himself. He did, but he still couldn't believe what he was seeing.

The chunks of debris tumbling to the ground had

slowed and were now reversing their course, flying back *up* into the sky. Trees, water, dirt, rocks, houses, hover cars, and everything else gradually followed, lifting off and swirling in circles below the gaping hole in the sky.

An inverted tornado. Lucien watched as it gathered strength, quickly darkening into a black funnel. The oily tip snaked up and touched the hole in the sky, where it remained.

"No!" Lucien slapped the window with his palms as hard as he could, vainly hoping that the stinging pain would wake him up.

But the chaos only amplified, quickly reaching clear across Fallside. Wind roared deafeningly around the hover once more, and writhing tentacles of water snaked up from lakes and rivers; waterfalls pouring from Hubble Mountain inverted their course, falling *up* into the spinning vortex in the sky.

The hover shuddered and the engines moaned as the driver program tried to compensate. It was like wading to shore against the backwash of a tidal wave, except the ocean they were being carried into was cold hard vacuum.

Hover cars were atmospheric vehicles, not spacecraft. If they got sucked out, they'd be dead within seconds.

Lucien fumbled with his seat restraints, hands shaking as he unbuckled.

"Death comes for usss," Brak hissed.

"Death can go frek itself!" Lucien replied as he broke free of his restraints. He jumped up and grabbed the bottom of the bench seat facing theirs. Folding it to either side and folding the seat back down into that space, he revealed a narrow passage leading into the cockpit.

Lucien crawled through. It was cramped inside the

cockpit, built for one rather than two to maintain the patrol hover's speedy, aerodynamic profile.

He managed to wrestle himself into place, legs in their slots, feet resting over rudder pedals. Reaching around he unfolded the back of the pilot's chair, blocking the passage behind him once more. All patrol model hover cars had space for a human pilot in addition to the nine seats in the back—six for officers, three for detainees.

Lucien deactivated the autopilot and grabbed the flight yoke. He slammed the flight yoke down and pushed the throttle up past the stops into overdrive. The hover shook like a leaf, and the thrusters screamed, but the range to Hubble Mountain began dropping steadily.

Thunk! A rock bounced off the nose of the hover. Then a handful of pebbles and leaves skittered across the windshield, followed by a curling column of water, invisible until the last second. It splashed over them, slapping the hover with a noisy *bang*. Collision alert warnings screamed belatedly. Another rock hit, this time slamming into the canopy and drawing a spider's web of fractures in the glass.

Lucien grimaced and activated a sensor overlay to shade and highlight the debris. Fuzzy red clouds of dirt appeared; larger specks for pebbles and rocks; a writhing red tentacle of water...

A spinning boulder the size of a house sailed up in front of him, and the cockpit turned solid red. Lucien jerked the yoke to starboard and rolled in the same direction. A collision alert screamed, and Lucien fired the grav lifts at full strength.

They bounced off the boulder with a brief crushing sensation, and then the rest of *Astralis* snapped into focus once more. Lucien breathed a sigh of relief—

But it caught in his throat. The inverted pyramid of the Academy was cracking away from its perch atop Hubble Mountain. A shattered rain of glinting blue glass fell from its walls.

Lucien felt a flash of satisfaction as the symbol of his wife's abandonment was ripped away. Then he remembered that there were thousands of people inside that building, and all of them were about to suffocate in the dark. He grimaced and dove for the base of Hubble Mountain, heading straight for Shelter Twelve.

Debris continued to assault the car on the way down, but the effects were milder closer to the surface. The shelter's garage doors swept up in front of him, and Lucien fired the grav lifts to halt his momentum, followed by a steady blast from the dorsal jets to keep the car hovering in front of the entrance.

He keyed the comms. "Shelter Twelve, this is Chief of Security Ortane, requesting emergency landing clearance. Please respond, over."

Static hissed back at him over the comms. Something scraped by the hover car, pushing it out of line. Lucien compensated with both lateral and dorsal jets. A second later he caught a glimpse of a tree branch waving at him as it sailed by the port side of the cockpit.

"Shelter Twelve, I repeat this is Security Chief Ortane, requesting emergency landing clearance, Over!"

More static...

And then a reply slithered back: "I read you, Lucien. Please proceed." That was not the voice of the shelter's comm operator. The voice was androgynous and silky smooth, with an accent like nothing Lucien had ever heard before.

"Who is this?"

The static was back. In lieu of a reply, the garage doors began rumbling open.

Fear clawed at Lucien's heart as he realized he must have just spoken with one of the aliens. They'd taken over the shelter. Lucien keyed the comms once more and switched channels to his station's band. "Central, this is *Sierra one zero,* requesting backup at Shelter Twelve. Hostages taken. Over."

Lucien throttled up and glided forward, fighting unpredictable gusts of air to keep them from slamming into the roof of the garage on the way in.

A reply came, but the comms crackled with a burst of interference that garbled the message.

"Say again, Central," Lucien commed back.

Another crackle of interference came, but this time Lucien heard the message. "Sierra one zero, this is Central. Cannot comply, all units grounded due to hull breach. Do not engage. Marines en route ETA ten minutes. Over."

"Negative, Central. Marines too slow. *Sierra one zero* responding." Lucien switched channels to the inside of the patrol car before the dispatcher could reply. "Listen up, Brak: we've got a hostage situation in the shelter. No backup from Central, but Marines are on their way. ETA in ten. I can't wait; my kids are in there, but you don't have to follow me in, buddy."

Brak replied, hissing into the comms, "You insssult my honor, *Bud-dee.* I follow you."

"Copy that," Lucien said as he set the hover down in the garage. The doors rumbled shut behind them with a resonant *bang,* sealing the shelter's atmosphere against the raging vortex outside. Lucien unbuckled and popped the canopy open. The thin air rushed in, making his head spin. He stood up carefully and grabbed the rim of the canopy overhead to hold himself down while he climbed out of the cockpit. In zero-G every step threatened to launch him to the ceiling.

Using the rungs on the side of the cockpit, Lucien rotated his body until he was facing the aft of the hover car, where the equipment locker was located. Pushing off carefully, he sent himself drifting to the back of the car. He managed to stabilize his trajectory and keep himself on course by grabbing hold of intake vents and control surfaces along the way.

Hang on girls, Daddy's coming...

CHAPTER 10

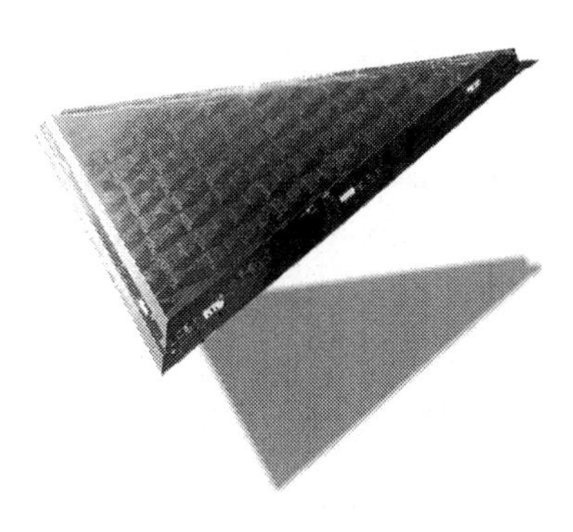

Astralis

"What do you mean Fallside is *depressurizing?*" Admiral Stavos demanded.

"It's exposed to vacuum, sir," the chief engineer, Lieutenant Ruso, said. "There was a massive detonation somewhere between decks twelve zero five and twelve fifteen soon after we turned off the gravity."

Tyra listened to the exchange with growing horror from where she sat belted in at an auxiliary control station. Someone had snagged a pair of mag boots for her before they'd shut off the gravity, but she was in no rush to test them out. Her stomach was still adapting to zero-G, and she didn't think walking around was going to help.

"Was the explosion caused by the faulty reactors?" Chief Councilor Ellis asked.

Admiral Stavos shook his head. "No, two or three

reactors going critical wouldn't cause that kind of damage. This was a bomb. They baited us and we fell for it—got us to turn off the gravity so their bomb would do maximum damage when it ripped open the sky."

"Then turn the gravity back on!" Ellis said.

Stavos shook his head. "We can't. Everything in the whole damn city is halfway into space already. We turn the gravity back on now and all of the debris goes plummeting to the ground, causing even more damage. Whatever went up must *not* come back down."

General Graves waved to them from the holo table in the center of the command deck. "Admiral, you need to see this!"

Both Admiral Stavos and Chief Councilor Ellis hurried over to the table.

Tyra's thoughts went out to Lucien, and she mentally placed a call to reach him, but it just rang and rang...

That pushed her anxiety into overload, and she couldn't sit still any longer. She unbuckled from her control station and followed Stavos and Graves, walking gingerly across the deck and trying not to make any sudden movements that might encourage the contents of her stomach to make a dash for freedom.

Tyra reached the table in time to see the general pointing to a group of about ten red dots surrounded by a few dozen green ones on a map of one of the ship's lower decks. "They're in the sub-levels," Graves explained. Already down to sub four hundred. We shut down the elevators before they could get any further, but they're still on the move, using the stairwells now."

"On the move to where?" Admiral Stavos asked, while

running a hand through his beard.

"Based on their proximity, and their consistent downward push..." Graves looked up from the holo table. "I'd say they're on their way *here,* sir."

Admiral Stavos straightened and turned to address his crew. "Lock down the bridge!"

"Aye, sir!" someone replied.

Klaxons blared and crimson lights flashed.

Turning back to the general, Stavos said, "Get as many squads down here as you can. We hold the bridge at all costs."

"Yes, sir."

Graves got on the comms to his men, barking out orders in his raspy voice.

Tyra turned in a slow circle, watching the frenzy of activity going on all around her. A Marine sergeant and a pair of bots ran from station to station with armfuls of equipment that she couldn't quite make out in the dim light. Then one of the bots came clanking up to her and held out a plasma pistol with a belt and holster attached.

She hesitated.

"For your protection, ma'am," the bot explained, its glowing red eyes insistent.

"Take it," Ellis said as he accepted a matching pistol from another Marine bot and belted it on. "If they get through those doors, we're going to need all the firepower we can get."

Tyra reached for the weapon. The cold weight of it felt strange in her hands. She was a politician, not a soldier. What was she supposed to do with a gun? It had been so long since she'd trained to use a weapon that she'd probably have more luck using it as a bludgeon. Then again, from what she'd seen and heard of their weapons' effectiveness against the enemy, it probably wouldn't matter anyway.

"How many of them have we killed?" Tyra asked.

Ellis stared blankly back, unable to answer.

General Graves looked up from the holo table, his eyes gleaming blackly. His features were all stark blue shadows in the light of the table, while his bristly dark hair blazed red in the flashing lights of the lock-down. "None yet, ma'am."

Tyra did a double take. "*None?*"

"Every time we think we've put one down, it heals itself and comes back to life. All we've managed to do so far is slow them down."

Tyra turned away in shock, her eyes drifting to the doors of the bridge. If these *Faros* were that hard to kill, then it wouldn't matter how many Marines the general sent to defend the bridge. They'd never be able to hold it.

* * *

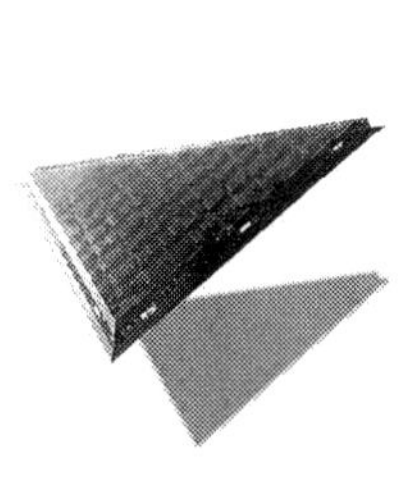

Astralis

Lucien opened the equipment locker at the back of the patrol car, clinging to the door like a life raft in a stormy sea. Brak stood effortlessly beside the engine cowling, already wearing his mag boots.

Lucien gazed into the locker, trying to decide what he'd need. Fortunately, this car had come fully equipped. Boxy black shield packs hung from racks. Matching flak jackets and plates of mirror-smooth refractive armor accompanied those, along with mag boots and helmets. Lucien took off his comfy shoes in favor of the over-sized metal boots and hurried to activate them. His boot soles hit the deck with a comforting *clu-clunk,* and Lucien released his death grip on the door.

Next he donned a flak jacket, followed by the refractive torso armor, and finally one of the shield packs. None of it seemed to weigh anything at all thanks to the zero-G environment, but when he tried leaning and twisting his torso, he felt the weight of the equipment resisting his movements. He grabbed a helmet and strapped it around his chin before selecting a weapon from the rack on the inside of the locker door.

Brak passed over the choices of armor—he was fresh off patrol and already wearing his own custom-fit flak jacket and shield pack, which he wore in reverse, over his broad chest.

Lucien selected an automatic laser rifle and a stun pistol; then he clipped a pair of stun grenades to his belt, as well as a pair of the deadly plasma version.

Turning to Brak, he noted that the Gor hadn't selected any weapons yet. Lucien scowled. "Hurry up!"

Brak nodded wordlessly and pushed him aside to look through the options in the locker.

Lucien imagined the blue-skinned aliens somehow finding his children and singling them out for some horrible fate. The one at the comms had somehow known his name, and it had spoken *Versal*. Lucien had heard the initial news reports back at the station, so he already knew to expect that, but what he didn't know was how any of them could possibly know his name.

Brak bent to retrieve a giant rifle from a case in the bottom of the locker.

Lucien blinked. "You can't take that."

"Why not?" Brak asked, hefting the massive weapon.

Lucien shook his head. "Because you won't just take out your target—you'll also kill whoever is standing next to them. Take something smaller."

Brak snatched a stun pistol from the rack and clipped it to his belt. "Now I have something smaller. Happy?" Brak made no move to put the cannon back.

Lucien frowned. "We don't have time to argue. Just watch your aim, okay?"

Brak hissed and bared his teeth. "Okay." With that, he slung the cannon over his shoulder and grabbed a bandoleer of stun balls—seeker drones that would roll or fly out to their targets, latch on, and stun them into submission.

"Follow me, and keep it quiet. We don't want them to hear us coming."

Brak clicked his comms to acknowledge, and Lucien picked his way through the parking garage, sticking to the shadows behind parked hovers and support columns. Up ahead the doors to the shelter gleamed. Lucien armed his rifle, expecting to see blue-skinned aliens come boiling out through those doors at any second.

But nothing happened, and they made it to the doors without incident. Lucien checked the control panel. The doors weren't locked. Before keying them to open, he ran a scan of the compartments beyond. He saw an empty corridor leading to a large chamber with a blurry smear of heat signatures huddled together on tiered seats. Shelter Twelve was a concert hall when it wasn't being used as an emergency bunker. Lucien's sensors weren't calibrated to differentiate between humans and humanoid aliens, but he did spot a few heat signatures down on the stage that were noticeably cooler than the rest—three cold ones standing beside two smaller warm ones. *Three aliens and two small human hostages? Children?*

Half-turning to Brak, Lucien whispered, "I'm reading three potential hostiles through the doors, on the other side of a short corridor, in the auditorium. They have two hostages, so we're going to have to stick to non-lethals."

Brak hissed and set his cannon on the ground. His hands free, he drew his stun pistol in one hand and a stun ball in the other. Lucien shouldered his own rifle in favor of a stun pistol, too.

"Take cover. I'm opening the doors."

Brak ducked behind the bulkhead and crouched. Lucien mirrored his position on the opposite side of the doors as he keyed them open. They parted with a *swish,* and Lucien peeked around the frame into an empty corridor. Another set of doors stood between them and the auditorium. "Clear," Lucien whispered, and stalked toward the second set of doors. They took cover behind the bulkhead again, and Lucien keyed open the second set of doors. As soon as they slid open, Lucien heard the sounds of children crying and adults pleading, followed by another sound—the silky smooth, androgynous voice he'd heard over the comms.

"Welcome, Lucien! We have been waiting for you."

Brak bared his teeth and his muscles bulged, his body a tightly-wound spring. Lucien gave a slight shake of his head, and mouthed: *no*. Then he stepped into view, his pistol up and tracking...

He found the aliens up on the stage, three of them as expected. They held their hands out to the crowd, clutching dazzling balls of light.

Weapons? Lucien wondered. There was a giant black scorch mark on the floor between the stage and the tiered seats around it, which seemed to confirm that thought.

The three aliens stood easily on the stage. They must have some kind of mag boots on.

"How do you know my name?" Lucien demanded, his aim finding the alien in the center of the three, assuming that must be the one who'd addressed him. The alien wore flowing gray robes, and a forked golden crown that rested just above a pair of glowing, ice-blue eyes. The other two with him sported bald blue heads and flowing *black* robes. Their eyes also glowed—one's green, and the other's yellow.

Lucien did a double take. These did *not* look like the technologically-advanced, space-faring aliens he'd expected. Where were their pressure suits? Their weapons?—glowing balls of who-knew-what notwithstanding. Lucien's mind flashed back to news reports that said *Astralis's* weapons seemed to have no effect against the alien boarders, and his brow furrowed, unable to believe that could be true. They weren't even wearing any armor, let alone anything that might be analogous with a shield pack.

"How do I know your name... well, we have met before, you and me," the crown-wearing alien said.

Of course, the Inquisitor, Lucien thought. His copy—*original*—had run afoul of these aliens eight years ago.

"But I knew your name before we met. After all, it is *my* name, too." The alien grinned and licked his black lips with an equally black tongue.

Lucien blinked in shock. It could be a lie. But if it wasn't, what did it mean that he shared a name with this blue-skinned monster?

CHAPTER 11

Astralis

Whether we share the same name or not, it doesn't matter, Lucien decided. His police training took over: *keep them talking. Distract. Get into position.* Lucien shrugged and edged casually closer to the aliens—*Faros,* he remembered they were called from the initial reports.

"So, we share the same name," Lucien said. "It's just a name." He kept his aim steady on the leader's chest. *King Faro,* he nicknamed that one, noting the crown, and the fact that he seemed to be in charge of the others.

"Oh, it's more than that," King Faro said. "I wonder, have you ever met a human with that name?"

"No," Lucien replied, and realized that it was true. He began to wonder how his parents had chosen that name, but he pushed his curiosity down. King Faro was starting to distract *him*. "My turn for a question: what do you want? You said you were waiting for me. You haven't killed anyone yet, so you must have demands."

"Very astute of you to notice the lack of corpses," King Faro replied. He made a gesture to one of the other aliens, and a glowing ball of energy leapt from the being's hand. It slammed into a man in the front row with a dazzling burst of light and a sound like thunder cracking. People sitting around the man screamed as the blast knocked them free and sent them sailing toward the walls and ceiling. The man who'd been hit drifted slowly above his broken seat. His chest was a black and sunken ruin: white ribs protruded, and glittering beads of blood dribbled out and hung in the air.

"Hold your fire, damn it!" Lucien roared, shock turning to outrage.

"I wanted to make sure you'd take me seriously," King Faro replied. "We're going to play a game."

"No games, tell me what you want."

"Yes, games." The alien said. He reached behind him and hoisted a little girl high above his head. Her hands and feet were bound with glowing cords, and a translucent patch covered her mouth, making it impossible for her to scream. Lucien recognized her instantly. It was Atara. Her cheeks were wet with tears, her green eyes wide with terror.

No! His irrational fear that the aliens would somehow find and single out his children had just been realized. It wasn't possible. How could they even know who his children were?

Coincidence. It had to be.

"Let the girl go," Lucien ordered, hoping to hide her relation to him, but the quaver in his voice betrayed his fear.

King Faro grinned. *"The girl?* Don't you mean, Atara?

Your daughter?"

Lucien's blood ran cold. He knew *her* name, too. "You heard me," Lucien said. "Let her go." It took a supreme effort not to pull the trigger and shoot the alien in the chest.

"Not so fast," King Faro replied. "First, you have to choose. Save your daughters, or save everyone else in this room. Two lives for a thousand."

Lucien blinked in shock. "Daught-*ers?* Where is Theola?"

"Right here." King Faro hoisted her into view, also bound and gagged, baby blues red from crying.

Lucien lost it. He shook his pistol at the monster standing in front of him. "Let them go!"

"Just say the word, Lucien. I'll let them go and kill all of the others instead."

"You can't make me choose between my children and a thousand strangers!"

Hushed murmurs spread through the room. Someone cried out, "We have children, too!"

Another cried, "Frek him! He's going to kill us all, anyway! We'll resurrect when this is over."

King Faro inclined his head to that. "Wrong. I will abide by your decision, Lucien. But that man is correct about one thing: you'll all be resurrected, so what does it matter who I kill? Really, it's just a question of suffering. Would you want your children to go through the trauma of death—no matter how brief? Wouldn't you rather spare them that?"

"Why me?" Lucien demanded. "What the frek does it matter? What do you care who lives and who dies?"

"I don't, but I *do* care about your choice. It is of personal interest to me. Nature versus nurture."

"What are you talking about?" Lucien said.

The alien shrugged. "I already know what *I* would choose..." King Faro replied. "But your choice—" the alien broke off suddenly, his mouth forming an *O* of surprise and pain as he rocked forward on his heels, as if he'd been kicked in his spine. Both of Lucien's children broke free and drifted off behind the aliens, bobbing through the air and heading backstage at a rapid rate.

Lucien blinked. His children shouldn't have been able to move through the air like that. Then he saw the pair of mag boots walking by themselves across the stage, and he realized what was happening. Brak had stripped naked, using his cloaking ability to creep up behind the aliens and steal Atara and Theola away. The boots hadn't cloaked with him, but they were easy enough to miss.

Lucien snapped out of it, and fired a stun bolt at King Faro's chest. It was a direct hit. Electric blue fire crackled over bare blue skin, but the alien's body didn't convulse as Lucien expected. Instead, King Faro recovered with a scowl and turned to watch as Lucien's daughters disappeared backstage.

The alien gestured to one of his guards. "Get them back—alive! And *kill* the one who took them." The black-robed alien inclined its head and ran backstage.

Lucien ran after him, discarding his apparently useless stun pistol in favor of the laser rifle dangling from the strap around his neck. He fired a flurry of dazzling red lasers at King Faro as he ran after his kids. Three bolts hit, splashing crimson fire across the alien's chest—again to no effect.

"You can't hurt me," the alien said, and held out a glowing hand to track Lucien. "But *I* can hurt you. Stop where you are, or I'll do it myself, and then I'll kill everyone else—

your daughters included."

Lucien skidded to a stop. A sharp pang of despair stabbed his heart, and it took a physical effort to look away from the spot where Brak had taken his daughters off the stage.

A stampede of metallic footsteps sounded behind Lucien, and he saw King Faro's gaze drift to the entrance of the shelter. "I was wondering when you would get here!"

Three squads of Marine bots piled into the concert hall, accompanied their human sergeants.

One of the sergeants nodded to Lucien and said, "Back away from the stage, sir."

Lucien hurriedly side-stepped to get out of their line of fire.

"Get down from the stage with your hands above your heads!" the same sergeant barked, now speaking to the aliens.

"Like this?" King Faro asked, raising both hands slowly, his palms glowing.

Someone shouted a warning. Too late. Two shimmering balls of energy leapt out and hit the sergeant in the chest. Explosions boomed and the room flashed white. When the glare faded, the sergeant's body appeared bouncing off the far wall of the room, his armor a blackened, molten mess.

The Marines opened fire with a thunderous roar, but King Faro was no longer standing on the stage. The black-robed alien who'd been standing beside him took the brunt of the barrage. Laser fire rippled across his chest, and bullets sprayed shrapnel as they exploded on some unseen shield. Then someone shot a pair of AP rockets—

Skrsssh...

The explosion boomed, and the alien's chest burst open in a spray of black blood. The imparted momentum shattered the mag-lock of the alien's boots, sending it tumbling backward.

Lucien scanned the room for King Faro, using his helmet's sensors to aid his eyes. After just a second, he found the alien's cold heat signature standing up on the tiers of seating amidst the crowd.

"We're going to play a new game!" King Faro said, and hoisted a young boy above his head. "The soldiers leave, or I kill the boy." The kid kicked him in the throat, but the alien didn't even blink. "Well, Sergeants? What do you say?"

CHAPTER 12

Astralis

Tyra could hear the *thudding* of heavy cannon fire and the high-pitched screeching of lasers even through the heavy blast doors of the bridge. A squad of bots and their sergeant stood behind those doors, weapons raised and waiting for the enemy to come bursting through.

"We're taking heavy losses," General Graves reported from the holo table. "We're down five squads and we've only taken down one enemy."

"One squad?" Tyra asked.

"No, just *one,*" Graves replied.

"What about our reinforcements?" Ellis asked in a panicky voice. "We have a lot more than five squads of Marines on this ship!"

"They're all too far away to reach us in time, and they have their own lines to hold."

"If this line falls, none of the others are going to matter," Admiral Stavos added. "Have the reinforcements fall back to the nearest quantum junctions and jump here *now!* We'll try to buy them some time."

"Yes, sir," Graves replied.

Tyra watched green dots winking off the table as a group of seven red dots stormed the bridge. *Wink, wink, wink...*

Now the odds were even. Seven to seven.

Seven to six—one of the enemies fell.

Zero to six—all of the remaining Marines went down as the enemy reached point-blank range. Tyra imagined shimmering alien swords cutting the marine bots and their sergeants to pieces.

Bang, bang, bang.

All eyes turned to the doors of the bridge. The alien's were knocking.

"Put me in touch with them!" Admiral Stavos ordered.

The comms officer nodded. "You're live, Admiral."

Admiral Stavos spoke, his voice echoing out over the ship's intercom. "This is Admiral Stavos, we have hundreds of squads incoming as we speak. You won't stand a chance against them. Surrender now, and I promise we will be merciful."

Silence answered that ultimatum, but Tyra spotted the red dots on the holo table backing away from the bridge.

"They're leaving!" Ellis said, his voice cracking with relief.

"No," Graves whispered. "They're not." He pointed to the map. The red dots had stopped moving a fixed distance from the doors.

BOOM! The doors shivered and glowed brightly at the seams, as if struggling to hold back a fire-breathing dragon.

"Here they come!" Graves roared. "Take cover!"

BOOM! The doors exploded in a fiery rain of shrapnel. Tyra hit the deck, using the edge of the holo table to hold herself down. A molten orange sheet of metal whizzed through the space where her head had been a second ago.

Weapons fire screeched, and blinding flashes of light tore through the bridge with deck-shaking *booms*. Marine bots *clanked* as they dodged and fell. Waves of heat swept over Tyra and an acrid smell filled her nostrils. She risked raising her head to look.

Smoke swirled in the entrance of the bridge, and the squad of Marine bots who'd been standing there floated in a cloud of glowing shrapnel. Their sergeant drifted with them, his face a rictus of horror and pain behind the shattered faceplate of his helmet. It was Sergeant Ikes.

A group of blue-skinned aliens stormed in, swatting away broken pieces of bots like flies. One alien strode to the fore. He wore gray robes and a golden crown. Tyra was surprised to see how human he looked, but his hairlessness and glowing blue eyes were decidedly alien.

"Where is the one who calls himself Admiral Stavos?" the alien demanded in a smooth voice. His accent was strange, but he spoke Versal clearly enough.

"Here," Stavos said. Tyra craned her neck to see him stand up from behind the holo table.

"Who else is in charge?" the alien asked.

For a moment no one replied. Then the alien thrust out a hand in the direction of the nearest control station. A ball of light shot out and exploded with a blinding flash of light a deafening *boom*. The control station flew apart, and the man sitting there went flying over the railing to the far wall of viewscreens.

Tyra felt something hot and sharp bite into her thigh, and she bit her tongue to keep from crying out.

"I'm in charge of the Marines," General Graves said, also standing up from behind the holo table, his sidearm in hand, but not aimed.

"Anyone else?"

Tyra raised her hand and gingerly climbed to her feet, making sure to keep contact between her mag boots and the deck. "I'm the councilor of Fallside."

"Councilor... this is like a lord?" the alien inquired. His voice was gender neutral, but his facial features were decidedly male. "Yes... you are a civilian leader. Where is your king? The one who calls himself *Chief Councilor Ellis?*"

Ellis made no move to stand up.

"If I have to ask again, someone else will die," the alien said, his hand already glowing with another ball of energy.

Tyra used her ARCs to find Ellis cowering behind the holo table. She glared in his direction, and General Graves hoisted him up by the collar of his white ceremonial robes. "Here he is."

The alien licked a set of perfectly straight white teeth with a black tongue and grinned. "Amazing how quickly you will turn on each other, isn't it?"

Councilor Ellis struggled free of the General's grasp and planted his mag boots firmly on the deck. Taking a moment to straighten his robes, he walked around the holo table to face the aliens.

"What do you want?"

"You three," he wagged a long index finger tipped with a sharp golden claw to indicate Stavos, Graves, Ellis. "I will commune with you." As he said that, two more aliens stepped through the swirling clouds of smoke and debris in the entrance of the bridge. They were identical copies, complete with matching gray robes and glowing golden crowns.

"Commune?" Ellis asked, his eyes skipping from one alien clone to the next. "What does that mean?"

All three spoke as one, "Come here and we will show you."

CHAPTER 13

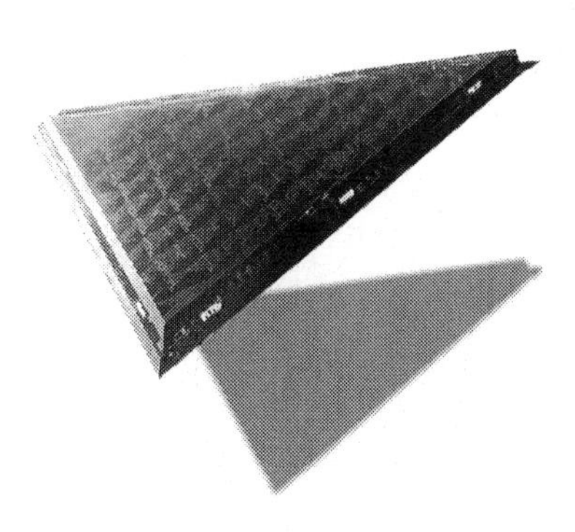

Astralis

Lucien watched King Faro hold the young boy above his head, kicking and screaming, impervious to the those kicks. The boy's parents snapped out of their shock and began beating the alien with their fists. In response, the alien grabbed the boy's mother in his free hand and held her up by her throat.

"Touch me again, and she dies," King Faro warned, nodding to the father.

Both he and his son subsided, and the alien directed his attention to the Marines standing in the entrance of the shelter. "Well? Are you going to leave, or should I start killing?"

Lucien ran through the list of options in his head. Stun weapons did nothing, and it took heavy weapons fire to overwhelm the Faros' personal shields. With this one surrounded by civilians, the Marines couldn't risk bringing that kind of firepower to bear. They had no choice.

"Fall back," one of the remaining two Marine sergeants said. He flicked a quick glance at Lucien, as if to ask, *what's he want with you?*

But Lucien was still wondering the same thing. Why had he and his children been singled out? As the Marines left, Lucien's gaze strayed to the back of the stage. His whole body itched with the urge to run after his children.

The doors to the concert hall slid shut with a *swish,* and King Faro said, "Looks like it's just the two of us again. Have you made up your mind yet?"

Lucien's head snapped around and he glared up at the alien king. "You're not holding my children hostage anymore, so you can't make me choose between them and a room full of strangers."

"I am holding someone else's child," the alien pointed out. "But you're right, it's not the same thing." King Faro released the boy and his mother with a shrug, and the father hurried to pull them back down to their seats.

"We will wait until Hassan recovers them."

Lucien glanced back to the stage, and he took a quick step in that direction, unable to help himself.

"No," King Faro said. "Let's see how Brak does on his own. One on one is a fair fight, wouldn't you say?"

Brak. The alien knew his name, too. *Buy time, just buy time, keep him talking, distracted...* Lucien thought. Maybe the Marines would come up with something.

Lucien turned to gaze up at the alien once more. "You want a fair fight? Deactivate your shield and face me yourself. No weapons. Hand-to-hand only."

"I fear that wouldn't last very long..." King Faro said, and the corners of his mouth drooped in an exaggerated frown.

Lucien was about to argue with more false bravado, but the alien grabbed the back of the seat in front of him and casually ripped the whole thing free of its bolts. The chair floated up in front of him, its occupant still clutching his seat and looking terrified.

"Strength alone isn't enough to determine the outcome of a fight," Lucien argued.

"No?" the alien replied. "When your face caves in under my fist, you may have trouble supporting that argument..." King Faro trailed off with a frown. His glowing eyes slid away, and the crowd gasped.

Lucien followed the alien's gaze to the stage and saw that the black-robed alien, *Hassan,* had returned. One hand still held his shimmering sword, dragging it behind him, the tip sizzling across the stage, while his other hand, and *arm,* were missing at the shoulder. He stumbled across the stage with black blood gushing from his open shoulder socket like party streamers. The alien staggered twice and shook his head. It said something in a sibilant language of hisses and sneers.

Despite the gruesome scene, Lucien felt relief spreading in his chest. Brak had somehow gotten the better of Hassan.

"I am disappointed to hear that," King Faro said, replying in Versal—*for my benefit?* Lucien wondered. He glanced back at King Faro in time to see the alien leap over the rows of seats and sail down to the stage, propelled by some unseen means—*grav boosters?* Lucien wondered as the alien king touched down in front of Hassan. The king drew a shimmering blade of his own from a scabbard on his back, and Hassan growled out something else, looking suddenly frightened. The king swung his sword, and Hassan lifted his to parry, but weakly. A sizzle of energy sparked, and Hassan's blade bounced away, flying out of his hand, while King Faro's blade sailed on to slice Hassan's head off.

"Mercy? Death is your mercy," the king said as the head floated away, its glowing green eyes wide and staring as the light slowly faded from them.

Silence rang, and King Faro rounded on Lucien. "Don't go anywhere. I'll be back." With that, he vanished from the stage in a blur of gray robes, moving impossibly fast.

Frek that, Lucien thought, and sprinted after him. Upon reaching the chest-high stage, he deactivated his mag boots, jumped, and activated them again, touching down on top of the stage. His rifle whipped around his neck, throwing him off balance and rocking him back on his heels. He shrugged out of the strap and let the weapon drift free. It was next to useless anyway. Instead, he cast about for Hassan's shimmering sword. He found it drifting at the edge of the stage, and ran to catch it.

The blade was almost invisible, and no longer shimmering, but as Lucien's hand wrapped around the hilt, it hummed to life, vibrating against his palm.

It was strange in an age of high technology to be reduced to melee weapons, but Lucien didn't have time to wonder about it. He ran backstage, using his helmet's sensors to track King Faro's cool heat signature through walls and doors.... Lucien ran past audio equipment, through a make-up room, and on down a hall past private dressing rooms. He turned sharply at the end of the corridor and started down another one. King Faro stood in front of a shut door at the end. Lucien slowed his approach, realizing it might not be the best strategy to charge.

"You refused to make your choice," the alien said as Lucien drew near. "So I'm going to make it for you." With that, he turned and opened the door, revealing at least five squads of Marine bots and their sergeants. King Faro rushed them.

Anticipating the Marines' reaction, Lucien took cover, plastering himself to the wall as they fired a blinding, deafening volley of lasers and cannons.

The alien king glowed brightly as his shield deflected everything. He ran through the ranks, sword flashing. Severed bits of bots went drifting out above the chaos, and the alien ran on, unfettered.

The weapons fire abruptly ceased as King Faro burst out the other side of the Marines' formation. As soon as that happened, Lucien lunged out of cover, giving chase once more. Up ahead he saw that all of the Marines had turned to face the rear now, weapons tracking, but none of them firing.

As Lucien drew near, a familiar, hissing roar reached his ears. Metal arms and legs were a forest, blocking his view, but he managed to steal glimpses of Brak's naked gray bulk streaking out and slamming into the alien king.

There was a brief struggle before Brak went spinning away, clutching a gash in his side, and hissing in pain. King Faro sailed on, heading for a group of corpsmen attending to a familiar pair of young girls.

"No!" Lucien ran as fast as he could, but there was no way he would reach them in time. His mind raged: *Why aren't the Marines firing!?* But he knew why. They couldn't shoot without risking the lives they were trying to save.

Lucien hit the ranks of Marine bots, forced to slow down as he waded through their rigid, unyielding lines. "Get out of the way!" he screamed. He was caught in one of those feet stuck-in-molasses nightmares where no matter how fast he tried to run, he couldn't go faster than a crawl.

One of the corpsmen stepped between Lucien's children and the alien. King Faro stopped and swung his sword, lopping off the corpsman's head.

Atara screamed, and Theola stared wordlessly.

Blood streamed from the lifeless body, held erect and swaying on its feet by the zero-G environment. King Faro shoved it aside, and reached for Atara with a glowing palm.

The Marine bots belatedly parted ranks, and Lucien broke free. He pounded across the deck, teeth gritted, eyes wide with rage and horror, unable to do anything but watch as King Faro wrapped his glowing palm around Atara's face like a squid and lifted her off the deck. Atara's feet dangled, and her muffled screams stabbed Lucien's ears repeatedly. He ran faster still, every second a lifetime while Atara suffered.

As he drew near, Lucien thrust out his stolen sword, using his momentum to put some weight behind the weapon. The sword sunk up to its hilt in the alien's back, but King Faro didn't release his daughter, or even cry out in pain.

Shoving off from the blue-skinned monster, Lucien screamed and ran him through again and again until black blood streamed from half a dozen slits in the alien's gray robes. But still the alien wouldn't let his daughter go. To his horror, Lucien saw one of the gashes in the alien's blue skin seal up before his eyes.

He swept the sword down through the alien's knees, and was gratified to see both legs severed and the alien king drifting free in a gushing stream of black blood. *Heal that, you frekking kakard!* Lucien thought. But the alien king clung to Atara as if his life depended on it, and Atara's muffled cries were ominously silent now.

Desperate, Lucien reached up and pulled the alien down to eye-level with him. He stared into those glowing blue eyes, their depths inscrutable. "How's this for a choice," he said as he ran the sword across the alien's throat with all his strength. The blade flashed clean through, and the alien's mouth popped open in a silent scream as the light left his eyes and his head drifted free in a torrent of black blood that splashed Lucien's helmet. He grimaced and shoved the body away from him, wiping the blood on his sleeve. Then he whirled around to find Atara drifting peacefully behind him, her eyes shut and a serene expression on her face.

"Atara!" Lucien dropped the sword and reached for his daughter, pulling her face down to his. When she didn't react, he slapped her cheek. "Wake up!"

Still nothing.

A navy corpsman appeared beside them and ran a scanner over Atara's body with a flickering blue fan of light.

"She's alive... but comatose," the corpsman declared. "We need to get her to hospital." He turned and snapped his fingers at another corpsman, a young woman. Her uniform was splashed crimson with blood from the one who'd been killed in front of them. She shook herself out of an apparent state of frozen terror, but made no move to assist.

Lucien saw why a second later. Theola stood beside her, clutching the woman's hand in a tiny fist. Lucien ran to his other little girl. He dropped to his haunches in front of her, about to fold Theola into a big hug—

But she screamed in terror and ducked behind the woman's legs.

Lucien blinked and whirled around, expecting to see another blue-skinned alien standing behind him, but there was nothing there.

The woman holding his daughter's hand spoke in a trembling voice: "She's afraid of you, sir."

Lucien turned back to her, his brow furrowed in shock. "Me?"

Black alien blood still smeared his faceplate, reminding him why his daughter might be afraid. Theola watched him with huge eyes, peeking between the woman's legs. Covered in Faro blood, he must have looked like another monster to Theola, maybe even more terrifying than the one who'd grabbed her sister.

A lump rose in Lucien's throat as he stood. "Look after them please, ma'am. I need to go wash up."

The female corpsman nodded woodenly as Lucien turned away. His whole body shivered with fury as he stalked back to the concert hall. Seeing the terror in his one-year-old's eyes, and knowing she was afraid of *him,* had hurt more than any injury the Faros could have inflicted. Add to that the psychological damage of what she'd witnessed, and whatever the frek they'd done to Atara...

Lucien shook his head, and his hands balled into fists. He'd make the Faros pay if it was the last thing he did.

CHAPTER 14

Astralis

"Come," the trio of identical blue-skinned aliens intoned in a single loud voice.

"And if we refuse?" Chief Councilor Ellis asked. He drew himself up and puffed out his chest, trying to look defiant, but to Tyra he looked like a boy pretending to be a solider.

"Then we kill everyone on the bridge," the aliens replied. "Your choice."

Tyra watched from the sidelines as Admiral Stavos stepped forward. "You can start with me."

"All three," the aliens replied.

Ellis glanced to General Graves and then to Admiral Stavos, his eyes pleading. Graves walked over to him with a tight smile, and placed a hand on his shoulder. "We'll go together," Graves said, and pushed Ellis along in front of him.

Admiral Stavos kept pace beside them, and Tyra watched in horror as the leaders of *Astralis* approached the alien clones to *commune* with them—whatever *that* meant.

They stopped in front of the aliens, each of them facing off with a different clone, and then the aliens raised glowing palms in front of their human counterparts' faces.

Graves arched an eyebrow at this, his eyes squinting into the light. "If you're expecting a high-five, you're about to be disappointed."

"Shut u—" Ellis began, but he was abruptly cut off as some unseen force yanked him face-first into the alien's palm. Graves and Stavos were also yanked forward, and glowing alien hands wrapped around each of their faces like luminous squid.

Ellis gave a muffled scream, and one of the bridge crew gasped. Murmurs of concern rose from the crew, and the comms officer rose halfway out of his chair, his hand on his sidearm.

"Wait!" Tyra said. She listened with growing apprehension to Ellis's muffled screams, but she thought it noteworthy that neither Graves nor Stavos were screaming. If they were in pain or danger, surely they'd at least grunt, or call out orders to the crew. All three of the Faros stared fixedly ahead, unblinking and unmoving.

Adrenaline sent sparks shooting through Tyra's nerves, urging her to act, while cold beads of sweat slipped down her spine. "What are you doing to them?" she demanded.

No reply.

She felt for her sidearm with a clammy hand, and cold metal kissed her fingertips. With the aliens so utterly distracted, this might be their only chance to take them by surprise...

Then she remembered that *six* aliens had made it to the bridge. That meant that these three had to have another three guarding their backs. Tyra caught a meaningful look from the comms officer, and she realized she wasn't the only one thinking about attacking. She gave her head a slight shake.

At best they had six crewmen with a clear shot right now, and none of them was as heavily armed or armored as the Marines who'd been defending the bridge. Opening fire with nothing but pistols would be suicide—not to mention they'd probably kill their leaders in the process.

The sound of weapons fire reached the bridge, and Tyra's breath caught in her throat. Should she dive back into cover, or remain standing?

The three Faros in front of her made no move to turn and face the threat, but the weapons fire grew louder and more insistent. Explosions *boomed* and roared. Acrid smoke gushed in.

The aliens appeared to snap out of their reverie, and finally they released *Astralis's* leaders. Tyra couldn't tell if it was because of the fight going on behind them, or because they'd just finished whatever they were doing.

Stavos, Graves, and Ellis stood statuesque on the deck, swaying in zero-G, pinned in place by their mag-boots. Their backs were turned to her, but Tyra suspected their eyes were shut, and they were asleep. She had a feeling that they'd just been subjected to the Faros' equivalent of a mind probe.

Tyra sucked in a breath and shook her head, wondering what to do. The three Faros turned to leave, their backs clearly exposed, offering tempting targets.

The ship's gunnery chief jumped up from his chair,

sidearm out. "Open fire!" he yelled, and pulled the trigger three times fast. Bolts of red-hot plasma shrieked out and slammed into one of the aliens—

To no effect. That same alien whirled around and launched a blinding ball of energy plasma from his palm. It hit the gunnery chief and exploded with a blast of heat that sent him flying over the railing to join the other dead crewman floating near the viewscreens.

No one else tried anything, and the aliens raced off the bridge. Tyra waited until they were gone before checking on Ellis and the others. She rounded their backs to face them, only to find exactly what she'd expected—eyes shut, faces expressionless, relaxed in sleep. They looked so peaceful that they might even be dead.

Fear stabbed Tyra's heart, and she reached up to check Ellis's pulse. The ship's science officer joined her and checked Stavos's life signs with a handheld scanner.

"Ellis is alive," Tyra said, feeling his carotid artery jumping steadily under her fingertips.

"So is Admiral Stavos," the science officer said. "But he's in a coma." She ran her scanner over Graves and Ellis next. "They all are."

Tyra grimaced. "We need a medical team down here."

"They'll never make it. The Marines need to open a clear path to the bridge first." The science officer nodded to the entrance of the bridge to indicate the sounds of battle still drifting to their ears. The weapons fire sounded more distant now.

Tyra hurried back to the holo table to check on the situation. She saw *four* red dots—no longer six—racing away from the bridge at an impossible speed, followed by a swarm of slower green dots.

The science officer joined her by the table. "They're outrunning *bots,*" she breathed.

Tyra glanced at her and took a moment to look up the woman's name via her ARCs. It flashed up above her head in a green bar of text—*Lt. Cmdr. Esalia Wheeler.*

"They're obviously not biological," Tyra replied. "No biological being can shoot plasma from their bare hands."

"Or perform mind probes," Lieutenant Wheeler added.

Tyra acknowledged that with a nod. She tracked the enemy's progress with her index finger. They'd just reached a stairwell and now they were flying down the stairs to even lower sub levels. "Where are they going?" Tyra wondered aloud.

"No way to know for sure," Wheeler said, "But I have a guess."

Tyra sought the other woman's gaze, and Wheeler looked up from the holo table with a grim frown. "They came here, mind-probed our leaders, and now they're fleeing with the intel they gathered."

"Or they found a weakness they can exploit in our ship," Tyra suggested.

"Either way, we have to stop them," Wheeler replied.

"How?"

"We have superior numbers and access to the ship's quantum junctions. We jump ahead of them and box them in."

Tyra nodded. "Who's going to coordinate that?"

"Graves, but since he's out of action someone probably already picked up the slack for him in the operations room. Hang on, let me check."

"Bridge to CIC, this is the acting CO. Is the acting CMO on deck? Over." Wheeler paused and waited for a reply, but none came.

"Bridge to CIC, how copy? Over."

...

"They're not answering," Tyra said, and pulled up a schematic view of the Operations Room. It looked fine to her.

"They're all dead," Wheeler whispered.

Tyra flinched. "What?"

The science officer pointed to the schematic of the operations room, but Tyra still didn't see anything. Then she saw what she'd missed: there should have been at least a dozen green dots spread through the room—officers at their stations, but there wasn't even one.

"We're going to have to coordinate from here," Wheeler said. Then a moment later, "Bridge to unit forty-nine. How copy? Over."

"*Sierra Four Niner,* solid copy. Need to speak with *Actual* for sitrep, over."

"Sierra Four Niner, this is Lima One. Actual is down. Sitrep is four bandits on sub five twenty, sector thirty-seven, section thirteen, sub-section F, heading down stairwell number four in alley beside the Pharma and Drug Store. How copy? Over."

Tyra tuned out the ensuing conversation to rather watch the action play out on the table. Sierra four niner called in backup and hundreds of green dots began pouring out of quantum junctions above and below Sub Level 520. Dozens more streamed into the stairwell in question and cornered the fleeing aliens. Tyra watched simulated weapons fire flash across the schematic. Green dots winked away in droves, but more kept streaming in to replace them.

After about a minute the first red enemy signature winked off the grid, followed by two more, and then the last one vanished.

"Sierra Four Niner here—we're all clear."

"Good to hear Four Niner," Wheeler replied. "I've got twelve more bandits on sub nine sixty, also heading down."

"We're on it, Lima One, moving out!"

A collective sigh rose from the bridge. The immediate danger was past.

Tyra glanced over her shoulder at the comatose leaders of *Astralis*.

Lieutenant Commander Wheeler followed her gaze and she snapped out a new order over the comms. "Bridge to Medical, we need immediate assistance, over."

The reply crackled out from overhead speakers. "Medical here, what's the nature of your emergency?"

"The CO, CMO, and Chief Councilor are all comatose after direct contact with the enemy."

"Acknowledged. A team is on their way. Advise you arrange a Marine escort."

"Roger. Escort will be waiting. Bridge out," Wheeler said. She turned to Tyra and nodded. "Until the CO and Chief Councilor wake up and are cleared for duty, the chain of command falls to me and you respectively."

Tyra nodded. She hadn't thought about that.

"You might want to check in with the other councilors and come up with a plan of action for after we neutralize the remaining invaders."

"Good idea." It was hard to think long-term when the short-term was still so uncertain. She remembered the empty operations room. The CIC was buried deep inside Hubble Mountain—not too far from the shelters in the base of the mountain. If the Faros had made it that far, then Lucien would have run into them, and if that were the case... then it might explain why he hadn't answered her comms call earlier. Her worries about Lucien and her daughters surged to the surface, and Tyra placed a call to Lucien once more.

This time he answered, and relief washed over her. "Tyra—I was just about to call you. I'm on my way down to the hospital with Atara."

Tyra's relief evaporated in an instant, and her heart leapt into her throat. "What? What happened?"

"The Faros took over the shelter. Their leader had some kind of personal vendetta with me or... something. He claimed we share the same name, and he wanted me to choose between saving our girls and all of the other people in the shelter."

Tyra's whole body went cold. The air felt thick. It was suddenly impossible to breathe. "What did you choose?" she whispered.

"I didn't. Brak took him by surprise and rescued the girls. The alien went after them, and so did I. I managed to kill the Faro, but not before he got his hands on Atara. He did something to her, and now she's in a coma."

Tyra glanced back to Chief Ellis and the ship's commanding officers. Whatever the aliens had done to them, they'd done to Atara as well.

"Which hospital are you going to?" Tyra asked.

"Winterside General."

"I'm on my way," Tyra replied. "See you soon." She ended the comms there and turned to Commander Wheeler.

"It's my daughter, she's..."

Wheeler nodded curtly. "Go. There's not much you can do here, anyway. I'll get you on the comms if I need you."

"Thank you," Tyra breathed. She ran off the bridge in an awkward loping gait thanks to her mag boots, but before long she had the hang of running in them, and she was pounding down the corridors faster than she'd ever run in her life.

CHAPTER 15

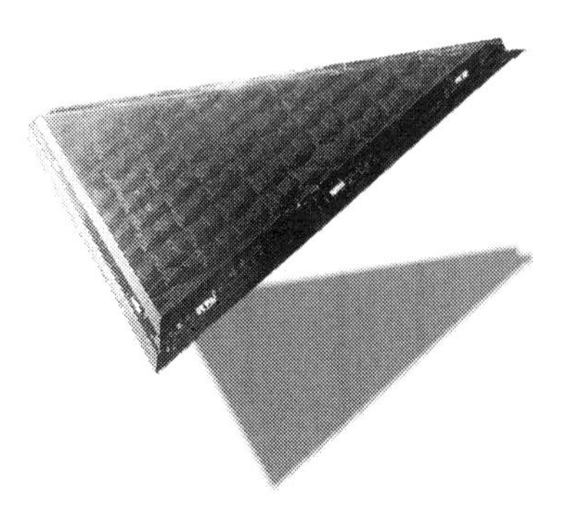

Astralis

Lucien watched as the door swished open and Tyra burst into the room. Her eyes met Lucien's first, then found Theola in his arms.

She reached with chubby baby arms for her mother. "Mama!"

"I'm here, sweetheart!" Tyra ran to them and folded them both in a big hug. She kissed each of them and then took Theola from Lucien.

Lucien smiled tightly and returned his attention to their other daughter, lying in the bed in front of him. Her eyes were shut, and her expression peaceful, but carved in stone. She hadn't so much as twitched since arriving at the hospital half an hour ago. Wires and an IV line trailed from her bed. Monitors beeped rhythmically around her, indicating that her life signs were strong. There'd been no signs of injury, and her brain scans had come back clean, but if all of that was true, then why hadn't she woken up? So far none of the doctors could answer that.

Tyra walked quietly around the bed and placed a hand on Atara's forehead. "Oh, Atty..." she whispered as tears fell from her cheeks and landed on Atara's pillow.

Theola reached down, as if to place a hand on her sister's forehead, too. Theola was back to her usual self, having somehow forgotten all about the gruesome events she'd witnessed. Lucien hoped it would stay that way.

"Do they know what's wrong with her?" Tyra asked.

He shook his head. "We're still waiting on the results from the latest tests. The doctors say she should wake up soon, but..." Lucien trailed off, not wanting to give voice to more negative possibilities.

"Well, whatever it is, there are a lot of people working on the problem by now. The Faros did the same thing to the command staff on the bridge."

Lucien blinked. "What? Why didn't you mention that when I called?"

"I was worried about you and the kids at the time."

"That might change the prognosis," Lucien said.

"How?" Tyra asked, wiping her cheeks on the back of the hand that wasn't holding Theola.

Lucien grimaced, wondering how much he should say. "Before that alien ran after the girls, he threatened me, saying because I couldn't make my choice, he was going to make it for me."

Tyra scowled. "What choice? Our girls' lives for the lives of the other hostages?"

Lucien nodded. "The implication is—"

"That he *killed* my little girl?" Tyra's cheeks flushed and her eyes flashed. She turned and pointed to Atara's brain monitor. "She's not brain dead, Lucien! And I don't see any mortal wounds, so she's *fine.*"

"No, you're right." Lucien nodded quickly. "But if they did the same thing to the command staff, then what do you think it was?"

Tyra hesitated.

"Mom...? Dad?" It was Atara's voice.

Lucien's heart jumped in his chest, and he ran to Atara's side to hold her hand. She raised her head, blinking bleary eyes as she looked around the room.

"It's okay, Atty," Lucien said. "We're here."

Tyra's tears fell anew as she stroked her daughter's head. "You're awake," she said, smiling broadly.

"Agaga!" Theola blurted.

"What happened?" Atara asked.

"You don't remember?" Lucien asked.

"I remember Brak carrying us, then the medics talking to me..." Atara's eyes flew wide and her whole body tensed. She grabbed fistfuls of the sheets. "You were in my head!" she said, gazing accusingly up at her father.

"Who was?" Tyra asked.

"Dad!"

"It wasn't me, honey. That... *thing,* claimed we share the same name, but it wasn't me. I killed him and rescued you."

Atara frowned uncertainly, but she nodded slowly, and her body relaxed.

"I'm going to go get your doctor," Lucien said. "He needs to know you're awake."

"No need for that." A new voice joined theirs, and Lucien turned to see the man in question come striding into the room. He had dark straight hair, slanted orange eyes, a moderate build, and golden skin. "Her monitors were set to alert me as soon as she woke up," the doctor explained as he stopped in front of Tyra and held out a hand. "I'm Doctor Fushiwa."

Tyra shook his hand in a reversed, left-handed grip, since her right arm was still holding Theola. "Tyra Ortane," she replied. "My husband tells me you were waiting on some more test results. I assume they came back fine?"

"Yes, all normal. Whatever those Faros did to your daughter, it doesn't appear to have harmed her. But..."

"But?" Tyra demanded.

Lucien's guts clenched in anticipation of the bad news.

"We'd like to submit her to a mind probe just to be sure. We need your consent for that."

"Absolutely not!" Tyra replied.

"It won't hurt her," Doctor Fushiwa insisted.

"You just said she was fine, so what's the point of a probe?"

The doctor glanced at Lucien, then Atara, and back to Tyra. A nurse strode by them, her mag-boots clomping noisily, on her way to check Atara's IV.

"Perhaps we should discuss this out in the hall while the nurse attends to your daughter?" Doctor Fushiwa said.

Tyra scowled, and Lucien frowned. "We'll be right back, Atara," he said.

She nodded weakly. "Okay..."

Lucien felt a knot of tension forming between his eyes as he and Tyra followed the doctor out. As soon as they were in the hallway, Lucien jerked his chin to the doctor and crossed his arms over his chest. "So?"

"We can't tell what that alien was trying to do to Atara. As far as we can detect, it didn't do anything besides put her into a coma."

"And that's a bad thing?" Lucien asked.

"No, but it *is* odd. According to the report you gave, the alien held her in some kind of trance, with his hand wrapped around her face, and neither your daughter nor the alien were responsive to external stimuli."

"What's your point?"

"There has to have been a reason that alien would risk its life and ultimately lose it just to reach your daughter."

"I don't think he *knew* he was risking his life," Lucien said. "He couldn't have known I would steal one of their swords and use it to chop off his head."

"Yes, there's that, which is encouraging, but the fact remains, he was trying to do something to her. Since it's apparent that the alien only interacted with Atara's mind, we need to get in there and see if anything changed. We'll compare her probe data to the last backup of her memories and personality."

"Her last backup was a month ago, *before* we reached the cosmic horizon," Tyra said. "A lot can change in a child's brain over the course of a month."

The doctor inclined his head to that. "Agreed. The analysis will likely take some time."

"And what if you find that he *did* change something?" Tyra asked.

"Then we'll see the changes and undo whatever it is that he did. If need be, we'll simply restore those areas from backups," the doctor replied.

Tyra looked as skeptical as Lucien felt.

"Wouldn't you rather know if there's something wrong with your daughter?" the doctor pressed.

"What about the others?" Tyra asked. "The command staff were subjected to the same *trance* that Atara was. Are you going to put them through mind probes and comparative analyses, too?"

"Actually, *their* doctor is the one who suggested the procedure. He contacted me a few minutes ago, following up on a request I'd put in asking for information about any other cases of alien contact that resulted in the victim losing consciousness. Apparently, your daughter was the last to wake up. Admiral Stavos, General Graves, and Chief Councilor Ellis all woke up en route to the hospital, and they've already signed off on the mind probe."

Tyra chewed her bottom lip. Theola slipped down her hip, making a break for the floor, but Tyra adjusted her grip and pulled her back up, to which Theola screamed and struggled.

"What happens if we say no?" Tyra asked.

"I'm not sure I understand the question," Doctor Fushiwa replied.

"If we refuse the probe, will Atara be detained or kept under some kind of surveillance?"

"I can't comment on that, ma'am. For the time being there would be no consequences that I'm aware of."

"We'll sign the consent forms," Lucien said.

Tyra turned to glare at him. "Just like that?"

"There *will* be consequences if we don't do this. You know that. Atara will be under suspicion forever. Do you want her to have to live like that? With everyone treating her like an outcast?"

"No one needs to know what happened to her."

"They'll find out. There were plenty of witnesses. It'll be on the news if it isn't already, and she *will* end up on a police watch list. If we have the probe report, all of that changes. We'll have something to show nosy reporters and the police—even neighbors."

Tyra hesitated. "Fine. I'll sign."

"You made the right decision, ma'am," Doctor Fushiwa said. He held out a palm-sized holo projector and activated it. A blue-skinned alien strapped to a gleaming steel table sprang to life above his palm. Theola screamed and writhed in Tyra's arms, trying to get away. Doctors walked up to the alien with gleaming scalpels and saws.

"Sorry, sorry!" Doctor Fushiwa said, and waved quickly past the image to the consent form. "I was watching one of the alien autopsies."

Tyra glared at the doctor and cooed reassuringly in Theola's ear, bouncing her to calm her down.

Lucien glanced at the form before signing at the bottom with his index finger; then Tyra passed Theola to him and added her signature beside his. Theola whimpered in Lucien's arms, the sound muffled by the thumb in her mouth.

"I want something in exchange," Tyra said.

The doctor regarded her with eyebrows raised. "Yes?"

"I want your best therapist to come see my daughters."

"That's a good idea," Lucien said as he kissed Theola's tears away. "I killed that alien right in front of Theola, and before that, he beheaded a corpsman in front of both our girls."

The doctor grimaced. "They might require more than simple therapy. You may wish to have their memories of the events erased via another probe, but that's a topic to discuss with a therapist. I'll make sure that one gets in touch with you right away."

"Thank you," Tyra replied.

The doctor nodded and walked off. Lucien took Tyra's hand and started back to Atara's room, but after just a few steps in that direction, Tyra stopped to answer a comm call.

"Acting Chief Councilor Ortane speaking..." she said.

* * *

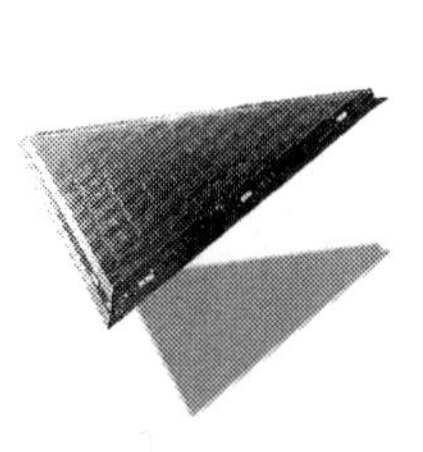

Astralis

"All hostiles have been eliminated, ma'am. *Astralis* is clear."

Tyra felt some of the tension in her chest release. "That's a big relief, Commander. How are repairs to the hull breach in Fallside going?"

"The Academy solved the problem. Literally. The whole building broke free and got sucked into the breach. It plugged the hole and repair bots welded it into place. Rescue efforts are underway to see about extracting the survivors trapped inside."

Tyra shook her head. "Incredible. We'll figure out how to make more permanent repairs later. Do we have any idea about casualties yet?"

"According to ship's sensors, our population is down by more than five million. Most of those people were from Fallside."

Tyra blinked. "That many?" There were only nine million people in the entire city of Fallside. That meant more than half the people who'd lived there were now dead. She shuddered to think what her beloved city must look like now. "The Resurrection Center is going to be working around the clock to bring that many people back."

"Aye, it will. What are your orders, ma'am?"

Tyra took a moment to consider that. "We stay where we are and lick our wounds. Prioritize getting the reactors online so we can turn the gravity back on. And keep jamming outbound comms. We don't know if they planted a tracking device somewhere."

"Aye, we'll do that, ma'am."

"I'll get in touch with the other councilors and see about long-term plans, but with any luck, the Admiral and Chief Councilor will be cleared for duty soon."

"Hopefully, but it may be a while before that happens."

"Time will tell. Thanks for the update, Commander. Keep me posted." Tyra ended that comm call, and a split second later another one started ringing inside her head. She answered it with a sigh. "Acting Chief Councilor Ortane speaking."

"This is the Resurrection Center. We have a priority update for you, ma'am."

Tyra's brow furrowed. She hadn't lost any loved ones. Besides Lucien and the girls, the rest of her family was back in the Etherian Empire. "What's the update?"

"We received a manual memory dump from you before *Astralis* jumped away, but it didn't come from *you*, exactly... the transmission source was from somewhere off *Astralis*. Do you know anything about that?"

"Are you sure the memories are mine? Maybe there was some kind of mix-up."

"The ID code and encryption checks out. The memories are definitely yours. I could look into them if you want to make sure, but I'd need your permission for that."

"No, that's fine. Hold the data in my archive. I'll be down to check it out as soon as I can."

"Yes, ma'am."

Again, Tyra ended the comm call. Lucien stood in front of her, his green eyes wide and his brow furrowed. "What was all of that about?"

"The acting commander called to tell me the aliens have all been eliminated."

Lucien's shoulders slumped. "Thank Etherus for that."

Tyra arched an eyebrow at him. "You mean thank the Marines."

He waved a hand to dismiss that distinction. "What was the other call about?"

"It seems like my clone from the *Inquisitor* may have transmitted her memories to *Astralis* before we jumped away."

"What?" Lucien shook his head. "Well... what are you going to do about that?"

Tyra shrugged. "Assuming it's true, I'll likely have to

integrate her memories and consciousness with mine."

"You don't *have to* do anything," Lucien replied. "This is unprecedented. We're not supposed to have simultaneous clones, so there are no laws to govern what should happen when we do. She's lived eight years without you! You won't even be you anymore if you integrate with her."

"Actually, she only has about a month of memories that are different from mine. She spent the rest of the time in stasis. Any changes to my personality would be very minor."

"Still..." Lucien shook his head. "We need to think about this. Maybe you should be cloned and she should be revived in a new body."

Tyra frowned. "That might set a dangerous precedent for others to start copying themselves. Besides, would you want a copy of me running around on *Astralis*? What if she decides to fight for custody of our kids? Or tries to steal *you* from me."

Lucien frowned. "No one would give her custody, and she wouldn't be able to steal me. Besides, are you the kind of person that would try to steal someone else's husband?"

Tyra narrowed her eyes at him. "It's a gray area for both of us since it's technically still me. How can you cheat on wife with your wife?"

"Ever hear of role-playing?" Lucien asked, with a crooked smile.

"Ha ha. I was being serious. You can't be sure that you wouldn't like her better. It'll be me, but eight years ago. The exact same woman you met and fell in love with. How do you know you wouldn't like her better?"

Lucien's smile flickered as he appeared to think about that.

His expression said it all. He *would* prefer that Tyra. Of course he would.

Putting those thoughts out of her mind, she went on, "Regardless of the personal consequences, legally this comes down to consent, and since we can't get Captain Tyra's consent, we'll need to get a ruling from a judge before I do anything."

Lucien nodded slowly and held out his hand to her. Theola mimicked him, holding out one of her hands, too. "All of that can wait. We need to see if anything is wrong with Atara first."

Tyra took Lucien's hand and allowed him to guide her back into Atara's room. Doctor Fushiwa was there, along with two more nurses, and a probe technician with his probe machine. Tyra released Lucien's hand and hurried to her daughter's side, pushing Doctor Fushiwa out of the way.

"I'm scared," Atara whimpered.

"It's okay, darling," Tyra said, and grabbed her daughter's hand. "You won't feel a thing." She rounded on Doctor Fushiwa. "What do you think you're doing?" she demanded.

He flinched and confusion flickered through his eyes. "You gave your consent..."

"And you couldn't wait *five minutes* for us to get here before you got started?"

"I'm sorry, ma'am. I didn't think—"

"Damn right you didn't think."

"Do you want a moment alone with your daughter?"

"And draw this out more? No, let's get it over with."

"Yes, ma'am."

Turning back to Atara, Tyra said, "Everything's going

to be fine, sweetheart."

Atara had the bedsheets pulled up under her chin. She'd managed to un-tuck them, and now they were floating above her in the zero-*G* environment. "You promise?"

"I promise," Tyra replied, and squeezed Atara's hand.

"We'll be right here," Lucien added, and walked around her bed to take her other hand.

The probe technician finished configuring his machine and said, "We're ready. Atara, would you please start counting backwards from ten?"

"Ten, nine, eight, seven..."

CHAPTER 16

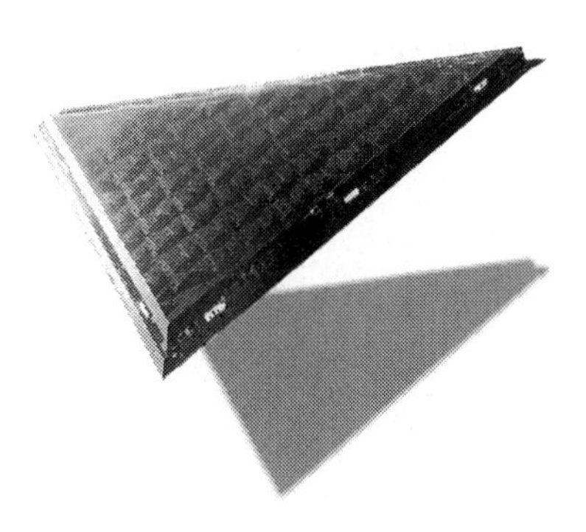

Astralis

Atara's eyes rolled up in her head and her eyelids fluttered shut. Her eyes roved rapidly behind their lids, as if she were in the middle of a REM sleep cycle.

"I'm going to begin by asking you a few questions, Atara," the probe technician said. "What happened to you when the alien touched you?"

"He said he was going to kill me."

"But he didn't."

"No, because I told him that if he killed me, my daddy would kill *him*."

"And how did he react to that?"

"He said that his name was Lucien, and he was my daddy."

"What did you say?"

"I told him he was a liar, because my daddy would

never hurt me. And he said he was only joking about killing me."

"Did you believe him?"

"I don't know... maybe."

"What happened next?"

"He asked me about grandpa Ethan."

"What did he want to know?"

"He asked if grandpa was a good person."

"And what did you answer?"

"I said yes. I've never met him, but my dad's told me stories."

"And then?"

"He didn't say anything else, but I could feel him there, watching me."

"Can you still feel him?"

"No."

"Has he said anything to you since you woke up?"

"No."

"Did he do anything to you while he was in your head?"

"No... I don't think so."

"Okay, Atara. Thank you for your help. I'm going to download the data from your brain now. When you wake up, you'll be back with your parents and your sister."

"Okay."

The remainder of the procedure was silent, and didn't take more than a few seconds. The technician raised his visor and nodded to them. "We're done. She should wake up at any moment."

"How long before we'll know the results?" Lucien asked.

"Given the volume of data to sort through... at least two or three days."

"That long?" Tyra asked. "You expect us to wait two or three days before we can take our daughter home?"

"Assuming we have a home to go back to," Lucien pointed out. Tyra turned to glare at him and he held up his hands in defense. "Not the point. I get it." He turned to the doctor. "Isn't there something you can do to get her released sooner?"

Doctor Fushiwa glanced at the probe technician, and the technician gave a slight shake of his head. "I'll see what I can do, but for now you should make the most of your time here. I'll have the therapist you requested meet with you to assess treatment options for your daughters."

Lucien nodded. "Thank you."

The medical staff turned and left the room. A few seconds after they'd left, Atara's eyes cracked open.

"Did they find something wrong with me?" she asked.

"No, sweetheart. There's nothing wrong with you," Tyra said and leaned down to kiss Atara's forehead.

On the other side of the bed, Theola started screaming in Lucien's arms. She was hungry and needed changing. Tyra looked pointedly at Lucien.

"I'll go get her a bottle and a clean diaper," he said, and headed for the door.

"Try maternity," Tyra suggested, and he nodded. Turning back to Atara, she looked for a chair she could pull up to sit beside her daughter's bed, but the only chair was floating up near the ceiling in the far corner of the room. No point sitting down in zero-*G* anyway. She stood beside Atara's bed, stroking her daughter's hair and answering questions that only a five-year-old would ask.

"Is daddy a murderer?"

"Why would you ask that?" Tyra replied.

"Because he killed the alien with his name."

"It's not murder to kill someone if it's in self-defense. He was protecting you and your sister."

Atara nodded slowly. "Are the aliens going to come back?"

"We'll make sure they don't."

"How do you know if they got them all?"

"Because *Astralis* has sensors that can detect every living thing on board. We know exactly how many people there are on the ship."

"Aliens, too?"

Tyra smiled. "Yes, Aliens, too."

"I feel like he's still here, watching me."

Tyra's brow furrowed. "When the technician asked you, you said you couldn't feel him anymore."

"I did?" Atara asked.

"Yes. It's just your imagination, honey, don't worry. Nobody's watching you."

Atara nodded slowly and appeared to relax. Her eyelids grew heavy, and her eyes drifted shut. Tyra watched her with a worried frown.

It wasn't strange that Atara didn't remember the questions the technician had asked—no one remembered what happened during a mind probe. But what was strange was the discrepancy in her answers during and after the probe. It was supposed to be impossible to lie during a probe. Had Atara somehow defeated that, or had she simply told the truth as she saw it in the moment?

Tyra hoped those feelings of being watched really were just Atara's imagination.

She glanced at the door, willing the therapist to hurry up. Whoever it was had their work cut out for them.

All of a minute later, the therapist did arrive, as if she'd somehow read the urgency in Tyra's mind, which was ironic, because this particular therapist actually could read minds.

"It is good to be seeing you again, Tyra."

"Troo?" Tyra said, looking the Fosak up and down. She was covered in black fur. Prominent fangs protruded from her upper jaw, and huge green eyes blinked as she approached.

Tyra held out her hand in greeting, and Troo offered a three-fingered, two-thumbed paw in exchange. The alien grinned with a mouth full of sharp teeth. Standing on her hind legs, Troo was almost as tall as her.

"It's been a long time," Tyra said. "You're working as a therapist now?" Troo and Lucien had a long history together, but they'd lost touch over the years.

Troo nodded once. "Yes, I is being therapy now. I see that you is being politics."

"A politician," Tyra corrected. "Councilor of Fallside."

Troo nodded, and released her hand. She walked to Atara's bedside and hissed quietly as she gazed down on Atara. "She is being largeness now. How many years?"

"Five," Tyra said.

"What happens to her that she is needing to speak with me?"

Tyra explained what had happened, and Troo listened carefully.

"I is needing to touch her mind to feel her pain," Troo explained.

Tyra nodded her consent. "Do you need me to wake her first?"

"No, that is not being necessary," Troo whispered as she placed a hand on Atara's forehead. The alien's green eyes drifted shut, and she mewled softly.

"There is much anger..."

Tyra nodded, her anxiety mounting. "What else?"

"Pain... hatred... death. Your daughter is deeply troubled..."

Tyra was saddened to hear that. It made sense given what Atara had been through, but she'd hoped the emotional damage wouldn't be that bad. "What do you think we should do? Erase her memories?"

"We is speaking in a dream now. She says that she is being scaredness... and that she is not being alone."

"Did she say who is with her?"

"I is asking her..."

"And?" Tyra prompted.

"She says it is *Death* that is with her, and that he is to be coming for us all."

CHAPTER 17

Astralis

Troo spent nearly half an hour working with Atara, during which time Lucien came back with Theola, his police chief's uniform covered in spit-up.

"Zero-G feeding is not recommended," Lucien said before she could ask. Then he noticed the furry therapist standing on the other side of Atara's bed. "Troo? Is that you?"

The alien turned to him with a grin, and he walked over to give her a one-armed hug. Theola took advantage of her proximity to stroke Troo's fur.

Troo withdrew, hissing, her nose scrunched up, and eyes accusing. "You is being wetness! And you smell like rotten fish."

"It's good to see you, too," Lucien replied, still smiling. He turned and nodded to Atara. "How is she?"

Troo shook her head. "She is not being well. She is

thinking someone else is being with her, someone called Death."

Lucien frowned. "Is that true?"

"I is not feeling any presence besides hers," Troo replied. "I is thinking it to be a symptom of her trauma, a suggestion that the alien made perhaps."

"Well, we'll know soon enough," Lucien said. "The mind probe will tell us exactly what changed inside her head."

Troo nodded and pointed to Theola. "What about this one? She is new. Is she to be needing treatment?"

"That's Theola," Tyra supplied. Troo had never met her.

Lucien nodded. "She's still badly frightened."

"May I?" Troo asked, and extended a paw toward Theola's forehead.

Lucien nodded, and Theola giggled and squirmed under Troo's paw. She grabbed it with both hands, and tried to push it away.

"Shhh... be calmness little one," Troo said as her eyes drifted shut, and Theola subsided. "She is being more resilience, this one.... She is not understanding what she saw, but she is having great fear of the blue ones."

Troo's eyes popped open.

"That's it?" Tyra asked.

Troo nodded. "She is to be fine. Her fear of the blue ones may be giving her nightmares, but I is not thinking there to be any other lasting effects."

Tyra sighed. "That's a relief."

"Thank you, Troo," Lucien said. "Since when did you become a therapist?"

A comm call trilled in Tyra's head and the comms icon flashed in the top right of her ARCs. "Excuse me," she said, and walked by them to the window in the far corner of the room. A curtain of icicles hung from the top of the windowsill, glittering in the sun. Far below, stretched frozen forests and icy lakes. Thankfully, Winterside was cut-off from Fallside by the shield walls that contained the climate zones on *Astralis,* so none of the chaos from the hull breach had touched the city.

"Acting Chief Councilor Ortane speaking," Tyra said as she took the call.

"Chief Councilor, this is Doctor Fushiwa."

"Doctor, any news from Atara's probe yet?"

"I haven't checked. I'm calling about an autopsy we performed on one of the aliens. I thought you might want to know what we found."

"I see. Go on."

"It might be better if I showed you. Can you meet with me now?"

"I suppose."

"Good. We're down in the morgue. Sub Level two of the hospital. I'll send the location to your ARCs."

A data transfer request popped up before Tyra's eyes, and she accepted. The green diamond of a waypoint appeared along a pale green compass/heading indicator bar at the top of her field of view.

"Got it. I'll see you soon, Doctor."

Tyra turned back to Lucien and Troo. "I'm sorry, I have to go."

Lucien regarded her with a frown.

"Duty calls. I'm the acting Chief Councilor," she

explained, but somehow that explanation didn't seem good enough. Lucien nodded and looked away, and Tyra felt her mood darken. What did he expect her to do? Resign in the middle of a crisis?

Shoving those thoughts aside, she went to kiss Atara on the forehead and then kissed Theola on the cheek. She waved goodbye to Troo on her way out.

"Bye," Lucien said accusingly as she left.

She'd deliberately not said goodbye to him. Despite her best efforts, she was fuming at him all the way down to the morgue. Lucien had this unrealistic, romantic idea about life and marriage, that it should all be one long honeymoon, with them spending every waking minute together, and to the netherworld with mundane concerns like paying for a mortgage or expensive private schools.

She emerged from the elevator and walked down a corridor to the examination room that Doctor Fushiwa had marked on her ARCs. He was waiting for her outside the door.

"Doctor," she said.

He nodded in lieu of a reply and waved the door open to reveal a room crowded with more doctors in operating gowns—as well as Marine bots and a human sergeant. Everyone was clustered around a steel operating table with a naked blue-skinned being strapped to it.

As they approached the table, the crowd parted to let them in, and Tyra eyed the Marines, wondering what they were doing there.

She turned her attention to the dead Faro. Anatomically, the alien had no visible genitalia, but the body looked male in terms of its shape and musculature. "What is it you wanted me to see, Doctor?"

"This." Doctor Fushiwa took a scalpel from one of his colleagues and ran it across the alien's chest. The skin flayed open and black blood oozed out. Silvery bones peeked out at Tyra, and she frowned, wondering what they were made of. While she was wondering about that, the wound sealed itself before her eyes.

Tyra jumped back from the table, and her eyes darted to the alien's face, expecting to see its eyes pop open.

But nothing happened.

She blinked and shook her head. "How did he do that?" And right on the heels of that question came another: "He's *alive?*"

"He wasn't when we began the autopsy," Doctor Fushiwa explained. "He woke up with his chest open and started screaming. We had to induce a coma for our own safety, but we're having to administer high doses of three different sedatives in order to keep him under."

"You're saying he was dead, but then he somehow resurrected *himself?*"

"Yes."

"Are you sure he really was dead? What was the cause of death?"

"We assumed that he bled out from all the bullet wounds, but by the time he got here, those wounds had sealed, and the bullets had been pushed out."

Tyra shook her head. "By what?"

"Their blood appears to be filled with billions of microscopic machines."

"Nanites," Tyra said.

"Yes."

"Then the Faros are actually bots?"

"They're genetically-enhanced cyborgs as near as I can tell. The level of biological and mechanical integration is astounding, far beyond anything we've been able to manage."

"Well, that explains the lack of genitalia," Tyra said, nodding to the alien's crotch.

"Yes," Doctor Fushiwa replied with a grim smile. "It also explains why they don't wear any visible technology, yet seem to receive all the benefits of doing so."

"Have you found a power source? It must be very dense for them to be able to shoot bolts of plasma from their hands and have such strong shields."

"The power source is more or less where you'd expect to find our heart and lungs."

"So they don't have a heart and lungs?" Tyra asked.

"They do have something analogous to a heart, but smaller. It circulates their conducting fluid, which doubles as coolant to keep them from overheating. And they *do* have a kind of lung, but they don't breathe in and out as we do—they circulate air constantly with a turbine, and they don't appear to require oxygen or any other type of atmosphere. Their air circulation system seems to be part of a secondary cooling system."

"They sound more like bots than organics to me," Tyra said.

"Indeed, that may well be the case."

Tyra jerked her chin to the Faro on the table. "How did you learn all of that if the subject woke up while it's chest was open?"

"We did have about ten minutes to examine the alien's internal structure before it woke up, and we've taken scans since then to model that structure without having to open him again. There are also other autopsies being conducted in other hospitals, and we were able to collate their findings with ours. For example, not all of the patients woke up. The ones who were beheaded, for example, never revived themselves."

"So the only sure way to kill one of them is to lop off its head."

Doctor Fushiwa nodded. "That, or to critically damage the power supply in their chests, but to do that you have to get past their breastbone—not an easy feat. We had to use laser scalpels on full power, and it still took us half an hour to cut through."

"I saw silvery bones when you ran your scalpel through his chest," Tyra mentioned. "I'm guessing they're not like our bones."

"A metal alloy, lightweight and porous, with an extremely strong molecular structure, at least ten times stronger and a hundred times lighter than solid duranium steel."

Tyra slowly shook her head. "I want a full work-up on the abilities of these aliens. Analyze them for weaknesses. There must be some way to get past their shields besides overwhelming force. We can't always assume we'll have them outnumbered."

"We're working on it, ma'am," Doctor Fushiwa said.

"My husband mentioned using one of their own swords to kill them. That might be a good place to start looking for weaknesses."

The Marine sergeant was the one who replied to that, "We don't know how those swords work, but they do appear to be able to get past the Faros' shields—and ours," he added with a grimace. "Our own razor swords might offer a similar advantage."

Tyra nodded to the sergeant. "That's progress. Who's in charge of reverse-engineering the Faros' technology?"

"Last I checked, the Marines were, ma'am."

"I'll ask Commander Wheeler about it, then." Tyra redirected her attention to Doctor Fushiwa. "Thanks for showing me this."

"Of course."

Tyra's gaze slid away from his, back to the impassive face of the Faro on the operating table. "Keep an eye on him. I'm going to see about moving the captives to a more secure facility—stasis maybe. We don't need them waking up and breaking free."

"Second that," the Marine sergeant said.

Tyra turned and left, wondering as she went if it wouldn't simply be safer to cut off all the Faros' heads and be done with it. She grimaced at the gruesomeness of that thought, but it might be the lesser of evils. One of the most hateful truisms of war is that you have to kill in order to stop the killing.

May the universe have mercy on our souls... were that we had them.

CHAPTER 18

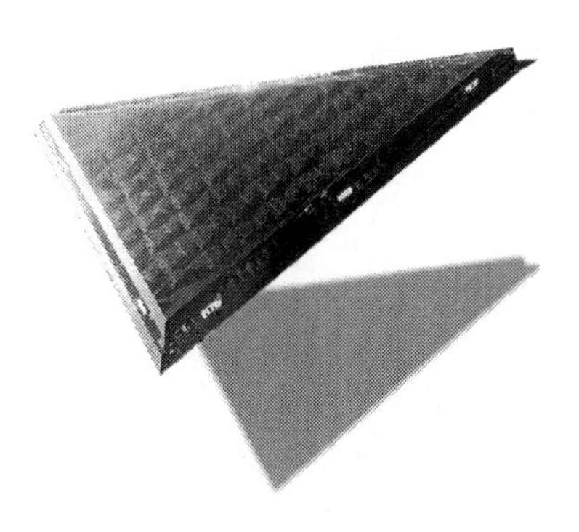

Astralis

SEVERAL HOURS EARLIER...

Nora Helios ran down the stairs to her basement. Her mag boots were set to grav-mode to keep her feet rooted. Nora had been watching the news when the gravity had turned off, and just a few seconds later she'd seen the fiery hole open up in the sky. She'd known what that meant even before the reporter figured it out.

Upstairs she heard windows exploding as the air pressure in Fallside abruptly dropped with the city's atmosphere streaming out into space. If she didn't do something soon, she'd suffocate.

Nora ran through the basement to her safe room, already hyperventilating at the thought of the air getting too thin to breathe.

She shut the door, sealing herself in with whatever was left of the air. The room was designed without any ventilation, so would-be abductors couldn't inject poison or sedatives into the air. Being the director of Astralis's Resurrection Center was a heavy burden. Enterprising criminals could extort just about anything from anyone if they could find a way to threaten their lives *and* the backups of their memories and consciousness in the Resurrection Center. Nora was one of the few people with administrative access to those records, so she had to live in a fortress.

Her eyes skipped around her safe room. It was a home within a home: a kitchen, living room, bathroom, bedroom... and to one side of the living room, sat the mirror-smooth golden dome of her own private quantum junction. It was locked down to prevent unauthorized entry, but it would work just fine to jump her away in an emergency.

Nora considered using it now. That would probably be the safest option. With all of the chaos in Fallside, her security team had probably been forced to evacuate the premises.

Bang, bang, bang!

Nora whirled around, eyes wide as she stared at the door to her safe house. Maybe her security hadn't all left. They couldn't seriously expect her to open the door so they could ride out this disaster with her. "Who is it?" she demanded.

No answer.

BOOM!

The shiny metallic surface of the door shivered, and glowed a faint, molten orange around the edges.

Nora's heart started pounding in her chest. "I'm calling the police!" she said. "You won't be able to get in before they arrive!" It was an empty threat with all of the chaos in the city, but maybe whoever it was would believe her and leave.

Unless it was one of those aliens.

BOOM!

The door shivered once more, and glowed a brighter shade of orange.

Nora shook her head. It was supposed to be impossible to break through that door. The security company had assured her... It didn't matter. She could sue them later. She turned and ran for her quantum junction, using her ARCs to activate it as she approached. The shiny golden dome of the junction hovered up on four shimmering pillars of light. Underneath that was a black podium with two glowing circles: one red, running around the outer edge of the podium, and a smaller green one inside of that. Nora just had to make it into the green circle and activate the junction...

BOOM! Superheated shrapnel went whizzing by her ears, and some of it bit into her back. She stumbled and cried out, but managed to keep moving. By now her security system had to have alerted the authorities about the break-in, but Nora doubted any officers would still be at their posts to see the alert.

Nora reached the edge of the junction and lunged for the green circle of safety in the middle of the podium...

She jerked to a sudden stop as if she'd hit an invisible wall. An unseen hand had grabbed her and pulled her inexorably back toward the open doors of the safe room. She twisted around to look, and saw a blue-skinned humanoid alien standing in the doorway with one, glowing hand raised toward her. He wore gray robes, a luminous golden crown, and a horrible grin. She couldn't see a grav gun in his hand, but somehow he was pulling her toward him all the same.

"Hello, Director," he said over the whistling noise of air being sucked out and up the stairs.

"Who are you?" Nora demanded.

His grin broadened until she could see his black tongue. His palm glowed even more brightly, dazzling her eyes as she drew near. "Let me show you," he said as her face hit his palm with a meaty *smack.*

Stars burst inside of her head. A flood of awareness filled her. Suddenly she knew exactly who this alien was. She could see his every thought. She knew what he knew, and felt what he felt. They became one and thought as one. Her fear vanished, replaced by simmering resolve and a surety of purpose. She had an important mission to accomplish.

Nora felt herself falling even as her consciousness faded. By the time she awoke, she was breathing hard, gasping for air in the thin atmosphere.

This is what it is like to be human? she thought, her lips curling in disgust as she stumbled back to the quantum junction. *Pathetic creatures.* Once she was standing inside the green circle under the hovering dome of the junction, she used her ARCs to set the Resurrection Center as her destination, and activated the junction. The dome began glowing brightly overhead, and a *whirring* noise filled the air, quickly rising in tempo and pitch. Then the dome fell with a *boom,* and it became painfully bright to look at. The air inside the dome whipped around violently, ripping at her hair and clothes. Then suddenly the light vanished, and she was left blinking spots as it rose on four shimmering pillars of light once more. Now she was in the Resurrection Center, in the middle of the center's ostentatious lobby on Sub Level 150.

The lobby was deserted, and the facility was in the middle of a security lock-down. Nora strode through the lobby to the elevators at the back. A security bot moved to stop her.

"Access to the center is restricted during lock-down, ma'am."

"Override. Code zeta, sixteen, forty-seven, nine, nine, seven six, alpha, one."

The bot scanned her with a flickering blue fan of light, and then stepped aside. "Welcome back, Madam Director."

"Thank you," she said, and proceeded to the nearest elevator. Once inside, she selected the records room from the control panel.

At the entrance of the records room she had to get past another bot and another routine security check. She pretended to look bored by the procedures, but once she was inside, she smiled. The plan was working flawlessly so far.

When infiltrating an enemy base, the easiest way to do so was to have a man on the inside who already knew how everything worked. Sergeant Garek Helios just happened to be that man. Sadly, he was no longer alive to appreciate the brilliance of the plan he'd been forced to come up with. *Thank you, Garek, for your insight—or should I say, thank you,* Dad.

Nora was, after all, Garek's daughter.

It took barely half an hour to reach the data terminal in the records room and to download her consciousness and memories to the Center's records. Once she'd done that, she isolated the recent changes and copies them to the most recent records of all the others who'd been touched by Abaddon.

Nora smiled as she finished her work. When she was done, she covered her tracks by hacking the *last changed* timestamps on the records she'd altered, and then she left the records room as if she'd never been there. With everything going on, no one would even bother to check the Center's surveillance tapes, and even if they did, she'd be able to explain herself easily enough. There'd been a sync error, and she'd come to make a manual backup of her own consciousness in case something happened to her. The changes she'd made to her own records would corroborate that. No one would think to look any deeper. They'd never suspect that she, Director Helios, would compromise the system.

But really, it wasn't her who had compromised the system; she wasn't even a *she*, and her name wasn't Nora.

It was Abaddon.

Abaddon smiled to himself as he went to Nora's office in the Resurrection Center. He disengaged his mag boots and jumped up to float above the director's desk, arms crossed behind his head, feet stretched out... basking in the glow of his plans.

After billions of years of waiting and raging impotently against his enemy, it was all finally coming together. Soon everyone would know that Etherus was a fraud. Abaddon would return to Etheria, not as an exile, slinking back meekly, but as a conquering king come back to claim his rightful throne.

CHAPTER 19

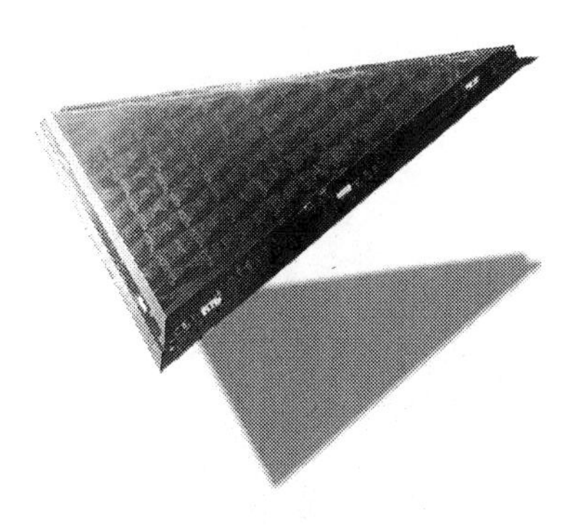

Astralis

—TWO DAYS LATER—

Tyra answered the insistent trilling of an incoming comm call. It was from Winterside General. "Hello?"

"Chief Councilor, it's Doctor Fushiwa. I have your daughter's probe results."

"And? What are they?" Tyra's heart thundered in her ears.

"She's fine."

"Thank goodness," Tyra breathed. "That is very good news, Doctor! You've just made my day. What about the others?"

"Apparently all of them are fine, too."

Tyra's brow furrowed. "Then what were those aliens doing to them? What was the point of it?"

She could almost hear Doctor Fushiwa shrug. "To gather intel, if I had to guess. Their version of a mind probe. They must have been planning to escape *Astralis* with whatever they'd learned. Thankfully none of them did. Who knows how we might have been compromised if they had."

Tyra nodded slowly. It made sense. She'd also thought they might have been gathering intel. "We got lucky."

"Indeed."

"When can Atara be released?"

"Your husband is already signing her out."

"Without me?"

"I suppose so."

"I'd better go find them," Tyra said. "Thank you for calling, Doctor."

"Of course."

Tyra hung up, and hurried from her office to the nearest quantum junction. It was expensive to use the junctions all the time, but she made six figures as a councilor, so she could spare a few thousand now and then.

She arrived right outside Winterside General in front of the ER, behind a group of EMTs pushing a grav gurney with a burn victim on it.

Tyra ran through the ER to the nearest bank of elevators. There she rode up to Level Four where she ran into Lucien, Atara, and Theola already on their way out.

"Mama!" Theola said, bouncing in Lucien's arms at the sight of her.

"I thought you had urgent business to take care of?" Lucien said.

Tyra shot him a look as she dropped to her haunches in front of Atara. "Nothing's more urgent than taking my daughter home. How are you feeling, sweetheart?"

"Fine," she said.

Tyra folded Atara into a big hug. "I'm so happy you're okay."

"I wasn't okay? What was wrong with me?"

Tyra winced, and Lucien made big eyes at her. They spent the past two days erasing Atara's memories of the trauma she'd been through, and here Tyra was trying to remind her.

Atara looked to Lucien for an answer, and he covered his shock with a smile. "Remember how we said you needed to stay in the hospital and rest because you weren't sleeping well?" he said.

"Because of the nightmares," Atara said, nodding.

"Exactly. Well, now you've had enough time to rest, so you can go home," Lucien said.

"But I'm still having nightmares," Atara objected.

"They'll go away in time," Tyra said.

"Promise?"

She nodded. "I promise." Tyra stood up and took Atara's hand to walk her to the elevators.

"Will I still get to see Troo?" Atara asked.

"Yes, you will," Tyra said. "She'll be coming to our house to visit you."

"Forever?"

"Well, no... just for a while," Tyra said.

"Can't we keep her?"

Lucien laughed, and Tyra smiled. "She's not a pet, honey."

"But she's furry!"

Tyra punched the call button for the elevator, still

smiling. *How do you explain the difference between pets and sentient beings to a five-year-old?* she wondered.

The elevator opened and they waited while a group of doctors and visitors filed out. While they waited, an incoming call trilled in Tyra's head, and she sighed. Ellis couldn't get back on the job soon enough as far as she was concerned.

"Acting Chief Councilor speaking," she said.

"Mrs. Ortane, it's Director Helios from the Resurrection Center."

Tyra nodded, her brow furrowing at that. "It's good to hear from you, Madam Director. I'm guessing this is about my clone's data."

Lucien and the girls were about to pile into the elevator, but Tyra stopped them with a hand on Lucien's arm. He frowned, watching as the elevator doors slid shut.

"Yes. The judicial department has made a ruling."

"I see. And? What was their decision?"

"It's been decided that the data does not belong to you. Your clone has been granted equal rights as a citizen of *Astralis,* and she will be revived at once using the clone you have waiting in stasis. Of course, we'll start growing another one for you immediately."

Tyra nodded, her head spinning with the thought of a copy of herself running around *Astralis*. "What will her legal rights be with respect to me?"

"She's entitled to half of whatever you owned at the time she left *Astralis*—minus half of the cost of your clone, which she will be using to resurrect."

"I see. And what about custody of my children?"

"She won't have any rights where they're concerned, since they were born after she left."

"And I assume likewise for my husband."

"Exactly."

"So... how do we establish what I owned at the time she left?"

"There should be bank records to help establish that, but she will have to appoint a lawyer to defend her claim to your estate."

"Of course," Tyra nodded, meanwhile thinking: *I'm getting a divorce from myself! That's got to be a first.* "Did the judicial department offer any justification for their ruling?"

"You mean besides the fact that she and you haven't shared the same life or body for the past eight and a half years?"

"Besides that."

"They did offer an explanation as to why she would be given your clone rather than be forced to wait while we grow a new one."

"And that is?"

"She's thought to possess valuable information about the Faros, and about whatever went wrong during first contact. If there was some kind of misconduct that led to war, then she may be tried for negligence."

"They're looking for someone to blame," Tyra said.

"Exactly."

Tyra sighed. "And I suppose I can't be held responsible for whatever happened, since she's being treated as an individual."

"Correct."

"Well that's a relief at least. Thank you for the information, Madam Director."

"You're welcome. Would you like to be here when she

wakes up?"

Tyra frowned. Usually only family members were allowed to be present during resurrections, but this copy of her wouldn't have any family. "Is that allowed?"

"Well, she is your clone, so I don't see why not."

"Under the circumstances, I think that might be confusing for the both of us. She can look me up through appropriate channels if she wants to see me."

"As you wish. Give me a call if you change your mind. Resurrection is scheduled for one hour from now."

"That soon? They really are in a rush to find out what happened. I'll let you know, Madam Director. Thanks again for the call," Tyra replied.

"Of course," Director Helios said, and ended the comm call from her end.

"What was all that about?" Lucien asked.

Tyra explained everything as briefly as she could.

The news left Lucien slowly shaking his head in disbelief. "This is crazy. How can they make a decision like this without consulting either her or you?"

"They have to bring her back to consult with her, and I guess my vote isn't worth much without hers. The ruling makes sense. We're not really the same person anymore."

"No, you're *exactly* the same person—just separated by eight years of life. She's the old you, and you're the old-*er* you."

Tyra glared at Lucien, pretending to be annoyed. "Cute. Never tell a woman she's old. Especially when you have to live with her."

Lucien grinned and winked at her. "Sorry."

"Let's get Atara home. I'm not sure how long I'll have

before Ellis calls an emergency meeting of the council."

Lucien's playful grin vanished, and the light left his eyes. "Duty calls."

Tyra scowled. *This again.* "You of all people should get that. You're the chief of security for Fallside, for Etherus' sake!"

"Etherus has nothing to do with it, and I'm not the chief of anything anymore. Fallside is a wasteland, remember?"

"That's like saying I'm no longer a councilor."

"It's different. You still represent the interests of your constituents, whether they're alive or dead, but the dead don't need policing."

"They're not dead."

Lucien waved a hand. "Waiting to be resurrected—same thing."

"The situation is temporary. We're rebuilding. As soon as Fallside is permanently sealed and the atmosphere is restored, people will start coming back, and you'll be back on the job."

Lucien shook his head. "We still have to find a planet with an appropriate atmosphere to supply the missing air. That could take some time."

"I'm sure that will be one of the first things we discuss at the emergency council meeting."

"Sure. And anyway, the argument is flawed. My job isn't like yours. I don't have to work all day and all week, never showing up to spend time with my family. If my job were like that, I'd quit."

"That's what you think I should do? Resign?"

Theola began fussing, and Atara jerked impatiently on

Tyra's arm. "Let's go!" Atara said.

Lucien nodded absently, and Tyra was left to wonder if he were nodding his agreement with Atara's sentiment or hers. He punched the call button for the elevator, and they waited in a heavy silence. A split second later the doors opened and another group of people piled out.

"So, where's home now?" Lucien asked, changing the topic to ease the tension.

They walked into the elevator together and Tyra breathed out a quiet sigh, wishing she could expel her frustration along with the air in her lungs. "I found us a three bedroom rental in Winterside."

Lucien's nose scrunched up. "You couldn't have picked a place in Summerside?"

Tyra mentally selected the ground floor from the elevator's control panel. "I couldn't be sure how long Atara would be in the hospital, and I thought we'd want to be close to her. Besides, Winterside is the only city with enough vacancy to house all of the people who evacuated Fallside, and I have to be close to my constituents."

"It has enough vacancy because no one wants to live there," Lucien said. "They should just make it into another Summerside."

"Their economy would crash. They'd lose all the tourists going there to ski and experience winter."

It was Lucien's turn to sigh. "Well, I guess I could take the girls sledding."

Tyra nodded. "That's a good idea. It might take their minds off things."

"Blaba!" Theola interjected enthusiastically.

"My sentiments exactly," Lucien replied, and kissed

her cheek.

CHAPTER 20

The *Specter*

OUTBOUND FROM FREEDOM STATION...

Lucien stared at his hairless blue skin in the bathroom mirror of the quarters he and Addy shared aboard Katawa's ship. He slowly shook his head. "I think this disguise would even fool my own mother." The words rolled easily off his black tongue, and he knew instantly what they meant, but it still sounded to him like someone else was speaking—a fact which the mirror seemed to confirm. Besides being *blue* his face was more angular than his real one, and his head was completely bald—along with every other part of his body. A holoskin did most of the work, projecting a hologram seamlessly over his body from the glowing golden bands on his arms and legs—Faro jewelry modified to conceal advanced holo projectors. As for his hairlessness, that was unfortunately real. He'd had to practically bathe in a foul-smelling depilatory gel, but Katawa assured them that the effects would last for at least six months.

Lucien walked from the en-suite bathroom to the sleeping quarters that he and Addy shared aboard the *Specter*.

They'd left Freedom Station just a few minutes ago, having spent the past two days since meeting Katawa sharing a hotel room at his expense while he stocked his ship and got it ready for visitors. During that time they'd used a helmet-shaped device that Katawa called a *Mind-mapper* to re-train their brains to speak Faro. After that, they no longer needed the translator bands to speak with Katawa, since Faro was his native language, too.

Lucien found Addy sitting on the edge of the bed, frowning at her reflection in a handheld mirror. She was as bald as he was, and her face was also more angular than it used to be. She looked up as he approached, staring at him with a face that was now only vaguely familiar. At least her eyes were still green.

"I'm ugly!" she said.

Lucien went to sit on the foot of the bed beside her. "You still look beautiful to me."

"Liar."

He placed a hand on her bare shoulder, and squeezed reassuringly. They were both wearing Faro robes. His was beige and just covered his shoulders, leaving his arms bare, while hers was white and purple and held itself with a strap around her neck.

The robes were adaptive and surprisingly comfortable. When it was cold they expanded, growing long sleeves, pants, and hoods, and when it was warm, the garments retreated, becoming thicker, but shorter and more porous.

"I mean it," Lucien said, making a point of examining her. She *was* still beautiful, despite her lack of hair and her now-alien features.

"Then you're blind."

He held up his hands in surrender. "I give up. You can always turn off the disguise while we're on board the ship."

"That's not any better. At least this way I look alien enough that being bald isn't so bad, but if I turn off the skin, I'll have to wear a wig—and I don't have one. How do you think they tell each other apart? The males and females?"

"Not all of them have a gender. According to Katawa, Abaddon and the Elementals are all neuters."

"Yeah, they're also half machine. I'm talking about the natural-born Faros, the ones we're trying to imitate. Look at me! If their women are all this ugly, it's no wonder the Elementals decided they could do without."

Lucien smiled and shook his head. "You'll get used to it."

"I doubt it."

"I'm going to the bridge," Lucien said. "You coming?"

"I guess I can't hide in here forever."

The door opened for Lucien as he approached, and Addy slid her hand into his as they walked out.

Katawa's ship was old and run down. The corridors were badly lit and discolored with patches of rust and greenish stains that looked suspiciously like they might be alive.

Lucien heard a water pipe *drip-drip-dripping* in the distance. The sound echoed through the ship, making it impossible to tell where the leak was.

The deck thrummed and vibrated underfoot, setting Lucien's teeth on edge and assaulting his ears with the constant roar of an over-stressed reactor and drive system. They walked beneath a rattling ventilation duct with a squeaky fan.

"This ship is falling apart," Addy said.

Lucien nodded. "That should help keep us safe from pirates. No one's going to bother boarding a piece of junk like this."

Addy snorted and rapped her knuckles against a bulkhead that had rusted straight through to the compartment on the other side. "And what's going to keep us safe from the ship?"

How do you get rust in space? Lucien wondered. "Might be a good idea to sleep in a pressure suit."

Addy gave him a rueful smile. "And here I was planning to sleep naked."

"Actually—sleeping in a pressure suit would probably be overkill," he amended.

Addy grinned. "Too late. You put the thought in my brain. On the bright side, it won't be long before you can walk around without a holoskin."

Lucien shook his head. "How's that?"

"Because you're going to turn blue all by yourself."

"Very funny."

They reached the bridge where they found Garek—also bald and blue—and Brak, a living shadow in his shapeless smock. It covered every inch of him, including his head. Lucien found himself wondering how the Gor could breathe—or see—in that disguise. Katawa sat cross-legged in the pilot's chair, not yet wearing his shadowy garment. He still wore the same loose-fitting black tunic he'd been wearing when they met him.

"Where are we going?" Lucien asked as he stopped behind Katawa's chair and looked out at the handful of stars he could see from the cockpit. Out here, at the edge of the universe, they were so close to the Great Abyss that space seemed even more desolate and forbidding than usual.

"To the Gakol System," Katawa replied.

"Where's that?"

"In the Gethari Galaxy."

"And that is..."

"In the Tosivian Supercluster."

Garek shot Lucien a smirk. "I got the same runaround a few minutes ago."

"Maybe I should ask a different question," Lucien said. "How far is the Gakol System from where we are now?"

"More than five million light years."

"And how long is it going to take to calculate a jump there?"

"Two hours."

"Five million light years in two hours. That's..." Lucien trailed off as he ran the numbers in his head.

"Over five times faster than *Astralis's* jump tech," Garek put in.

"Incredible," Lucien said.

"And this bucket is apparently slow as far as Faro ships go," Garek said. "Katawa was telling me one of their top-of-the-line destroyers can calculate more than two thousand light years per second. That's seventy-five billion light years in just one year, which is about the distance from here back to the Red Line."

Lucien didn't miss the meaningful tone in Garek's voice. If they couldn't find this lost Etherian fleet, taking one of the Faros' ships and running back to Etherus for help was a good backup plan. Although, something told Lucien that if Etherus hadn't already gone to war with the Faros to emancipate all the other sentient races that they'd enslaved, then he might be equally indifferent to the enslavement of a bunch of faithless human scientists. All of which raised the age-old question: *how can a good God be so seemingly indifferent to suffering?*

"What's the Gakol System like?" he asked, putting that troubling thought from his mind.

"We will soon see," Katawa replied.

"You mean you haven't even been there before?" Addy asked.

"No."

"Then how do you know to look there for this lost fleet of yours?"

"Because it is the last location where the fleet was rumored to have been."

"Ten thousand years ago," Garek replied dryly.

"Yes."

"By now that trail is colder than space," Garek said.

Lucien frowned. "You said you kept notes of your search. I'm assuming that most of them are rumors like this one."

"Correct."

"So how many rumors have you collected?"

"The ones that I have been unable to investigate, or in total?"

"The ones you haven't already checked," Lucien replied.

"Five hundred and sixty-two."

"That many?" Addy blurted.

"The guy's been searching for ten thousand years," Garek said. "That's not a lot of leads considering how long he's been at this."

"I was a slave for much of that time," Katawa said, as if he felt the need to justify his lack of progress.

"It could take us years just to follow up on all of these rumors!" Addy said. "At that rate it could be a century before we find anything!"

"That would be wonderful," Katawa replied. He turned from his controls to face them, his giant black eyes blinking and his small mouth slightly agape. "Do you really think you could get such fast results?"

Lucien stared at Katawa. To him, a century was fast. How long was he expecting this search to take? A thousand years? Another *ten* thousand? Lucien's heart sank. *What have we gotten ourselves into?*

CHAPTER 21

The *Specter*

"Still think this was a good idea?" Garek asked, looking smug despite the alien features projected by his holoskin.

Lucien glanced at him. "Your objection was based on not trusting Katawa, not on the viability of his search."

"It was based on both, but you didn't give me a chance to voice my concerns," Garek replied.

"Well, now you've got your chance. Voice away," Lucien replied. They were all sitting in the galley at the back of the ship while Katawa finished whatever he was doing on the bridge.

"Too late now," Garek replied. "We're at Katawa's mercy, trapped on his ship. How do you think he's going to react if we have a change of heart after all the work he's put into our disguises? Assuming he doesn't kill us, he might just dump us on the nearest uninhabitable planet and let nature take its course."

"He's from Etheria, so he's incapable of doing anything wrong," Lucien said.

"Assuming he told us the truth about that," Garek pointed out.

"This isn't the time for *I-told-you-so's,*" Addy put in. "We need to figure out what we're going to do. We can't spend the next few millennia searching for a lost fleet that might not even exist."

"No, we can't," Lucien agreed. "So what do we do?"

"This is still a good opportunity to learn about the universe," Garek said. "Your plan of signing on with a Marauder crew to find out where the slave markets are is even more workable now that we look and sound like Faros. We might even be able to legitimately purchase some of our people—assuming we can find a way to make enough money."

"That's true..." Lucien said. "All right, new plan—while we're following leads and rumors to search for Katawa's lost fleet, we do some investigating of our own to find our people, and maybe find a way to make some money on the side."

Garek nodded.

"Agreed," Addy said.

"Brak? Do you have anything to add?"

The Gor stood in the far corner of the galley, a hulking shadow, easy to miss in the poorly-lit confines of the *Specter.* "I like this plan," Brak replied, speaking barely passable Faro. He'd learned the language, but not the accent. He was posing as a Faro slave, so no one would expect him to be fluent.

"We're all agreed, then," Lucien said. "We help Katawa as best we can, but we help ourselves while we're at it."

Everyone nodded along with that. Lucien felt bad using Katawa, but in a way he was also using them. The trick would be making sure the little gray alien didn't find out what they were doing.

"Jump is calculating."

Lucien jumped at the sound of Katawa's voice and turned to see him standing in the entrance of the galley. "Great," Lucien said, with an innocent smile.

"What were you talking about?" Katawa asked as he entered the galley.

"We were trying to guess what we'd find in the Gakol system."

"Oh. Dangerous place," Katawa said, shaking his oversized head as he went to sit beside Addy in one of the galley's two booths.

"I thought you said you haven't been there," Addy said.

"I have not. Others have. Much is written about Gakol in the ship's databanks."

Lucien blinked. "Why didn't you say so?"

"You did not ask," Katawa replied, blinking innocently up at him.

Lucien offered the alien a dry look. "Where can we access the ship's databanks?"

"In the data center."

Lucien stared a while longer, waiting for Katawa to anticipate his next request. When he didn't, Lucien asked,

"Could you take us there, please?"

"Of course. This way," Katawa replied, walking back through the galley.

They all followed him to a small room with a data terminal and one chair. Katawa showed them how to use the terminal—by wearing a band much like the universal translator bands, and thinking their queries at the console. The console responded with holographic texts, holo-videos, and a variety of other multimedia.

Lucien sat at the terminal first to peruse the data on Gakol. There were seven planets, of which three were inhabited by three different sentient alien races, each of them more barbaric than the last. They lived in hostile environments where everything was constantly trying to kill them, so of course they'd evolved with the same killer instinct. Their cultures were obscene, and they'd apparently escaped slavery to the Faros by offering their services as mercenary soldiers and assassins. Making matters more complicated, none of the three alien species were humanoid.

The lizard-like Deggrans from Deggros lived in burrows underground, never seeing daylight on their scorched desert planet. The Mokari from Mokar, were avian, and had their nests high in the mountaintops overlooking the plains where they hunted. And the third species was even less relatable: the Kivians from Kiva were Crab-like monsters that stood on two legs, four, or six. Each of them was the size of a hover car, and they could live interchangeably on land or in the tropical waters of their archipelago planet.

None of the three races liked each other, but since all three depended on the Faros for high technology like spaceships, they'd been unable to go to war with one another.

Lucien asked the obvious question after scanning through all the data. "How can any of these species know about a lost fleet of starships if they're not independently space-faring?"

"There are legends on all three worlds about small gray gods from the sky."

"If the fleet went there, wouldn't the Faros have captured it?" Addy asked.

Katawa shook his head. "Ten thousand years ago they had not yet discovered Gakol. I believe the fleet stayed here for some time before the Faros arrived."

Lucien nodded, trying to hide his disappointment. According to the ship's databanks, the Faros didn't have a colony in Gakol. That meant no slave markets.

"Even if the fleet was here, what makes you think we'll be able to find any clues about where it went next?" Lucien asked. "They probably left in a hurry once the Faros arrived."

Katawa inclined his head to that. "I believe that is what happened, yes, but the Mokari have a song about one who flew among the stars with the gray gods from the sky. This legend is much more recent. Only one hundred and sixty years old."

"A song?" Lucien asked.

Katawa nodded. "That is how they tell their legends. In song."

"Bird songs," Lucien pressed.

"Yes," Katawa replied.

"So you think the fleet took one of the locals with them and he came back to tell about it?"

"Correct."

Lucien had to admit that was a lot more promising as

far as rumors went.

"You think that Mokari will still be alive?"

"They are immortal."

"Then it sounds like Mokar should be our first stop," Garek said.

"It is," Katawa replied.

"The bird people are hunters," Brak put in. "I shall enjoy hunting with them."

"We're not going there to sample the local cuisine," Lucien said.

Addy turned to him. "Maybe not, but we'll need to make friends if we're going to find this Mokari who *flew among the stars with the gray gods from the sky*. And to do that, it's not a bad idea for us to look for things we might have in common."

"I think there might be an easier way," Lucien replied. "They're all immortals, so they should recognize your species, Katawa—assuming the *gray gods* that visited them really were your people."

"They will have forgotten, but perhaps they will recognize me from their songs."

Lucien frowned. "What do you mean they will have forgotten? How do you *forget* first contact?"

"No one can possibly remember everything that happened over ten thousand years," Garek said. "Immortal or not, biological beings only have so much capacity to remember things. That's part of the reason we take backups of our memories and keep the old ones in storage."

Addy sighed. "So we have to find one bird in particular on a planet of millions by asking about a hundred and sixty year old bird song that may or may not even be true."

"Why would the Mokari lie?" Katawa asked.

"Not lie," Lucien explained. "But over time and countless re-tellings, some details of the events might have been altered."

Katawa nodded. "This is possible. Let us hope enough details remain factual for us to find the fleet. I will leave you now. I must rest before we arrive. Feel free to stay here or use any of the other facilities on my ship."

Lucien nodded. "Thank you."

After the alien left, he turned to Garek and said, "If he were hiding something, he wouldn't let us wander around his ship without supervision."

"Hiding something?" Addy asked. "Like what?"

Garek shrugged. "He's lying about something."

Lucien shook his head. "And you're basing this on what exactly? A gut feeling?"

"How about this: Katawa offered to give us an entire fleet of a thousand advanced warships in exchange for our help in finding them. Does that sound like a fair trade to you?"

"That depends how long it takes us to find the fleet," Addy replied dryly.

Garek waved that concern aside. "I'm telling you, he's up to something. He's got shifty eyes. Maybe he wants us to help him find the fleet so he can take it for himself and sell it to the highest bidder?"

"It's possible," Addy admitted.

"The point is, we only know what Katawa's told us, and without being able to verify his story, the truth could be very different. He might not be trying to get back to Etheria at all."

Lucien nodded, his lips pressed into a grim line. "Fair enough. We'll keep our eyes open. Is that good enough for you, Garek?"

He grunted. "No, but it'll have to do."

CHAPTER 22

Astralis

—TWO HOURS LATER—

Chief Councilor Ellis called an emergency session of council as soon as he was released from hospital. Not long after that, gravity was restored to all of *Astralis,* with the exception of Fallside, where it was being ramped up very slowly to prevent more damage from falling debris.

Tyra took a quantum junction up to the Council chambers at the zenith of the artificial sky, on Level One, directly above Hubble Mountain. The room had a heavily reinforced and shielded glass floor, giving an unparalleled view of all four cities on the surface below (as well as a bad case of vertigo).

Tyra reached the double-story golden doors of the room to find a full platoon of Marine bots and their sergeant guarding the entrance. She stopped in front of them and waited while a pair of bots scanned her from head to toe. Ellis wasn't taking any chances after what had happened on the bridge.

The doors swung wide, revealing a vast chamber, and Tyra sucked in a shuddery breath. Even after all these years, the chamber still inspired awe and fear. The glass floor made every step feel like her last, while the dome-shaped, star-studded ceiling reminded her how much more there was to the universe than this tiny speck they called *Astralis.*

Tyra headed for her chair, empty and hovering above the glass floor. All of the other councilors had already arrived—one from each of the surface level cities, as well as another eight—four for the districts in the fifteen hundred levels above the surface, and four for the sub-districts in the fifteen hundred levels below.

The councilors sat on floating grav chairs around the circumference of the chamber, thirteen in all counting Tyra, but this time the circle was wider than usual with the addition of extra chairs for Admiral Stavos and General Graves, seated on either side of Ellis. There were also two strangers in the center of the chamber: a woman sitting on a grav chair with her back turned to Tyra, and the other, a doctor in a white lab coat standing beside her with a gurney full of medical equipment.

As Tyra took her seat, her gaze flicked back to the woman in the center of thc room. That woman was dressed in a naval officer's white uniform, and her black shoulder boards were marked with the four white bars and golden star of a captain's insignia. If that wasn't enough to identify her, the woman also had familiar raven black hair, tied up in a bun at the back of her head.

"Thank you for joining us," Ellis said, with a hint of annoyance at Tyra's tardiness. She was twenty minutes late—Lucien's fault. He'd insisted she finish lunch with him and the girls before she left. "Council is now in session," Ellis said. "First on the agenda, we have—"

"What's she doing here?" Tyra demanded, pointing to the woman in the center of the circle.

The woman turned around, her grav chair rotating soundlessly. One look at her face confirmed Tyra's suspicions about her identity. "Way to make a woman feel welcome. I believe we spoke earlier on the comms, Madam Councilor."

Tyra nodded slowly. "A lot has happened since then."

Her clone nodded back. "I got the summary from a nurse after I woke up."

"If you're both done trading pleasantries, we have some serious issues on the agenda," Ellis said.

"What is she doing here?" Tyra asked again.

"She is the sole surviving witness of first contact with the Faros, so it's fair to say she knows more about them than any of us, and hopefully, she also knows something more of what they want."

"They want to make us all their slaves," Tyra's clone said.

"Captain Forster, please hold your answers until the probe has been initiated," Ellis said.

"Sorry," the captain replied.

"You're subjecting her to a mind probe," Tyra said, noting now that the doctor standing beside Captain Forster was actually a probe technician.

"It's the only way we can be sure she's telling the truth. Doctor Exeter, you may start whenever you're ready."

The doctor nodded, and took a moment to configure his probe machine on the gurney beside Captain Forster. The probe would be conducted via her AR implant, so no invasive mechanisms or scanners were required, just programming one machine to talk to another. When he was finished, he turned to Captain Forster and said, "Please lay back and count backward from ten."

Captain Forster reclined her chair and began counting. "Ten, nine, eight..." When she reached five, she stopped talking, and her eyes glazed over. She stared fixedly at the stars shining down from the ceiling.

"She's ready, Chief Councilor," Doctor Exeter said.

"Good. Miss Forster, please tell us exactly what happened during first contact with the Faros. Don't leave anything out."

The captain explained how they'd landed on a jungle world and found a holographic history of a race of sentient spiders. The history depicted them being enslaved by a sentient humanoid race, and it marked the planet where they'd been taken. Captain Forster and her crew had decided to follow them and meet the slavers. The slavers' fleet was waiting for them when they arrived, and one of the humanoid aliens contacted them, speaking in Versal. He claimed his name was Lucien and that his people were called Faros. The alien asked to meet with the crew of the *Inquisitor* on the surface of the planet where his fleet was orbiting. They agreed to meet with him, whereupon Faro-Lucien explained who the Faros were and all about their long history with Etherus and the Etherians.

Apparently the Faros had been created by Etherus to be the army of Etheria. Back at the beginning of the universe they'd argued for the creation of a free, chaotic universe, while Etherus and the majority of the Etherians had envisioned a paradise like Etheria. The Faros insisted on a vote, and the majority decided in favor of paradise, but the Faros hadn't been allowed to participate in the vote. Feeling overruled, they started the Great War and tried to take over Etheria for themselves. The entire galaxy of Etheria was decimated by the war, but the Faros lost that war, and the Etherians exiled them beyond the Red Line.

With the majority of the universe at their disposal, the Faros went on to create the free, chaotic place they'd envisioned—except their idea of *freedom* was to enslave all other sentient races, including a green-skinned caste of their own people, making them the only free beings in the universe. When Captain Forster raised objections to the Faros' selective application of freedom, and indicated that she and her crew were leaving, Faro-Lucien gleefully informed them that they could not leave because he'd decided to make them slaves of the Farosien Empire, too. They'd barely escaped with their lives, and two of them had been killed.

They successfully fled in their ship, evading the Faros; but the aliens repeatedly chased them until they finally realized they had a spy in their midst. They managed to extract the timer implants that should have killed them after a month by making first contact with a friendly species of what they assumed to be higher-dimensional beings.

Soon after that, the entire crew submitted themselves to stasis, obviating the need to find the spy and leaving their navigator bot at the helm to guide them to *Astralis's* destination at the cosmic horizon. When they arrived, they arranged for a rendezvous with *Astralis,* thinking that they'd left the Faros far behind them, but of course, that hadn't been the case.

Councilor Ellis leaned back in his hovering chair and folded his hands in front of his mouth, both forefingers pressed to his lips as if to shush anyone who might dare to interrupt his thoughts.

Tyra nodded slowly to herself. This was all consistent with what they'd already learned.

Ellis stopped making the shushing gesture. "Quite an elaborate tale, Captain, but I suppose we can't doubt any of what you've said, since you're under the influence of a probe. It sounds to me like there's no case for misconduct here. The Faros are slavers; when you refused to condone their culture, they decided to subject you to it."

Captain Forster gave no reply, since no one had asked her a direct question.

"There is one other matter that needs answering, and I'm afraid this one is far more serious. You had a spy on board the *Inquisitor*. I understand that even after waking from stasis you took appropriate measures to isolate the crew from the *Inquisitor's* systems, but somehow the spy still managed to give away your location. Is that correct, Miss Forster?"

"Yes."

"Did you learn who the spy was?"

"We did."

"And who was that spy?"

"Pandora, our nav bot. She confessed soon after the Faros arrived at the rendezvous."

"The *bot* gave you away?" Ellis sounded surprised. "Was it infected with a virus?"

"In a way."

"And you didn't consider the possibility sooner? You should have scanned the bot for alterations to its code."

"We did, but the scans came back clean," Captain Forster replied.

"Then how did the Faros turn your navigator into a spy?" Ellis asked.

"While we were making first contact with the Faros, they apparently slipped a data probe aboard the *Inquisitor* and made physical contact with Pandora. They managed to insert another layer to her programming that we were unable to detect, a kind of multiple personality lurking below the level of her primary programming, which was able to take control whenever it liked."

"I see. Then none of the human or alien crew were responsible for the Faros finding us."

"No."

"And the Faros followed you for eight *years?* Why didn't they ambush you sooner? While Pandora was at the helm and everyone was in stasis it would have been easy to capture the ship."

"Their goal was to get to *Astralis.* They were using the *Inquisitor* as bait. And they didn't follow us for eight years. The Farosien Empire appears to span the entire universe beyond the Red Line, so they simply sent the nearest fleet to intercept us once Pandora alerted them to our location."

Silence fell in the council chamber.

After a few moments of digesting what Captain Forster had said, Ellis spoke in a hushed voice: "You're telling me that they have an empire spanning tens of billions of light years in all directions?"

"That is what Pandora implied."

"The *bot* told you this?"

"We asked how and why they followed us after eight years, and she confirmed that they didn't have to follow us, because the Farosien Empire is just that big."

The councilor of Winterside, Corvin Romark, blew out a breath and shook his head. "Then we don't stand a chance against them!"

"I think that's a given," General Graves added. "Look how much trouble they caused on *Astralis* with just a few hundred soldiers. That proves that even if we had equal numbers, we'd lose."

"Yes, that seems to be the problem..." Chief Councilor Ellis agreed. "So we avoid contact with the Faros. It's a big universe. We did it for eight years already after our first battle with them. And if it weren't for the *Inquisitor* leading them straight to us, we probably would have gone unmolested for another eight years—or even eight hundred!"

Tyra nodded her agreement, as did several of the other councilors.

Ellis was making that shushing gesture again. Apparently lost in thought contemplating their situation.

They'd established strict safety protocols ever since their first meeting with the Faros had almost resulted in the destruction of *Astralis.*

The protocols called for sending out disposable probes ahead of *Astralis,* using them to scan for safe systems. If a probe detected unknown alien starships or technology, it would self-destruct immediately and never live to tell *Astralis* about it. (They couldn't risk comm signals being detected and tracked back to either the probe or to *Astralis,* so comms silence was one of the safety protocols.) If, on the other hand, a probe encountered an uninhabited system, it would jump back to *Astralis* and report its findings. *Astralis* would then review the safe systems marked by its probes and pick the one they thought was least likely to result in contact with an advanced alien race.

It was a practically fool-proof system, but one which left little room for exploration along the way. They did get to explore the systems that *Astralis* jumped to, but all those barren rocks, frozen ice balls, gas giants, and toxic wastelands blurred together over time.

"Doctor Exeter, you may end the probe and wake the patient. Thank you for your assistance," Councilor Ellis said, having apparently returned from whatever far off place his thoughts had taken him.

The doctor nodded and set about terminating the mind probe. Captain Forster's head lolled to one side and her eyes fluttered shut. The doctor pushed Captain Forster's grav chair from the room, and his hover gurney floated along behind him like an obedient pet.

Once they were gone, Chief Councilor Ellis sat forward in his chair. "Next on the agenda... what do we do about the Faros we captured? Almost half of the ones we thought we killed later came back to life during their autopsies. Two of which escaped and were subsequently killed. We're keeping the surviving prisoners sedated in a maximum security prison, since we can't figure out how to disarm them."

"Do we even know *how* to kill them?" Corvin Romark from Winterside asked.

"The surest way seems to be by cutting off their heads," Ellis replied.

"Then I move that we behead them all before one of

them escapes and finds a way to call for help."

"I second the motion," Councilor Kato S'var of District One said; half his face was still bandaged from third degree burns he'd suffered during the fighting.

Ellis shook his head. "They're too valuable alive. If we can find some way of getting inside their heads, we'll be able to find out exactly what we're up against—maybe even which systems are safe for us to travel to, and which ones aren't."

"I agree..." Tyra added slowly. It was a risky proposition, and Tyra wasn't entirely sure it was the right move, but Ellis had a point: they couldn't afford to pass up the chance to learn something from the prisoners. "We keep them sedated and double their security."

"We need to vote on it," Romark said. "All in favor of executing the Faro prisoners?"

Six councilors raised their hands.

"All against?" Ellis asked.

Seven raised their hands, including Ellis himself.

"Then we keep them alive," Ellis said.

Romark's eyes narrowed, but he held his tongue.

"Moving on..." Ellis began. "We need to decide our course of action going forward. Do we press on to the new cosmic horizon, or do we turn back and return to the Etherian Empire?"

The councilors voiced their opinions, all of them talking over one another.

Ellis waved a hand for silence, and called on them one at a time, in clockwise fashion, to voice their arguments.

"The mission was to reach the cosmic horizon," Corvin Romark said, when it was his turn to speak. He shrugged his broad shoulders. "We've already done that. It's time to go home."

Tyra gaped at him. Unable to wait her turn, she blurted out, "We've only begun to explore! Thirty billion light years from here is a big stretch of empty space that we've never even conceived of. What *is* that emptiness? What caused it? For all we know it's the physical edge of the universe, and anything that goes beyond that point drops off into another dimension! Or maybe it really *is* just *empty* space. If so, we don't know how far that emptiness extends, or even if it is a uniform phenomena that surrounds the universe on all sides. It could be like a lake, or an ocean, and on the other side of it is another part of the universe. Our real mission was to explore and to learn the true nature of the universe, not simply to reach one horizon and stop there. We've only just begun our mission, and at this point, home is even farther away than the *Big Empty* ahead of us."

"But one direction will take us deeper into enemy territory, and the other will return us to safe harbor," Corvin replied.

"Romark is right," one of the district councilors put in. "Safety should be our primary concern right now."

Tyra shook her head. "There's no guarantee that we'll be safe if we return home, or that we won't be if we press on, and we only have the word of a spy to say that the Farosien Empire really does span the entire universe beyond the Red Line. It might have been a lie, designed to intimidate us so we wouldn't try to resist. Just because we can't conceive of a race so dogged that they would follow us for eight years doesn't mean they aren't, in fact, that obsessed with us. The Faros are immortals, and by all indications they've always been immortals, which means that they've been alive for *billions* of years. Eight years is a blip to them, as insignificant as a second would be to us. Time is relative. These Faros could be extremely patient beings."

Several councilors murmured their agreement with that, and a few of the ones who'd come out in favor of turning back looked thoughtful, as if they might be reconsidering their opinions.

"Don't you want to know what else is out there?" Tyra pressed.

"But that's just the thing," Councilor Romark said. "We can't afford to explore very much along the way, so there's only so much we can learn. We've been forced to jump to uninhabited systems for the past eight years, treating all alien races as if they were equally hostile."

"What if we change that?" Tyra asked. "Instead of sending out disposable probes to clear a path for *Astralis,* we could send out galleons again, like we used to."

"And just look where that got us!" Romark boomed.

"It's too dangerous," councilor Gavin Luprine from Summerside added, shaking his head.

Tyra frowned, and Ellis held up a hand to forestall further argument. "I have been thinking a lot about the problem of exploring safely over the years, and I believe there is a way to do what Councilor Ortane is suggesting without putting ourselves at risk. We could use our galleons in the same way we currently use disposable probes."

Councilor Romark shook his head. "How? We can do that with probes because they're automated—if we lose one, it's no big deal, so we can afford to have them self-destruct at the first sign of trouble. Besides, if we change our criteria for what constitutes *trouble* and allow manned expeditions to inhabited systems, we won't know what kind of trouble we're in until it's too late. We'll be opening the door for exactly the same kind of ambush that the *Inquisitor* brought to us. Maybe it won't be the Faros this time, but it will be someone, sooner or later."

"Not so," Ellis replied. "If you'll allow me to explain, there *is* a way to accomplish this and still keep *Astralis* safe."

Romark sat back and spread his hands in invitation. "By all means, tell us what you've come up with."

Ellis smiled. "Transferring consciousness from one body to another is child's play to us. We were doing it for ages on Avilon, and then again on New Earth when we left our galaxy. The technology is well understood, but perhaps not fully utilized."

Tyra leaned forward. "What else could we do with it?"

"Funny that *you* should ask, Councilor Ortane, since we've just resurrected an identical clone of you, giving her equal rights as a citizen of *Astralis.* This sets a legal precedent for something we could do to conduct safe exploration of civilized alien worlds."

Councilor Romark snorted. "I don't see how simultaneous copies of people can help us."

"You will, Councilor," Ellis replied, flicking him a smug look. Turning away to address the others, he went on, "We could send out the galleons again, but this time with no bots on board, since we now know that's how we were compromised the last time. But this time," Ellis raised a finger to indicate an important point, "the human crews will all be duplicates, identical copies of people already living on *Astralis,* whom we've determined to have the necessary skills and experience."

Ellis went on, "These clones will explore as safely as they possibly can, and then fall back to pre-determined safe systems where we will have disposable probes waiting to receive a data-only transfer of the memories and consciousness of the crews. The probes will then return to *Astralis* with the data, and their copies living on *Astralis* will integrate the new memories with their own, so that we can learn what they learned. Once they've been debriefed, we'll send their consciousness back out there to the galleons they left waiting, and their memories will be re-integrated with their bodies aboard the galleons. They will then continue exploring, with updated instructions and mandates from *Astralis,* and new pre-determined safe rendezvous with the disposable probes further along *Astralis's* path.

"Like that, the Galleons need never physically return to *Astralis.* They don't even need to know where *Astralis* is—only where the disposable transfer probes are waiting for them, and those probes will self-destruct at the first sign of trouble, so they can't possibly be hijacked. If that should happen, the galleons will be on their own until we can re-establish contact and set up a new rendezvous with another disposable probe. In the very worst case, we'll lose contact with a few galleons and their crews, but life will go on as usual for their clones living on *Astralis,* so there's technically no risk to them or their families."

Silence reigned in the council chamber as everyone processed the implications of that plan. Unlike the Etherian Empire, they had no religious or moral compunctions about creating simultaneous copies of people, so it was really just a matter of over-turning old laws, and placing limits on new ones to prevent people from copying themselves for unethical or criminal purposes.

"What if one of the galleons is captured and the Faros hijack the system to transmit *themselves* to *Astralis?*" The woman who'd asked was the councilor from Sub-District Three, Jilian Kia.

Ellis answered her, "It wouldn't do them any good. As soon as we receive the data from one of the returning crews, we'll compare it to their last backups in the Resurrection Center, look for differences, and then analyze those differences to make sure that we aren't integrating an alien consciousness with one of our citizens. It's exactly the same system we just used to clear myself, Admiral Stavos, and General Graves for duty after our contact with the Faros."

Tyra nodded and added, "They performed the same procedure with my daughter, too."

A few of the councilors glanced her way before returning their attention to Ellis.

"When did you come up with this plan?" Corvin Romark asked.

"As I said, I've been working on this idea for years already, but the pieces all finally snapped into place with recent events."

"It sounds fool-proof," Tyra said. "I can't think of a way that this would place us at any additional risk. It's really just an extension of the safety protocols we've observed over the past eight years. Our only point of contact is still with disposable probes."

"Probes that could be hacked to give us away," Romark said.

"How?" Tyra demanded.

"A virus could piggyback in on one of the data

transfers from the crews, masquerading as a memory."

Ellis shook his head. "That's not so easy, but we can make sure that all of data goes to isolated storage inside the probes and that it remains in isolated storage when it reaches *Astralis.* We'll submit the data to rigorous checks before we integrate it with anyone. We could even devise a system whereby the explorers don't need to be integrated or resurrected on this end for us to be able to debrief them—some kind of virtual brain, perhaps."

"You mean an AI," Tyra said.

"More like a VI—a virtual intelligence," Ellis replied. "But another possibility is to keep cloned bodies waiting in stasis on this end and use them to resurrect the crews so that we can debrief them. Then when they leave, those bodies go back into stasis."

Several councilors nodded and voiced their agreement. They already had the mechanism in place for that system, so it would be the easiest and fastest to implement.

Tyra thought to add, "That way their copies living here on *Astralis* won't be affected by their experiences, and we'll also be able to physically isolate them, just in case something goes wrong."

"What kind of life is that?" Romark demanded. "Who would ever agree to become such an explorer? They'll effectively be exiled from their own homes. We'll be using them like bots."

Ellis shifted in his chair. "Wouldn't you agree to allow a *copy* of yourself to be created for the purposes of exploring the universe, if you knew that doing so would never affect you personally?"

"No," Romark replied. "Because someday that copy

will have to come home, and then it might think it has some legal claim to my life."

Tyra nodded along with that. "That's exactly what the judicial department ruled in my case. I'm going to have to share my assets from eight years ago with my clone."

Ellis waved a hand at her. "That's different. She left *Astralis* with legal ownership of your assets, and when she returned, one could make the case that *you* are the clone who stole *her* life."

"Except that she wasn't meant to live. She should have died when her timer implant ran down," Tyra said.

"Obviously your case is more complicated than what I am proposing," Ellis said. "These clones would be created with the express purpose of exploring the universe safely, and we can have them sign away any legal claims they may think they have to their other halves' possessions and lives. That way, when the time does someday come to integrate them with the population, there won't be any problems."

"What about their freedoms?" Corvin Romark asked. "We can't force them to explore until we decide they should stop."

"That's the beauty of it," Ellis said. "We won't have to. All you need to do is ask the originals if they want to go, and then get them to sign on for a specific period of time with the Navy or the Marines. Because they and their clones will be one and the same—one mind in two bodies—they'll make all of the same choices, so no one should have a change of heart. And besides, anyone who wants out of the Navy early would be guilty of desertion. If they want out after their commission or term of enlistment is up, well, then they should be allowed to leave and re-join the population—after appropriate security checks, of course."

"That won't fly with the judiciary," Romark replied, shaking his head. "It's still a violation of rights. You can't ask the original to sign up on behalf of his clone and then still treat them as individuals. And yes, lots of people will have a change of heart. The originals will know that *they* won't actually be the ones going, so of course they'll say *yes*—what's it to them? But when you resurrect them as copies, the copies will know that they are actually the ones leaving. They'll think about their wives and children, their homes and jobs, and all of the other roots that tie them down, and they'll decide not to go."

Ellis just smiled. "Ah, but that's the beauty of it: they'll wake up, and they'll *think* they have families and homes and jobs, but then they'll find out that they're *clones,* and *they* don't actually have anything. They were created for one purpose: to explore."

Rumblings of discontent spread through the room.

"That's all highly unethical!" Aria Calias, the councilor of Springside said.

Ellis shook his head. "It will all be voluntary, so there's nothing unethical about it. We'll ask the originals if they want to go, as a matter of screening. Then if we must, we'll ask them a second time after they wake up as copies. As Councilor Romark says, we can't dismiss the possibility that some of the clones will have a change of heart. So if that happens, we'll ask them to re-integrate with their originals immediately—with the understanding that each of them will have to pay for his or her clone, which was created for use with the program. It won't be a total loss for them, however, since they can always put those clones in stasis in the

Resurrection Center to use as spares."

Tyra nodded along with that. She couldn't see any human rights violations anymore.

"But I assure you," Ellis began, "if you woke up tomorrow to learn that you'd been created with the express purpose of exploring the universe, and you suddenly had nothing to physically or emotionally tie you down to *Astralis*—you'd go in a heartbeat!"

Several councilors bobbed their heads in agreement with that.

"Well?" Ellis prompted. "Are there any other reasonable objections?"

The councilors conferred amongst themselves, while Ellis sat back and smiled. Admiral Stavos and General Graves conferred with him quietly, making it look disturbingly like this was a plan they had come up with together.

And maybe they had, Tyra decided. But what did it matter who'd come up with it? It was a brilliant plan.

Tyra raised her voice, "In light of this proposal, we should take a vote on *Astralis's* course of action going forward."

"That would be premature," Corvin Romark said, shaking his head. "We'll need a ruling from the judiciary to decide if we're allowed to use clones like Ellis is saying, and even if they rule in favor, we'll still need a whole new set of laws to govern cloning and the transfer of consciousness. We can't allow people to clone and copy themselves for just any reason. The consequences would be dire. Imagine what you could get away with? Commit a crime and blame it on your clone!"

"Mind probes would reveal the truth," Ellis replied,

"But I agree. Reasonable limits must be set, and particularly for ordinary citizens."

"Then before we decide anything, we should wait for the judiciary to make a ruling," Romark insisted.

Ellis shook his head, "And do what in the meantime? Send *Astralis* home? Press on? Or wait here? If everyone is in favor of returning home, there's no sense in asking the judiciary for a ruling, or even in writing new laws. What would be the point?"

"We could also explore on our way home," Romark pointed out.

"True," Ellis said. "But that only confirms that these are separate issues."

Tyra spoke next. "I move that we stay where we are until we can get a ruling from the judiciary. At that point we can vote to decide where we should go next."

"I second the motion," Aria Calias from Springside said.

"Third," Jilian Kia of Sub-District Three added.

The other councilors murmured their agreement.

"All in favor, raise your hand," Ellis said, and raised his own hand.

The vote was unanimous, with the exception of Corvin Romark, who had the look of someone who had been thoroughly outmaneuvered.

"It's settled then," Ellis said.

They spent the next hour going through the remainder of the agenda. Tyra spent the whole time puzzling over the implications of what Ellis had proposed. She put it in a personal context, asking herself what she would do if she were asked to join the explorers. Would she consent to send a copy of herself out into the unknown? And if she did, what would she get out of it? Would she be allowed to integrate her memories with those of her clone?

If they both consented to it, probably, but would she really want to have all of her explorer-clone's memories? The longer her copy was away, the more their lives and personalities would diverge. She might not even recognize herself when she returned.

Then there was the matter of how hard it would all be for her clone, knowing she had kids and a husband that weren't really *hers* unless she decided to integrate, and even if she did, she wouldn't even get to see them again for... what? A month? Two months? More?

Maybe they wouldn't ask *her* to join the explorers, so she wouldn't have to deal with the dilemma personally, but Tyra found herself torn, half-hoping that they would ask her and half-hoping that they wouldn't.

Then she realized that they wouldn't need to; they already had a copy of her that they could ask, and *she* had all the requisite experience. She was even already a Captain in the Navy, so there'd be no need for her to sign a commission.

It was unlikely they'd want more than one of her to go, and if they did, they'd ask the Captain to send a copy of *herself*. No, they wouldn't ask *her* to be an explorer.

But they might ask Lucien. He had the training for it. He'd been a Paragon back in the Etherian Empire, and he'd been one of the original crew aboard Captain Tyra Forster's ship.

What would Lucien say? she wondered. Would he consent to join the program? And if he did, how would his copy handle the knowledge that he had two daughters and a wife that he was leaving behind?

It needn't be a permanent separation, Tyra realized. If both Lucien and his copy were willing, they could integrate at some point in the future. The problem was, then she and the girls would be at the mercy of utterly unpredictable changes in Lucien's personality. He could wake up after integration only to tell her that he'd fallen in love with one of his fellow explorers and he wanted a divorce. She could lose him like that.

Tyra's imagination ran away with those fears, and suddenly she saw herself and Lucien exploring the universe together—except that it wasn't really *her* and it wasn't really *him*. It was a *copy* of each of them: Captain Forster, and her XO, Lucien Ortane. He'd already been her XO aboard the *Inquisitor*, so Captain Forster would probably look him up and ask him to pick up wherever they'd left off.

She probably had a big fat crush on him. Forget *probably*. Tyra had fallen in love with Lucien eight years ago, and Captain Forster was that same exact woman, so she would have all the same feelings, and now he was older and wiser, which made him arguably even more attractive. And as for Lucien... Captain Forster was the exact same woman he'd fallen in love with: a younger, more fun-loving, and more adventurous version of her, his wife. What man could say no to that?

Tyra shivered. But there was one silver lining in all of those dark and confusing thoughts: if their clones fell in love with each other, then it almost certainly wouldn't affect Tyra's family. The only way it could affect them was if Lucien and his clone decided to integrate, and why would they want to do that? She nodded slowly to herself, comforted by that thought.

It was a good thing that the Lucien from the *Inquisitor* hadn't survived. Dealing with the implications of two identical copies of him was bad enough—but *three?*

The universe couldn't handle that much Lucien.

CHAPTER 23

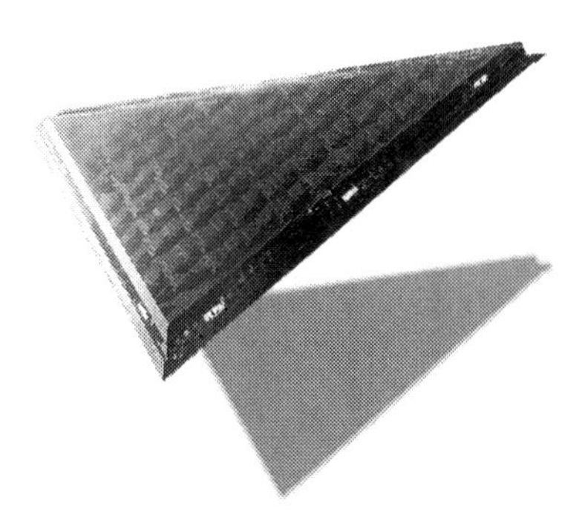

Astralis

Chief Councilor *Abaddon* sat by his pool on the roof of his penthouse apartment in Summerside, sipping a cocktail and drying in the sun. The view of Archipelago Lake from the fortieth floor was startling. The golden shores and lush green foliage of dozens of islands sprawled out to meet the distant walls of *Astralis*. The artificial sun was about to set, casting everything in a rosy hue. Potted palm trees flanked his pool, their fronds rustling in a warm breeze.

These humans can even rival us when it comes to luxury, Abaddon thought. It was nicc to stop for a moment to enjoy the spoils of victory—but only for a moment. There was still so much to do. So far things were going very well. No one seemed to suspect him, and the council had been receptive to his plan to send out manned missions. Now all he had to do was get the judiciary department on his side. Fortunately for him, he'd already done so. High Court Judge Cleever had been intercepted by one of Abaddon's clones and had befallen the same fate as Director Helios of the Resurrection Center. With the two of them, himself, the chief councilor, as well as Admiral Stavos and General Grave under his control, there was almost no limit to what they could accomplish. It would be easy to lead these humans around by their collective noses in order to reach his goals.

Abaddon smiled and took another sip of his cocktail—a delicious fruity concoction made from tropical fruits native to galaxies within the Red Line. He had never had the pleasure of tasting such fruits before. He had to hand it to Etherus: guiding the evolutionary process did seem to yield more satisfying results. But who had the time to micro-manage the development of trillions of different ecosystems?

Let Etherus do it. Besides, if all went according to plan, it would all belong to Abaddon soon, anyway.

Abaddon drained his drink and walked up to the glass railing running around his rooftop terrace. The tropical blues and verdant greens of Summerside sprawled before him. Quaint little villages and towns pricked holes in the lengthening shadows as people turned on their lights. Unbeknown to them, all of this was now a part of the Farosien Empire and little more than a fresh mat for Abaddon to wipe his feet on.

He smirked and tossed his empty cocktail glass over the railing. He watched it tumble to the ground, wondering absently if it might hit some blithe pedestrian on the head and temporarily end their meaningless existence. If it did, they might tie some saliva-coated fragment of the glass to him and bring him up on charges for manslaughter. Of course, with

Judge Cleever in his pocket, it would be all too easy to have those charges overturned.

If these humans only knew what their ruler was thinking... Abaddon supposed they might call him evil, but that was naive. One day humanity would have to grow up and learn what he had learned. They would uncover the great lie of Etherus and finally know the truth: there was no such thing as good and evil.

Abaddon smiled. *Someday they will learn the truth... and the truth shall set them free.*

*   *   *

The *Specter*

Lucien stood on the bridge of the *Specter,* gazing down on the brown fields and wrinkled black mountains of Mokar. Green-blue rivers snaked down from the mountains through dark brown canyons to what looked like an ocean. Bright blue and red growths of who-knew-what blotted and hedged the brown fields, making the entire planet look diseased with some kind of alien fungus.

Lucien's brow was furrowed all the way up to his shaven scalp. "Is the whole planet like this?"

Katawa's head turned. "I do not know. I have not been here before."

"Right," Lucien said.

"I can't wait to get down there," Addy put in.

"I don't know..." Garek said. "The Mokari are basically sentient birds of prey, right?"

"Right," Lucien said.

"So what's to stop them from thinking we're their prey?"

"They know the Faros are their masters," Katawa replied. "They do not like the Faros, but they have a healthy respect for them."

"Have you met the Mokari before?" Garek asked.

"Oh yes. They serve as private security and soldiers all over the Farosien Empire. The ones I have met are aggressive and forbidding, but they do as they are told. I am sure we won't have any problems."

"Still," Garek said. "If they're the Faros' slaves, what makes you think we're going to get anywhere with them? They might feign ignorance when we ask them about the lost fleet."

"We must convince them to speak with us," Katawa replied.

Brak hissed. "They will speak with me. I do not appear as one of the blue ones, and I am a hunter like them."

"I'm starting to think you've got a point there, buddy," Lucien replied. He turned and patted Katawa on one of his bony gray shoulders. "Take us down, K-man."

"K-man?" Katawa asked, as he broke orbit and began their descent toward the planet's surface.

"It's a nickname," Lucien explained.

"A pejorative? Did I do something to offend you?"

Lucien favored the little alien with a sympathetic frown. Katawa had spent so much of his life as a slave to the

Faros, he was probably used to being belittled and insulted. "No, a nickname is something humans use as a way of establishing camaraderie and familiarity with one another."

"Oh, I see," Katawa replied, blinking huge black eyes at him. "In that case, I will have to come up with a name for you."

"Sure," Lucien replied. "I can give you a few suggestions."

"Such as?"

"How about Mr. Magnificent. Mr. M. for short."

"Okay, Mr. M, I will call you this," Katawa replied.

Lucien smiled.

"Hold on a second—" Addy said. "—he doesn't get to pick his own nickname, especially not after he picked all of ours. He called me *Triple S.* One of those S's stands for sexy, and since he's my superior officer, it's a blatant case of sexual harassment. If he weren't so damn sexy himself, I might have pressed charges."

"I did not know this," Katawa replied. "I will call you *one who harasses his mates.*"

Lucien's nose wrinkled. "That's a mouthful."

"Forget the nicknames," Garek said. "We have bigger issues to discuss—like what kind of atmosphere Mokar has, whether or not we'll be using exosuits, and what exploring with a limited supply of air will mean for our goals on the surface."

Lucien nodded soberly. "True. Katawa, does Mokar have a safe and breathable atmosphere, or will we need to use our exosuits?"

"No suits. The Mokari will expect the Faros to be able to walk around freely on their world, and they do not trust people who wear *false skins.*"

Garek snorted. "That's ironic, considering we're actually wearing holoskins."

"They will be unable to detect the holograms," Katawa replied. "The holoskin masks your scent and simulated that of a Faro. It will convince them."

"That's what that stink is?" Garek demanded.

"I don't smell anything..." Lucien replied. He walked over to Garek and sniffed the air around him—only to pull back sharply. "Never mind." Garek stunk of a sweet odor that reminded him vaguely of some of the *medical* herbs he'd smoked back in school.

Lucien sniffed himself, but didn't detect the same smell. "I can't smell myself," he said.

"Mated Faros do not give off the odor. It is meant to attract a mate. Faro females find the scent irresistible."

"Great," Garek said. "So I'm going to be fighting off bald blue witches with a stick wherever I go,"

"Faro females are not magical," Katawa objected, "but they will appreciate your concept of carnal discipline."

"No sticks, then. Got it," Garek muttered.

Addy whispered in his ear, "Maybe you could try that."

Lucien felt his cheeks warm, and cleared his throat, "Back to the issue of Mokar's atmosphere. If we're not expected to use suits, the air must be breathable and safe."

"It is breathable, yes, but it may be dangerous to humans," Katawa said. "I will perform a scan of the atmosphere and develop the necessary inoculations and treatments for you with the fabricator in the med bay," Katawa replied.

"Just like that? Won't it take too long?" Addy asked.

"A few minutes. No more."

"That fast?"

"Faro technology is far more advanced than what you are used to," Katawa replied.

Lucien marveled at that. Back in the Etherian Empire Paragon medics and bio-engineers took weeks to come up with treatments to allow human colonists to live on new worlds without pressure suits, and there were usually hundreds of them working together in each new colony.

"Amazing..." he said, shaking his head. "What about gravity? How's it compare to what you've set on the *Specter?*"

The ship's gravity felt lighter than human standard, but not uncomfortably so.

"Sensors report Mokar's gravity to be one point two times standard," Katawa replied.

"You mean *your* standard, which I'm assuming is what you've set the ship's gravity to simulate?" Lucien asked.

"Correct."

"So Mokar's gravity is probably just a little less than our standard gravity," Garek concluded.

Lucien nodded. That helped to explain why they wouldn't need exosuits. Close to standard gravity was a necessity for humans, because a planet's gravity also determined how thick the atmosphere was. If the gravity were much less than standard, the air would be too thin to breathe.

They rode the rest of the way down to Mokar in silence, watching as wisps of pinkish clouds swept up, and a peach-colored haze of atmosphere clouded their view. A fiery glow wreathed the *Specter's* viewports as friction between the air and their hull lit the planet's atmosphere on fire.

As their speed diminished, that fire subsided, and finer details of the surface appeared—the most notable of which were the swarms of black specks circling the brown plains below.

Mokari? Lucien wondered.

Katawa leveled out, and they saw a range of obsidian-black mountains soaring to one side. The jagged spires and cliffs were wreathed in pink clouds against a salmon sky. A bright red sun simmered above the horizon, to one side of those mountains, while its twin hung directly overhead as a dim, hazy orange ball of light. The separation of those suns likely meant that night would never truly fall on Mokar since shadows cast by one sun would be illuminated (at least partly) by the other.

Katawa took them up to a sheer black cliff that must have plunged at least a kilometer straight down. A bright green river roared over that cliff to a darker emerald pool below. The pool was surrounded by some kind of blue and red vegetation.

"Where are we going to land?" Lucien asked.

Katawa flew on toward the cliff and raced over the top of the shimmering green waterfall. A broad, flat plateau opened up before them, and both banks of the river were speckled with strange brown mounds. Each mound varied significantly in size and shape from the next.

Katawa slowed the ship and hovered down for a landing. As he did so, a pair of giant black shadows passed over them and swooped down to land beside one of the brown mounds. Those had to be the Mokari. They became mere specks beside the mound where they'd landed, and yet their shadows had been big enough that Lucien thought the

Mokari had to be at least as large as humans.

"This must be a Mokari village," Addy said.

Lucien watched as more black specks picked their way along the ground from mound to mound, while others took flight, and still others landed in a constant bustle of activity. He nodded slowly. The mounds appeared to be made of mud and grass, and their size relative to that of the Mokari suggested that each of them was a nest. The larger mounds were likely larger nests for bigger families.

Katawa landed the *Specter* among the Mokari nests, some of which towered three and four stories high. Lucien marveled at how much work it must have taken for the Mokari to fly more than a kilometer up from the plains below, carrying that much mud and grass. They obviously didn't have things like hover trucks to make the job easier.

"It is time to prepare you for the surface," Katawa said. "Please follow me to the med bay."

Once they arrived there, Katawa took blood samples from each of them while they sat waiting on rusty metal examination tables that had probably been gleaming silver when they were new. They'd probably also come with mattresses, Lucien reflected as he tried to shift his weight in some way that didn't result in a stab of pain from his backside.

"Interesting..." Katawa said.

"What?" Lucien asked.

"Your biology. It is extremely flawed... almost intentionally so. It is a credit to your species that you have done so well in spite of your shortcomings."

"Thanks," Lucien replied dryly.

Within just a few minutes, Katawa announced that he

had finished testing their blood samples against air samples collected by intake vents in the ship's hull. His analysis revealed over three hundred potential vulnerabilities. Most of those were threats from alien microbes and viruses, and that was probably just the tip of the iceberg.

"What about water-borne microbes?" Lucien asked. "Or food-borne?"

"I have found an easy way to immunize you against any biological hazards on Mokar—as well as any other alien planet you travel to in the future."

"And that is?" Addy asked.

"A one-time injection of modified white blood cells from your own blood. Unlike your original cells, the engineered ones will be capable of reproducing on their own, and they will quickly populate your bodies to provide a second layer of defense against any biological threats you might encounter. In approximately forty-eight hours, you will never get sick again," Katawa announced. He withdrew four vials from the fabricator and slotted them into syringes and hypodermic needles. Then he walked up to Garek with one of the needles.

"You sure this is safe?" Garek asked as he held out his arm to receive the injection.

"Oh yes."

"What happens if we get infected before forty-eight hours?" Lucien asked.

"You may develop a few unpleasant symptoms," Katawa replied. "To avoid this, I suggest you don't drink the water, or eat any of the food."

Garek snorted. "Wasn't planning on it."

"Why don't we just wait until we're immunized to

leave the ship?" Lucien asked as he received his inoculation.

"The Mokari are not a patient species," Katawa replied as he moved on to give Addy her injection. "By now they will have our ship surrounded. If we keep them waiting, they may decide to push us off the cliff."

"They can do that?" Lucien asked.

"They are very strong, yes," Katawa said as he walked over to Brak and lifted the Gor's shadow robes to give him an injection in his thigh.

When Katawa was done, he went back to the fabricator and produced antihistamine tablets for them. He gave each of them a tablet, except for Brak, who apparently didn't need one. Gors were direct evolutionary descendants of Etherians who'd been stranded in the ruins of their galaxy after the Great War, so their bodies were much hardier than humans, whose Etherian DNA had been diluted with a local species of primates from ancient Earth.

"Take the pills now," Katawa said, and pointed to a sink.

Lucien and Addy both jumped down from their examination table to get some water, while Garek dry-swallowed his pill.

"What is the concentration of different elements in the atmosphere?" Lucien asked, as he filled a cup with water and took his pill.

"The air is breathable, but richer in carbon dioxide than you or I are used to," Katawa replied.

Lucien nodded along with that. Most alien species were carbon-based, and as a result, their body chemistries required both water and oxygen to function, so almost all of them had evolved on worlds with both readily available.

Despite that encouraging fact, different planets had different concentrations of oxygen and carbon dioxide in their air, not to mention different levels of toxicity in the water. The water problem was easy to solve—bring their own supply from the *Specter*, but the air was more complicated. Paragons were all trained to recognize the symptoms of respiratory acidosis, which was the most common malady caused by exposure to 'breathable' alien atmospheres.

Katawa walked over to a cold storage bin and withdrew five silver flasks with breather masks attached, one for each of them, including himself. He made a few adjustments to the flasks via holographic control panels, and then passed them out, keeping one for himself.

"We're supposed to wear these the whole time?" Addy asked, trying to figure out how to secure the mask, and accommodate the flask without its weight ripping the mask off her face.

"No." Katawa's voice was muffled by his mask as he put it on. "You must inhale the contents. It will help your lungs to process the air and give you the appropriate concentration of gasses for your bodies," Katawa replied.

Lucien watched as Katawa depressed a silver button on the back of his flask and took a deep breath. The alien held his breath for a moment, then removed the flask and exhaled.

They each mimicked Katawa, emptying their flasks.

"How does it work?" Lucien asked while Katawa collected the empty flasks.

"The particles will assemble a synthetic lung inside of your airways to filter the air."

"You mean a machine?" Garek asked.

"A living machine," Katawa corrected.

"How's it going to power itself?"

"It is highly adaptive," Katawa replied. "The lung will feed off the glucose in your blood. It may make you hungrier than usual, but otherwise you shouldn't notice that you have a new organ inside your bodies."

"It's *alive?*" Addy asked. She looked like she was about to be sick.

"It is not in any way autonomous or harmful. Do not be alarmed," Katawa replied.

Lucien nodded, quietly amazed by the Faros' mastery of biotechnology. "Now what?"

"Now, we go to meet the Mokari before we anger them any further."

They followed Katawa to the ship's rear airlock. Before cycling the airlock, Katawa retrieved a shadow robe like Brak's from a locker and pulled it over his head. The garment automatically shrank and adhered to his body until he became a shapeless shadow like Brak. Not even Katawa's giant black eyes were visible through the garment, but Lucien assumed he must be able to see and breathe somehow. Brak had been wearing one of those robes ever since boarding the ship, and he hadn't been stumbling all over because of it.

Katawa began passing out translator bands, and Lucien realized he and Addy had left theirs in their quarters.

"It does not matter. Use these for now," Katawa said, and handed two of the bands to each of them.

"Why two?" Addy asked.

"So you can give the spares to the Mokari when you need to speak with them."

Lucien nodded and slipped one of the bands behind his head, above his ears. He put the other in one of the inner pockets of his robes.

Katawa opened the airlock and ushered them inside. The door irised shut behind them.

"Shouldn't we bring weapons?" Garek asked.

"Faros do not need weapons when dealing with previously-subjugated populations," Katawa replied. "Their most effective weapon is fear, and it is far deadlier than any sword. Besides, I was unable to procure Farosien weapons for this trip."

"Great," Garek muttered.

The airlock cycled quickly, and Katawa explained that the Faros didn't bother with decontamination procedures.

Lucien was horrified. Maybe they didn't care if they infected indigenous populations with deadly diseases, or maybe they weren't carriers of such pathogens. Still, that didn't mean they couldn't transfer them from the worlds they visited, and there was plenty of ecological damage they could do by allowing biological contaminants to travel on their ships from one world to another. It was yet another example of the Faros' careless disregard for all species besides their own.

When the outer door of the airlock irised open, a wave of hot dry air gusted in and took Lucien's breath away. The alien smells were overpowering but also fascinating—sickly sweet, gamy, and acrid all at the same time.

Something in the scenery beyond the airlock shifted and *clicked* in Lucien's brain, and suddenly he saw the host of nightmarish black birds waiting for them on the plateau where they'd landed; their dark leathery skin made them blend almost perfectly against the gleaming black rocks of the mountains.

Lucien waited for Katawa to lead them down the ramp from the airlock. Garek nudged him between the shoulder blades, and he remembered that Katawa was supposed to be posing as a Faro slave.

Lucien took the lead, He started down the ramp toward the assembled aliens, trying hard to hide his growing unease. If the Mokari killed him, he wasn't going to come back to life in a cloned body like he would on *Astralis,* or like a real Faro probably could.

One of the Mokari stepped forward to greet him. It walked on two skinny, multiply-jointed legs, using the bony tips of its wings for added stability to give it what seemed to be four legs instead of two.

Besides the obvious difference of *wings*, the Mokari had startlingly humanoid bodies: two eyes, two arms, two ears...

The differences were almost easier to count than the similarities; they had big, sunken red eyes, and bony faces with protruding, beak-like mouths, and sharp white teeth that were always bared in a predatory grin.

Lucien was already wearing a translator band, but the Mokari wasn't, so he produced the spare from his robes and held it out. The alien tossed its head and clacked its teeth, followed by a loud chittering sound.

The sounds automatically connected to meaning in Lucien's brain thanks to his translator.

"No need Faro magic," the Mokari said. "You leaving now, or dying now. Choose."

Lucien blinked, taken aback by the alien's hostility. The databanks on the *Specter* said that the Faros had subjugated the Mokari. They should be more deferential—unless something had changed since the records had last been updated. He hadn't thought to check the date stamp.

Or maybe this Mokari was testing him. Lucien decided to gamble on that. He stood his ground and shook the translator band at the alien.

The Mokari tossed its head again and screeched.

This time the sound didn't connect to meaning in Lucien's brain, but he didn't need a translation to understand that he was in trouble.

The bird jumped up and flapped its massive wings with a violent gust of air. It hovered easily in front of him, buffeting him with gusts from its massive wings. Its wingspan had to be at least thirty feet. It hovered there, studying him with those red eyes, and cocking its head from side to side, as if trying to decide which part of him would be the tastiest.

That went on for only a second or two before another untranslatable screech tore out of the Mokari's chest, setting Lucien's teeth on edge. He felt Addy's hands on him, pulling him back.

"Get back inside the airlock!" she whispered.

But Lucien held his ground. He shook the translator at the Mokari once more. "Take it, you ugly kakard!" he roared. The alien wouldn't understand him, but he hoped it would grasp something from his tone.

The Mokari's red eyes flashed like daggers in the night, and the alien swooped forward. It knocked him over and stood on his chest, threatening to break his ribs with its weight. Its talons stabbed through his skin, drawing hot rivers of blood. Lucien gasped from the pain, but found he couldn't suck in another breath. The Mokari was too heavy. He couldn't breathe!

The monster regarded the crimson pools of blood

around its feet, its head cocked curiously to one side, and jaws slightly agape. The Mokari's red eyes were narrowed, as if with intense interest. Addy ran behind the creature and began beating it on the head with her fists, but the Mokari took no interest in her. It was fixated on him—on his blood. It could probably smell it.

Lucien's whole body went cold. He'd miscalculated, and badly. Addy screamed and intensified her assault. Both Garek and Brak ran into view, and grabbed the Mokari by its wings to pull it off him, but they were too late.

The Mokari's head snapped down, jaws gaping wide, and Lucien cringed, waiting for the searing bite that would rip out his throat and end his life.

CHAPTER 24

Mokar

A long green tongue flicked out of the Mokari's mouth. It lapped Lucien's blood from one of the pools around its feet, and withdrew sharply, chittering at him.

"Blood red. Not blue. Or black. Taste good," it said.

Lucien grimaced from the pain still radiating from his chest. Brak, Garek, and Addy were pulling on the Mokari's wings as hard as they could to get the creature off him, but they weren't getting anywhere.

The Mokari glanced over its shoulder at them, and flapped its wings to shake them off. All three went flying.

The alien returned its full attention to Lucien, its head cocked curiously. It chittered something else. "Not Faro?"

Then Lucien got it. His holoskin did nothing to disguise his blood. It was *red, not blue, or black* as the Mokari had said.

Lucien decided to take a risk. Using what little air he'd managed to suck in despite the crushing weight of the Mokari standing on his chest, he croaked out, "Not Faro. Human."

The Mokari cocked its head to the other side. "Look like Faro." Lucien's head swam and dark spots crowded his vision. He had no strength left for a reply.

Addy ran up and crouched beside him. "It's a disguise!" she screamed, and deactivated her holoskin, revealing her human features once more.

The Mokari screeched and rocked back on its heels. Its talons dug even deeper into Lucien's chest as it did so. A guttural cry burst like a living thing from his lips, taking what little air he had left.

"Get off him!" Addy said. "We're not your enemies! We come in peace!"

The Mokari stepped off Lucien's chest, and he sucked in a deep breath. His ribs ached sharply as his lungs filled with air, and more blood bubbled from his stinging wounds, hot and wet, soaking his robes.

A small shadow came and crouched on the other side of him—Katawa. The little alien wiped away Lucien's blood with the beige fabric of his robe, and sprayed his wounds with an aerosol of some kind.

The wounds bubbled, then sealed with a translucent resin, and the pain was replaced by a pleasant tingling.

Lucien sat up and glared at the Mokari who'd attacked him. Addy helped him to his feet.

"Are you okay?" she asked.

Lucien shook his head. "Fine," he grunted. Then added in a softer tone, "Sorry. Thank you for defending me."

Addy nodded mutely, her eyes full of concern. Garek and Brak walked back up the ramp and stood to either side of them.

Lucien found his spare translator band lying a few feet down the ramp and went to retrieve it. The Mokari watched him curiously out of one eye as he walked by.

Lucien held the band out to the alien once more. "Take it," he insisted.

And to his surprise, this time the Mokari did so, grabbing the band in over-large, three-fingered hands that tapered into vicious-looking claws. The alien placed the band behind its head, above its dish-shaped ears. Apparently this Mokari already had experience using the translators.

"Finally," Lucien breathed, wincing as that exhalation provoked a sharp ache from the right side of his rib cage. He clapped a hand to that side and leaned the other way to take the weight off his injured ribs.

"Death final. Not dead. Not final." The Mokari said, proving it could finally understand him—but obviously only in the most literal sense. "What you?" it asked.

Lucien struggled with the clipped phrases of the Mokari. Clearly universal translators weren't a panacea for language barriers.

"What am I?" he suggested.

The Mokari chittered. "Yes. What you?"

"I'm..." Lucien trailed off, noting that his holoskin was still active. He touched a hand to each of the glowing golden bands on his arms to deactivate the holoskin, and his true human features re-appeared.

The Mokari screeched and glanced sharply at Addy. "False skins. Evil Faro magic. Why use? Not Faro."

Suddenly Lucien found himself wondering the same thing. After the dubious welcome they'd received while disguised as Faros, it seemed like they'd have had better luck greeting the Mokari as humans to start with. He glanced at Katawa, who lifted the top of his shadow robe to reveal his over-sized gray head.

The Mokari took a quick step back, and almost fell off the ramp. It had to flap its wings to regain its balance.

"Gray god!" it chittered, bowing its head and kneeling before Katawa.

Lucien glared at Katawa. "You almost got us killed for nothing! The Mokari obviously hate the Faros, but not other aliens, and they *do* recognize your species."

The little gray alien blinked its giant eyes at him. "I was mistaken. I apologize."

The Mokari raised its nightmarish head and snapped its jaws at Lucien, glaring at him with one red eye. "Respect gray god. Or death."

Lucien scowled. "Of course." He turned back to Katawa and mimicked the Mokari's submissive posture, all the while fuming inside.

"How do you know about us—the gray gods?" Katawa asked.

"Many songs."

"Your songs about us are very old, some as old as ten thousand years," Katawa objected. "You should have forgotten by now."

"Some songs old. Some songs new. Songs still sung. Gray gods recent. Hard forget."

Katawa nodded and turned to Lucien. "My people were here recently. That explains why I heard of a Mokari legend about us that is only one hundred and sixty years old. The implication is that my people stayed here in the Gakol System for a very long time."

"If that's true," Lucien said, "and the Grays left because the Faros found them here, then the Faros must know these Mokari songs, too, and that means they've already followed them to wherever they lead."

Katawa turned back to the Mokari. "Have the Faros heard your songs?"

"Not worthy listen. Why gray god return Mokar?" The Mokari asked, its head canting from side to side.

"I returned to hear your songs about the gray gods, and of the one who flew with them among the stars."

The Mokari tossed its head. "You seek others like you."

"Yes," Katawa replied.

"Not see Gray Gods for many suns."

"What does that mean? Many suns?" Addy asked.

"Many years," Katawa replied. Nodding to the Mokari, he asked, "What is your sound?"

The Mokari threw back its head, and uttered a loud cry. Lucien guessed that the question was analogous to *what is your name?*

The Mokari's *sound* was impossible for him to repeat exactly, but Katawa gave a good approximation. "*Aakee?*"

The Mokari canted its head to one side and nodded once.

"Can you help us, Aakee?" Lucien asked.

The Mokari glared at him for an uncomfortably long second, then turned back to Katawa. "Come gray god. We sing. You listen. We eat. Our honor you stay."

Katawa smiled. "My honor to listen," he replied.

Aakee turned and walked down the ramp, back to the waiting ranks of his fellows. Katawa followed, and the rest of them trailed a few steps behind. The Mokari parted for them as they approached. Garek deactivated his holoskin to avoid ruffling their feathers—so to speak—and Brak lifted the top of his robe to reveal his skull-shaped head. The Mokari saw Brak for the first time and screeched at him. He roared back, and they spread their wings in agitation. They watched him, red eyes glaring and heads cocking every which way.

Brak bared his black teeth in a grin. "I like these Mokari," he said. "They want to eat me, and I want to eat them. It is good to be among like-minded beings."

Lucien frowned. "If you say so."

Garek glanced at them. Between his bald head and scarred face he looked fearsome enough that he seemed to fit right in with the Mokari's eat-or-be-eaten culture. "We should go back for our exosuits," he said in a low voice.

"And leave Katawa alone with the Mokari?" Addy asked.

"He seems to be able to handle himself," Garek replied. "They think he's a god. They're not going to eat *him.* We'll catch up."

"Your suits will anger the Mokari and make them more likely to attack you," Katawa said. "False skins, remember? Stay. They will not harm you as long as you are with me."

"For someone who's never been here before, you seem pretty confident of what to expect," Garek replied.

"I have met their people before, on other worlds. One of them shared the same master with me. He was an assassin. I was a doctor. We used to share meals together. That is how I first heard of their legends and songs."

"A killer and a healer became friends," Garek said. "Sounds like the proverbial lion and the lamb to me."

"The what?" Addy asked.

"Am I the only one who's read the Etherian Codices?"

"If we were faithful enough to do that, we wouldn't have left the Etherian Empire in the first place," Addy replied.

"Katawa, what exactly do the Mokari legends say about you?" Lucien asked, while keeping an eye on the unending lines of Mokari to either side of them. Aakee seemed in no hurry to get wherever he was going. They walked past one mud-grass mound after another, heading for one of the larger mounds on the plateau.

"They say that we are the creators of their world, that we created the Mokari suns and the stars, and that we control fire, wind, and rain."

Garek snorted. "I wonder how they got that impression."

Katawa glanced at him. "Legend says that when we came here with the Etherian Fleet, we made the stars fall. Mokar still bears the scars of that incident. Since then, the Mokari have a healthy respect for us."

"Falling stars, huh?" Garek mused. "I bet that was just—"

"Let's talk about it later," Lucien said, cutting Garek off before he could poke a hole in the Mokaris' beliefs. "We came to listen to what the Mokari have to say."

"Yeah..." Garek nodded, while watching the serried ranks of Mokari to either side of them. "Point taken."

They could all guess what *falling stars* meant. There had been a battle and the debris had rained down over Mokar—or maybe one of the Etherian ships had experienced a critical failure after reaching orbit that resulted in it falling from the sky and breaking up in the atmosphere. Whatever the case, the devastation had obviously been significant enough to trigger Mokari superstitions.

Later on, taking one or more of the Mokari on board the Etherian ships had probably only reinforced their ideas about the Grays' deity. If the Grays had arrived on Earth and taken primitive humans into space, whole religions would have sprung up around them, too.

Aakee reached the mud-grass mound that was their destination and disappeared through a large circular opening near the ground. More circular openings pocked the outside of the mound at various heights for windows or possibly higher-level entrances.

They passed inside the mound and found the floor padded with dried grass. The structure was huge. Dozens of mud-grass *chairs* adorned the space, each of them piled high with dried grass. Aakee went to sit on one of them. He folded his legs and wings, seeming to shrink into himself as he settled into the chair.

Mokari came streaming in on all sides—some swooping in through circular holes in the dome-shaped ceiling, others walking in at ground level. The other Mokari joined Aakee, quickly occupying all of the empty chairs. Katawa went to what was roughly the center of the room, and took a seat in one of the few remaining chairs, leaving Lucien and the others to stand around him. Katawa glanced their way and gestured for them to sit.

Lucien did as he was told, and promptly winced as his bruised ribs reminded him they were there. Addy and Garek sat on either side of him, but Brak remained standing, despite a scathing look from Katawa.

A few moments later, the Mokari began to sing. It started with just one of them raising its head to the ceiling and exhaling with a sound like a flute. Then another joined in, and another, followed by a dozen more. Their voices rose and fell in perfect, melodic harmony.

To Lucien's surprise, his translator began assembling lyrics in his brain, and a kind of story emerged.

Mokar is all.
One nest. One people. One sky.
Sky is torn.
Stars fall and fires burn.
Life is lost and ashes fly.
Death and sadness.
Gods appear from sky. Gray as smoke. Tiny.

Mokari lifted up, higher than sky.
Sky turns black.
Stars bright and many.
Mokar small.
Mokar gone.
New nests. New peoples. New skies.

Everything different.
All is new.
Mokari see.
Mokari know.
Mokar not all.

Gray gods return.

Death no more.
Life forever.
Life for all.

Death no more.
Life forever.
Life for all.

The song went on, speaking about how great and wonderful the gray gods were.

"What the is all that krak supposed to mean?" Garek muttered.

Lucien shook his head. "I can't make sense of it."

"I can," Addy said.

Both of them turned to her.

"Well—I think I can," Addy said. "They're talking about how the Mokari thought their world was the only one, and they thought their people were the only people. Then the Grays came, raining fire on their world—debris maybe?"

Lucien nodded.

Addy went on, "A bunch of them died. Then one or more of them got to ride in the Grays' spaceships. They went up to space, *above the sky,* and traveled to new *nests.* They got to see *new skies* and meet *new peoples*. Then they returned to Mokar and the Grays made all of the Mokari immortal—that's what the chorus means: *death no more, life forever, life for all.*"

"I guess that makes sense," Lucien said. "If you're right, then the Mokari weren't always immortals. I bet that's even news to Katawa."

"I don't see how any of this helps us," Garek said, shaking his head. "Katawa basically told us all of this already, and he didn't need to spend half an hour singing about it," he said, jerking his chin at the alien *a cappella* group. They were busy still singing the Grays' praises.

"Maybe we'll get some kind of clue if we keep listening," Addy said.

"Yeah, or we'll go deaf," Garek replied, wincing at the growing volume of the Mokari's voices.

They were starting to sound shrill.

Lucien gave his attention to the lyrics once more, hoping Addy was right. They were singing something about *magical keys* and *blue devils,* which Lucien could only assume were the Faros.

He listened for a while longer, then turned to Addy. "Translation?"

"They're talking about how the Grays suddenly left them after the *blue devils* came, but they left a... *magical key* to open a *doorway* to a new *nest*—another world. The key was hidden in the *underworld* to keep it safe. The Mokari were supposed to find it after the blue devils left...."

Addy stopped to listen some more, then continued with her summary, "The key was supposed to open the doorway to bring the Grays back, but none of the *Mokari* who went into the underworld to find it returned, and the key was never found. They say that Death found them, and the underworld is where Death went after the *Gray Gods* sent it away."

"So all we have to do is go into their underworld and find this key?" Lucien asked. "I'm assuming their underworld must be a physical place. Maybe a network of underground caves or caverns?"

"Must be," Addy said.

"So why haven't the Faros gone down there themselves and found the key?" Lucien asked.

"Who says they haven't?" Garek asked. "That *magical key* probably leads the way to a quantum junction that goes to whatever planet the Grays went to next, but Katawa told us that the Grays became slaves of the Faros, so the Faros obviously found them there."

Lucien frowned. "I guess so."

"Like I said, this trail is colder than space," Garek said.

The songs ended, and several Mokari came in carrying shadowy, foul-smelling burdens. One after another they dropped their burdens in the center of the room, piling them high. A sound like swarms of flies buzzing filled the silence, and one of the Mokari chittered: "Eat!"

At that, the Mokari bounded out of their chairs and fell upon the shadowy pile with enthusiastic chittering and screeching. Wet tearing noises followed.

The foul smell grew fouler, and Lucien's guts clenched. The smell was so bad that he grew dizzy and had to stumble outside before he added to the stench with the contents of his stomach.

Addy burst out after him. "Whew!" She fell on her hands and knees outside, gasping for air. Then her body heaved, and she did throw up. Lucien stumbled over to hold her hair—but then he remembered she didn't have any.

It was dark outside, and the air was cooler now. The warmer sun had sunk below the horizon, while the more distant one still hung high overhead, a dim orange eye, casting everything in a flat, reddish gloom. It was hard to see more than a few dozen meters, and only a handful of stars were visible. Mokar's twilight had begun.

Lucien heard feet trampling the grassy floor of the Mokari dwelling, and he turned to see Garek and Katawa emerge from one of the circular doorways.

"Well?" Lucien asked, his eyes on Katawa. "You ready to go chasing the next rumor?"

"Not until we go to the underworld and find the key," Katawa said.

Addy s and wiped her mouth on her sleeve. "You didn't hear us talking in there? The Faros must have already found the key. How else did they find and enslave your people?"

"You do not understand—the key leads to the lost fleet, not to my people. My people were found and enslaved, but the fleet was never found. Only the caretaker knew where it was hidden, and he has made himself to forget."

"How do you know that?" Addy asked.

"Because I am the caretaker."

Lucien blinked in shock. *"You?"*

"Yes."

"Well, you really frekked yourself over," Garek said.

"That is anatomically impossible," Katawa replied, his huge eyes blinking slowly.

"He means all of your precautions have made your life difficult," Addy said.

"Oh. Yes. I thought you knew this."

"I do... I was re-stating the problem for effect," Garek said.

"Do humans all waste their air by repeating what is already known? Perhaps I am not the only one who has a problem remembering things."

Garek's eyes narrowed to slits, and he looked away.

Lucien followed his gaze, out over the dark emerald river swishing through the Mokari village, past the black cliffs, and out to the hazy red sky.

"Come, we must rest," Katawa said. "The Mokari will not take us to the underworld until morning."

"Why not?" Addy asked. "Is it far from here?"

"Yes, but that is not why. Twilight is dangerous on Mokar, even for the Mokari. They live in the mountains for good reason." Katawa left them on that note, heading back to the *Specter*.

"How do you know all of that if you've never been here?" Garek called after him, suspicious as ever.

"It is in the ship's databanks!" Katawa called back, his voice muffled by the *swishing* of the river.

"You still don't trust him," Lucien said.

"I trust him about as far as I can fly by flapping my arms," Garek replied, and started after the little alien.

Lucien turned to Addy. "Where's Brak?"

She looked around. "I don't know... Brak?" she called.

A moment later he emerged from the Mokari's dwelling, rank with the smell of raw, gamy meat. Flies, or the Mokari equivalent, buzzed around him while he munched on a giant leg or arm of something.

"Uck!" Addy said as he stopped beside them. "I'll see you back in our quarters, Lucien," she said, and took off at a run.

"What did I say about sampling the local cuisine?" Lucien asked.

The leg fell dramatically from Brak's mouth. "I could not resist. The smell was too much."

"You can say that again," Lucien said.

Brak grinned and held the leg out to him. "Try some. It is like nothing you've ever tasted."

Lucien's guts clenched in warning. "I'll pass," he said. He was starting to feel dizzy again. "I need to go," he managed, and then turned and ran after Addy. To his horror, Brak came running up beside him, still munching.

"Throw that thing away!"

Brak grunted. "Fine."

Something wet and noxious hit Lucien in the side of the head, almost knocking him over. "The frek...!"

"You say to throw it away," Brak replied.

"Not *at* me!" His cheek itched maddeningly where the meat had hit him. He scratched it, and his fingers came away sticky and smelling like rotten krak.

Lucien's head spun with the smell, and there was no getting away from it now. It was stuck to him. "You did that on purpose!" he accused, breathing hard through his mouth.

"Maybe, yes," Brak admitted, and let loose a booming laugh.

"You'd better watch your back," Lucien warned.

"I will watch my front, also," Brak replied, and laughed again.

CHAPTER 25

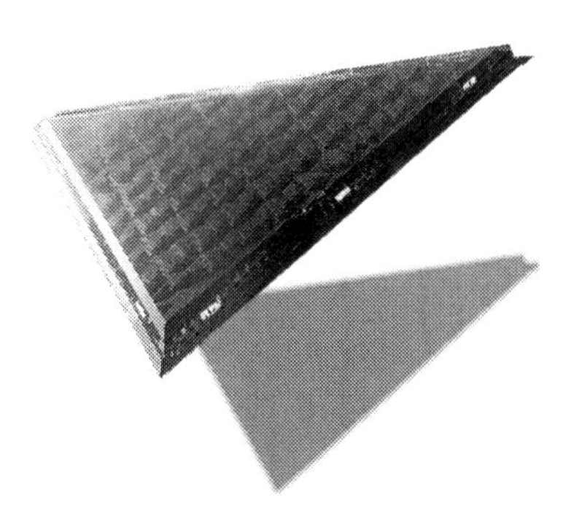

Astralis

Lucien waited until late for Tyra to come home, watching holo-cartoons with the girls to pass the time. Theola succumbed to sleep first, sucking her thumb, her eyes slowly drifting shut. Seeing the glazed look in Atara's eyes, Lucien realized she wasn't far off, so he put them both to bed, carrying Theola, and taking Atara by the hand. He tucked Atara in and kissed her on the forehead. "Goodnight, Atty," he whispered. "I love you."

"Night, Daddy..." she mumbled back.

He shut thc door softly behind him and went to the living room for a drink—his nightly ritual. It was almost midnight and Tyra still wasn't home. He'd probably be in bed himself by the time she returned.

Lucien poured himself whiskey, neat, and went to sit in an armchair by the picture windows, in front of a crackling fireplace. He sat sipping his drink, allowing his stress to melt away. Orange tongues of electric-fueled flames danced over convincing metal logs, mesmerizing him. The window beside him seemed to radiate cold.

He looked out that window, into the night. Just like their home in Fallside, this one was situated on the side of Hubble Mountain, looking out over the city. Giant snow flakes tumbled from a black sky, accumulating on the deck. Street lights shone intermittently through the falling snowflakes. The view was as mesmerizing as the fire.

Lucien reclined his chair and balanced his drink on his stomach, allowing the warmth of the fireplace and the crackling sound it made to lull him to sleep...

He awoke to desperate screaming.

The girls.

Lucien bolted out of his chair, sending his glass and drink flying. He ran down the hall to the bedrooms, his heart pounding in his chest. As he drew near, he recognized those cries.

It was Theola.

Lucien collided with the door, unable to stop in time. He turned the handle and opened the door. Theola's cries became ten times louder.

The room was still dark. He couldn't see a thing. "Lights!" he roared.

The overhead lights snapped on, and he blinked the spots from his eyes, searching desperately for his daughters. Atara was in bed. She sat up and rubbed her eyes. "Dad?"

Lucien hurried over to Theola's crib. She was writhing on the mattress, making a mess of the sheets. Her face had flushed bright red, and tears streamed down her cheeks. He picked her up in shaking hands.

"She won't go to sleep," Atara explained.

"Shhh... it's okay, it's okay," he said as he bounced Theola in his arms, but she refused to be comforted. He kissed her forehead—

And promptly recoiled from her. Theola's skin was like ice. His heart leapt into his throat. He placed a hand on her forehead. "She's freezing!" Lucien said, shaking his head in disbelief. The room was cold, too. He turned to Atara. "Did you mess with the temperature in here?"

She shook her head quickly.

Not buying it, Lucien stalked over to his eldest and felt her forehead, but she was warm.

Lucien's brow furrowed in confusion.

Theola was calming down now. She had her face buried in his chest.

"Maybe she's sick?" Atara suggested, her eyes wide and blinking. "Is she going to be okay?"

Lucien felt Theola's forehead again. It was warmer now. "She'll be fine..." he said, trailing off. He glanced at the window beside Atara's bed and went to check it. The window was shut and locked, but looking closer he found greasy fingerprints around the latch.

"She might have a fever," Atara suggested.

He rounded on her and pointed to the window. "Did you open this?" he demanded.

Atara's bottom lip began quivering. "Why are you yelling?"

"Yes or no, Atara!"

"I was hot!" She cried, and dove under the covers.

Lucien felt a pang of regret for getting so mad. He went

over and sat on the edge of her bed. He placed a hand on the sobbing lump under the covers.

"Atara," he said in a gentle voice. "You could have made your sister sick. You can't open the window again, do you understand me?"

"I was allowed in Fallside!"

"This isn't Fallside, sweetheart. It's too cold here for you to open the window. If you're hot, then throw off one of your blankets, but don't open the window, okay?"

Atara said nothing for a moment, but at least he could tell that she wasn't sobbing anymore.

"Can you come out, please? I'm sorry for yelling."

Atara popped her head out of the covers, and beamed up at him. "I forgive you."

Lucien blinked, taken aback by Atara's abrupt change of mood. Her eyes were dry, and so were her cheeks. Was she just pretending to be upset?

"I'm going to take Theola with me for a while..." he said.

Atara nodded. "Okay."

He leaned in and kissed her on the forehead. "Good night, sweetheart."

"Good night, Dad," Atara said as he was leaving.

"Lights off," he said, and closed the door behind him.

Theola sighed and snuggled into his chest, already asleep. Lucien walked carefully back to the living room with her, trying not to wake her.

He puzzled over what had just happened, and why he felt so troubled by it. Atara had opened the window because she was hot, and even if she hadn't been genuinely sobbing, that wasn't anything to worry about. Kids learned to manipulate their parents from a young age. Maybe Atara was learning how to fake her tears.

Lucien sat in his armchair by the fireplace once more. He reclined the chair with Theola on his chest. She stirred sleepily and popped her thumb in her mouth for a good suck. After a few moments her features relaxed in sleep and she stopped sucking. He smiled, watching her, and his thoughts turned idly back to the incident....

Something clicked.

Theola's crib was far from the window, tucked away in the corner of the room. Even with the window open, it would have taken a while for her to freeze like that. Atara's bed, on the other hand, was right next to the window. If anyone should have been ice-cold with the window open, it was her.

Unless...

Unless Atara had taken Theola out of her crib and held her up to the open window. Or left her on the window sill...

Lucien shuddered at the thought. It was a long way down the mountain from their house. Anyone who fell out that window wouldn't just fall one story to the ground, they'd fall more than two, because of the walk-out basement, and then they'd still roll a few hundred feet until a tree or another house stopped them. Not that a baby could survive a two-story fall to begin with.

Lucien shook his head. He was being crazy. Atara wouldn't even be able to reach Theola to get her out of her crib. She wasn't tall enough. She'd probably just opened the window and then pulled the covers over her head when she got cold. Later she must have got up to shut the window again when even the covers weren't enough to keep her warm.

Being a baby, Theola hadn't been able to adjust her blankets properly, so she'd frozen in a matter of minutes.

That was the most reasonable explanation. Nothing sinister. *Just parental paranoia,* he decided, and let out a sigh.

He wrapped both his arms around Theola, hugging her to his chest to keep her from rolling off, and then he lost himself in the warmth and rhythmic crackling of the fire. The flickering flames had him mesmerized before long, and his eyelids grew heavy with sleep. He let the warmth carry him away, and this time there weren't any screams to wake him.

* * *

Mokar

"We're wasting time chasing our asses like we have tails," Garek said, picking through a plate of bland-looking food that he'd selected from the *Specter's* meal fabricator.

"Colorful," Lucien replied, picking at his own food with dismay. He'd chosen some kind of eggs with a side of meat strips, but the eggs tasted sour and the meat... Lucien's stomach clenched and he set his fork down.

"Look, I'm all for being neighborly and helping a down-on-his-luck alien find his way home," Garek said, shaking his fork at Lucien, "but this whole thing stinks, and you know it."

"I've been feeling uneasy, too," Addy admitted.

Lucien looked at her. "You didn't say anything to me."

"Because I know how much you want Katawa's story to be true. I get that you want to go on some crusade against all the evil in the universe, but Garek's right, why would anyone hand us a fleet of a thousand warships as payment just for finding them?"

Lucien shook his head. "It's not about crusades. That fleet is our best chance to rescue our people. We can't go in guns blazing and rescue them without any guns."

"So we find or steal some guns along the way," Garek said. "We can start by stealing Katawa's ship."

Lucien scowled. "I'm going to need proof that he's planning to betray us before I agree to go along with a plan like that."

"By the time we have proof, he's going to have us over a barrel of antimatter," Garek replied.

Lucien shook his head. "Let's follow this Mokari rumor first. Go to their underworld and see what comes of it. If it's a dead end, then we convince Katawa to take us somewhere that has a Faro slave market, so that we can do something to advance *our* goals. I'm sure he won't say no to that."

"And if he does?"

"We'll cross that wormhole when we get there."

"Fine," Garek said. "But don't say I didn't warn you when the krak hits the turbines."

"Let's hope it doesn't," Lucien replied.

Brak walked up, wearing all but the hood of his shadow robe, his plate piled high with foul-smelling raw meat.

"Ugh!" Garek said as Brak sat down. "What the... I'm done," he said, and dropped his fork.

Lucien clapped a hand to his face and pinched his nose. "Where'd you get that?"

"Mokar breakfast," Brak said, grinning as he picked up a foot-long bone and ripped off a giant chunk of bloody meat. "They agree to share with me."

"Isn't that the same krak they were eating last night?" Garek asked. He was leaning as far away from Brak as he could without falling out of his chair.

Brak chewed twice and swallowed the massive bite. "Yes," he replied. "Want some?" He held the bone out.

"No!" Garek almost fell out of his chair in his hurry to leave the table. He left the mess hall at a run.

Brak heaved his massive shoulders. "More for me."

Lucien left the table next, taking Addy with him. They went to sit in a booth at the far end of the mess hall, as far as they could get from Brak without physically leaving the room.

Addy grabbed his hand and laced her fingers through it.

"I've been thinking about what we're doing—starting a war and rescuing our people. Maybe we should set our sights somewhere closer to home."

Lucien regarded her with eyebrows raised. "What's home? The Etherian Empire? *Astralis?*"

Addy placed her free hand over his heart. "Here."

He smiled wryly and leaned in for a kiss, but she pushed him away after just a moment. "I mean it, Lucien."

"So do I," he said, matching her tone.

She frowned and looked away, placing their hands on the table in front of them. She spent a moment studying the way their hands locked together, her gaze far away. "I think I'm in love with you," she said.

Lucien blinked. He hadn't expected that. "I..."

"Can't bring yourself to say it back?" she asked, turning back to him.

"No, it's not that. It's... I just haven't had a chance to stop and think about *us*. It's been one crisis after another since we left the Etherian Empire and you and I met, and most of the time we've spent together since then has been in bed."

Addy nodded slowly, her hand leaving his. "I get it." She sighed. "Story of my life. I find a great guy, and he just wants to have fun."

Lucien found her hand again. "That's not true. I want more than that. I could actually see us together fifty years from now, a ship of our own, exploring the universe together, seeing things no one has ever seen before."

"Sounds amazing," Addy said, smiling dreamily at him. "So why don't we do that? Forget *Astralis,* the Etherian Empire, Etheria, Etherus, Abaddon, the Faros—forget everything but you and me."

"I don't know if I can do that."

"Why not? Neither of us have ties to *Astralis.* And as for family back in the Etherian Empire... my ties to family were cut long before I left, and your family has probably forgotten you by now."

Lucien frowned and shook his head. "I don't know about that."

"It's been eight years, almost nine, since they've heard from you. They probably think you're dead. Maybe they've even convinced Etherus to let them bring you back to life from backups taken before you left."

"I don't think Etherus would agree to do that," Lucien replied.

"Regardless, nine years is a long time, and if your family ties were so strong, you wouldn't have left the Etherian Empire in the first place."

"Fair enough, but what's your point?"

"My point is we're free, Lucien! As free as two people can ever get. So why aren't we living like it?"

"Well, for one thing, we don't have a ship of our own to go exploring the universe with," Lucien said.

"No," Addy admitted, "But we could get one."

"How?"

Addy shrugged. "Work for a Marauder crew until we can afford our own ship."

"Become outlaw pirates, you mean. I don't think the life expectancy is very long in that job."

"We could find legitimate work, too. An empire as big as the Farosien Empire has to have plenty of work."

"But we're humans, not real Faros. We'll end up enslaved to them in no time."

Addy shook her head, smiling. "Thanks to Katawa, we look like Faros, we sound like Faros, and we even have fake ID-chips. We'll blend in perfectly no matter where we go."

"What about Brak?"

"We take him with us."

"And Garek?"

"If he wants to come."

"I doubt he'll be interested."

"That's fine," Addy said. "He has his own path to follow. Unlike us, he does have ties to *Astralis.* He has to go find and rescue his daughter."

Lucien nodded.

"So?" Addy prompted. "What do you think? Just you and me and the stars. No commitments—except to each other," she added with a wink.

"And to the netherworld with everyone else?" Lucien asked.

"Well, I wouldn't put it that way, but yeah. What makes you think it's our job to save them? *Astralis* left the Etherian Empire knowing the risks, and so did we. I don't want to be heartless, but I don't think there's actually anything we can do to help them. By now our people have been farmed out to slave markets all over the universe. Even rescuing *one* of them would be hard, but all of them?" Addy's eyebrows shot up, and she shook her head. "Garek has a reasonable goal: save his daughter and beat it back to the Etherian Empire, but even that won't be easy.

"You want to start a war and defeat an alien empire that spans the entire universe. Even if you find the Etherian Fleet and Katawa really does give it to you, a thousand ships are never going to be enough."

"We can't just give up," Lucien said.

"Why not? Look, I know you believe in Etherus. You think he's almighty God. Well, if that's true, then why doesn't *he* go wage a war with Abaddon? What's he doing hiding behind the Red Line?"

"That's neither here nor there," Lucien said, looking away from her.

"It's both here and there," Addy replied. She touched the side of his chin with her forefinger and turned his gaze back to her, forcing him to look into her bright green eyes. They weren't cold as he expected them to be, but warm and full of sympathy. "Who are you to do what even your God will not?"

Lucien frowned. "Let's break it down: you're saying we shouldn't fight evil because Etherus isn't out there leading the charge."

Addy shrugged. "Pretty much, yeah."

"What if he's waiting for us to do it?"

"So he's lazy?" Addy asked, her brow screwing up. "How's that any better?"

"What if Etherus created the Faros and the Etherians, knowing full well that they'd start a war with each other. What if he's testing them? Testing us. We used to be Etherians, after all. And if this *is* some kind of test, I don't think we're going to get full marks by leaving all the questions blank, and waiting for the teacher to tell us the answers."

"But the Etherians aren't free," Addy objected. "So how can he be testing them?"

"They have to be," Lucien said. "Maybe they're not tempted to do evil, but I think they still can, and the history we've learned about them supports that. Look at the Gors and the now-extinct Sythians. They were Etherians who fought with the Faros in the Great War. Their punishment was to remain stranded on the worlds they destroyed, and eventually they evolved into entirely different species."

"What's your point?" Addy asked, shaking her head.

"My point is, a long time ago some of the Etherians did choose to do something wrong. The Gors are living proof of that."

"Okay, so they're free-*ish*," Addy said. "But what does that have to do with anything?"

"Simple. The first time the Etherians did something wrong was back when some of them joined the war against Etherus, and now they're doing something wrong for a second time by not *starting* a war with Abaddon. The Etherians are just sitting there in paradise, content to forget about the rest of the universe and its troubles. Pacifism is their new sin, but what scares me is what their punishment might be."

"Such as?"

"The Etherians and all of the Etherian Empire are like a sand bar in the middle of an ocean. All it takes is one big wave, and they're gone.

"If you take the Red Line and everything in it, it's just a dot compared to the rest of the universe. The sheer difference in size and numbers between Etheria and the Farosien Empire makes them extremely vulnerable."

"But the Faros don't know where Etheria is."

"No, not yet, but the lost fleet might change that. If Abaddon stumbles on it before we do, he's going to use it to conquer Etheria. The war will be over before you can blink, and the Faros will lead everyone in the Etherian Empire into slavery—including the entire human race."

Addy looked skeptical. "New Earth is mobile. They'll just pick up and run."

"And just look at how that worked out for *Astralis.* You can't run forever."

"All right, let's say all of that happens. You think Etherus is just going to stand by and let his kingdom crumble? If he's the almighty creator of the universe, then you're worrying for nothing. He'll just wave his hands and the Faros will disappear."

Lucien stared at her. "And what if he's not really God?"

"Well..."

Addy didn't have a ready answer for that. She wasn't exactly a big believer, after all.

Lucien nodded slowly. "If Etherus isn't who he says he is, then this war that you're trying to convince me not to start is the only thing standing between our entire species and eternal damnation."

Addy blew out a breath. "So it's our job to find this fleet and use it against Abaddon to make sure that doesn't happen."

"Maybe. First we need to make sure the secret of Etheria's location stays safe. Then we can figure out how to use the fleet to get our people back, and after that, maybe we can start freeing other species, too."

Addy began shaking her head. "I love your idealism, Lucien, I *really* do, but I also love you, and I'm pretty sure this war is going to get you killed."

"Maybe. Maybe not. But if I do die, at least my life will have meant something."

"It already means something! To me. I need you." Addy's eyes were pleading as they searched his.

"I need you, too, Addy..."

"No, you don't need me. You need soldiers. And I'm not one."

Addy stood up and left the booth. Even bald as an egg she still looked amazing. Lucien felt something physically tugging him to follow her as she left, but instead of doing that, he just sat there and watched her go.

His heart hurt. They were at an impasse. She wanted

the two of them to go off exploring the universe with nothing to weigh them down, while he was itching for a larger meaning to life. This war with Abaddon was it: a real crusade, a holy war like the universe had never seen before.

Wars were rarely justified, their causes diluted by the blood of the fallen until they lost all reason, but every now and then there came a war that was different, a war that called out to the hearts of everyone who ever heard of it—a war to end all wars.

This was one of those wars. Lucien knew he couldn't walk away. He'd been born for this. The light-bringer. Somehow, even his name foretold his purpose. He was supposed to bring light to a dark universe, to help restore peace and justice for everyone, everywhere.

Maybe it was arrogant to think that was possible, or that he could somehow be instrumental in such a timeless struggle, but *someone* had to be, so why not him?

"We are ready to leave."

That voice stirred Lucien from his thoughts. He looked up and found Katawa standing in the entrance of the mess hall. Katawa's giant black eyes found him, and blinked. "Did you eat?" the little gray alien asked.

Brak grunted and pushed out his chair from the table at the other end of the mess hall, his plate was empty but for a few bloody scraps of gristle. "Too much!" he declared, and pounded his belly with a fist, knocking loose a thunderous belch.

Lucien smiled ruefully.

"Good. You will need your strength for the underworld. We must go. The Mokari are waiting."

CHAPTER 26

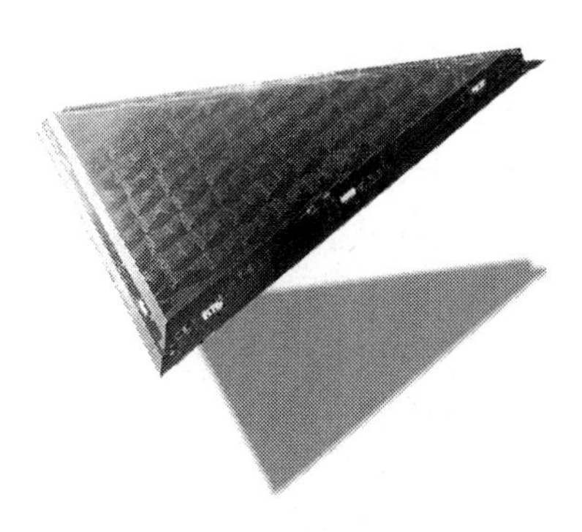

Astralis

Tyra sat in the armchair in the living room beside the picture window, wearing a sweater to help keep out the cold. She listened to the sound of the fire crackling in the hearth while she scanned the news headlines on her ARCs. Taking an absent-minded sip from her cup of *caf,* she promptly grimaced. The caf was cold—of course it was, Lucien must have brewed it hours ago when he got up to take Atara to her new school. *Typical Tyra, so distracted that you don't even remember to heat up your morning caf.*

She'd woken up at eleven o'clock, but she'd still only gotten five hours of sleep. She'd been in her office until early morning coming up with new cloning bills in case the judicial department approved Ellis's initial proposal.

Now she was scanning the headlines to see if the judicial department had delivered their verdict. Only a day had passed since Ellis had submitted the proposal, but the judicial department sometimes delivered verdicts within hours, so it wouldn't be strange to have one by now. *Astralis's* government was a hyper-efficient machine.

"Tyra? You mind un-plugging for a second? We need to talk about something." It was Lucien.

Tyra closed the least interesting of the two news feeds she had open, freeing up half her field of view. She spared a glance at Lucien. He sat beside her on the couch warming his hands around a fresh cup of caf. Tyra swallowed a sigh, instantly resenting him for the fact that he had time to make a fresh pot, while she didn't even seem to have the time to re-heat an old one.

"What's going on?" she asked, only half-turning to him so he wouldn't see the news feed glowing in her other eye. She took another sip of her cold caf and pretended to stare into the flames dancing in the fireplace.

"It's about Atara. Last night, some time after I put the girls to bed, Theola woke up screaming. I went to check on them and..."

There it is! Tyra thought as she read the headline.

Judicial Dept. Approves Use of Simultaneous Copies for Safe Exploration

Tyra scanned the story. It mostly detailed things she already knew, a summary of Ellis's proposal, and an explanation of how they would use clones to explore safely.

Then she got to the part of the Judicial Department's verdict. They approved the proposal, pending further legislation to place new limitations on the use of simultaneous copies. But the Judicial Department had placed a limitation of their own: the clones would be forced to integrate with their copies on *Astralis* each time they returned, and no more than two simultaneous copies of any given person would be allowed.

Tyra frowned, considering the implications of that. It meant more disruption to the lives of the people who agreed to send out clones. In a way that was better. It meant the clones wouldn't be leaving their families for good, since each time they returned they'd integrate their memories, and it would seem to them as if they'd somehow never left. They'd have all the memories of the time they'd spent with their partners and children, as well as all of the memories of the time they'd spent away, exploring.

Tyra nodded along with that. Assuming clones were never separated from each other for more than a few months at a time, it wouldn't be too shocking or disruptive for anyone, but it also meant that anyone who consented to send out a clone of his or herself would have to think twice about it, because doing so actually would affect their lives. Besides all of the new memories they'd have to cope with, they'd be accountable to their families for their actions while they were away.

Tyra became aware of eyes boring into the side of her skull. She hurriedly closed the news feed and turned to Lucien with a sheepishly-innocent smile.

"You didn't hear a thing I said, did you?" Lucien accused.

"Hmmm?" She took another sip of her caf and shook her head. "Of course I did. The girls woke up. Theola was screaming. Something about Atara... I missed that part."

Lucien scowled and shook his head. "You know what, never mind."

"Hey—" Tyra reached for his hand, but he moved it from the armrest of the couch to his lap. "I'm sorry."

Lucien's lips were twisted in a smile, but his eyes were cold. "Look, forget about it. You've got more important things to worry about."

"That's not fair. Nothing's more important to me than our family."

"Sure, in theory, but in reality..." He shook his head and got up from the couch.

Tyra felt guilt twisting her stomach in knots. "I'm sorry, okay? I was reading an important article about—"

Lucien held up a hand to stop her. "Save it. I've got a meeting to attend. Maybe we'll have time to talk about it tonight. That is—*if* you make it home tonight."

The knot got tighter, and Tyra nodded slowly, watching as Lucien turned to leave. Then something clicked and her brow furrowed with sudden interest. "What meeting? You're supposed to be on vacation until Fallside is repaired."

"Admiral Stavos called a meeting this morning for all of the ex-Paragons."

Tyra's eyes widened suddenly. She knew what that would be about. "You can't go," she blurted.

Lucien stopped and sent her an incredulous look. "What do you mean *I can't go?* I'm an ex-Paragon. I don't actually have a choice."

"Well..." Tyra faltered for words. "I meant you can't allow them to send out your clone on one of the galleons."

Lucien shot her a baffled look. "What clone? And since when are we sending out galleons?"

"Ellis proposed it all yesterday, and the judiciary just gave approved it."

Lucien came and sat back down. "Maybe you'd better explain."

So she did.

Lucien sat blinking in shock. "That's..."

"Crazy?" Tyra suggested.

"I was going to say brilliant. Finally we can get back to doing what we came out here to do!"

Tyra arched her eyebrows at him. "As opposed to... what? Playing house on a giant spaceship?"

Lucien frowned. "You don't get to play that card with me. I'm the one who's there every day, wiping noses and changing diapers."

"I'm sorry. You're right. Look you need to think about this, that's all. If you agree to go, you're going to be away from me and the girls for months at a time."

"Technically, I'll still be right here," Lucien said.

"But your clone will be out there, and as soon as he comes back, he'll be forced to integrate his memories with yours."

"Sounds like having your sweet tart and eating it, too. What's the problem with that?"

Tyra started to say something, but stopped herself and sighed. "Nothing." She looked away, out the picture window, out over a forest of evergreens caked with snow. Beyond that she spied a frozen lake crowded with stay-at-home parents and their children, all skating on the ice. It was a glimpse of the life she was missing, the one where she always seemed to be the spectator and never the participant. If anyone needed a clone so that she could be in two places at once, it was her.

How many others felt that way? No wonder the judiciary had ruled that clones had to integrate once they reached *Astralis*. If they didn't, it was just a short leap from there to living multiple lives at once. Things would get out of hand really fast.

"What are you worried about?" Lucien prompted.

Tyra turned back to him, her constant guilt and her secret fears made her feel suddenly intensely vulnerable. She tried to keep her expression neutral, but she felt naked, like every whisper of a thought was written on her face.

She lived with the waking dread that one day she'd come home late and find that Lucien wasn't there. She'd never voiced it to him. Weakness was a throat exposed, the jugular pulsing invitingly, and men were all hunters at heart. But if she didn't share her fears, she couldn't justify telling him to turn down the chance to get back out there and explore the universe.

Tyra took a deep, shuddery breath. "I'm worried about you. What if you fall out of love with me and in to love with someone else? What if you start to prefer your life out there, in the stars, with no responsibilities and no commitments? What if you get lonely and some woman seduces you?"

Lucien's brow was skeptically raised, but the grave look in his eyes told her the truth: he'd just admitted the possibility to himself, and he was busy thinking about it, weighing the risk that he might actually succumb to such temptations—an affair that wasn't an affair, his mind in two bodies, having your sweet tart and eating it, too, what happens in space stays in space....

Tyra swallowed a scream and did her best to look unconcerned.

"We're married," Lucien said finally. "We have two kids. They need their mother, not some other woman. I don't want to make our lives any more complicated than they already are."

"*They need* their mother. What do *you* need, Lucien?"

"I need you, too. But you're never here."

"I'm going to work on that. I promise. Things are going to be different."

"Good. Then maybe you won't need to worry about me having an affair, because you'll be confident in what we have."

Lucien's words stabbed straight through to her heart. "So you're saying I have a reason to be worried."

"No, I'm saying your worries are a direct result of your guilt and the fact that you're giving me more reason and opportunity than most men need. What you forget is that I'm not most men."

"Maybe not, but you're still human."

He sighed. "You're getting ahead of yourself. We don't even know why Stavos called the Paragons together."

Tyra snorted. "Yes we do. It doesn't take an astrophysicist to figure that out."

Lucien's eyes narrowed. Poor choice of words. One of his lesser issues with her was how she was always patronizing him with her education. She'd been an astrophysicist before she'd decided to run for political office, and while he wasn't un-educated, his education as a Paragon was only really applicable to expeditionary work, to exploring the stars and meeting new alien races, which he'd been unable to do for almost a decade.

Now he was about to get a second chance, and here she

was telling him not to take it because she was scared that whatever threads were still holding them together wouldn't be strong enough if he had some freedom.

She was being selfish and she knew it. "Look, just... consider the consequences, okay?"

Lucien nodded. "I will." He grabbed her hand and gave it a quick squeeze before getting up from the couch and leaving the room once more.

Almost as an afterthought, Tyra thought to ask, "Where's Theola?"

Lucien turned back to her from the front door, while he reached into the coat closet and withdrew his gloves and jacket. "She's at daycare. I signed her up for one after I got the notice about the meeting. I figured you wouldn't be able to watch her, so..."

Tyra nodded absently. "Okay. See you later," she said, as he finished putting on his coat and gloves.

"See you," he replied.

He opened the door and a blast of cold air gushed into the room, making Tyra shiver. He shut the door behind him, and Tyra sat staring at it for a long moment, her guts twisting with dread.

"I love you, too," she whispered.

CHAPTER 27

Mokar

The *Specter* flew low over mottled blue and red *forests* of strange, cauliflower-shaped trees and vast open plains dry brown grass.

Both of Mokar's suns were high in the sky, one as red as a Mokari's eyes, the other campfire-orange. The sky was pinkish, almost white, while the clouds were salmon-colored.

Mokar was as unique as any world or facet of New Earth that Lucien had ever been to, and it was a far cry from the blue skies, white clouds, and typically-green trees of *Astralis*.

Along the horizon a cloud of black specks led the way. Mokari. They were taking the *Specter* to their underworld.

"How is it possible that one sun sets and the other doesn't?" Addy asked, peering up through the top of the

Specter's canopy.

Katawa answered, "We landed at the North Pole. The planet's tilt and rotation are such that at this time of year the most distant sun only sets three times a year, while the other one rises and sets a hundred times as often."

"So twilight is going to fall again soon?"

"In five of your standard hours," Katawa said.

"And you know all of this because..." Garek trailed off. "Wait, don't tell me. The ship's databanks, right?"

"Correct."

"Is it much farther to the underworld?" Addy asked.

"I do not know."

After another few minutes of standing and watching their progress from the *Specter's* bridge, Lucien grew tired and took a seat in the co-pilot's chair.

Katawa glanced sharply at him as he did so, and Lucien held up his hands. "I won't touch anything. Promise."

Katawa looked away. "It is not that. You sat on my lunch."

Lucien felt around underneath his robes until his hand encountered something slimy and squishy. Lucien withdrew his hand in horror to find it coated with thick white slime. "Yuck!" He jumped up from the co-pilot's chair and saw a plate filled with an assortment of colorful slug-like creatures, all flattened into a sticky paste.

Lucien's nose wrinkled, and he used his clean hand to brush off the back of his robes. That hand came away dripping with slime, too.

"How is it possible that everyone this side of the Red Line eats such disgusting food?" Lucien asked, staring at his hands in dismay.

Addy laughed.

"It is not disgusting," Katawa replied. "Try one. They are delicious."

"I'm going to go wash up," Lucien said. He squeezed by Katawa's chair and hurried to the amidships washroom.

When he returned, he found Katawa devouring the remains of the slugs and licking his bony gray fingers. Addy sat beside him in the co-pilot's chair, trying not to notice, and both Brak and Garek were gone, probably back in their quarters.

There were only two seats on the bridge, so Lucien was forced to stand behind Addy's chair.

The three of them remained silent for a while, watching the scenery roll by below. Lucien noticed that every now and then the plains would part to reveal a gaping black hole belching steam. *Volcanic vents?* Lucien wondered. That got him wondering about the Mokari underworld. Would it be volcanically active? Too hot to safely explore? Or perhaps the air was simply toxic. That would explain why no Mokari who'd ever gone there had returned.

Eventually Lucien grew tired of standing and he sat down on the deck with his back to one of the curving bulkheads. After about an hour of sitting, Lucien's back and backside were aching enough to force him to his feet once more.

"I have a suggestion for you, Katawa," he said, looming between the pilot's and copilot's chairs once more.

"Yes?"

"Install some extra seating up here."

"Oh yes. That is a good idea. But we may have to survive on less appetizing meals from the fabricator in order to afford them."

"*Less* appetizing? If the meals get any less appetizing I'm going to starve. Forget the chairs." Lucien jerked his chin to the horizon where the Mokari were still flying on up ahead. "They haven't even stopped for a break."

"The Mokari are strong. They do not need breaks," Katawa replied.

"They must have heard you. Look—" Addy pointed out the canopy. "They're dropping down into that field. I guess they take breaks after all."

Lucien leaned over her chair and peered into the distance. She was right. The black specks were growing larger and closer, and they were circling down. "So what do we do while we wait?" he asked. "Stop and hover, or go down and take a look around?"

Katawa hauled back on the throttle until they were hovering amidst a swarm of Mokari, all swooping and circling around them. Katawa pointed to something on the ship's sensor display. "They did not stop for a break. They stopped because we have arrived."

Lucien spent a moment trying to decipher the sensor display while Katawa hovered down for a landing.

"I don't know what I'm looking at," Lucien said.

Addy sucked in a breath. "Then you're looking in the wrong place."

Lucien looked up from the display and saw what she was talking about. As the *Specter* dropped down, the ground opened up beneath them in an enormous, almost perfectly circular opening that plunged straight down into darkness. Lucien couldn't see the bottom of it. It just went on and on...

"How deep is that?" Addy asked.

"More than seven kilometers," Katawa said as the *Specter's* landing struts touched ground with a subtle jolt. The yawning hole leading into the Mokari Underworld was just a few meters from the bow of the ship.

"Seven *kilometers?*" Lucien asked. He imagined the edge of the hole crumbling and sending the *Specter* tumbling down. "Is it going to be safe down there? How thick is Mokar's crust?" He assumed there must be magma after a certain point, since they'd seen steam rising from smaller vents along the way.

"It will not be safe, but if you mean to ask whether or not you'll have to walk through magma, this will not be a concern. Thermal readings suggest that the crust is approximately fifty kilometers thick at this point."

"Even so, we'll need our suits. The temperature and air pressure are going to be a lot higher at the bottom."

"Yes," Katawa agreed.

Addy turned to him. "I thought you said the Mokari don't like *false skins*."

"They will not be going with you, so it will not be a problem."

Something about what Katawa had just said bothered Lucien, but he couldn't put his finger on it.

Addy figured it out first. "*You?*" she echoed.

That was it. Katawa's choice of pronouns. He hadn't included himself in that statement.

"You're not going with us?" Lucien asked, his eyes narrowing with sudden suspicion.

"No. I cannot."

"Why *not?*"

Katawa rotated his chair away from the ship's controls

to face Lucien. The alien's face was expressionless, but he sat with his hands folded in his lap, and big black eyes blinking lazily.

Lucien glared. "Well?"

"I am a god to the Mokari," Katawa explained, and left it at that, as if the rest should be self-evident.

"So what?" Addy said.

"So, I cannot go into their underworld. It would defile me, and they would no longer trust me to listen to their songs."

"You've already heard their songs," Lucien replied.

"They have others that may help us in our search. I will listen to them while I wait for you to return from the underworld."

Lucien snorted and shook his head. "And what if we don't return?"

"If you die, I will mourn your passing. As will the Mokari. Songs will be sung of you. I will make sure of it."

"Gee, thanks," Lucien said dryly. Suddenly he felt just as suspicious as Garek, and more. He had a bad feeling about this so-called *underworld,* and how Katawa seemed to know so much about Mokar and the Mokari, even though he'd supposedly never been here.

Maybe that was a lie. The truth could be far more sinister. They might be about to become Katawa's latest victims. For all they knew, he'd already lured dozens (or hundreds!) of others to their deaths in the Mokari underworld, all of them looking for the *magical key* that would open the portal to the planet where the lost fleet had gone.

Now that Lucien thought about it, that would make a lot more sense. Katawa had been looking for his people and their lost fleet for thousands of years, so how was it possible that he was only now starting to follow all the rumors and legends he'd heard? It was far more likely that he'd followed them all already, and this Mokari legend was the last and most promising one—the one he'd been unable to follow because everyone he sent into the underworld ended up dead.

Addy shot him a worried look, and he wondered if she was thinking along similar lines.

"We should not delay," Katawa said, after enduring the long silence of Lucien's thoughts. "There is much to do to prepare you for your journey." Katawa rose from his chair and walked by him, heading off the bridge.

"What if we decide not to go?" Lucien asked.

Katawa froze in the entrance of the bridge and slowly turned. "Why would you change your mind now, at the last possible second? Are you afraid of the underworld? I thought you were explorers. Paragons."

"*Paragons?*" Lucien asked, the word slicing through him like a hot knife.

Katawa nodded slowly. "Yes. Trained to explore the universe. Etherus trained you himself, did he not?"

Lucien couldn't believe what he was hearing, couldn't bring himself to speak. Katawa had knocked the air right out of his lungs.

Addy stood up beside him, took his hand and squeezed it—*hard.* "We *are* Paragons," she said. "We can handle this."

"Good. This is what I thought. I am glad to not be mistaken," Katawa replied. "Come, we must get the others."

"Wait," Addy said. "It would be better if *we* explained to them about you not coming with us—alone. If you're there, they might think we're being somehow coerced into this."

Katawa blinked. "Coerced?"

"Garek is suspicious by nature. It'll be easier to deal with his concerns without you there."

"I see."

"We'll get our equipment together and put on our suits and then meet you at the rear airlock, fair enough?"

"Yes. Fair. I will meet you. Do not take long."

"We won't."

Lucien watched Katawa leave, his thoughts racing and heart pounding. The little alien walked around a bend in the corridor and out of sight.

As soon as he was gone, Addy grabbed his arm and squeezed it to get his attention. "Garek was right," she whispered. "Katawa is up to something."

Lucien stared grimly back at her. "You figured it out, too."

She nodded. "We never told him we were Paragons. And he's been gone from the Etherian Empire for more than ten thousand years. The Paragons were only founded a little over *thirty* years ago, after we met Etherus for the first time. There's no way he could have found out what we are unless someone told him."

"And besides us, there's only one person who could have told him that we're Paragons."

"Abaddon," Addy breathed, her green eyes wide.

Lucien nodded slowly. "Abaddon."

"What are we going to do?"

Lucien thought about it. "I think it's time to execute Garek's plan. We're need to steal Katawa's ship and get the frek out of here before it's too late."

CHAPTER 28

Mokar

"I knew it!" Garek said, and lashed out at the nearest bulkhead with his fist.

"I crack his head like egg!" Brak added.

Lucien suppressed a chill at Brak's bloodthirstiness. "We don't have to kill him. Just kick him out the airlock and fly off."

Garek sent him a sour look. "It would be safer to kill him. What if he tells Abaddon we took his ship? We'll have every Faro in the universe looking for us."

"He might tell Abaddon what happened whether we kill him or not. For all we know he has a neural implant like ours that will transmit his consciousness to the nearest Faro ship when he dies."

"Well, whatever we're going to do, we'd better do it

fast," Addy said. "We're going to make him suspicious if we take any longer."

"You said we'd suit up and meet him at the rear airlock..." Lucien mused.

"So we'll be armed," Garek said, smiling wryly. "Smart move." He walked over to the closet and opened it to reveal the gleaming silver armor of his exosuit. They'd all met in Garek's quarters, so his suit was the one closest at hand.

"We'll meet you at the cargo bay," Lucien said. It was located right before the aft airlock where Katawa would be waiting for them.

"Actually, it might make more sense for you and Addy to head up to the cockpit and get ready to fly. Brak and I can deal with Katawa."

Lucien hesitated. "Are you sure?"

"It's one little gray alien against his much bigger and nastier cousin, plus me, and I can be pretty nasty myself."

Brak bared his black teeth in a grin. "We take care of the little gray one. Do not worry."

"All right, but be careful," Lucien said.

Garek nodded absently, already busy shucking his robes in favor of his Paragon-issue black jumpsuit and armor.

Lucien turned away before the sight of Garek's backside struck him blind. He and Addy hurried from the room and ran back the way they'd come.

"How do you know you can fly this thing?" Addy asked on their way to the cockpit.

"I don't," Lucien said.

Addy made a noise in the back of her throat. "We should have told Garek to capture Katawa, in case we need him to pilot the ship."

"Yeah..."

"We could end up stranded here."

"Go back and tell him," Lucien said. "I'll see what I can figure out in the meantime."

Addy nodded and ran back to Garek's quarters.

Lucien reached the cockpit a few seconds later and fell into the pilot's chair with a *whuff* of escaping air from the seat cushion. He scanned the holo displays in front of him. Thanks to his translator band he could understand the unfamiliar symbols perfectly, but that didn't turn out to be much help. He tried accessing the ship's engines, only to receive an error prompt:

Biometric profile not recognized.
Override code:

Lucien should have known better than to think Katawa would leave the ship's systems unlocked. Addy was right. They needed Katawa alive or they were going to be stranded on Mokar until the next Faro ship came to visit.

Lucien jumped up from the pilot's chair and ran back through the ship, heading for his and Addy's quarters to get his own exosuit. If Katawa had been careful enough to lock them out of the ship, then he might have taken other precautions, too. There was no sense taking chances and facing him without armor.

Lucien tried sending Addy a message to explain the situation and suggest that she put on her suit, too, but his ARCs reported a connection error. The *Specter* was jamming their comms.

Lucien's fingertips sparked with adrenaline as the

implications of that hit home. Comms jamming *and* a systems lockout? Both seemed to point to the same conclusion: Katawa *knew*. Somehow he'd anticipated them. They weren't going to take him by surprise with their ambush—it was the other way around: *they* were the ones being ambushed by *him.*

* * *

Mokar

Lucien ran back to his quarters as fast as he could. He stopped his momentum with the door, and a resounding *bang* shivered through it. He keyed the door open and hurried over to the closet to don his jumpsuit and armor.

Lucien had just finished putting on his jumpsuit when the door *swished* open behind him. He jumped and spun around, his heart beating in his ears. He half-expected to see a Mokari warrior come stalking in, jaws gaping for the kill...

But it was only Addy. Lucien blew out a breath. "You scared the krak out of me!"

She shook her head, breathless from running, and leaned heavily against the door jamb. Garek pushed in behind her, his armored boots *clunking* heavily on the deck.

His voice reverberated from his helmet speakers: "Katawa is gone. No sign of him on board."

Brak stormed in next, his chest and shoulders heaving, slitted yellow eyes wide with rage. He was still wearing his shadow robes. "I will eat him alive, and make him watch!"

Lucien grimaced and shook his head. "He locked us out of the ship and activated comms jamming."

"I know," Garek said. "I already tried to contact you via ARCs."

"We'll have to go outside and hunt him down with our suit sensors," Lucien said. "We're not going anywhere until he gives us the override code for his ship."

Addy ran her hands over her bald head, making the motions to tie her hair in a bun; then she seemed to notice that she didn't have any hair to tie, and her hands fell back to her sides. "What about the Mokari?" she asked.

"What about them?" Lucien countered as he lugged his exosuit out of the closet and lay it out on the deck. He keyed it open with a holographic control panel in the chest plate, and the suit flayed open with a loud *clicking* of metallic joints and seals. Lucien lay down inside the suit, lining up his limbs.

"You think this was all by chance?" Addy said. "I think Katawa planned the whole thing, and he locked us out of his ship to make sure that we'd have no choice but to go down into the underworld. There's supposed to be some kind of quantum junction down there, right?"

"Right," Lucien said as his ARCs connected to the suit's systems and he mentally sealed his armor. More *clicking* as it wrapped him up in a metal skin. At least the comms jamming didn't affect communication with his suit.

"What if Katawa's plan was to strand us here and then wait for us to go down and find the key to open that junction?" Addy continued.

"What's he get out of that?" Lucien asked. "He's looking for the lost fleet. If he betrays us and we find the fleet without him, we're not going to use it to help him find his way home."

"We might not have a choice. He's probably got some kind of tracking device on us," Garek pointed out.

"Or *in* us," Addy said. "We've been eating his food."

"So we're doubly frekked," Lucien said, standing up in his suit. He clomped over to the closet and retrieved his helmet. As soon as he slipped it over his head, HUD displays swarmed his view. He minimized the non-essential ones. "We can't take his ship and leave, and we can't go into the underworld to escape."

Addy nodded slowly.

"I find the little gray one and squeeze his head until he give me the code," Brak said.

Garek nodded. "That sounds about right to me."

Lucien pointed to the closet where Addy's exosuit was waiting for her. "Suit up and let's go hunting. Brak—you, too. You're going to need your suit for this."

Brak's predatory grin faded to a petulant frown. "I cannot rip out his throat with a helmet on."

"You can't rip out his throat period. He's going to need it to tell us that override code. Now go."

Brak hissed, but turned and left the room.

Addy hurried to undress, and Garek respectfully looked away. In less than a minute she was armored up and ready to go. A few seconds after that, Brak came hulking back into the room, his head now brushing the ceiling with the added inches provided by his armor.

"On me," Garek said, and marched out the door.

They fell in behind him and followed him back through the ship. Lucien was technically the ranking officer, but Garek had a lot more experience as a Paragon, so Lucien was content to defer to his leadership.

They reached the cargo bay and were just about to open the doors to get to the rear airlock when the deck shivered under their feet. The movement was accompanied by a sound like grass swishing against the hull. They all froze, their heads cocked toward the outer bulkheads, listening.

The deck shivered once more, again accompanied by that swishing sound.

"What the frek..." Lucien muttered.

Another shiver. More swishing.

"I think the Mokari are trying to push us over the cliff!" Addy said.

"Frek that!" Garek slapped the cargo bay door controls and raced through to the rear airlock. Lucien and the others ran up behind him as he cycled the inner doors open. Garek waved them through just as the deck started trembling again. "Come on!" he yelled.

Before Garek could join them, the deck kicked up, angling sharply and sending them all tumbling and sliding back through the cargo bay, picking up speed. With the ship's main reactor off, the inertial compensator and artificial gravity were offline, too.

Lucien fired the grav boosters in his boots to cushion his fall, but there wasn't enough time to react, and his knees still buckled with the impact. Brak landed on top of him with a loud *thunk* that knocked him over and left him seeing stars.

Garek stumbled to his feet and stood with one foot on the wall of the cargo bay and the other on the deck. "We're balanced on the edge of the cliff! We've got to get out now!"

Lucien scrambled to his feet and gazed up at the distant airlock. The deck was smooth as ice, and tilted up at a forty-five degree angle. There was no time to climb back up. They had to fly.

"Use your grav boosters," Garek said, and blasted off at an angle, heading straight for the open airlock.

It was bad timing. The ship shuddered briefly once more, and then fell. Lucien's stomach leapt into his throat as weightlessness set in. They all floated a few inches above the deck—except for Garek. He sailed up to the airlock with the momentum imparted by his grav boosters at nearly the same speed as the airlock was now *falling* toward him. He put out his palms and fired his grav boosters for braking thrust, but it was too late to slow down. His head clipped the top of the inner door frame, and then he slammed into the outer airlock doors with a resounding *thunk!*

"Garek!" Addy screamed.

Lucien drifted in shock, his feet dangling bare inches above the rusted metal wall. The sound of air rushing past the ship's hull was a constant roar in his ears.

Time seemed to slow, but Lucien's thoughts were racing at a lightning pace. Katawa had said the pit that they were now falling into was seven kilometers straight down. Mokar's gravity was a little less than a standard G, so maybe eight meters per second, per second, but it would take them just a few seconds to reach terminal velocity, at which point they'd no longer be accelerating, and the effects of the planet's gravity would be restored.

Lucien's feet touched down, his prediction fulfilled.

"What the..." Addy marveled at the sudden sensation

of normalcy. "Did we stop falling?"

Outside, the air was still roaring past the *Specter's* hull.

Garek came plummeting back down from the airlock, unconscious, and Addy screamed.

Lucien angled his body toward Garek and triggered a blast from his grav boosters.

They collided in midair, and Lucien got the wind knocked out of him, but he managed to slow Garek's fall from a deadly tumult to a hard knock. Garek landed on top of him with a loud clatter of armor, plastering him to the cargo bay wall for the second time in the past few seconds.

"We have to get out of here!" Addy said.

"Yess," Brak hissed. "This is a fool's death. No honor in it, only shame."

Lucien crawled out from under Garek and shook the veteran by his shoulders to wake him up, but he didn't even stir. Lucien's suit sensors reported Garek's life signs were strong, but he was out cold.

"Get over here and help me!" Lucien said. He took one of Garek's arms, and waited for Addy to take the other. As soon as she did so, he said, "On three! One, two, *three!*"

They boosted off at almost the same time, but *almost* wasn't good enough. A fraction of a second's difference in their timing sent them careening to one side of the open airlock. Lucien decreased power to his boosters and managed to correct their course just in time. They sailed into the airlock and landed on the inside wall of the door frame. Brak boosted in after them and landed on the other side of the door.

Lucien bent to reach the control panel at his feet and toggled the inner door shut. It irised closed, leaving them to figure out how to reach the panel for the outer door.

There were no zero-*G* rails in the airlock, just a few rusted out rivet holes to suggest where they used to be.

"How are we going to get out?" Addy asked, searching the airlock frantically. The outer door control panel was at least four meters above their heads.

Lucien scanned the walls, ceiling, and floor, but he couldn't see any kind of handholds. "Let me try something," Lucien said, and fired his boosters at ten percent thrust. He shot up faster than intended and had to put out his hands to cushion his impact with the door. Now he was pinned in place. He backed off his boosters to five percent and reached for the control panel with one hand...

But the movement threatened to overbalance him and send him spinning out of control. "Frek!" Lucien gritted out. He tried again, swiping desperately at the control panel. Again, he was forced to plant his hand against the door a split second later.

This was taking too long. Lucien couldn't be sure what their terminal velocity was, but even with seven kilometers to fall they wouldn't have more than a few minutes before the *Specter* hit the bottom. They needed some of that time to negate their momentum and to get to a safe distance from the *Specter* before it hit.

Addy hovered up beside him and mimicked his trick of holding himself in a powered handstand against the outer door. Luckily she'd managed to pin herself within closer reach of the control panel. She spared a hand to work the panel...

Come on... He thought, watching as her other arm trembled and her whole body arched against the forces now threatening to unbalance her.

They didn't have time for another attempt.

"I got it!" Addy said. Lights flashed briefly inside the airlock; then the outer door irised open and out from under their hands. Both Lucien and Addy were thrown free of the airlock, tumbling and breathing hard. Air roared in Lucien's ears. The black abyss below traded places with a bright circle of sky over and over again. This was the proverbial dark tunnel with a light at the end, except they were heading into the darkness—not the light.

Lucien threw out his arms and strategically fired the boosters in his palms to counter his downward spiral. After three more spins, he had his flight path under control and he fired his grav boosters at maximum thrust to climb back up.

"Addy!" he yelled, with his suit speakers at max volume to compete with the wind of his ascent. He desperately searched the hazy darkness for her as he shot straight up at high speed.

"Here!" she said, and came floating up beside him. She was barely visible in the dark. The only way he could see her at all was because of the dim blue glow of HUD displays radiating from her helmet.

Lucien breathed a sigh.

"Where's Brak and Garek?" Addy asked.

Horror sliced through Lucien's gut. He glanced down and saw the *Specter* vanish into darkness. "We have to go back!" Lucien yelled, already cutting the power to his grav boosters and orienting his body for a nosedive so he could chase after the *Specter*.

"There's no time!" Addy called after him as he began falling once more.

She was right. From the now tiny, thumbnail-sized

opening overhead and the sheer darkness all around them, it was obvious that they'd already fallen most of the way to the bottom of the pit.

Lucien gazed helplessly into the hazy black abyss where the *Specter* had vanished. It was gone. *They* were gone. Brak's words echoed through Lucien's head: *This is a fool's death. No honor in it, only shame. Shame on* us, Lucien thought. His conscience screamed at him, telling him all the things he could have done differently: while Addy was busy trying to get the doors open, he could have dropped back down and helped Brak carry Garek out. He could have—

A flash of light lit up the bottom of the pit, and a split second later the thunderous *boom* of that explosion rattled through Lucien's armor, shaking him down to his bones.

Fiery scraps of shrapnel streaked up like fireworks. Lucien re-oriented himself and fired his grav boosters once more to get some distance from the shrapnel.

As he rocketed up, his whole body felt cold and leaden with grief. He'd just lost his best and oldest friend, and it was all his fault.

Lucien glanced down to see a solitary speck of shrapnel sailing on toward him even as the glow from the others faded. That speck grew steadily larger, glinting with deadly promise.

Then came a soft *ping* from his sensors.

"They made it!" Addy said.

Lucien blinked in shock. That piece of shrapnel was Brak! Seconds later the Gor sailed up beside them, carrying Garek over one shoulder like a sack of taber roots.

"You ugly *kakard!*" Lucien roared. "What the frek took you so long?"

Brak grunted under the weight of Garek's unconscious body. "You leave me to carry this one out alone."

"We didn't mean to leave you behind," Addy said.

"Yess, I know. If you did, you would be sorry. We hunt the gray one now?" Brak asked.

"What for?" Addy asked. "His ship is gone!"

Lucien peered up at the growing circle of light overhead. They were rocketing back out of the pit at high speed. Their surroundings became progressively brighter, and sheer black cliffs snapped into focus all around them—as did the angry swarm of black specks circling the pale sky overhead.

"The Mokari are still there," Lucien said.

"Good," Brak said. "I break their wings, and then we see how *they* like being thrown off cliffs."

"I don't know..." Addy said. "There's a *lot* of them. I'm reading hundreds of signatures. We won't stand a chance against that many, not even in our armor. They'll rip us apart."

"Addy's right," Lucien said. "We need to go back down."

"Into the underworld?" Brak asked.

"Yes," Lucien replied, backing off with his grav boosters until he started falling back down.

"And then what?" Addy asked.

"Find the gateway," Lucien said.

"That's what Katawa wants us to do!" Addy objected. "He got the Mokari to push us off the cliff knowing full well that we'd find a way to escape before we hit the bottom. With no ship, there's no point in us going after him for the override code. He pushed us into this corner, and now he's waiting to follow us when we find a way out."

"I don't think we have a choice," Lucien replied. "Even if we find another exit to the underworld that isn't guarded by Mokari, there's no other ships on the planet. We're stranded unless we find the key and the gateway. So we do that, but first we find whatever Katawa's using to track us and we disable it. If it's something we ate, then it's only a matter of time before we pass the tracking devices in our stool."

"Uck," Addy said.

"We're going to krak out the trackers?" Brak asked.

"Hopefully," Lucien replied. "If not... maybe our suit sensors can find them for us."

"We're going to make Katawa pay for this," Addy said.

"The best payback will be to deny him his prize and make sure he can't follow us. Then *he'll* be the one stranded on Mokar."

"Something tells me Abaddon will come pick him up before long," Addy replied.

"Probably," Lucien admitted. "But he'll have to find a new group of suckers to go looking for his fleet. On the bright side, if Abaddon went to all this trouble, it means we're probably on the right track."

Their conversation lapsed into silence, and Lucien gazed down between his feet to watch as they slowly sank back down. The darkness swirled below them like a raging sea, ready to suck them under. *Smoke from the* Specter? Lucien wondered.

"What do you think is down there?" Addy asked, her voice barely audible above the muted roar of air rushing by them as they fell.

"Death," Brak said before Lucien could reply. "There will be much honor in it. A fitting end to Brak, son of Karva."

Lucien glanced at him, but it was too dark to see now. He turned on his helmet lamps, and the others followed suit. Six bright white beams of light appeared, sweeping through a glittering mist.

A panicked yelp came from Brak's direction.

"Mother*frekker!*" Garek roared.

"Stop moving or I drop you," Brak said.

"What happened?" Garek demanded.

"The ship crashed," Lucien said. "We barely made it out in time."

"Krak... the last thing I remember was making a break for the airlock. Hold up, why are we going *down?*"

Lucien explained their reasoning.

Garek's headlamps joined theirs and swept down to pierce the black. "So our best bet to escape is to walk straight into a trap. How does that *not* make sense?"

"That depends whether or not we can find whatever Katawa plans to use to track us," Lucien said.

"And if we can't? Or if it's *inside* of us and can't be removed?" Garek asked.

Lucien had no answer for that. He cast his headlamps back and forth, searching the impenetrable darkness at his feet, but there was still no sign of the bottom.

"We don't have a choice," Addy said. "We have to find that gateway, or we're going to be stuck on Mokar waiting for Abaddon to come get Katawa—and then us."

"Yeah," Garek growled. "So we're frekked if we do, and frekked if we don't."

Lucien nodded slowly. "Exactly."

CHAPTER 29

Astralis

A pair of Marine bots scanned Lucien at the door to the meeting room. As soon as they finished, the door slid open and he walked in. Admiral Stavos was seated at the head of a long, glossy black table.

"Welcome, Mr. Ortane," Stavos said.

All eyes followed Lucien as he approached the table and sat down in an empty chair beside Brak—

Only to do a double take as his wife's blue eyes met his across the table. Shock coursed through him, and he faltered for words. "Tyra...?" She hadn't mentioned that she would be attending this meeting.

Then he noticed the white Navy uniform and the Captain's insignia on her sleeves and shoulders.

This was her clone, Captain Forster.

"Hello, Lieutenant Commander Ortane."

"Lieutenant...?" Lucien trailed off, shaking his head.

"Trust me this is stranger for me than it is for any of you," she said, glancing around the table at each of them in turn. "None of you remember me—with the exception of Lucien here—who recognizes me as his *wife,* of all things." Tyra's mouth curved wryly at that. "But let me assure you, I know all of you very well already."

"We had a lill' somethin' goin' on, didn't we?" one of the men at the table said, flashing a lopsided grin at her.

"No, Tinker, we didn't. In fact you were killed by the Faros within days of leaving *Astralis.*"

"Damn," Tinker replied.

A striking blond-haired woman glanced at him and smirked.

"Perhaps you should make the introductions before we start, Captain Forster," Admiral Stavos said. He leaned forward and folded his hands on the table in front of him.

"It would be my pleasure." Tyra turned to the man sitting to her right.

He had thick, angry scars running all the way down one side of his face. His head was shaved, with a faint black shadow where his hair was supposed to be, and a matching shadow of stubble on his lower jaw.

"This is Garek Helios, who I'm told is the father of Director Helios from the Resurrection Center. We called him *The Veteran,* and he served as our medic on the *Inquisitor.*"

Garek grunted at his introduction, looking like he wanted to add something, but he settled for a scowl instead.

"Sitting next to him is Jalisa, our gunnery chief and demolitions expert, as well as our second-best shuttle pilot."

Lucien studied her: dark skin and intense violet eyes with long black hair wound into dreadlocks. She certainly looked like someone who knew her way around a weapons locker.

"Jalisa and Garek were something of an item on the ship," Captain Forster added.

Jalisa glanced at Garek in disbelief, and he winked at her. "Heya, sweetheart."

She rolled her eyes. "Another example of my poor taste in men."

Garek snorted, and Tinker chuckled.

Captain Forster went on, "Sitting on the other side of Jalisa we have Troo, a Fosak. She was our comms operator."

"I is being therapist now," Troo said.

"That only adds to your qualifications," Captain Forster replied, nodding. "Troo's telepathic abilities make her a unique asset to any mission, especially during first contact.

"On the other side of the table we have Teelo Ferakis, a.k.a *Tinker,* our chief engineer."

He raised his hand and waved dramatically to everyone at the table as if he might be about to get up and take a bow.

"He's also our resident comedian," Tyra added, frowning. "Tickets to his show are free, but nobody wants them."

"Ouch," Tinker said, holding a hand to his chest. "That stings, Cap'n."

Tyra nodded to Addy next. "Next up is Adalyn Gallia, or *Triple S,* our scout and sniper."

"Triple S?" Addy asked.

"Sexy sniper scout. You can blame Lucien for that. Feel free to come up with a new nickname. I believe it was Lucien's misguided idea of flirting."

Addy turned to Lucien with a disgusted look. "He's a married man."

"Indeed. *Now* he is, and with two young daughters, but he wasn't married when you met him."

Addy nodded slowly, her disgust fading to a furrowed brow.

Lucien's mind reeled. Addy was beautiful, no question there, but it was strange to be told that he'd been in a relationship with someone that he couldn't even remember having met.

"Sitting beside Addy is Brak, the Gor: violent, impulsive, and unpredictable to the point that I question the wisdom of asking him to join us again."

Brak hissed and bared his teeth at her.

"Nevertheless, Brak is a specialist in melee combat, which turned out to be extremely useful against the Faros, whose personal shields rendered all of our ranged weapons useless."

"Yeah, he'll definitely be an asset," Lucien agreed.

"And finally, there's Lucien Ortane, executive officer aboard the *Inquisitor*, commander of flight ops, and our best pilot."

Lucien shook his head, his jaw set and eyes thoughtfully narrowed.

"Is there something wrong, Commander Ortane?" Captain Forster asked.

"You're introducing us all as if we're still your crew, but we're not, and in a sense we never were. We have no recollection of each other or any of the time we spent together on the *Inquisitor*."

"That's correct," Admiral Stavos put in, "but we're

hoping to change that." He went on to explain what Lucien already knew about the proposal to send out clones to explore the universe.

"Woah, back that krak up," Garek said, holding up a hand to stop the admiral there. "You don't actually want *us* to go. You want our *clones* to go?"

"That's correct, but make no mistake, thanks to the Judicial Department's ruling on the matter, your clones will have to sync their memories with yours every time they return, so you will ultimately acquire all of the same experiences as them and vice versa. You will essentially be living two lives in parallel, one here on *Astralis,* and one out there among the stars."

"*Waa-how!* That's all kinds of frekked up," Tinker said.

"Please mind your language, Mr. Ferakis."

"Fine. It's all kinds of sexed up. That better?"

Admiral Stavos scowled.

Tinker turned to the rest of them. "What if we get all depressed after we sync because we're still waking up every day to our dull little lives?"

"It's better than living our dull little lives without even the memory of adventure," Addy replied. "This is the chance of a lifetime, and it's the whole reason we came on this mission. As far as I'm concerned, it's about time we found a way to get back out there. Where do I sign up?"

Admiral Stavos smiled. "Now there's the explorer's spirit we're looking for. What about the rest of you?"

Addy looked around the table.

"I'm in," Garek said.

"Likewisss," Brak hissed.

"Aww, sex it, I guess I can always pop some pills or

start smoking glow. Sign me up, too."

"You may go back to cursing now, Mr. Ferakis," Admiral Stavos.

Tinker just grinned.

"I is deciding to be joining this mission," Troo said next.

"That just leaves you, Mr. Ortane."

All eyes were on Lucien once more. His wife's words echoed through his head, urging him to consider the consequences of his choice.

"Commander?" Captain Forster prompted. "I'd be hard pressed to find a better XO, but I will if I have to."

Lucien gazed back into the Captain's blue eyes—his wife's eyes. Less than an hour ago they'd been pleading with him not to join this mission, and now here she was asking him to go for it.

Tinker's right, Lucien decided. *This is all kinds of frekked up...*

Ultimately, he found he had to agree with Addy: it was the chance of a lifetime and there didn't appear to be any kind of downside to it. "I'm in," Lucien said, nodding once.

Captain Forster grinned. "There's the Lucien I know."

And love? he wondered. Under different circumstances they'd ended up falling in love and getting married. How much of that potential had they explored while they were crewmates aboard the *Inquisitor?*

"That settles it," Admiral Stavos said, nodding. "Chief Ellis is working with the council to draft the legislation for all of this as we speak. If all goes well, we'll be able to send out the first Galleons within a month. That will give us enough time to grow a new clone for Garek, who recently used his to resurrect after being killed by the Faros."

"You don't have to wait for me, sir," Garek put in.

Stavos nodded to him. "We aren't, but I'm glad that you'll be able to join us all the same."

That caught Lucien's attention. "*Us*...? Are you coming with us, sir?"

Stavos grinned. "I wouldn't miss it for the universe."

"I thought Captain Forster was going to be in command."

"She is—of her ship. We're sending out the galleons in pairs for better security this time. Captain Forster will command the *Retribution,* with you as her crew. I'll have command of the *Harbinger,* as well as the overall mission."

Lucien began nodding. "I see."

"This is going to be one for the history books," Stavos went on.

"Sex yeah!" Tinker blurted out.

Everyone turned to glare at him.

"What?" Tinker asked innocently.

"I understand why the Faros kill you," Brak said.

Jalisa chuckled, and Addy laughed with her.

"So do I," Stavos said, his blue eyes glittering with amusement.

Lucien couldn't help feeling apprehensive now that he knew Stavos would be commanding his mission. For whatever reason, he didn't trust the admiral after the Faros had touched him. But he'd been cleared for duty by a mind probe and the subsequent comparative analysis. Besides, if Stavos or any of the others had somehow been corrupted by the Faros, they would have called in a Faro fleet by now.

Lucien leaned back in his chair with a sigh, and

allowed his suspicions to drift away. He was just being paranoid.

CHAPTER 30

Mokar: Underworld

They touched down in the still-smoking crater that the *Specter* had punched in the bottom of the pit. Heat radiated through Lucien's faceplate, scalding his skin and threatening to suffocate him.

"Shields up and weapons out!" Lucien said, his voice booming as it echoed off the sheer rock walls. Lucien armed his lasers, and the weapon barrels slid up out of his gauntlets with a whirring *click-click-click.*

"Way ahead of you," Garek replied, his voice echoing back.

As soon as Lucien activated his shields, the heat abated, and his suit's cooling system took over, making it easier to breathe. He swept his headlamps in a slow circle to get his bearings. Black rocks shone in the light, and gravel crunched under foot.

"Where to now?" Addy asked.

Lucien's lamps flickered over the opening of a passage, visible just over the rim of the crater. "Over there," he said, pointing and taking a step in that direction.

"Hold up," Garek replied. "Let's scan each other first. If we're carrying tracking devices we might be able to detect the signals."

Garek scanned Lucien with a flickering blue fan of light and spent a moment studying the results on his HUD.

"Well?" Lucien demanded.

"There's a problem..." Garek said.

Lucien was already imagining the worst. "What is it?"

"There's no signal, and I'm not detecting any foreign bodies inside of you besides your AR implant."

"So there's no tracker?" Addy asked.

"Try scanning me," Garek suggested.

Addy did so, and Lucien took his cue from that and scanned her while they waited. The results flashed up on his HUD a few seconds later.

"Same thing. Addy's clean."

"Thanks, I took a shower this morning," Addy replied.

"Ha ha."

"Garek's clean, too," she said. "Either Katawa isn't tracking us, or he is, but we can't detect it."

"The trackers could be cloaked," Lucien suggested. "The Gors are all born with self-replicating cloaking implants—that's how they can cloak themselves without armor."

"It *could be* cloaked," Garek agreed, "but we'd still be able to detect the tracking signals."

"Unless they're not actively transmitting," Addy said. "The trackers might be sophisticated enough to wait until we go through the gateway before they broadcast our location."

The beams of light from Garek's headlamps bobbed. "If that's true, then there's nothing we can do about it."

"We could do something if we had a comms jammer," Addy said.

"Or a spaceship," Garek pointed out. "While we're playing that game we may as well wish for an entire fleet. The lost Etherian fleet, maybe?" His mouth twisted sardonically and he shook his head.

Lucien sighed. "Whoever planned this, they really frekked us over. I can't see a way out. All we can do is hope the gateway takes us somewhere far enough away that Katawa won't be able to follow us before we can go somewhere else."

"That's not much of a hope," Addy said. "Especially not since we know how fast Faro jump calculations are."

"It's all we've go—"

"Shhh!" Addy whispered sharply. She turned slightly, looking at something, and stood perfectly still. Lucien followed her gaze. Bits of ash and debris fluttered down through their headlamps, but otherwise there was nothing to see—just more black rocks and gravel.

"What is it?" Lucien asked.

"Switch to comms!" Addy said, her voice no longer echoing, but canned by the limited acoustics of her helmet.

"What's going on?" Lucien snapped back over the comms while casting about with his headlamps and sensors.

"You didn't see that?" Addy asked.

"See what?" Lucien demanded.

"There's nothing on sensors," Garek added.

"It was up there," Addy insisted, pointing to the rim of the crater.

"What was?"

"I don't know.... a light. Something glowing."

"Which way do we go?" Brak interrupted.

Lucien found the Gor a hundred meters away, up on the rim of the crater. "It was light from Brak's headlamps reflecting off something," Garek suggested.

"I guess that's possible...." Addy said.

Lucien turned his attention to Brak. "Did you find any other paths leading out of here?"

"Many," Brak replied.

"Hang on, I'm coming up for a look," Lucien said, and blasted off the bottom of the crater with his grav boosters. He flew in an abbreviated arc and touched down beside Brak with a loud *crunch* of gravel. Sweeping his headlamps from side to side, Lucien saw no less than five tunnels leading away from the rim of the crater.

Garek hovered up silently beside them, and touched down just as quietly, his caution betraying his twenty years of experience with the Paragons. "Scanners show those paths connect to a larger network," he said. "Some kind of labyrinth."

"A maze," Addy said as she touched down beside them with another noisy *crunch*.

"It's *hot* in there," Garek added.

"It's *already* hot," Addy replied. "Over *350 K*."

"Well, it gets a lot hotter in those tunnels. I can only get readings up to a couple klicks from here, but we're talking at least *400 K*."

Lucien grimaced. "That's over a hundred degrees Celsius. I guess we're not going to find any water down here, then."

Garek nodded. "On the bright side that means we're less likely to find anything alive down here."

Lucien shook his head. "That's not much of a bright side. Our suits have limited cooling capacity. We can't stay down here for more than..." He queried his suit's systems to project how long they could last in a *400 K* environment.

"We've got about twelve hours before our cooling systems shut down," Garek said just as Lucien got the same result on his HUD.

"We'll run out of air before then," Addy said. "In just under six hours."

"The air's breathable down here," Lucien said. "We could open up our vents and run it through suit filters."

"That would overload our cooling capacity in minutes!" Addy said.

"Those might be the minutes we need to make a break for the surface," Lucien countered.

"Well, we're wasting them arguing about this," Garek replied. "Pick a tunnel and let's go."

Lucien checked his scanners and pointed to the one that seemed the longest and least winding. "That one," he said, his eyes still glued to his sensors.

"Wait..." Addy whispered and pointed. "Look..."

Lucien followed that gesture and promptly sucked in a breath. He was just in time to see a glowing ball of light with hundreds of luminous tentacles darting into one of the other tunnels.

"Did you see that?" Addy asked. "Tell me someone

saw it this time."

"I saw it," Garek said.

"That's one of those Polypus creatures we met eight years ago," Lucien said. "What are they doing all the way out here on Mokar?"

Garek shook his head. "If they're extra-dimensional beings as we suspect, then time and space might not mean the same things to them as they do to us. Two points halfway around the universe from each other might look close to them."

"They helped us the last time we met them," Lucien said. "They might be trying to help us again." As if to confirm his thoughts, the creature bobbed back into view, and hovered briefly in the entrance of the tunnel that it had darted down. "Look!"

"I think it wants us to follow it..." Addy said.

"What if it's a trap?" Garek asked.

"We're already in one," Lucien said. "What's the worst that could happen? Let's go," he said, and started toward the glowing creature.

* * *

Mokar

Just as they were about to reach the entrance of the tunnel, the Polypus darted inside.

"Don't let it get away!" Garek said, breaking into a run.

Lucien poured on a burst of speed, spraying gravel as he ran. He reached the tunnel entrance first and found the Polypus hovering just inside, waiting. As soon as he entered the tunnel, it zipped away. Lucien boosted his suit's power-assist to keep up. The creature darted around a bend in the tunnel and he careened into the wall with his momentum.

"Damn it!" he muttered as he bounced off into the opposite wall. He managed to keep running, but it was all he could do to keep the Polypus in sight. It kept darting out of view, around the next bend. "Slow down!" he called out over his external speakers, hoping the thing would hear him—but even if it did, how would it understand?

The creature raced on, not slowing down or stopping. Lucien glanced at his sensors to keep track of it, but of course the Polypus didn't appear on his sensors. He did, however, spot the others running up behind him.

"Don't let it get... out of your sight!" Garek panted over the comms.

"Why's it going so fast?" Addy asked.

"Perhaps it knows that our air is limited," Brak said, sounding barely winded.

"Or else it's trying to get away," Addy suggested.

"If it—" Lucien interrupted himself as he ricocheted off another bend in the tunnel. He glimpsed the Polypus darting down the rightmost of three branching paths, and he raced to follow. "If it were trying to get away from us, it would fly *through* the tunnel walls," Lucien finally said.

"Good point," Addy said, breathing hard.

In their initial encounter aboard the *Inquisitor,* the Polypuses had proven they could fly through walls, thanks to their extra-dimensionality. They were like ghosts, non-corporeal, but somehow capable of interacting with the three-dimensional universe when they wanted to—such as they had done to remove the timer implants in their brains.

They ran on for what seemed like hours, until Lucien's legs felt numb, and his lungs were screaming for him to stop. Sensors showed that Addy and Brak had fallen behind by about fifty meters—though in the Gor's case that was probably because he was keeping an eye on her.

"Where is it?" Garek asked as they rounded another corner only to find that this time the Polypus was nowhere to be seen. Lucien slowed his pace, almost tripping over his own feet. "Don't slow down!" Garek roared, and ran by him. Lucien let him go, and stopped to lean on the nearest wall and catch his breath.

Garek rounded the corner up ahead, and skidded to a sudden stop. "The frek...?" he trailed off.

"You found him?" Lucien asked.

Garek said nothing; he just stood there, frozen.

Seeing Garek's reaction, excitement stirred in Lucien's veins, spurring him to life. He poured on a final burst of speed and caught up fast—only to go skidding to a stop just as Garek had. Now he could see what had given Garek pause, and he was equally shocked.

They were still standing there by the time Addy and Brak caught up to them. Addy gasped at the sight.

At least three different tunnels came together where they now stood. It was a high-ceilinged chamber several hundred meters across, filled with the broken remains of colorful stalagmites and stalactites. The rocks shone red, blue, and orange in the light of their headlamps, but none of that was what had given them pause—scattered amongst that colorful rubble were hundreds and hundreds of *bodies.*

Some of them wore black suits of Faro armor, while others wore nothing but rough-hewn black and gray Faro robes, their bare blue skin exposed where their robes ended. An entire Faro army had died down here.

Lucien shook off his shock and walked up to the nearest corpse with his heart beating in his throat. It was a blue-skinned Faro, not wearing any armor. The body was half-buried in rubble, but from what he could see of it, it was in pristine condition, with no obvious signs of decomposition. He half-expected the Faro to leap up and attack him, but the body didn't so much as twitch. Then Lucien saw why—

It was headless.

"They must have died very recently," Addy whispered as she came to stand beside him. "They haven't even begun to decompose."

Lucien frowned. "We can't assume that. Oorgurak told us that Abaddon and the Elementals modified themselves to the point that they don't need exosuits or armor to survive in extreme environments like this one. That might also mean that their bodies don't decompose."

Garek joined them, holding a severed blue head. "This one looks like an Abaddon to me," he said.

Lucien examined the familiar features of that head and nodded slowly.

"How can we tell how old the bodies are if they don't decompose?" Addy asked.

"Carbon dating them might still work," Garek said.

"Let me see..." A fan of blue light flickered out from Garek's helmet, passing briefly over the head he was holding. "Damn it," he sighed after just a moment.

"What?" Lucien asked.

"We can't use carbon dating, because we don't know what the proper ratio of carbon-12 to carbon-14 is for a living Faro. I can tell you what the ratio is right now, but that's meaningless without a baseline to compare it to."

"What does it matter if they die yesterday or they die a thousand years ago?" Brak asked. "They are dead, and that is all that matters."

"But what killed them?" Addy asked.

"And is it a threat to us?" Lucien added, as he picked his way among the bodies. He shone his headlamps into the helmet of the nearest armored Faro and saw papery green skin barely clinging to jutting white bones. Hollow black eye sockets glared sightlessly up at the dripping fangs of stalactites above. The head looked shrunken, and very old. "This one's been mummified by his armor," Lucien said, noting that the soldier's armor appeared to be intact. "They definitely didn't die recently." He rolled the body over, looking for damage he couldn't see, but the glossy black armor was pristine.

"What are you doing?" Addy asked, her nose wrinkled with disgust as he rolled the body back the other way.

"I can't figure out what killed him," Lucien explained. He walked over to the next armored body. It was another green-skinned Faro, also mummified. He repeated his examination, and again found the soldier's suit of armor intact. He sat back on his haunches and shook his head. "I don't get it. There's no visible cause of death."

Garek walked over, his boots crunching through gravel. The sound echoed softly through the cavern. "What do you want, an autopsy report? Let's keep moving."

Lucien shook his head. "That Polypus led us here for a reason."

"Maybe he did, but I don't think that reason was for us to play forensic detective."

Lucien glanced up at Garek. "If we can figure out what killed them, we might also figure out what we're up against down here. The Mokari said no one has ever returned from the underworld, so whatever the threat is down here, it's obviously an ongoing one."

Garek shrugged. "Maybe the Polypuses are the threat."

Lucien frowned. "What do you mean?"

"Maybe they killed the Faros."

"But not us?"

"And *how* did they kill the Faros?" Addy asked. "There are no signs of injury on the armored ones."

"I can't pretend to understand their motives," Garek said, "but think about it: eight years ago they ripped the timer implants out of our heads without hurting us or even breaking our skin. So, what's stopping them from doing the same thing with vital organs?"

Addy looked horrified. She cast a quick look around the chamber.

"The Abaddon clone we found was headless," Lucien pointed out.

Garek shrugged. "It's just a theory."

"I find something," Brak said. "Come see."

They found the Gor standing about fifty feet away, gazing down at something by his feet. They all hurried over to see what had caught Brak's attention: a large white skeleton lay at his feet, as well as another, smaller and semi-translucent one. The skulls gave them away. The larger of the two had a pronounced snout with long, sharp white teeth, while the other skull was almost as big, but with a tiny mouth, giant eye sockets, and an over-sized cranium.

"It's a Gray and a Mokari," Lucien said.

"And another Abaddon," Garek added, pointing to another blue-skinned, gray-robed Faro, also headless, lying beside the skeletons.

"They all died fighting together," Addy said.

Brak nodded. "Yes."

"But were they fighting against each other, or with each other?" Lucien asked.

"Good question," Garek said.

"The dead cannot help us," Brak decided. "But I find something that might."

"What's that?" Lucien asked.

"Come." Brak led the way, picking his way through the ancient battlefield.

After a few minutes of walking, Lucien glimpsed a pinprick of light shining at the far end of the chamber, almost three hundred meters away, according to his sensors.

"What is *that?*" Addy asked, pointing to it.

At first Lucien thought it might be the Polypus who'd led them here, but one look at his sensors revealed that it was actually an opening into a much larger adjoining chamber. That chamber seemed to go on forever, expanding rapidly across Lucien's sensor display as they approached. It was almost perfectly spherical, and hollow.

"I'm getting some massive energy readings from that

direction," Garek said.

Lucien double-checked with his own sensors, and found the same thing.

"What is it?" Addy asked.

"It's too uniform to be naturally occurring," Lucien said, noting how perfectly spherical it was.

"Yes," Brak agreed.

"Those power readings could be from the gateway we're looking for," Lucien said.

"It can't be that easy," Addy replied.

"Why not?" Lucien asked.

"If it were so easy to find this gateway, then why didn't Abaddon just send another army down here and take it for himself?"

"It obviously didn't go so well for him the last time," Garek pointed out. They were still wading through Faro corpses.

"Something's obviously guarding the gateway," Garek went on. "My bet is it's the Polypuses."

Lucien considered that. "If they're against Abaddon, then why stop at guarding this place? Why not go fight him? We obviously can't hurt them, and if Abaddon's afraid of them, then that implies that he can't either. They'd be an invincible army."

"Maybe they're pacifists," Garek suggested.

"I'm reading lots of life signs on the other side of that opening," Addy said.

The circle of light in the distance had resolved into a pair of large metal doors that were deformed and scorched black. The doors were bowed inward, as if a plasma bomb had ripped them open. A faint blue haze rippled over the opening, indicating the presence of an atmospheric shield.

They slowed their pace as they reached the opening. The glare from it was dazzling, making it impossible to see what was on the other side.

"I'll go through first," Lucien said, and walked through before anyone could argue. He heard and felt the atmospheric shields sizzle against his exosuit as he crossed the threshold. Then his feet touched a hard, flat surface that echoed with his footsteps.

His eyes adjusted quickly to the brightness, and he saw that he was standing inside some kind of giant concourse. Dead ahead, a high wall of shattered viewports gazed out on a blinding sphere of light. The light was as bright as a sun, and painful to look at. Lucien's faceplate auto-polarized and more details of his surroundings snapped into focus.

"Lucien?" Addy asked over the comms.

"I'm fine..." he said.

He heard faint sizzling sounds as the others walked in behind him.

The walls and floor of the concourse looked like they might once have been opulent, but now they were discolored and broken. The floor was littered with shattered black rocks, more Faro bodies, and skeletons of Grays and Mokari. A thick layer of dust covered everything.

Looking out through the shattered viewports once more, Lucien saw that the blinding orb of light hung suspended between two giant black towers, one coming down from the ceiling of the spherical chamber, the other rising up from the floor. All around the light source, vibrant colors assaulted Lucien's eyes in a confusing tapestry that was somehow too intricate, or too distant to make sense of.

"It's incredible..." Addy breathed.

Lucien turned away from the glaring light to find her standing to one side of the concourse, looking out over a vibrant field of flowers. He went to stand beside her and admire the view, but he quickly noticed that there was something very wrong with that scene.

Somehow everything was turned on its end and wrapped around the inside of the spherical chamber. The landscape outside the concourse sprawled for tens of kilometers in all directions, defying gravity from every possible angle. A towering alien forest rose up beyond the flowering field, but it lay parallel to the floor of the concourse. Likewise for the sheer white mountains that peeked over the tops of those trees.

Lucien looked straight *up,* through a broken skylight, and saw a sparkling blue lake arcing overhead, wrapped concave against the inside of the sphere and surrounded by jungle.

The Mokari underworld was like a miniature planet that had been turned inside-out, and the only part of it where gravity still functioned the way it should was in the concourse where they stood.

"What's holding everything against the walls like that?" Addy asked.

"Something's warping the gravity in this place," Garek said.

"So why aren't we falling against that wall?" Addy nodded to the broken entrance they'd walked through. It lay along the inside of the sphere, parallel to the *ground* outside. If gravity were warped the way Garek was suggesting, then they should have been standing on the wall of the concourse, not the floor.

The whole setup confused Lucien's brain to the point that he suddenly felt like he was falling. He flinched and shook his head to clear away that sensation.

"This must be some kind of transition zone," Garek said. "I spotted what looked like a tram station down that way." He pointed to the viewports that looked out—*up?*—at the blinding ball of light in the center of the chamber.

Lucien nodded slowly. "This is the entrance to the underworld."

Addy snorted. "Under-*world*. I didn't realize the Mokari were being so literal when they named the place. Who do you think lived here?"

"The Grays, who else?" Lucien asked. "I bet they built it."

"Then Katawa was definitely lying about not being able to join us down here because it would *defile* his deity," Addy said.

Garek snorted. "I think that goes without saying. He didn't come down here because he was afraid of whatever killed that army outside."

"Afraid of the Polypuses?" Addy asked.

"Or something else," Lucien replied. "We shouldn't assume we're safe from them just because they helped us once. The one who led us here might not be as friendly. It may have *lured* us here."

"So it led us here to... what? Kill us? Eat us?"

Lucien shook his head. "I don't know."

"The temperature in here is a balmy *300 K*," Garek said. "And I'm reading breathable air."

"I guess we won't be suffocating after all," Addy said.

Garek nodded and twisted off his helmet with a *hiss* of escaping air. He took a deep breath, and a rare smile crossed his face. "Smells like a dream, too. Must be all those flowers outside."

Lucien shot him a frown. "Just because our sensors aren't detecting anything dangerous doesn't mean the air's safe to breathe."

"We'll know soon enough," Garek replied, and tucked his helmet under one arm. "Besides, Katawa fixed us up, remember?"

"Now you're trusting him?" Lucien asked dubiously.

Garek shook his head. "No, but Katawa has nothing to gain from the atmosphere killing us. He obviously needs us to find that key and open the gateway."

Lucien looked away, back to the overgrown field. "Any idea how we can get down there? We could jump out and use our grav boosters, but we're going to fall sideways. Landing on our feat might not be so easy."

"What about those?" Addy pointed to a row of circular openings to one side of where they stood.

Lucien spied translucent tubes snaking down from the openings to the ground. "They look like giant slides to me," he said, walking up to the nearest one.

Addy walked over to stand by the slide next to his. "On three?" she asked.

"On two," Lucien replied.

"One..."

"Two," Lucien finished, and dove head-first down the slide.

CHAPTER 31

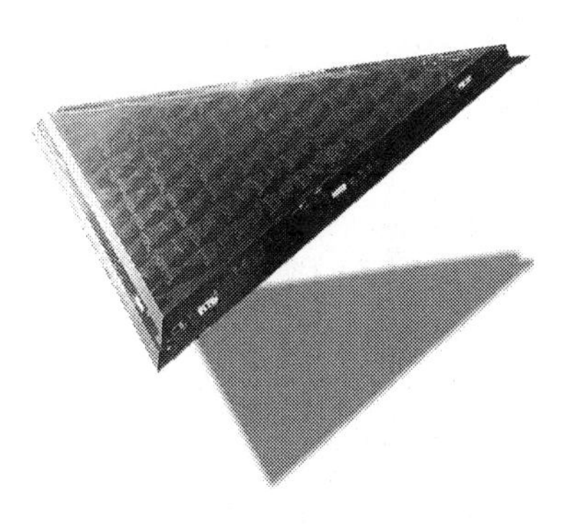

Astralis

Lucien busied himself while waiting for Tyra to come home by installing baby gates in their rental home. Atara stood over his shoulder, watching him work, while Theola was taking a nap in her room downstairs.

"Is it going to keep me from falling down the stairs, too?" Atara asked.

Lucien glanced over his shoulder at Atara while screwing the gate frame into the wall. He flashed her a smile and shook his head. "You already know how to use the stairs," he said.

"But what if I trip?"

"That's why you need to hold on to the railing."

Lucien finished driving in the last screw and sat back on his haunches to admire his work. A bead of sweat trickled down from his hairline, itching maddeningly as it went.

Lucien wiped his brow on his sweater sleeve, scratching the itch at the same time.

He swung the gate shut to test it, and the locking mechanism automatically *clicked* into place.

"How do I open it?" Atara asked.

"Like this. Watch." Lucien pointed to the sliding catch at the top of the gate. "Slide this, and pull up at the same time." He opened the gate and then shut it again with another *click.* "Now you try."

Atara had to use both hands. She was barely tall enough to pull up on the gate, but she managed to wrench it open, her cheeks bulging with the effort.

"Wow... it's hard," she said.

"Well, if it were easy, then Theola could open it, too."

Atara nodded sagely at that.

"Speaking of Theola..." Lucien checked the time on his ARCs. "We'd better go wake her up. She's not going to sleep tonight if I let her sleep any longer. I'd better make her a bottle first, though," Lucien said as he started down the stairs.

"If you don't, she's going to scream like her head's been cut off!" Atara suggested, walking down behind him.

"Exactly," Lucien said, frowning at the gruesome analogy.

"She always wakes up hungry," Atara said.

"Yes, she does," Lucien agreed absently.

"How can someone scream if their head is cut off?" Atara asked.

Lucien grimaced. "It's just an expression, Atty."

"Chickens can still run around without their heads," Atara mused on their way to the kitchen.

"All right, that's enough."

"It's true!" Atara insisted.

Lucien stopped on the landing halfway down the stairs and turned to her. "I don't care if it's true; that's not what I'm objecting to. You shouldn't focus on those things."

"Why not?" Atara asked.

"Because it's not okay. You might get desensitized."

"What's that mean?"

"It means... never mind. Just think about nice stuff, all right?"

"Fine." Atara went down the stairs in a huff, heading for the living room, while Lucien continued on to the kitchen. He made a bottle for Theola and then went to fetch her from her crib.

When he walked in, he found Atara standing beside the crib, watching Theola sleep.

"What are you doing?" Lucien asked, puzzled by her behavior.

Atara turned to him with a smile. "She looks so peaceful."

Lucien stopped beside the crib to admire Theola, too. "She does," he agreed.

"She's not even waking up," Atara said. Theola hadn't stirred at the sound of their voices. "It's like she's dead."

He shot Atara a cold look. "Why would you say something like that?" he demanded.

Atara's lower lip quivered. "Why are you yelling?"

Lucien scowled and shook his head. "You don't say things like that about your sister, do you understand me?"

Atara scowled right back, as if he was the bad guy. "Why not?"

Theola woke up at the sound of their arguing, and

immediately began to cry. She sat up and popped her thumb in her mouth, watching them with big, wary blue eyes.

Lucien turned to Theola. "Come here, sweetheart," he said, holding out his arms. She climbed to her feet and held out her arms in turn, waiting to be picked up. He scooped her into a one-armed embrace, and showed her the bottle of milk, and a smile sprang to her lips. She began bouncing on his hip trying to reach it.

"You want this?" he asked, shaking the bottle just out of reach.

Theola's smile faded to a dramatic pout when the bottle didn't immediately replace the thumb she'd been sucking. Her lower lip trembled briefly, and then she started crying.

Lucien laughed. "Okay, okay! Here you go." He gave her the bottle, and she grabbed it with both hands, stuffing it into her mouth.

Lucien turned back to Atara, but she was gone. He left the room with a frown, wondering if he had been too hard on her. She was only five; she was bound to say strange things sometimes.

He walked with Theola down the hallway to the living room as she gulped her milk.

"Atara?" he called.

No answer.

"Where are you?"

Just as he reached the living room, his foot hooked under something, and he tripped. He was going to fall on top of Theola! He couldn't put out his hands because one of them was holding her. He managed to thrust out his free hand to break their fall, and a sharp pain shot through his fingers as two of them bore all of his and Theola's combined weight.

He cried out and crumpled to the floor, being careful to roll onto his back as he did so. Theola landed on top of him, still holding onto her bottle, but no longer sucking it. She grinned and started bouncing on his belly. She thought it was a game.

"Giddy-up..." he muttered, and Theola giggled enthusiastically, bouncing harder.

His hand wasn't hurting anymore, but as he lifted it in front of his face, he saw that his pinky finger was broken—maybe his ring finger, too—and that whole side of his hand was swelling up badly.

Lucien grimaced. He wasn't feeling any pain because of the shock. Using his good hand, he carefully lifted Theola off his stomach. Cradling his injured hand to his chest, he sat up to look for what had tripped him, but there was nothing on the floor. He did, however, see Atara standing there, leaning against the wall and watching him.

"Are you okay, Daddy?" she asked, as their eyes met. "How did you fall?"

Suddenly he saw Atara's green eyes as cunning rather than innocent. First she'd frozen Theola with the open window, and now she'd tripped him—with Theola in his arms. It had to have been her. There was nothing on the floor, nothing else that could have done it. Was *he* the target this time, or was it Theola again?

Lucien felt a chill come over him. This was more than simple mischief or jealousy. Besides, Atara and Theola had more than a year together already, and Atara had never shown any signs of jealousy before. At least not to this extent.

"Atara..." he said slowly. She cocked her head to one

side, her eyes full of concern, and a glitter of something else...

Amusement.

The chill Lucien had felt turned to solid ice, and he went suddenly very still.

"Did you trip me, honey?" he asked, trying to keep his tone light and clear of accusation.

Atara's eyes flew wide and her lower lip began to tremble, but he could have sworn she was trying to hide a smile. "No!" she blurted out defiantly, and crossed her arms over her chest.

But he could see the lie gleaming in her eyes—the smug satisfaction. "Okay. I believe you," Lucien said, lying back, and trying to pretend everything was normal. Behind that pretense, his mind raced with terror—fear of his own daughter. The Faros had done something to her. Somehow they'd *changed* her when they'd touched her, and if that was true, then the others had been changed, too: Chief Councilor Ellis, Admiral Stavos, General Graves... and who knew how many others.

"We'd better go to the hospital," Lucien said slowly, trying to mask his thoughts before Atara realized he was on to her. "Daddy broke his finger, see?" he held up his hand for Atara to see.

She gasped at the sight of his swollen hand and crept forward for a better look. Stopping beside him, she leaned in and pressed his hand to her lips, smacking them in an exaggerated kiss. She retreated, grinning broadly at him. "All better!"

Lucien suppressed a shiver. Something told him her delight was in his pain, and not in the presumed healing powers of her kiss.

"I'm afraid it's not that easy," he said. "I'm going to need a doctor to fix this."

Atara's smile faded. "It's that bad?"

He nodded. "I'm afraid so, yes." Lucien cast about for Theola and found her pottering around the coffee table, sucking her thumb and shaking her bottle. She was spraying milk everywhere. Lucien grimaced. He walked over and scooped her up in a one-armed embrace, balancing her against a hip that wasn't designed for the task.

"Come on," he said, keeping an eye on Atara to make sure she didn't trip him again—or do something worse this time.

"Why do *I* have to go?" Atara whined.

Lucien's patience snapped. "Because you're five years old and I can't leave you alone! Now let's go! To the garage. March!"

Atara made a pouty face and walked through the living room to the foyer. Lucien made sure to keep her ahead of him, where he could watch her. When they reached the foyer, Atara opened the coat closet and pulled on her gloves and winter coat. Lucien gave the closet a skip, deciding to brave the cold. Between Theola and his broken finger, it would be too much trouble to put on his coat—or his gloves, for that matter. He cringed at the thought of squeezing broken fingers into a glove.

"Open the door, please," Lucien said, nodding to the garage door in the foyer. Atara did as she was told, and they hurried through the garage to their shiny new hover car; a midnight-blue six-seater that Tyra had somehow found the time to purchase this morning while he was at his meeting with the other ex-Paragons. The car had arrived on autopilot with a pre-recorded message from her, just in time for Lucien to use it to pick up the girls from school and daycare. The invoice from the dealer indicated she'd also bought a matching black car for herself. They'd lost both of their old cars with their home when Fallside had depressurized.

Lucien used his ARCs to open the car doors as they approached. As soon they were seated inside, the car greeted him, "Welcome, Mr. Ortane! Where would you like to go this afternoon?"

"Winterside General Hospital, please."

"Right away. Please buckle up," the car replied in a congenial voice. Lucien dropped Theola in the car seat on the row of seats in front of him and awkwardly buckled her in, wincing as he occasionally brushed his broken finger against something. Feeling weak, he slumped back into his seat in the middle of the front-facing row of seats. Meanwhile, the car had already powered up and hovered a few inches into the air.

"Is this an emergency?" the driver program asked, as the car rotated on the spot to face the garage door, which was already rising to reveal a bright bar of daylight at the bottom.

Snow swirled in underneath, dusting the entrance. As the door finished opening, Lucien saw that it was snowing hard outside, and the frozen lake below their home was barely visible beyond the snow-caked trees.

"My scanners report that your cortisol and adrenaline levels are elevated in a way that is consistent with a serious injury," the driver program went on, when Lucien didn't immediately respond. "I can have EMTs waiting when we arrive," the car suggested as it shot out of the garage.

"No, that's all right," Lucien said, and laid his head

back against his seat with a pained grimace. He allowed his eyes to drift shut, waiting for the trip to be over.

"Does it hurt?" Atara asked.

Lucien cracked one eye open to regard her. She was smiling faintly at him and reaching for his injured hand with her index finger extended, as if to poke his broken finger. He jerked his arm away and cradled his hand protectively. "Are you crazy?" he demanded.

Atara's eyes flashed with hurt, and her lower lip began to tremble once more.

He made an irritated noise in the back of his throat and shook his head. Forget his hand. The real medical emergency here was whatever the frek was wrong with Atara.

He was almost afraid to think about what that might be. They'd mind probed and scanned her thoroughly. She was supposed to be fine. Obviously they'd missed something. This wasn't the innocent, loving five-year old he'd raised.

This was a devil in a child's body.

CHAPTER 32

Mokar: Underworld

Lucien's armor screeched against the sides of the tube, but the friction was barely enough to slow his descent. He felt gravity shifting, as if the world were sliding out from under him. *Up* and *down* became *sideways,* and he lost all sense of direction, spinning and rolling as he fell. He caught a glimpse of green plants through the translucent walls of the tube, and suspected he was close to the ground. His suit clocked his speed at over forty kilometers an hour. He gritted his teeth, bracing for impact.

He flew out of the tube and landed hard in the overgrown field of flowers he'd seen from the concourse. The jolt of the impact was enough to clack his teeth together, but the vegetation provided a nice cushion.

Lucien stood up and struggled through waist-high

grass and flowers. He saw Addy get up beside him, and a split second later Garek and Brak both came flying out of tubes adjacent to hers.

Lucien activated his suit's sensory suite and an array of floral smells flooded his helmet, making his nostrils flare. The plants felt rough and prickly against his thighs and torso.

He reached out to touch a spiky blue flower the size of his head, and received a sharp stab of electricity—the simulated prick of a thorn.

The flower reared at his touch and let out a high-pitched whistle, blowing air in his face and shrinking into itself as it did so. Lucien regarded it curiously, and he felt as though it might be regarding him back, though he couldn't see any eyes.

"These plants seem more *alive* than usual," Lucien said. "And some of them have nasty thorns. Watch yourself, Garek. I wouldn't want to see what one of them could do to your exposed face. You might swell up like a puffer fish."

Garek barked a laugh. "Probably make me prettier."

Lucien snorted, but peripherally he noted that Garek was wearing his helmet again. He'd probably put it back on to avoid losing it on his way down the slide.

"Where to now?" Addy asked.

A piercing wail split the air, drawing their attention to a Mokari-sized bird circling the field up ahead. For all they knew it actually was a Mokari, but this bird was white rather than black, and it didn't sound the same.

"I don't know," Lucien admitted, turning to look around and get his bearings.

The inside of the underworld curved up and away to all sides of them, divided in a farm-like patchwork of different-colored vegetation. In the distance, giant trees soared, each with just a handful of branches and one or two over-sized, opalescent leaves per branch. Towering mountains peeked over the treetops, sheer white cliffs striated with purple veins that might have been rivers. All of it curved up sharply, clinging to the inside of the sphere.

Lucien turned and glanced up at the concourse where they'd been standing moments ago. From the outside it looked like a low-rise apartment complex, but the rows of broken viewports lay perpendicular to the ground rather than parallel.

Looking up, he saw the blinding ball of light in the center of the sphere. It hung directly overhead, at the zenith of the sky. Its radiance blocked their view of the other side of the sphere.

The two black towers that Lucien had seen before now seemed to traverse the sky like two halves of a bridge, with the light source suspended in the middle.

"Let's head for one of those towers," Lucien suggested. "Whatever is generating that light might also be used to power the gateway we're looking for."

"Looks like a long hike," Garek said, peering up at the nearest tower, and shielding his eyes against the glare of the artificial sun with one hand.

"We should boost up there," Addy suggested. "I doubt it will take more than a few minutes to get there like that."

"I agree," Lucien said, and powered his grav boosters at a modest five percent to send himself floating up above the field.

The others joined him, hovering up one by one.

"Let's not fly too high," Lucien said. "Keep to an

altitude of fifty meters just in case the direction of gravity doesn't hold constant all the way up."

"Roger that," Addy said, and Garek and Brak clicked their comms to confirm.

Lucien powered the boosters in his palms and used them to rotate on the spot, orienting his body for horizontal flight toward the nearest of the two black towers. He waited for the others to get into position, and then boosted off at ten percent thrust.

The ground swept up quickly with the curvature of the sphere, making it hard to maintain straight and level flight, but by angling his body upward, he was able to keep a constant altitude of fifty meters.

His forward velocity hit one hundred kilometers per hour, and he backed off the power to his boosters to maintain that speed. He didn't want to miss something important on the ground. The gateway they were looking for could technically be anywhere—not to mention the so-called *magical key* they needed to open it.

"Wow..." Addy breathed. "Take a look at that!"

Lucien cast about, looking for whatever had caught her eye. He didn't have to look for long.

A giant two-legged creature roamed the plains below, leaving a trampled path through the multicolored shrubs and flowers. It had a row of wicked-looking spikes down its hunched spine, and two massive arms that it used like extra legs to pick its way through the field. The creature's hide was dark brown and wrinkly, and probably very thick.

Lucien slowed down as they reached the monster, and its size relative to their altitude of fifty meters gave a sense of scale. It reached more than halfway up from the ground, making it at least thirty meters tall.

They could actually hear its footsteps booming as they approached. Lucien matched his speed with that of the creature at twenty klicks per hour. He hovered along behind it, watching it walk through the field.

Suddenly it stopped, and its head perked up, its attention fixed on a herd of bright green blobs rolling through a field of blue grass up ahead.

The monster suddenly leapt forward, bounding toward the herd of blobs at incredible speed. The air shivered with its footfalls, and the green blobs rolled away as it drew near, schooling like fish. The monster was too fast for them. It scooped up a pair of them in one giant palm.

But it wasn't a palm; it was a gaping mouth lined with rings of sharp white thorns. The blobs were impaled on those thorns.

Lucien slowed his flight and circled down for a better look. The monster's arms were like snakes, and the one that had impaled the two blob creatures was waving bonelessly in the air. Two large bulges inched down along its length with the help of gravity. It had swallowed the blob-creatures whole.

"Be careful..." Addy warned as he strayed within reach of the snake-armed monster.

It must have felt the pressure from Lucien's grav boosters, because it looked up as he passed overhead. Its entire head was a giant, blinking black eye on a flexible stalk, rimmed with long red thorns. The eye narrowed as it tracked him, and then both of the monster's arms shot up, swiping at Lucien's ankles with giant, sucking mouths. They barely missed him, and hot rancid breath whistled out of those orifices as the arms sank back to the ground. Lucien's stomach clenched with the smell and suddenly he wished he hadn't turned on his suit's sensory suite. He boosted up out of reach, trying to calm his heaving stomach. He did *not* want to throw up in his helmet.

"Are you okay?" Addy asked.

Lucien nodded slowly. "What *is* this place?"

"If I had to guess, I'd say it's some kind of zoo," Garek said.

"So why aren't the animals in cages?" Lucien asked, staring at the two-legged, snake-armed monster as it bounded after the schooling herd of green blobs.

"Maybe the Grays don't like keeping animals in cages," Addy said.

"Or else they found a way to break out in the long years of the Grays' absence," Garek added.

"Good thing we decided to fly to the tower," Lucien said. "There's no telling what we might have run into down there."

"Yeah, good thing..." Addy agreed.

They reached the end of the plains and flew over a rocky field of glowing blue crystals. Lucien couldn't see any animals walking between them, but the crystals periodically discharged bright bolts of electricity from one to another. Each time one of them did so, it grew momentarily dark and opaque, only to light up again as another crystal zapped it.

"I wonder if those are alive?" Addy asked.

"Silicon lifeforms?" Lucien suggested.

"Why not? We found a few of those immediately after we crossed the Red Line."

"Living rocks," Brak grumbled. "What good it is to be

alive if you are a rock? You cannot move. You cannot eat..."

"But you can think," Lucien said. "For all we know, they're more intelligent than we are."

Brak snorted. "What does a rock have to think about?"

"They might not be alive," Garek said. "Might just be part of the power grid that feeds this place."

Lucien nodded at that. The field of glowing crystals came to an end, and they arrived at the forest they'd seen from a distance. The trees were incredibly tall, their boles silver and leaves opalescent white. They were far enough apart they they could fly easily through the forest. As they did so, Lucien noted that each branch had just one or two giant opalescent leaves. Those leaves sparkled brightly in the sun, casting deep pools of shadow on the ground below. Lucien thought he spotted small creatures moving through the underbrush, but it was too dark to be sure.

Mountains soared up to the right, their steep white slopes clearly visible through the trees. Again Lucien noted the purple veins snaking down from their peaks. *Definitely rivers,* he decided.

"There's the tower," Addy said, as she zagged under a looming branch and over another one.

"I see it," Lucien said. The curvature of the underworld made for an odd horizon, where they could never see very far in any given direction. A moment ago, looking straight ahead, they'd only been able to see more silver tree trunks and glittering leaves, but now they saw the smooth black sides of the tower soaring to block their view. The closer they got to the tower, the more their perspective shifted so that the tower appeared less like a bridge traversing the sky, and more like a skyscraper, rising up to blot out the sun.

The trees fell away abruptly and then the tower was all they could see. Lucien banked sharply to avoid colliding with it. The others followed him through that maneuver, and they circled back, spiraling to the ground.

They landed in almost perfect unison on a castcrete pad surrounding the base of the tower. Beyond that, overgrown black and red shrubs rose in a tangled wall. The shrubbery flowed gradually *up* along the curvature of the ground to greet the silver trees just over a hundred meters from where they stood.

Lucien turned and looked up at the black tower. It was shaped like an obelisk, and tapered to a slender point almost ten kilometers up—according to the rangefinder on his HUD. At that point it reached the artificial sun and disappeared in the blinding light. Assuming a perfect sphere, that put the size of the underworld at around three hundred and fourteen kilometers in circumference—tiny as far as planets went, and even small when compared with the vast scale of *Astralis*.

"I'm detecting a lot of lifeforms down here with us," Garek said. "Medium to large. Most of them in the forest."

"The hunt beginsss..." Brak hissed, and drew the razor sword from his back. The blade shimmered, blurring with a faint blue glow as Brak activated it.

Lucien's scanned the wall of black and red shrubs running around the tower, his integrated lasers up and tracking.

"Form on me," Lucien said after a moment, and started walking around the tower. "Keep eyes on our flank."

The others fell in behind him, walking fast, their footsteps *thunking* against the castcrete foundation. The tower walls looked seamless, with no windows or doors. They walked around the tower for several minutes before they returned to their starting point.

"That was a nice stroll," Garek said. "Didn't find my tail, though."

Lucien turned to peer up at the tower again, squinting against the light pouring from the top.

"I don't get it," Addy said, and rapped a fist on the side of the tower, eliciting a hollow bang from it. "There has to be a way in."

"Brak?" Lucien asked, turning to find the Gor half-crouching by the shrubs at the edge of the pad around the tower, as if he were hunting something.

"Yess?" the Gor answered belatedly.

"Get over here and see if you can cut a hole with your sword."

Brak straightened and strode up to the tower. Addy knocked on the side of it a few more times to sound out the bounds of the hollow area.

"There—" Addy pointed to the center of the area she'd identified.

Taking his sword in a two-handed grip, Brak reared back and delivered an impaling thrust.

Lucien expected to see the sword sink in up to its hilt. Few materials were strong enough to resist molecular-edged razor shields. But as soon as the tip of the weapon touched the side of the tower, there came a *bang*, and an intense flash of light, and Brak went flying backward. He skimmed over the castcrete and crashed into the dense tangle of vegetation running around the tower. The shrubs parted for Brak, only to spring back a moment later, seeming to swallow him whole.

"Guess we should have scanned it first," Garek said.

Lucien gaped at the spot where Brak had disappeared. "Are you okay?" he called over the comms.

No reply.

Then came a flash of crimson light from within, accompanied by the tell-tale shriek of lasers discharging. Black smoke curled from the vegetation, and the field of shrubs seemed to explode as Brak blasted straight up into the air. The plants lunged after him, unfurling like coiled snakes and waving at his departure, as if beckoning for him to come back.

Brak landed with a grunt and cast about for his sword. He found it lying at the edge of the shrubbery, the dead-man's switch having turned off the blade as soon as it had left his hand. He walked over to collect the weapon.

"Any other bright ideas?" Garek asked, turning to Lucien and Addy.

"I think this might be the gateway that the Mokari were talking about," Addy said.

"That's a bit of a leap," Lucien replied.

"Not really. Think about it. This tower is the only unnatural structure we've found besides the concourse where we entered the underworld."

"The whole place is an unnatural structure," Garek pointed out.

"True," Addy agreed. "Anyway, from the look of it, there's no way into the tower, which is where I think that *magical key* comes in."

"So where do you suppose we should start looking for that key?" Garek asked. "We could spend a lifetime searching for it if we have to turn over every stone, and uproot every bush."

"Well..." Addy trailed off. "I haven't figured that part out yet."

Lucien was distracted, gazing at the artificial sun shining overhead. He could have sworn it was dimmer now than it had been a moment ago.

Sure enough, as he watched the brightness faded to the point that it was no longer painful to look at. Now he could see the second tower, as well as a ball of clouds forming around the fading sun. Behind and around those clouds, Lucien saw a patchwork quilt of alien vegetation on the other side of the sphere.

"I think night's about to fall," he said.

Garek snorted. "That should make searching for this key easier."

A shrill cry sounded from the direction of the trees, followed by growling and snarling sounds, and then more cries—frantic, and growing softer by the second.

A chilling silence fell, broken by the soft trilling of nocturnal creatures waking with the night.

Darkness gathered swiftly, and a thick white mist descended on them. Lucien glanced up once more and saw that the artificial sun was now a faint blue-white orb, shining through the mist—*an artificial moon?* Lucien wondered. Smaller white orbs detached from that one, floating down from the light source like balloons.

Lucien pointed to them. "What are those?"

"Looks like the Polypuses," Garek said.

They came flowing down the sides of the tower in rivers of light.

"They're headed this way..." Garek said slowly.

"An extra-dimensional party and we're the guests of

honor," Lucien mused.

A whistling shriek split the air, and the ground shook, followed by a sound like dry palm leaves rattling.

Boom. More leaves rattled.

Lucien froze and turned toward the sound. Sensors marked a large lifeform approaching from the direction of the forest.

"Is that..." Addy trailed off in a whisper.

"We've got incoming," Garek warned as he brought his arms and integrated laser cannons up, aiming between the trees.

"We should get on the other side of the tower," Lucien said.

Boom. Boom. Boom. The footsteps were falling faster now, as if whatever beast was headed their way knew its cover was blown.

"No time to run... it's almost here," Garek said. "Take aim!"

Lucien brought his cannons up and targeted the incoming lifeform. It was huge, at least as big as the snake-armed monster they'd seen hunting in the field around the concourse. Lucien's heart jumped against his sternum as the red-shaded outline of his target appeared, descending the curve of the underworld. The creature was bipedal... and it used two long arms for added balance as it walked.

The monster burst from the trees and into the surrounding field of shrubs. Both arms snapped up and waved through the air, giant pink mouths snorting and whistling as they sampled the air. A giant eye swiveled on the end of a fat neck stalk, gleaming in the moonlit night.

It was the same monster they'd seen hunting the blobs

in the field.

They all stood frozen in shock, afraid to move for fear of setting off whatever hunting instincts the creature might have. The monster's arms gradually undulated to the ground, until the gaping mouths were at eye-level with them. Those arms drifted closer, sniffing the air around them in phlegmy snorts

"Fire!" Garek said as one of the mouths came within a few feet of him. He fired into the mouth with both cannons. Crimson beams of light flashed down the monster's throat, illuminating it from within and revealing spidery networks of red and blue veins.

The monster let out a piercing scream as the lasers struck inside its throat, and it thrashed the castcrete, shaking the ground and crumbling the foundation where they stood.

Lucien dove out of the way as it slapped the ground where he'd been standing. He rolled back to his feet just in time to see the monster's other arm come sweeping in, its mouth gaping for the kill.

CHAPTER 33

Mokar: Underworld

Before Lucien could react, he was tossed high into the air and then falling straight into the gaping maw of the beast. It sucked him into its rancid depths, and everything went dark. Haptic sensors relayed sharp pricks to Lucien's skin as the monster's thorn-shaped teeth ground against his armor.

Then he felt those rings of teeth sweeping him back, deeper into a smooth-muscled throat, and soon he was cocooned by clenching bands of muscle.

He was trapped.

Waves of noxious alien breath assaulted his nose. Feeling his stomach clench up, Lucien mentally turned off his sensory suite and sucked in a deep breath of mercifully odorless air.

"A little help here!" he called out over the comms as he

felt iron bands of muscle contracting above his head and squeezing him down the length of the monster's throat.

"Hang on!" Garek commed back.

Lucien heard the muffled screeches of laser fire and saw the accompanying flashes of light periodically illuminate the inside of the throat. The arm thrashed and bucked in time to each shot, but the creature's reaction wasn't as strong as it had been when Garek had fired directly down its throat. It's hide was probably tough enough to buffer the effects of their lasers.

That gave Lucien an idea. He strained against the bands of muscle contracting around him, trying to get his arms into a position that would enable him to fire without shooting off his own feet.

He managed to get one arm angled slightly away from his body, and fired three times in quick succession. The monster bucked violently, and a muffled shriek sounded from the monster's other mouth.

The muscles inside the beast's throat spasmed so tightly that his suit's shields overloaded with a loud *pop.*

Now he couldn't move at all, not even with his suit's power-assist boosted to the max. Damage alerts began streaming across his HUD, accompanied by a computerized voice: "Warning, armor integrity dropping to sixty-two percent."

"Guys?" Lucien called in a gasping voice as he began to feel the pressure constrict his chest. It was like being squeezed by a boa. His armor groaned ominously in time to each muscle contraction. With his lungs burning for air, Lucien was forced to exhale, but he was unable to suck in another breath. Dark spots swarmed his vision, and he knew he was going to pass out soon.

"Brak's going to try to cut you out!" Addy said, her voice sounding dim, even though it came from speakers right beside his ears.

"What the frek?" Garek exclaimed.

The sounds of laser fire stopped, and then there was nothing... just a ringing silence and an angry roar of hypoxic blood.

"Armor integrity at twenty-seven percent."

Lucien fought impotently against a wave of dizziness. Everything faded, and the raging concerns of the present were gone, sinking fast into the utter dark of oblivion. Lucien felt himself falling into that abyss.

A meaty *smack!* and a ground-shaking *boom!* awoke him. Lucien gasped, and sucked in a deep, desperate breath. The ever-tightening cocoon of flesh around him had relaxed. Now it was a limp, but heavy weight pressing him down, loose enough for him to breathe freely and for to move his arms and legs, but not by much.

"What just happened?" Lucien asked, still breathing deeply to clear his muddled thoughts.

"I don't..." Addy trailed off.

Lucien was about to try shooting his way out when a glowing blue blade appeared, slicing through just above his head. Red blood gushed, splattering Lucien's faceplate.

Once the gash was a few meters wide, the sword withdrew and an armored hand appeared, reaching blindly for him through a crimson cascade of alien blood. Lucien grabbed that hand, and felt himself sliding up and out. The flooded throat slurped disgustingly as he left.

Lucien's feet touched castcrete and he furiously swiped

away the blood from his faceplate so that he could see.

He saw Brak's grinning face staring back at him. "This is a tale to tell your children's children," he said. "And when you tell it, remember Brakos, the hero."

Lucien grinned and slapped Brak on the back. "You bet, buddy." He turned to see Addy and Garek crouching beside a big, bloody red mound of flesh that Brak must have hacked off some other part of the beast. He walked over to them. "What were you two doing? Providing moral support? A few more seconds and I'd have been swimming in a pool of digestive fluids."

Addy stood and turned to him with a look of mingled horror and awe. She slowly shook her head. "Brak didn't save you."

Lucien frowned. "What do you mean he didn't save me?"

Garek straightened, too, and jerked his chin up to indicate something in the sky. "They did."

Lucien followed that gesture and saw four Polypuses floating down, their hair-like tentacles waving in an imperceptible breeze.

"How?"

"They ripped out its heart," Garek replied.

Lucien blinked in shock, and his gaze strayed back to the bloody mound of flesh beside Garek and Addy. Now he saw it for what it really was: a giant heart.

* * *

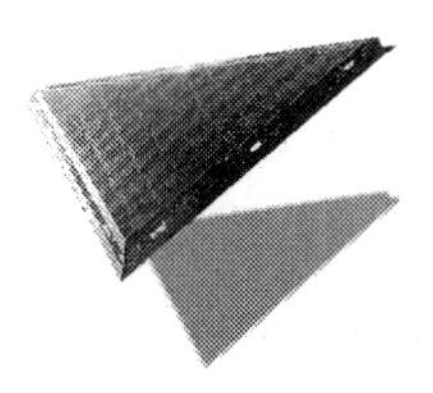

Astralis

"This emergency session of council is now in session," Chief Councilor Ellis declared.

Tyra resisted the urge to sigh. Her gaze wandered to the bird's eye view of the four cities through the transparent floor of the council chamber. Her inattention was a silent form of protest. Here she was, attending yet another emergency session of council—two in as many days. The last one had dragged on for almost six hours, and she'd been falling asleep by the time it had ended. After that, she'd still had to work well into the morning coming up with new legislation to regulate cloning in the wake of Ellis's proposal. Hopefully this time they'd be able to get through the agenda faster. Tyra dragged her eyes up, forcing herself to pay attention to the proceedings.

"...are well on our way to getting back out there. I'm told that all of our former Paragons have agreed to have their clones join the new expeditionary force, and we have hundreds of other applicants signing up by the hour. At this rate, we'll have to start putting them on reserve for future missions."

"*All* of the Paragons agreed?" Tyra asked, blinking in shock.

"That's correct," Ellis replied.

Tyra accepted the news with a shallow nod. She felt an accompanying flash of anger at her husband. They'd talked about it just a few hours ago, right before he'd left to attend the meeting with the other Paragons. She'd explained all of her concerns to him, but he'd decided to go ahead and sign up, anyway.

"First up on the agenda, I have a motion from Councilor Kato S'var of District One, petitioning for a formal declaration of war against the Farosien Empire," Ellis said.

Kato nodded, half of his face still pink where the flesh had been re-grown after he'd suffered third degree burns in the Faros' attacks. District One had been hit the hardest by the bomb that had ripped Fallside open, and Kato was understandably biased against the Faros, but Tyra didn't think any of the other councilors would be against formally declaring war.

"Let's vote on it, shall we?" Ellis asked. "All in favor?" He raised his hand, and so did everyone else. "It's unanimous, then. Let the record show that *Astralis* is now officially at war with the Farosien Empire."

The councilors nodded and murmured their agreement.

"Moving on, we have another motion from Councilor S'var, calling for the execution of the Faro prisoners we have on board... I believe we addressed this issue in our last emergency session of council. There were six votes for and seven against dispensing with the prisoners. Are you suggesting we retake the vote?"

Councilor S'var nodded. "They must be made to answer for their crimes. Publicly if possible."

Ellis arched an eyebrow at S'var. "All right. Let's have

another vote."

The vote came out exactly the same as it had the last time, with six in favor and seven against.

"It's settled, then. I trust that we won't need to re-take this vote again tomorrow?" Ellis asked S'var. He responded with a scowl and looked away.

"Good..." Ellis trailed off and cocked his head, as if listening to something only he could hear. "Well, that's good timing," he said after a moment.

"What's good timing?" Councilor Romark of Winterside asked.

"The Speaker of the House just informed me of the result of their deliberations. They've approved the Emergency War Measures Act, which I suppose will be going into effect now thanks to Councilor S'var's motion."

The councilors shot each other bewildered looks.

"What War Measures Act?" Tyra asked.

Ellis frowned and met the councilors' confusion with a measure of his own. "The one we all drafted in our last session of council..."

Looks of dawning realization replaced the councilors' confusion, and they began nodding slowly, murmuring at their absent-mindedness. Tyra wasn't so easily assured.

"What War Measures Act?" she insisted.

"Since everyone seems to be having so much trouble remembering..." Ellis reached into one of the pockets of his ceremonial robes and withdrew a holo projector. He tossed it toward the center of the room, and it hovered into place. A moment later, the document in question appeared as a three-dimensional hologram that seemed to be facing everyone at once. Ellis made a scrolling gesture with one finger until he reached the bottom of the document, where all of the councilors' signatures appeared, followed by hundreds more signatures from the House of Representatives.

Tyra blinked in shock. Now she remembered, but somehow the memory felt alien and *wrong*. Signing the act didn't sound like something she would do, and she found it hard to believe that any of the other councilors would sign it either. The Emergency War Measures Act gave Ellis the ability to overrule the council unilaterally in the event of war on all defense-related decisions. With that act in place, his only advisers would be Admiral Stavos and General Graves.

The council had essentially handed all of their political powers and responsibilities to Chief Councilor Ellis during wartime, and now conveniently, a war had been declared.

It smelled like a setup to Tyra. One by one, she glanced at the other councilors, her gaze challenging each of them as it traveled around the room. "You *all* remember signing this?"

The councilors' heads bobbed, but confusion warred on their faces, belying those acknowledgments.

"I understand we've all been under a lot of pressure and stress lately," Ellis said. "Perhaps this should be the last emergency session of council for a while. I think a good night's rest is in order for all of us."

Tyra turned back to Ellis, working hard to conceal her shock and suspicion. She failed utterly. "I guess we *will* be able to get more sleep now that you'll be making all of the decisions for us."

Ellis smiled thinly at that. "Not *all* of the decisions, Councilor Ortane. Just the war-related ones, and you can rest assured that even with those decisions, I will still value all of your input."

Value, but not listen to? Tyra wondered. Dread wormed through her stomach.

Somehow Ellis had managed to strike a killing blow against democracy while everyone was watching. They'd all literally signed off on it, but Tyra could barely remember giving her signature, and she obviously wasn't alone.

But that wasn't even the strangest part. The majority of the House of Representatives had also signed the War Measures Act, and there were more than four hundred representatives in the House. How was it possible that all of them had consciously voted for the proposal, knowing full well that they'd be paving the way for a military dictatorship?

Thanks to the War Measures Act and subsequent declaration of war, Ellis, Stavos, and Graves were now the sole authorities on *Astralis*. As far as Tyra was concerned, that was no coincidence. Those three were the same three that the Faros had fought so hard to reach. All three of them had been touched by the Faros.

And Atara. Horror and outrage flashed through Tyra with renewed force, but she clamped down on it, determined not to draw attention to herself.

She looked around the council chamber, watching the other councilors' faces as Ellis went blithely through the rest of an otherwise mundane agenda.

Every single councilor wore an expression that reflected some part of what Tyra was now feeling. And yet, no one said anything.

Tyra had already challenged Ellis once, sarcastically, but he'd pretended not to notice. What would happen if someone challenged him again, but more forcefully this time? Would Ellis call in security and have them escorted from the room? Or would he appear to tolerate dissenting voices only to have them conveniently silenced later?

It was finally clear what the Faros had been after when they'd invaded *Astralis.* They were slavers through and through, but when they'd realized they didn't have the numbers to take the ship by force, they'd decided to do so politically by subverting their leaders. An insidious plot if there ever was one. But if that was true, they could have called in reinforcements to finish the job long ago.

So why hadn't they?

What else were they planning?

And was it too late to stop them?

Tyra considered what had happened so far. Twelve councilors, including herself, *remembered* signing the War Measures Act, and four hundred plus representatives from the House had just done the same thing, but had anyone actually signed anything? The signatures could have been forged, the memories of signing planted via their AR implants.

In order to do that, there needed to be more Faro agents on board besides Ellis, Stavos, and Graves. One of them had to be a high-ranking official in the Resurrection Center. Someone with high enough clearance to get in while no one was watching and alter people's memories—maybe even their personalities—in a way that no one would notice.

One name jumped to mind: Nora Helios, director of the Resurrection Center. It had to be her.

Now all Tyra had to do was prove it before Ellis realized she was on to him. But even if she succeeded, she needed someone else waiting to wrest control of the military from Stavos and Graves, to make sure they didn't get out a comms message calling for reinforcements from the Faros. Lieutenant Commander Wheeler, the one-time acting Commander of *Astralis* might be able to do that.

The pieces of a plan began sliding into place in Tyra's brain, but she stopped those thoughts in their tracks. She felt watched. If memories could be planted in her brain without her permission, then maybe someone could read her thoughts, too.

Just in case, Tyra went about de-activating her AR implant, and then her ARCs, but just before she deactivated them, an urgent message came in from Lucien—text only. She hurriedly scanned the contents, her horror mounting with every word: it was about Atara....

CHAPTER 34

Astralis

"You're the one who got hurt," Atara whined. "Why do I have to get an injection?" She struggled violently against the pair of nurses holding her down.

The probe technician stood off to one side, looking uncertain. "I thought you said she agreed to this? I can't administer a probe against her will without parental consent."

"I already gave you my consent," Lucien insisted. Theola began squirming in his arms, unsettled by her sister's cries.

"I'm afraid I need *both* parents' consent if the child is unwilling, Mr. Ortane. I only have your word for it that your wife has agreed to the treatment."

Atara went on kicking and screaming on the examination table, her back arching as she struggled to break free. The two nurses holding her down each received a couple of kicks for their trouble before they gave up. Atara sprang up from the table, sobbing, and ran out of the probe room.

The nurses both followed Atara out, sending Lucien dirty looks as they left.

He turned to the technician. "Look, it's going to take too long to get my wife's signature. I already explained what's been going on. Atara was touched by one of the Faros, and she hasn't been herself ever since. She's a security risk to everyone on board this ship."

The technician looked unimpressed. Images flickered over his eyes as he looked something up on his ARCs. "Your daughter's file says she lives in Fallside, is that correct?"

"Used to."

"Of course," the technician said, nodding sympathetically. "And I assume she's going to a new school, has to make new friends, and has a new home..."

Lucien's eyes narrowed, and he leveled an accusing finger at the technician. "I see where you're going with that, but I know my daughter, and she's *not* herself."

"I'm sure you do know her, Mr. Ortane, but you need to understand that she's suffered multiple traumas and dramatic life changes over the past few days." More images flickered across the technician's eyes. "I see here that there's even a psychiatric evaluation on file. It details an incident whereby Atara witnessed a Navy corpsman beheaded right in front of her."

Lucien gaped at the technician, who began nodding with the wisdom of his own reasoning.

"Given all of that, it would be strange if Atara *weren't* acting out. Perhaps you need to schedule extra sessions with her therapist? I see she's being seen by a doctor by the name of... *Troosssaka'arrr.*" The technician's brow furrowed as he failed to pronounce the name. He repeated it to see if he could do better justice. He didn't. "Troo, for short," he decided, giving up. "She's an alien, but her references and credentials are excellent. Shall I call her for you? Or would you prefer that Atara be seen by a human doctor this time?"

Lucien shook his head and glanced over his shoulder to the door, wondering where Atara had run to. "I'd better go after her," he said.

The technician inclined his head agreeably. "Of course. If there's nothing else..."

Lucien started to leave, and the technician followed him out. Once they were in the hallway, Lucien saw his daughter seated in the waiting room a few feet away, her head in her hands, sobbing. One of the nurses who'd been the recipient of Atara's kicks was sitting beside her, a hand rubbing Atara's back. The nurse saw Lucien, and glared.

"You should see to your daughter, sir," the nurse said. "She is extremely distraught."

Lucien took half a step in their direction, and Atara looked up. Her eyes were dry, the hint of a smirk on her face.

Lucien spun around to look for the probe technician, to point out his daughter's disingenuous behavior, but the man was already walking away, off to see his next patient.

That's it, Lucien decided. He held up a hand to the nurse sitting with Atara, indicating that she needed to wait. Then he texted Tyra over his ARCs to make sure Atara didn't overhear what he said. He explained the situation, and the fact that he needed Tyra's consent to perform the probe. He finished by saying, *Atara isn't herself. First Theola, then me. I'm afraid to take her home and find out what she'll do next. Have any of the others who were touched been doing or saying anything strange?* When he was done composing his message, he marked it *urgent,* hoping Tyra would answer him promptly.

To his relief, she texted him back almost immediately.

I'm in a meeting. Can we talk about this when I get home?

Lucien frowned. *I'm at the hospital now. It would be nice not to have to come back again tomorrow.*

Atara's behavior is something we should discuss together before we submit her to more tests. I need to go, but we will talk about this later. I promise.

Lucien sighed. *Fine.*

I'll get home as soon as I can. I love you.

Love you, too... Lucien replied.

He turned back to find Atara sitting alone in the waiting room, the nurse having moved on with her day.

"Ready to go home?" he asked brightly.

Atara regarded him warily as he approached. "What about the probe? Who were you talking to?"

Lucien frowned. "Your mother."

"You told her."

"Of course I did. You tripped me and I broke a finger!"

Atara's eyes narrowed swiftly at him, and she crossed her arms over her chest. "I didn't trip you."

Lucien swallowed a sigh and took a seat beside Atara. Theola started smacking her sister and giggling.

"Stop it!" Atara snapped. "Dad!"

Lucien grabbed Theola's hand to stop her, and she started crying and struggling to break free of his grip. He let go of her hand, and she began smacking her sister again.

"Theola's being bad, too," Atara said, leaning away, out of her sister's reach. "Maybe you should have *her* probed."

Lucien shook his head. "No one's getting probed. Let's go home."

Atara re-crossed her arms over her chest and looked away, pouting. "Not until you say sorry."

"Okay... I'm sorry, Atara."

She glanced at him, then broke into a grin and wrapped him in a fierce hug. "It's okay. I forgive you."

Something melted inside of Lucien, and suddenly he felt bad. Maybe he was imagining things. Maybe Atara hadn't tripped him. Maybe he'd tripped over his own feet. And maybe her opening the window and freezing Theola hadn't been deliberate. Maybe it was all in his head and *he* was the problem.

Theola started crying again as the hug lingered and invaded her personal space. Lucien eased away and took Atara's hand to lead her back through the hospital. As they went, Atara skipped along beside him, looking like any ordinary five-year-old.

I'm definitely imagining things, he decided, but his instincts said otherwise. He decided to put them to the test. *Any good police officer knows how to coax a confession.*

"You know, Atara," he said slowly, his tone as mild as he could make it. "I know you tripped me by accident. You were just scared to tell me, weren't you?"

Atara stopped skipping and looked up at him, her eyes wide.

"You can tell me. I won't get mad. I promise."

A sly look crossed Atara's face at that. "You promise?"

He nodded, smiling. "I promise."

"No matter what?"

Lucien's instincts were screaming again, but he tried not to let it show. "No matter what, sweetheart."

"Okay. In that case, it wasn't an accident." Atara went back to skipping again.

Lucien's hand felt suddenly cold and numb. Her hand went sliding out from his as he stopped walking. "You did it on purpose?" he asked, frozen in shock.

Atara stopped and turned back to him, her brow knitted, and lips pressed in an angry line. "You promised you wouldn't get mad."

He nodded woodenly, and then switched to shaking his head. "I'm not mad... why would you want to trip me?"

"You're always yelling," Atara explained. "You hurt my feelings. I wanted you to hurt, too. I'm sorry now, though."

"Why's that... why are you sorry?"

"'Cause now you're being nice."

Lucien nodded as if that made all the sense in the world.

"Let's have ice cream!" Atara said.

"Maybe later," Lucien said, walking on in a daze, and reaching for Atara's hand again.

"No, now!" Atara screamed, and punched his leg.

Lucien took a deep breath and counted to three. It took all of his will to smile sweetly at Atara and hide what he was really feeling. His instincts had been spot on, but now they were telling him something else: his daughter was a sociopath, and you don't challenge a sociopath until you're safe from reprisals. "Okay. Let's go get ice cream."

"Goody!" Atara grabbed his hand and tugged on his arm, pulling him along behind her. They left the hospital without further incident. A blast of frigid air took Lucien's breath away as he exited the ER, but it was nothing compared to the cold he felt spreading inside of him. He withdrew his hand from Atara's to hug Theola close and keep her warm—and safe.

They crossed the hospital parking lot with Atara skipping again, once again looking like a normal, carefree five-year-old. Anyone watching them would have seen exactly that.

But Lucien knew the truth.

The Faros had done something to her. There was no more room for doubt about that. Lucien bit down on his lip to the point of pain, clamping down on the wave of misery and despair that thought sent coursing through him. He would find a way to bring her back.

He had to.

CHAPTER 35

Mokar: Underworld

The Polypuses hovered, their luminous bodies peeling back the night with a dim blue-white glow. Their hair-like tentacles waved in a breeze that only they could feel.

"What are they doing?" Addy whispered.

"Waiting for something," Garek said.

Lucien stepped to the fore. "Thank you for your help," he said via his suit's external speakers, and subsequently wondered if they would understand him. He was wearing one of the Faro translator bands, but none of them were.

"I don't think they can hear you," Addy said. "They exist in a higher dimension."

"But they can obviously still interact with our dimensions," Lucien pointed out.

One of the four Polypuses floated out to greet him.

That's progress, he thought.

"We don't mean you any harm," he went on. "We want to know more about you and your species."

The light emanating from the creature dimmed and then brightened a few times, but there was no way to know what that might mean. Maybe it was some kind of visual language? If it was, his translator wasn't picking up on it.

Lucien shook his head. "I'm sorry, I don't understand."

The creature brightened and dimmed once more, then it began drifting closer.

"Lucien..." Addy said, her voice rising in warning.

"If they wanted to kill us, they could have done it a long time ago," Lucien said.

He waited for the Polypus to reach him. As it did so, it reached out with a pair of tentacles. They skittered over Lucien's face, raising the hair on the back of his neck. Lucien took deep breaths to calm his racing heart while he waited for the creature to finish its examination.

"Ask it to remove our tracking devices," Garek suggested.

Lucien's eyes darted to Garek. One of the creatures was creeping up behind him, while the other two appeared to be circling around behind Addy and Brak. Four Polypuses for the four of them. Somehow Lucien didn't think that was a coincidence.

"Why don't you ask them yourself?" Lucien suggested, and gave a shallow nod to indicate the alien creeping up behind Garek. The Veteran whirled to face the creature, both arms snapping up to track the threat with his laser cannons.

Brak drew his sword and faced the Polypus approaching him, while Addy began retreating slowly from hers.

"Our weapons won't do anything to them," Lucien said. "Besides, they're not going to hurt us."

"You don't know that," Addy said. "They might be what killed all of those Faros we found."

"I bet they are," Lucien said, as his Polypus went on examining him with its tentacles. "But we're not Faros, and we don't have the same intentions that they do."

"These guys might not know that," Garek said, but his arms fell reluctantly to his sides.

Brak swiped his sword at the Polypus that had chosen him, but the blade passed right through the creature and out the other side.

Meanwhile, Lucien's Polypus crept closer still, completely filling his field of view with its light. Lucien saw swirling currents and patterns in the light, but that brightness quickly swelled and overwhelmed him, making it impossible to see anything but blinding white. Lucien felt a spreading warmth and a profound sense of peace course through his entire being.

The brightness faded dramatically, and images began flashing through his mind's eye; he saw Abaddon. The Faro King was seated on a throne, his glowing blue eyes sharp, his regal features stretched into a broad grin.

Lucien recognized that throne and its surroundings. It was Etherus's throne from the Etherian palace in the facet of *Halcyon,* back on New Earth. Lucien shook his head, but he couldn't feel the movement. It was as though he was no longer in his own body.

"What is this?" he asked aloud, but the words reverberated back to his ears a hundred times, echoes piling on top of echoes.

The image faded, and Lucien saw another place he recognized: a clear blue sky overhead, and white cobblestone streets sparkling in the sun below. The street was lined with picturesque cafeterias, restaurants, and shops, and colorful blossom trees from a dozen different worlds spreading intermittent shade. Hover cars landed and took off from rooftops almost-soundlessly in futuristic ballet, and Etherian families strolled lazily down the street.

This was the city square on Ashram, the planet in Etheria where his half-brother, Atton, lived with his family.

While Lucien watched, the scene flashed white, as if from an explosion. Details gradually re-emerged, but now the blue sky was black and clogged with smoke. Ash fell like snow, dusting the pristine white cobblestones. The blossom trees were on fire, and so were the buildings to either side of the street. Etherians lay dead and dismembered under thickening blankets of ash, while groups of Faros in black robes picked their way through the carnage, their transparent swords drawn and shimmering. Elementals. Up ahead a familiar gray-robed figure stood on a mound of bodies. He raised his sword and pumped it in the air, shouting, "Vengeance is *mine!*" The crowd of Elementals stopped and cheered, pumping their swords in the air, too.

Lucien felt a growing sense of bewilderment and despair as he watched the Faros cheer. This couldn't have already happened. The Polypus was showing him the future, or at least a *possible* future.

Lucien felt a comforting warmth spreading through him with that thought, as if to confirm it.

We're not going to let this happen, Lucien said. He felt

another flash of warmth from the Polypus, and the scene faded to a new one. He saw a vast fleet of hundreds of starships floating in space with nothing around them, and barely enough light from the nearest sun to illuminate their shining silver hulls. Those mirror-smooth, highly-reflective hulls were a trademark of Etherian starships. *The lost fleet,* Lucien thought, marveling at the sight. As he watched, the ships vanished, having engaged some type of cloaking shields.

Lucien shook his head at that, but again he felt no movement to accompany the gesture. *We need to get to that fleet,* he thought. *We have to take it back to Etheria so the Faros can't find it.*

Another flashed of warmth. The Polypus seemed pleased with that idea.

The scene of the fleet faded, and back was the blinding white light of the extra-dimensional alien. The light retreated slowly, and once again Lucien saw currents and patterns in the Polypus's radiance. Once the creature had retreated to about an arm's length, something small and metallic fell out of it.

Lucien bent to pick it up. He examined it in the light of the creature hovering before him and saw what looked to be a small disc-shaped microchip, no bigger than the tip of his pinky. He rubbed it between his fingers and found that it was flexible, easily deformed into different shapes. It would have been easy to swallow something like that in his food and not notice.

"Looks like they found my tracker," Lucien said. He turned to find Garek and Addy each examining matching microchips. Brak either didn't have a tracker or hadn't bothered to pick his up after the Polypus had extracted it.

Garek snorted and dropped his microchip to crush it under the heel of his boot.

Addy tossed her microchip aside, and Lucien did likewise.

"Did anyone else just experience some kind of vision?" Addy asked.

"Yesss," Brak hissed. "I see the Faros reach New Earth. I see them round up the Gors and take them away as slavesss."

"I saw my parents in Etheria," Addy put in quietly. "The Faros killed them. And everyone else."

"They showed me *Astralis*," Garek put in. "It was surrounded by Faro ships, but then it somehow managed to jump away and escape."

"I wonder if that's what actually happened?" Lucien mused.

"What did you see?" Addy asked, nodding at him.

"I saw Abaddon in Halcyon, sitting on Etherus's throne, and then I saw a city from Etheria. It was in ruins with Faros standing over dead Etherians and cheering."

They spent a moment trading solemn looks with one another, while the four Polypuses hovered just a few feet away, waiting.

"What does all of it mean?" Addy asked.

"I think they were showing us the future," Lucien said. "Except for Garek. He might have seen the past." Lucien turned to the Polypus in front of him. "I'm right, aren't I?" The creature grew momentarily brighter.

"How do we know if that's a yes or a no?" Addy asked.

"Good point." Facing the Polypus, he said, "Yes is brighter. No is darker."

The Polypus glowed brighter once more.

"So they can predict the future?" Garek asked, sounding skeptical.

Lucien considered that. "If they exist outside of time, or can somehow see the future, it would make them gods."

"Then maybe they *are* gods," Addy said. The creature in front of her glowed darker. "Or not..." Addy amended, glancing at the Polypus.

"Gods or not, their extra-dimensionality makes them a force to be reckoned with," Lucien said. "Maybe Etherus sent them to guard the lost fleet?" The Polypus in front of him glowed brighter at that.

"What are you?"

"I don't think that's a yes or no question," Garek said.

"They can show us things in our minds," Lucien replied. "They could explain with pictures. Show us who or what you are," Lucien suggested, trying not to sound too demanding.

The creature in front of him grew darker.

"I think they're done with explanations," Addy said.

Her Polypus glowed brighter.

"Then what are they waiting for?" Lucien asked.

"They want us to decide what we're going to do about what we saw," Addy suggested.

Again, her Polypus glowed brighter.

"I told them we wouldn't let what I saw come to pass," Lucien said, "that we'd take the fleet back to Etheria to make sure the Faros couldn't use it."

All four Polypuses glowed brighter at that, and more of

the extra-dimensional aliens came drifting down from the sky, out of the silver-treed forest, and *through* the seamless black walls of the tower beside them. Now the Polypuses were a dazzling sea of light everywhere Lucien looked.

"I think they like your idea," Addy said slowly.

"What about *Astralis?*" Garek asked.

"You saw them escape, right?" Lucien said.

"Right..."

"Then they're safe for now. We need to return the fleet to Etheria before we go looking for them."

All of the Polypuses glowed brighter at once, making Lucien's eyes ache. His faceplate auto-polarized in response.

"And after that? How do we get back to rescue them?" Garek demanded.

"We can ask Etherus to help us," Lucien suggested. Again the Polypuses glowed brighter.

Garek snorted. "By sending another fleet that could be traced back to Etheria? Sounds like going in circles to me."

The Polypuses darkened.

"Maybe Etherus will ask New Earth to send a rescue fleet instead," Lucien said.

The aliens glowed brighter.

"These guys seem to know a lot about what Etherus would and wouldn't do..." Garek said. "How do we know we can trust them?"

"They saved our lives once," Lucien pointed out. "And they saved mine twice."

"Maybe they saved us so we could come here and relieve them of guard duty," Garek said. "I'm sure extra-dimensional aliens have better things to do than hang around here, waiting for Faros to show up."

"There's no way they could have planned for us coming here," Addy said. "That was Katawa's doing. And probably Abaddon's."

Another flash of brightness from the Polypuses.

"It doesn't matter how we ended up here, or why," Lucien decided. "If we don't take the lost fleet back to Etheria, Abaddon might find it, and then the future we saw will come to pass. There are trillions of lives at stake in Etheria and the rest of the Etherian Empire, and only a few hundred million on *Astralis*."

"Fine. You win," Garek said. He turned in a circle to address the waiting aliens with an open-handed shrug. "So? How do we get to this missing fleet?"

One of the Polypuses bobbed to the fore and dropped something at Garek's feet. It hit the ground with a *thunk,* and rolled to a stop at the tip of his left boot. It was a glossy silver ball, just big enough to hold comfortably in one hand.

That done, the Polypuses began swarming back up into the sky, streaming toward the blue-white ball of light at the top of the tower. Lucien watched them go, marveling at how many of them there were. At least a thousand. Probably more.

Garek bent to examine the ball at his feet, but made no move to pick it up.

Lucien walked over to take a look, and Addy and Brak joined him. Soon they were all standing over the device, trying to figure out what it was.

"That must be the key to the gateway," Addy said.

"You sure about that?" Garek asked, arching an eyebrow at her.

"Pretty sure. What else could it be?"

"If it is a key, then how do we use it? And where is this

damn gateway, anyway?" Garek replied.

Lucien reached out to touch the silver ball. As soon as his fingertips grazed the mirror-smooth surface of it, an image flashed into his mind's eye of him flying up to the top of the tower and throwing the ball into the light source at the center of the underworld. Moments later, the artificial light exploded to a hundred times its size, becoming a shimmering, spherical portal—a window into the bridge of a starship, an *Etherian* starship, if the familiar glossy white deck and the simulated, dome-shaped viewport above that were anything to go by.

"I know what to do," Lucien said, and snatched up the silver ball.

"Yeah?" Garek asked, sounding more skeptical than ever. "Did one of your extra-dimensional squid friends whisper something in your ear?

"Follow me," Lucien said, ignoring Garek's sarcasm. He triggered his grav boosters at max thrust and shot into the air. Glancing at his sensor display, he noticed the others were flying up after him.

"Where are we going?" Addy asked over the comms.

"Through the gateway to the lost fleet," Lucien replied, as if that should be obvious. He looked up, keeping his gaze fixed on the blue-white orb of light overhead. The smooth black sides of the tower raced by, faster and faster as he picked up speed.

Thanks to their grav boosters, they didn't need to get inside that tower to use the key. The Polypuses must have known that, because they hadn't bothered to show them a way inside.

In a matter of minutes, Lucien reached the top of the tower and stopped to hover directly in front of the artificial moon, but it no longer looked like a moon. Light flowed in rivers from the tops of the two towers, racing in circles to form a swirling vortex. The gravity here was almost non-existent, but Lucien could have sworn he felt a subtle tug pulling him *toward* the light. He gazed into the vortex, momentarily mesmerized by it.

The others came hovering up beside him.

"Now what?" Addy asked.

Lucien glanced at her, and then threw the silver ball as hard as he could into the vortex. It quickly vanished against the glare.

"What did you do that for?!" Addy screamed.

He had just enough time to question himself, imagining their one and only key to the gateway dropping straight down ten kilometers, and picking up speed on its way to shatter on the castcrete below.

But then the swirling vortex of light rippled, and abruptly expanded to a hundred times its size, just as he'd seen it would do when he'd touched the key. Now a shimmering, translucent skin was all that remained of the artificial moon, giving them a clear view into a giant, spherically-distorted portal. On the other side of that portal lay the bridge of an Etherian starship.

"Well, that's new," Garek said, sounding taken aback.

"Yesss..." Brak agreed.

Lucien understood those sentiments perfectly. This wasn't a quantum junction that would teleport them from one place to another after making the necessary spatial and quantum calculations. It wasn't even one of the antiquated SLS space gates that the Imperium of Star Systems had left littering the Milky Way before the Sythian invasion.

This was an entirely new technology, a persistent portal from one place to another, a doorway that could be opened and shut at will—just as long as you had the key.

Lucien turned to regard the others. "Ready?"

"On three," Addy replied.

Lucien flashed her a grin. "On two—one... two!"

And with that, they all boosted straight into the shimmering portal.

CHAPTER 36

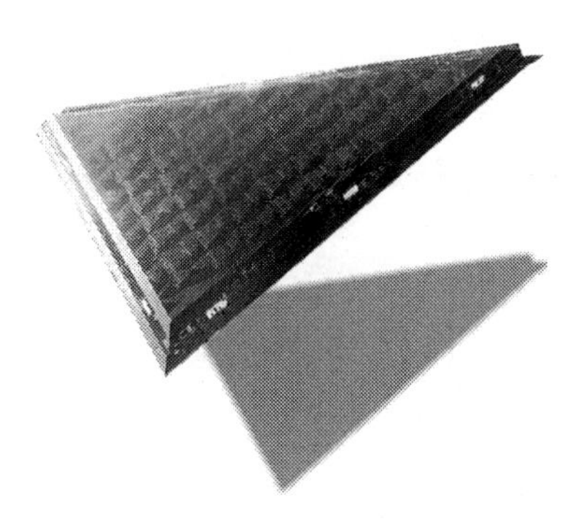

Astralis

The room was utterly dark. Chief Councilor Ellis sat in an armchair beside a real, floor-to-ceiling viewport in the outer hull of *Astralis.*

And so, too, sat Abaddon.

He'd booked this luxury hotel suite in District One under the guise of showing his support to residents who'd lost their homes and businesses when the Faros' bomb had ripped a hole in the hull.

Abaddon gazed out the viewport, surveying his kingdom. Countless bright specks of light gazed back at him, but he barely noticed. Most people looked out at space and saw the stars, their eyes drawn to those comforting specks of light, but when Abaddon looked out, all he saw was a vast sea of darkness, gathering to snuff out the light.

Abaddon smiled—or tried to—the corners of his mouth

refused to obey, twitching reluctantly as Ellis resisted, but that battle of wills only lasted for a second. *He* was in control of this body, just as he was now in control of *Astralis.* In just one day he'd gone from the glorified mouthpiece for *Astralis's* bloated representative democracy to its sole ruler.

It was almost depressing how easy it had all been, but Abaddon had to remind himself that the real challenge lay in defeating Etherus—not in subjugating this small band of humans.

Now that Abaddon and his like-minded cohorts were in sole command of *Astralis,* they could proceed more openly with their plans.

Just over an hour ago, Abaddon had ordered General Graves to head over to Hangar Bay 18, where the Farosien boarding shuttles were being kept; there he had Graves retrieve a portable long-range comms unit from one of the shuttles and deliver it here.

The blocky unit now sat on the table beside his chair, its green status lights glowing—ready and waiting. Faro comms technology was a lot faster than the human variety. Unfortunately, it could still be jammed and detected, so Abaddon had needed to make a few arrangements before using the device.

First, he got Admiral Stavos to turn off *Astralis's* outbound comms jamming. Next he'd arranged for a power surge to take down the power in District One, so that his use of the device and the message he sent wouldn't be detected by *Astralis's* comms operators.

Now, with that done, Abaddon was ready to send his message. He turned and activated the comm unit. A holographic control panel sprang to life above the device, and he hurried to enter the coordinates for Mokar. When he was finished, he recorded his transmission.

"Katawa, it's Abaddon. What news do you have of your search for the lost fleet? I have a brief window to speak without being detected. Do not transmit more than once, and do not send a reply if it will arrive more than an hour after this one." Abaddon sent the message.

The comm unit estimated the arrival time to be just a little under fifteen minutes. That was remarkable considering the tens of billions of light years between *Astralis* and Mokar. That feat of near-instant communication wasn't accomplished by the Faro's superior technology, but by their application of it.

Abaddon's message would be relayed to Mokar along the *quantanet,* a network of relays with pre-calculated connections that provided a hyper-fast solution to interstellar travel and communications in the Farosien Empire. Of course, the *quantanet* was too dangerous to let just anyone have access to, so Abaddon reserved use of the network to himself and those he personally authorized.

Barely half an hour later, the comm unit chimed with Katawa's message, and Abaddon queued it for playback. Katawa must have seen his message and replied almost immediately. The little gray alien's halting voice rippled out of the unit's speakers moments later.

"Abaddon. The humans became suspicious of me. I was able to strand them in the underworld. They reached the gateway and made contact with the guardians, who then found and removed the humans' tracking devices just as you predicted. Two of the trackers survived removal, and I was able to detect the opening of the gateway. You were right about that as well. The guardians only attack when they read bad intentions in the minds of those who would use the gate."

Who needs bad intentions when you've got good ones? Abaddon thought, smiling. *The road to the netherworld has to be paved with something.*

Katawa went on, "I do not understand how this helps you reach the lost fleet, but I have done my part. You will release my people now and grant them full citizenship in the empire. I await news that this has occurred. If it does not happen promptly, I will go down to the underworld and warn the guardians myself."

Abaddon's lips curled into a sneer at the threat, but he had no intention of reneging on their deal. What did emancipating a few billion slaves matter? There were countless trillions more where they'd come from, and soon he'd have the Etherians to replace them, anyway.

Abaddon hurriedly composed two more messages: one to Katawa, reassuring the spiteful little alien, and another to issue the emancipation order for the Grays, and to request that a ship be sent to Mokar to pick up Katawa.

He sent both messages and then shut off the device. That done, he reclined his chair and folded his hands over his chest. Everything was proceeding according to plan. Now all he had to do was wait for the Etherian Fleet to come to him.

It was a detestably passive plan, but thanks to the mind-reading ghosts guarding the gateway, there was no active way to reach the fleet. Until now, everyone he'd sent after it had been killed—Faros, Elementals, Abaddons, Grays, Mokari... It didn't matter who he sent, the problem was that *he'd* sent them, and the guardians of the gate could tell.

This time was different. This time, the people he sent

weren't working for him. Perhaps even more importantly, they were humans, and citizens of the Etherian Empire, so the guardians weren't suspicious of them.

But that would be their undoing. Abaddon knew Garek well enough from having looked into his mind that he'd use the fleet to come straight to *Astralis,* and as for Lucien, Abaddon didn't even need to look into his mind to know what he would do. He knew Lucien as well as he knew himself.

Wipe a man's memories and give him a fresh slate, and watch him slide back into his old ways. Abaddon, Lucien, the Devil... Ellis, Stavos, Graves... he went by many names, and all of those instances of his existence had a common body of experiences and memories to draw upon. All except for a few scattered individuals in human bodies.

Etherus had told him what he was doing, recreating him in human bodies to see what they would do. When those people hadn't turned into sociopaths, Etherus had shared the results of the experiment, as if to say, *this is who you could have been.*

Abaddon sneered.

Etherus thought he was proving a point with that, but it proved nothing. The experiment was still in its infancy. It had taken more than a billion years before he'd grown bored enough with paradise to rebel against Etherus.

And how long had humans been around? Better yet, how long had they been immortal, with lives long enough to truly appreciate the fathomless boredom that he had suffered?

No, Etherus hadn't proved anything yet. Lucien Ortane and his father, Ethan, might have had all the same initial conditions as he, but they were missing the critical factor of his experiences.

Give them the same life to live, and they'll make all of the same so-called evil choices as I have.

But where was the root of that evil? In the choices that he, Abaddon, had made? Or in the person that Etherus had created to command his army?

The problem was simple: if Etherus was good, and God, and all-powerful, then how was it possible that he had created Abaddon, who was evil?

It was nature versus nurture. If the flaw lay in Etherus's creation and the initial characteristics of Abaddon's being, then Etherus was to blame, but if the flaw lay in Abaddon's choices, then Abaddon was to blame.

But of course, then comes determinism to prove that free will doesn't exist, and therefore good and evil don't exist, so either way Etherus can't judge me. Deep down he knows it. That's why he and his people are all hiding in a corner while the rest of the universe burns. It's impossible to lead a crusade without the strength of true conviction.

In that moment the lights snapped back on, and the darkness fled. Blinking spots from his eyes, Ellis arched an eyebrow at the ceiling. *Listening to my thoughts, were you?*

But he smirked at the absurdity of that thought. He'd long since stopped believing that Etherus was the almighty deity he claimed to be. Ghostly extra-dimensional allies notwithstanding, Abaddon was far more powerful than Etherus. Of the two of them, the only one who'd achieved anything close to omnipresence was *him*, Abaddon, with his billions of simultaneous instances.

Yet another reason for you to hide in your corner, Abaddon thought. *But you won't stay hidden for long. I'm coming for you,*

Etherus.

CHAPTER 37

The Lost Etherian Fleet

Lucien emerged from the portal a split second before the others did. The negligible gravity in the center of the underworld was suddenly replaced by a much stronger force, pulling him down to the deck of the ship. He tried to land feet-first, but ended up on his back, sprawled out against one of the bridge control stations. He watched as the others fell out of the shimmering portal, their arms and legs windmilling. Garek and Brak landed one on top of each other in a pile of tangled limbs and clattering armor, while Addy managed to perform a controlled somersault. She brushed off her suit and offered a hand to help Lucien up.

He took her hand and stood up, surveying the bridge. It was a perfect circle with two levels separated by a short flight of stairs. A dome-shaped viewport lay overhead, revealing a vast sea of stars and space. Lucien felt as if he were standing on an airless platform, adrift in deep space. Unnerved by the sensation, he walked around aimlessly to remind himself that there was gravity. He noted the warm glow of lights emanating from control stations, and from the glow strips in the floor. Gravity and lights meant power, so they weren't adrift in space. Looking behind them, Lucien saw the portal to the underworld shimmering, still open.

"I don't get it," Garek said. "This ship looks as new as the day it was built. I thought it's supposed to have been here for over ten thousand years?"

Lucien nodded and looked away from the portal. Had they left the lights and gravity on all this time? Did Etherian ships have unlimited fuel in their reactors? Most ships that Lucien had encountered ran on fusion power, but even fusion required a ready supply of fusionable materials.

"Do you think there's anyone on board?" Addy asked.

"There might be an easy way to find out," Lucien replied, and went to the control station in the center of the bridge. It was on the upper level where they'd emerged, and he guessed it had to be the captain's station.

He took a seat there, and holographic displays sprang to life all around him, emitted from projectors in the floor. The alphabet and language was Etherian, but thanks to the translator band he wore under his helmet, he was able to understand everything perfectly.

Lucien located the ship's sensor display where a *3D* star map appeared, crowded with green icons of friendly vessels. At the center of the map was a particularly large vessel, highlighted white. Lucien selected it, and found that the ship was called the *Gideon.* Ship schematics and technical readouts appeared on that screen. Lucien scanned through the information until he found what he was looking for.

"The ship's sensors show exactly four lifeforms on

board," he said.

Garek and Addy walked into Lucien's periphery, appearing to either side of his chair.

"What else can you see?" Garek asked, while peering over Lucien's shoulder at the sensor display.

Returning to the star map with all the green icons on it, he found a *contacts* panel in the top left of the display. A long list of contacts appeared, all of them green and friendly.

"There's one thousand and fifty seven friendly ships around us," Lucien said, reading the total number of friendly contacts at the bottom of the *contacts* panel. Sensors indicate they're all cloaked."

"Obviously not very well if we can detect them from here," Garek said.

Lucien nodded, still scanning the contact panel. "Most cloaking shields only hide ships from a distance. The fleet looks to be in a close formation..." Lucien trailed off. "These ships are all named after prominent figures in the Etherian codices."

"Makes sense, given where they came from," Garek replied.

Lucien selected the fleet as a group. It was called *Gideon's Army.* A table with information about the fleet appeared, giving each ship's name, range away from them, mass, ship class, shield strength, hull integrity, and crew.

Lucien scrolled through the list and found all of the ships to be in pristine condition with hull integrity and shields at a hundred percent. He also found the active crew count for each of the ships to be 0/###. The second number varied, but the first was always zero and highlighted in red. All except for one ship—the *Gideon.* It had a crew count of

4/9750. There were just four people on board the entire fleet—the four of them. "The fleet really is abandoned," Lucien said.

"How big are the ships in the fleet?" Garek asked.

Lucien turned back to the display. He tapped the top of the column labeled *mass,* and a set of alternative categories for size appeared—*beam, draft, length,* and *tonnage.* Lucien selected *length* and tapped the little arrow beside the column, assuming it would order the list by that category.

It did. "The smallest ships are only a few hundred meters long..." he said, scrolling down again, "but it looks like most of them are over a kilometer long." As he reached the bottom of the list he found more than a dozen ships that were even larger than that. "The biggest ones are over ten kilometers from bow to stern, and we're sitting on the largest of those, the *Gideon,* at fourteen kilometers long."

Garek nodded. "Well, well, looks like Katawa held up his end of the deal, after all. We've got our fleet: one thousand capital-class ships. I think it's time we go find *Astralis* and take the fight to the Faros, don't you?"

Lucien turned to Garek. "The Polypuses were clear. They only let us get here because we agreed to take the fleet back to Etheria."

"And we'll do that, but why not go get our people first? Then we won't have to come back and rescue them later."

"Because we might be detected by the Faros while we're out looking for them," Lucien said.

"We might also be detected along the way to Etheria. And if we are, it would be good to have these ships properly crewed so we stand a fighting chance."

Addy began nodding. "Garek has a point."

"The Polypuses wanted us to go straight back to Etheria. They showed us what would happen if the Faros found the fleet."

"And they showed *me* that *Astralis* escaped," Garek replied. "They must have known how I would react to that. If they're safe, then what's the harm in us going there first?"

"They showed you that they're safe to put your mind at ease, so you wouldn't think there was an urgent rush to go rescue them. We talked to the Polypuses about this. They clearly told us to go back to Etheria first."

Garek snorted. "Yeah... it was like having a conversation with a light bulb. How do you even know they understood us? Or that we understood them? What if they thought brighter was *no* and darker was *yes?*"

"You're deliberately confusing the issue," Lucien said. "I get your personal stake in all of this, but we're going to Etheria first. You want to do something else?" Lucien turned and pointed to the open portal behind him. "Go ahead. The door's still open."

But just as Lucien said that, the shimmering portal vanished. "Someone must have heard you," Garek said, smiling. "I guess they don't want me to go back."

"I think it is my fault," Brak said, and Lucien turned to see him on the level below, holding up the silver ball that was the key to the gateway.

Garek barked a laugh. "Nice job, big guy."

"There might still be a way to open the portal from here," Lucien said. "Anyway, it doesn't matter. We're not going back—and we're not going to *Astralis*."

"How about we vote on that?" Garek suggested. "We voted to join Katawa on this crazy quest in the first place, so it seems only fitting that we should vote to decide where we go next. All in favor of going to find *Astralis?*"

Garek raised his hand.

Addy's eyes flicked from him to Lucien and back. "I think Lucien's right. If the Polypuses can see the future and they wanted us to go to Etheria first, then it must be for a reason."

"Brak?" Garek prompted. "What do you think?"

"My people must never become slaves again. If that is what we risk by Abaddon finding the fleet, then we must return it to Etheria as quickly as possible."

"Fine," Garek gritted out and thrust an accusing finger in Lucien's face. "But if something happens to *Astralis,* it's on all of your heads!" With that, he stalked away, fuming.

"What's that?" Addy asked, as Lucien closed the contacts panel and returned to the star map. She pointed to one side of the cluster of green blips that was the Etherian fleet, to a region of brightness that dominated the right side of the map. "Are we orbiting a sun?"

"I don't know," Lucien admitted. He zoomed out the display until all one thousand and fifty seven green blips clustered together into a single green speck. From there he continued zooming out until that region of brightness coalesced into the familiar shape of an accretion disk. "Uh oh..." Lucien whispered.

"*Uh oh,* what? What's going on?" Garek demanded, stalking back over to them. Upon seeing the map, he went suddenly very still. "Krak..." he whispered.

Brak came up from the lower level of the bridge to see what had everyone so concerned. When he saw the display, he hissed with displeasure.

They all had enough experience with space travel to know what they were looking at. Accretion disks formed around black holes. Lucien tried selecting the black hole, and a pair of brackets appeared around it. Sensors reported its size to be more than a hundred million standard solar masses. Making matters worse, this black hole was spinning very fast.

Lucien remembered dealing with this type of black hole on a theoretical level at school while he'd been training to become a Paragon. They were dubbed *time machines* because the time dilation around them could be severe even at the range of safe, stable orbits. Most black holes only had extreme time dilation close to their event horizons, where the orbital velocity required to maintain a stable orbit was too high for any ship to safely reach.

"What's our time dilation?" Garek asked quietly.

Lucien spied a link at the bottom of the sensor display to something called *gravimetric readings.* He touched that with his index finger, and the display changed, showing a wireframe visual of the black hole's gravity field. The field was depicted as an infinitely deep funnel, which was technically only accurate in two-dimensions, but it worked well enough to illustrate the shape of space-time around the black hole. The green dot that represented the Etherian fleet lay along the steep, inward-sloping curve of the funnel. Radial lines in the wireframe were each marked a value for t=___, and according to the legend at thc bottom of the display, the "t" was for the *time dilation factor.*

The *t* values grew progressively larger as they approached the red radial line that coincided with the event horizon of the black hole, while the line closest to the fleet's location was marked with t=700, but they were sitting just past that line, heading toward the next one, marked t=800. Lucien tried selecting the green dot that represented the fleet, and he got a new value for *t*.

"Seven hundred and seventeen..." Garek whispered, reading the value. "So every second we spend here is..." he trailed off, and Lucien saw images flickering over his eyes as he ran the calculation on his ARCs. "Almost 12 minutes for a stationary observer!" Garek burst out.

"That means every minute is almost twelve hours," Addy said.

"What if we have to spend a day trying to figure out how to fly the fleet out of here?" Garek demanded. He paused, and Lucien saw images flickering over his eyes once more. "Almost *two years* will have passed for everyone on *Astralis!"*

"And Etheria," Addy said.

"Yeah, and then we still have to calculate the jump to Etheria for more than a thousand ships, and who knows how long that will take," Garek said.

Lucien shook his head, speechless. This definitely threw a corkscrew in their plans.

"What's ten thousand years with that time dilation factor?" Addy thought to ask.

Lucien ran the calculation on his ARCs—10,000 divided by 717. "A little less than fourteen years."

"So that's how long the fleet has been here from its own frame of reference," Addy said. "No wonder the Grays left the lights on. By the time these ships run out of power, another hundred thousand years will have passed for the rest of the universe."

"We'd better get started, then," Lucien said. "Every

moment we spend here trying to figure out how to get the fleet back to Etheria, Abaddon's going to have seven hundred and seventeen moments to find us. Addy—see if you can find the nav station."

"What's the point?" Garek demanded. "We can't move more than a thousand ships by ourselves! Even if we could, it would take too long."

"The Polypuses must have thought we could do it," Lucien countered. "I'm betting the ships are all set to follow each other, and since the gateway led to the largest ship in the fleet, it's probably the one that all the others are set to follow."

"That's just a wild guess!" Garek said. "The Grays might have had a pilot on board each of these ships when they maneuvered them into position."

"I found the nav station!" Addy called out.

Lucien turned from Garek to see Addy now seated at a control station on the level below. "Good. See if you can break orbit—*away* from the black hole."

"That goes without saying... powering engines..." A *whirring* noise started up somewhere deep below their feet, and quickly rose in pitch until it became a steady *thrumming* sound. "Setting thrust to seventy-five percent, and nosing up twenty degrees."

"What's *up?*" Lucien asked.

"*Away* from the black hole," Addy replied.

"Just checking."

Addy was figuring out the nav systems fast. As a Paragon she had plenty of flight training, but Lucien was surprised that the Etherian control systems were so intuitive.

"And?" Lucien prompted after a few seconds had passed. It was hard to believe each of those seconds was twelve minutes back on *Astralis.*

"You were right!" Addy said. "The other ships are following us!"

Lucien flashed a triumphant grin at Garek. "What'd I tell you?"

"Lucky guess," Garek mumbled.

Lucien shrugged. "It's what I would have done if I were planning to leave just one person at the helm of an entire fleet. He would have needed to be able to move the fleet easily by himself in case its location was discovered."

Garek snorted and turned his attention to Addy. "See if you can figure out how to plot a micro-jump and get us out of the time dilation zone."

"Yeah... I've already figured that out."

"That was fast," Lucien said.

"The controls are highly intuitive," Addy said. "Anyway, that's not the point. We can't jump out of here. Not yet, anyway."

Garek's eyes narrowed to slits. "Why not?"

"We're inside the magnetic field of the black hole."

Lucien grimaced.

"How far does the field reach?" Garek asked.

"That depends how much of a risk you want to take," Addy replied. "The chance of scattering if we jump from here is sixty-five percent."

"We can't risk that," Lucien said.

"The chances drop the farther out we get. If we plot a jump at five hundred light seconds from here, the probability of scattering drops to just ten percent."

"Five *hundred* light seconds?" Garek echoed. "What's our ETA to reach that point at max thrust?" Garek asked.

"Almost a full standard hour," Addy replied. "And that's probably an *Etherian* standard hour, which is even longer. By the time we get there, a month or more could have passed on *Astralis*, but that's probably a lot less than the overall time it will take for us to get this fleet back to Etheria."

"And just where is Etheria?" Garek asked. "Have any of you thought to check that yet?"

Lucien shook his head. "We're probably going to have to dig through the ship's star charts to find it. Why don't you and Brak go find control stations and help us look? We've got an hour to kill, we may as well use it for something."

Garek didn't need to be told twice. He stormed over to the nearest control station and took a seat. Brak hesitated for a moment before doing the same, and Lucien busied himself looking through various holo displays for the Etherian star charts.

After a few seconds, he found a link to something called *Universal Map.* He opened that, and was immediately greeted with a kind of pinched sphere, wrapped with stars. He blinked in shock, his heart suddenly racing with excitement. With all the drama surrounding their dealings with the Faros, they'd lost sight of their original goal in traveling beyond the Red Line. *Astralis's* mission was to discover the true nature of the universe, its shape, extent, and whatever else they could learn. And here, both its shape and extent were clearly marked.

The universe appeared to be wrapped around a distorted sphere, pinched together at the poles, and bulging out at the rim/equator, with an infinitesimally small hole in the center. It was a type of torus.

"I don't believe it..." Lucien whispered.

"What?" Garek called back.

"The universe," Addy replied. "It's... a donut?"

Lucien smiled at that. "A *horn torus*, actually, but yeah I guess that's kind of a donut." Lucien zoomed in on the torus and manipulated it with his hands, watching the stars glitter. "This is a *2D* simplification," he realized. "We can't picture a *3D* torus from the outside. We'd need to be able to see an extra spatial dimension to do that."

"Maybe we can ask the Polypuses what it looks like," Garek said.

"I don't think we'd understand their description even if they could explain," Lucien replied.

"Simplification or not, it conveys the concept clearly enough," Addy said. "Why's the bottom half of the map dark and fuzzy?"

Lucien studied the torus and frowned. Addy was right. The top half was bright with stars, but the bottom half was blurry and kind of grayed-out.

"I bet that's the *universe on the other side* that Oorgurak mentioned," Addy said.

Lucien nodded slowly. "I forgot about that."

"Whatever it is, it looks like not even the Etherians have been there," Garek said.

"I wonder why," Lucien mused. "Seems like you could get there easily enough..." Then he noticed the dark band of empty black nothingness running around the equatorial rim of the torus, separating the top from the bottom.

"The Great Abyss lies between the two universes," Addy said, again noticing the same things as him.

"So maybe it can't be crossed?" Garek suggested.

Lucien shook his head. "Maybe..." He found a search

button to one side of the display, and tapped it. A holographic keypad appeared in his lap, and he typed in *Etheria.*

A green dot appeared near the center of the torus, in the funnel-shaped hole leading up from the fuzzy bottom half.

"Etheria is—"

"On the other side of the universe," Addy finished for him.

"No wonder we've never been able to find it on our own," Lucien said.

"Fascinating. How long will it take us to get there?" Garek asked. "Try plotting a jump, see what the ship says."

"Hang on," Addy replied.

While he waited, Lucien played around with the Universal Map, zooming in to smaller and smaller scales. He picked a random spiral galaxy, and from there a random star...

Only to be assaulted by a plethora of information about the system, its sun, planets, moons, intelligent species, governments, space stations... even large starships were listed on the contacts panel of the star system. As he watched, one of those ships disappeared, and the locations of the others shifted subtly as they moved through space.

Lucien blinked in shock. The system wasn't inside the Red Line, so where had all of that information come from? More importantly, how could any of it be *live* data?

He tried searching for Laniakea, which the Red Line encompassed, just to be sure that the system he'd chosen wasn't inside of it. The map zoomed all the way out to show him a red dot at the center of the universe.

"Ah... guys, try searching for Laniakea."

"Why?" Garek asked. "Where is it?"

"At the center of the universe," Lucien replied.

"*What?*" Garek asked. "You're joking."

"No, he's right..." Addy replied.

"It would be funny if it weren't so sad," Lucien said. "Galileo must be rolling in his grave."

"Gali-who?" Garek asked.

"Galileo. The inventor of the telescope... he was the first person to propose that Earth wasn't the center of the universe."

"Actually that was Copernicus," Addy said.

"I'll take your word for it," Garek replied. "It's been a long time since I studied any of that stuff."

Lucien tried zooming in on another random system, and this time he made sure that it was far from the red dot of Laniakea at the center of the universe.

The system was called Tekken Prime. It had two suns, six planets, and twenty-seven moons, with just one intelligent species—the Tekken—and a unified feudal government. The Faros were not mentioned, which Lucien took to mean that they hadn't found or enslaved the Tekken yet. Again the contacts panel for the system was populated with *live* data for all the ships and space stations in the system.

"That's impossible..." Lucien breathed, shaking his head.

"What's not possible?" Garek asked.

He explained what he was seeing, but it sounded even more absurd when he said it out loud.

"There's no way our sensors can detect that level of detail from here," Addy said.

"Exactly—there's no way, and yet the Etherians seem

to have found one," Lucien replied.

"Then maybe Etherus *is* God. Or at least *a* god. He has to be," Addy said.

"Maybe, yeah..." Lucien replied. "At the very least, it means the Etherians have found a way to tap into a truly instantaneous form of communication."

"I wonder if the Faros have this technology?" Garek asked.

"If they did, then they wouldn't need to find the lost fleet in order to find Etheria," Lucien replied.

"Then I guess they don't have the same tech. You realize what this means," Garek said.

Lucien shook his head. "No, what?"

"It means we can probably find *Astralis* from here. We don't have to *risk* looking for them by jumping to random systems around their last known location. And it also means we can identify a safe route to get there, checking systems for signs of the Faros before we make a jump."

"Garek's right," Addy said. "This changes everything. Now we have a clear tactical edge over the Faros."

Lucien frowned, unconvinced.

"I think we need to re-take the vote," Garek said.

"Hang on," Lucien said. "Before we get carried away, let's be sure we really can find *Astralis*. It's a big universe. Searching every system for it will literally take forever."

"Found it!" Garek crowed.

Lucien's frown deepened. He tried searching for *Astralis* this time. Almost instantly, a new star system appeared, and sure enough, his view of that system was centered on a green dot labeled *Astralis*. Lucien selected that contact to read more about it, just to be sure.

"The size and shape match," Addy said, beating him to it. "It's them all right."

"They're twenty-nine billion light years away," Lucien pointed out. "It could still take a long time for us to reach them."

"Plotting a course..." Addy said. "Got it!"

"You calculated a jump there already?" Lucien asked, suddenly wondering if Etherian jump tech was somehow instant, too.

"The *route* is finished calculating—" Addy clarified. "—not the actual jumps. There's over a hundred stops along the way, and the time to reach our destination is estimated at... twenty-six days, eight hours, and thirty-eight minutes."

"Less than a month!" Garek said.

Lucien's brow felt heavy, his eyes tight. "We'd have to make sure all those stops are safe before we jump to them."

"We can adjust the route as we go," Garek suggested. "Zigging or zagging by a few light years here or there isn't going to make a difference to our arrival time. So?" Garek prompted. "All in favor of going to *Astralis,* and *then* Etheria?"

Everyone stuck their hand up except for Lucien. Seeing that, he gradually raised his own hand.

Garek twisted off his helmet and set it beside him. "It's unanimous," he said, looking around and nodding with a rare smile on his face. "We're going home."

"Yeah..." Lucien replied, feeling unsettled by that decision. If this was such a good idea, then why had the Polypuses been so adamant about them going to Etheria first? Lucien had a bad feeling they were making a big mistake. "What if *Astralis* overrules our decision to take the fleet back to Etheria?" he asked. "They might want to use it to continue their mission. With perfectly accurate recon data we wouldn't have to worry about running into Faros again."

"There's an easy solution to that—don't give the fleet to them," Garek said. "By rights of salvage it's ours, so they can't force us to hand it over. After we arrive, we can ask the people of *Astralis* to join us, or not. Anyone who wants to come, can, and those who don't are welcome to stay. It'll be a second chance for everyone, a way to go back safely. After everything we've been through with the Faros, I think most people will want out of *Astralis's* mission. Besides, with what we've learned from the Etherians' *Universal Map*, *Astralis's* mission is somewhat redundant now, anyway."

"Agreed," Addy said. "I can't see any risks associated with this plan. In fact, right now we're sitting along the outermost edge of the universe, near the Great Abyss. By flying back to *Astralis* first we'll be covering almost half of the distance back to the Red Line. *Astralis* is actually on the way to Etheria, so there's no reason not to go there first. In fact, if our comms are instant, we could use them to send *Astralis* a message," Addy suggested. "Let them know we're coming."

"Bad idea," Garek replied. "Instant or not, we don't know if the Faros will be able to detect any message we send."

"True," Lucien said, and let go of his misgivings with a sigh. As he did so, a smile crept onto his face. "I guess it will be nice to see some fresh faces."

"What's wrong with our faces?" Addy asked, arching an eyebrow at him behind her helmet.

Lucien laughed. "You know what I mean."

"Yeah, I do," she replied with an audible smile. She twisted off her helmet, and Brak did the same.

Lucien followed suit, and took in a deep breath of the ship's air. Despite how stale and sterile it smelled, somehow it still smelled sweet. "We're going home," he whispered.

CHAPTER 38

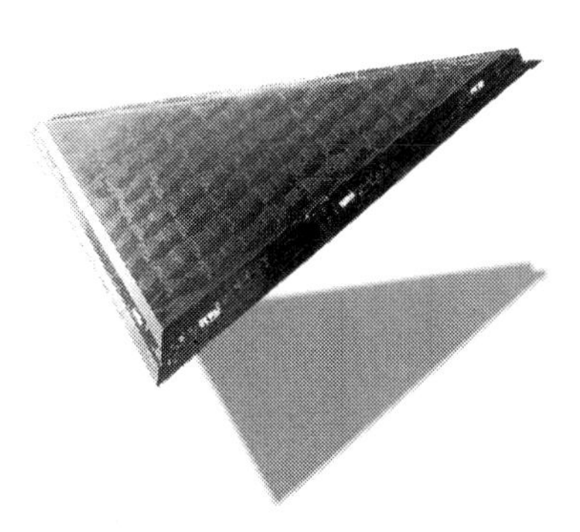

Astralis

"Is something wrong?" Atara asked, her gaze flicking from her mother to her father and back again.

"No sweetheart, I just need to have a talk with your father about grown-up stuff. We'll be right outside on the deck, okay? If you need us, all you have to do is come get us."

"How come Theola gets to listen?"

Lucien adjusted his grip to keep her from sliding down his hip.

"Because she's just a baby, and you're too young to babysit," Tyra explained.

"It's about me, isn't it." Atara crossed her arms over her chest and pouted.

"No, sweetheart, it's not," Tyra replied, shaking her head. "Why don't you go play in your room? We won't be long." With that, Tyra led the way to the balcony. She opened the sliding door and a blast of frigid air hit them.

Lucien shivered as he turned and shut the door behind them. Tyra wasted no time activating the balcony's heat shield. While she did that, Lucien waved at the fire pit to ignite it. The artificial logs burst into flames, and they sat on a bench by the fire, warming their hands and feet. The sky was clear and blue today. No wonder it was so cold.

"Are your ARCs offline?" Tyra asked.

Lucien nodded.

"Good. Then it's safe to speak."

"What are we going to do?" Lucien asked.

Tyra appeared to consider that. "We don't know how many people have been affected by this, but we do know who the key ones are."

"Chief Ellis, Admiral Stavos, General Graves... and someone in the Resurrection Center, possibly Director Helios," Lucien said.

"And Atara," Tyra said.

"But why her? She's just a kid. What's she got to do with anything?" Lucien asked.

Tyra shook her head. "I don't know, but I do know how to fix it. We need to get to the Resurrection Center. From there we can roll back the changes to the people we know are infected."

"We're not going to have an easy time securing the Resurrection Center," Lucien said. "It has better security than almost anywhere else on *Astralis,* and you can bet that as soon as we trip the alarms, General Graves is going to send thousands of Marines in after us."

"How long do you think we'll have?"

Lucien shook his head. "Not long enough to get access to the data or roll back any changes."

"Maybe we don't need to. All we really need to do is prove that there's been tampering with people's memories, and identify what the Faros did to Ellis and the others. At that point even the Marines will stop following their orders.

"You haven't had a lot of experience with military discipline, have you? The squad sergeants aren't just going to take our word for it."

"So we show them," Tyra said. "We find a way to convince them. We have to. The question is how do we hold them off until we've had a chance to find incriminating evidence?"

"Hold the center ransom," Lucien decided. "If we're threatening to destroy everyone's clones and the backups of their consciousness, the Marines will have to negotiate. We demand that one or more of them come and witness what we've found, giving us a chance to prove our suspicions. That should get their attention. What kind of terrorists would make demands like that? At the very least they'll have to concede that *we* believe *Astralis* has been taken over by Faros."

"That might just work," Tyra said. "But we're going to need help, and we don't even know who we can trust."

"We know we can trust ourselves, and I know I can trust Brak."

"How do you know that?" Tyra asked.

"He was with me the whole time when the Faros were invading, and they never touched him."

"Are there any others you could ask?"

"That I know for sure haven't been compromised?" Lucien shook his head. "No."

"I might know someone," Tyra said. "Commander Wheeler. She was with me on the bridge when the others were affected. They didn't get to her. She was the acting commander of *Astralis* while Admiral Stavos was out of commission."

"You think you can convince her to help us? If you can't, she could have us arrested."

"Then we'll have to make sure we're convincing," Tyra said.

"What would she add to our team?"

"She has access to the bridge. She could let us know when the Marines have been alerted, how many, and where they're coming from," Tyra said. "She might even be able to help us get into the center."

"She's an asset, then. What about you?" Lucien asked, staring pointedly at her.

Tyra blinked. "What *about* me?"

"You're not trained for this kind of thing. You're a politician, and before that, a scientist."

"I'm not sitting on the sidelines."

"I didn't say you were, but you could compromise the whole operation by coming along."

"So what do you propose I do?"

Lucien considered that for a moment. "We could use a distraction, something that will also allow us to get Ellis, Stavos, Graves, and maybe even Director Helios all in one place. Can you think of anything that might work for that?"

Tyra's brow furrowed. "They've all been subverted by the Faros, so we might just raise their suspicions by trying to do that."

"There's got to be some kind of legitimate excuse to get them all in one place, but not *just* them."

"What about a charity banquet to raise funds for the

families who lost their homes in Fallside?"

Lucien smiled. "That sounds perfect. And as the councilor of Fallside, it makes sense that you'd suggest and organize such an event. While you're hosting the banquet, you'll be able to keep an eye on everyone for us. At the same time that you're doing that, Brak and I will find a way to sneak in to the center and plant our bomb."

Tyra blinked. "I thought you were just going to *threaten* to blow the center?"

"I am, but if it's a bluff, it won't be long before the ship's cameras and sensors give us away and Marines storm the place. We need a *real* bomb, or this isn't going to work."

Tyra's eyes went huge. "Where are you going to get a bomb?"

"I know a few illegal arms dealers."

"Aren't all of them in the correctional center?"

"Some. Not all. One guy was particularly slick. We couldn't pin him with anything. Joe Coretti."

Tyra's eyes got even bigger. "Of the Coretti Brothers?"

"Yeah."

"They're responsible for half of the crime on *Astralis!*"

"More than half on a good day," Lucien said.

"Why would they want to help you?"

"Because I can take the heat off them for a while."

"You can't promise that."

"I can in Fallside, after it's rebuilt, but if that's not good enough for them, then I'll appeal to their sense of greed. Alien dictators are bad for business."

Tyra didn't look convinced.

"Don't worry, I'll have Brak with me," he said.

"Another cop."

"A scary cop."

"What about the girls? What do we do with them?"

"They'll stay with you at the benefit."

"And how are we going to explain the fact that *you're* not there?"

"Food poisoning."

"Why don't you just get an injection?"

"Bad timing. Even injections take an hour or two to purge the toxins."

Tyra still didn't look convinced.

"You're the politician. Come up with something that sounds good to you."

"All right," Tyra said. "Fine." Theola began to complain, squirming in Lucien's arms. "She must be hungry," Tyra said.

Lucien passed Theola to her and stood up from the bench. "I'm going to get Brak and go see Joe."

"Now?" Tyra asked.

"The Corettis are easier to track down at night. They're usually hanging out at one of their clubs. Meanwhile, start getting that charity banquet organized—and talk to Commander Wheeler, but feel her out first before you tell her about our plan. We don't need her trying to stop us."

Tyra nodded, and Lucien leaned in for a quick kiss.

"Be careful," Tyra said as he withdrew.

"I will," Lucien said as he went back inside.

"What were you and Mom talking about?"

Lucien froze, and turned to see Atara watching him from the armchair in the living room. She'd turned it away from the fireplace to face the deck. She'd been watching them all this time. *Reading our lips?* Lucien wondered. Atara didn't know how to read lips, but without knowing what the Faros had done to her, it was hard to be sure what she was and wasn't capable of.

"Grown-up stuff," Lucien said.

"Like what?" Atara asked, hands folded over her chest, looking too grown-up for her age.

Tyra came in then. "I thought I told you to go play in your room," she said, putting on her best Mom voice.

Atara shrugged. "Didn't feel like it."

"I'm going to let you deal with this," Lucien said, and breezed on through to the front door. As he went, he heard Tyra switch from bad cop to good cop, offering ice cream to distract Atara. That seemed to work, but Lucien couldn't get over the feeling that he was somehow exposed, like Ellis already knew what they were planning.

He pushed those thoughts aside. Ellis wasn't god. He couldn't have eyes and ears everywhere at once. And Atara, even if she could read lips, couldn't have caught more than a handful of words from their conversation on the deck. Not enough to string together their plot.

They still had the element of surprise.

For now.

* * *

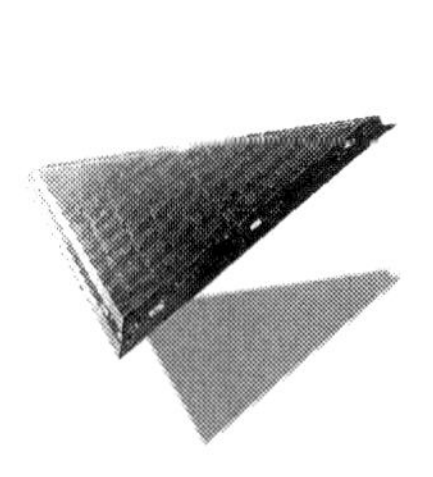

Astralis

Lucien interrupted Brak just as he was sitting down to dinner—a pile of fresh-grown, uncooked steaks. "Come in," Brak said, waving him through the door as he bit off a chunk of one of the steaks.

Lucien looked around as he walked inside. There wasn't much to the place. One small room for a cooking, eating, and living space. A door led to what might have been an adjoining bedroom. Lucien took a seat in an old chair beside the couch where Brak had sat back down to eat.

"Nice place," Lucien said.

"Liar," Brak replied, while biting off another chunk of steak.

A holoscreen in front of the couch showed Ellis, making an announcement about the War Measures Act. Based on the color of the sky, this particular press conference had obviously been taped earlier in the day. Ellis was busy promising to use his new political powers to keep *Astralis* safe.

"You believe this?" Brak asked, pointing to the screen with a bloody hand.

Lucien began nodding slowly. "Power can be good in the right hands. At least he's getting us back out there with the changes he's making to the cloning laws." While he said that, Lucien mimed with his hands, indicating his own eyes with two fingers, then Brak's, followed by a cutting-off gesture at his throat. Brak got the idea, and his eyes grew dark as the subtle glow of light from his ARCs disappeared.

"Speak," Brak indicated.

And Lucien did. He explained about Atara's strange

behavior, followed by Tyra's planted-memory experience with Ellis's War Measures Act.

"I kill him. I rip out his throat," Brak said, baring his bloody black teeth in a fearsome display.

Lucien shook his head. "Assassination will get you blown out the airlock with no chance of resurrection. And it won't do any good, because they'll just bring Ellis back the very next day. Not to mention he's not the only one we have to worry about."

"Then what can we do?"

Lucien explained the plan he and Tyra had come up with.

"Yesss, this could work..." Brak agreed, and absentmindedly bit off another chunk of steak.

"Glad you approve, because I need your help."

Brak grinned, revealing red bits of raw meat stuck between his dagger-sharp teeth. Blood dribbled down his bony gray chin. He wiped it on a massive forearm. "Where do we start?"

"Now. Tonight. We need to go get a bomb from Joe Coretti."

"Joe?" Brak's enthusiasm disappeared. "We're going to criminals for help?"

"We're about to *become* criminals, so getting help from them seems appropriate."

"I do not think Joc will hclp us," Brak said.

"Well it's our job to convince him."

"Hmmm. I do not like your plan."

"Got a better one?"

Brak tore off another giant bite of steak while he thought about it. He chewed briefly, then swallowed. "No," he decided. "I do not."

"Then let's go."

CHAPTER 39

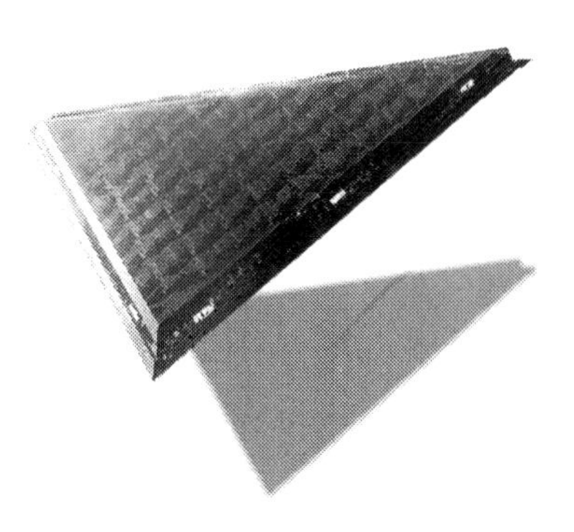

Astralis

Joseph Coretti wasn't hard to find. Lucien and Brak had each spent plenty of time tracking him and his brothers across *Astralis,* so they already knew all of the Corettis' favorite haunts.

This particular club, the Crack of Dawn, was located in Sub-District Two, the same district where Brak was currently renting his apartment. As Lucien walked in, he was greeted to a dozen topless girls in thongs, all wrapped around poles, swinging their hips and baring everything but their souls for the men drooling into their drinks around the stage.

This was definitely one of the sleazier joints that the Corettis owned. Music thumped in a fast, primal beat, setting the pace for the patrons' racing hearts. Illuminated strips lit the floor, but overhead lights were nonexistent—except for up on the stage, where they glared at the dancers from every possible angle. The setup was meant to give the illusion of a private show and to protect the anonymity of the club's patrons by reducing them to ambiguous shadows.

These guys could have been literally anyone—councilors, lawyers, security officers... even Ellis could have been there, but Lucien didn't think he'd risk coming to a place like this. If he wanted a show, he could afford to order a truly private one.

As they walked through the club to the back, two illuminated waitresses with hovering trays of drinks wove to intercept them. The waitresses were clothed with clinging, transparent dresses and illuminated by hovering spotlights that followed them wherever they went. The waitresses, one brunette and one blond, sauntered up to him and Brak.

"Hey there, big guy," the brunette said while rubbing Brak's arm. "You look *thirsty,*" she licked her lips as she said that, and stretched sensuously. All of that was lost on Brak. He leaned into the cone of light projected by her spotlight, revealing his skull-shaped gray face, and bared his black teeth at her. The girl paled dramatically, and her mouth popped open in a silent scream.

The blond actually did scream, and she ran back through the club with her spotlight chasing after her. The commotion was all but swallowed by the thumping music, but a few heads turned from the bar to watch her run. For her part, the brunette was frozen in place.

Lucien leaned into view of her spotlight and smiled reassuringly. "We're looking for Joe Coretti. You know where we can find him?"

The girl shook her head, and Lucien shrugged. "Thanks, anyway."

They continued through the club, and this time no waitresses appeared to offer them drinks, but Lucien spied the blond they'd scared talking to a pair of hulking shadows at the back.

After just a second, those goons peeled away from the wall and came to block the way in front of Lucien and Brak.

"We don't want trouble in here, boys," one of them said in a gruff whisper that was somehow audible above the music.

"Neither do we," Lucien said. "We're looking for Joe."

"He's not in."

"I saw his car out front."

The goons had no reply for that.

"Look, it's business. He'll be happy you sent me."

"He expectin' you?"

"Not exactly."

"Then you're not gonna see him. I suggest you leave. Or stay and enjoy the show. Up to you."

Lucien grew tired of the runaround. He elbowed Brak in the ribs, and the Gor took a long step toward the two men. He grabbed the one who'd been talking and hoisted him off his feet, letting him dangle by one arm.

The guy cursed and yelped, making a grab for his gun, but Lucien kicked his hand and snatched the weapon for himself. He aimed it at the other goon's head before that man could draw his weapon.

"You two are dead," the second one gritted out.

Lucien took his gun, too, and said, "Either you can lead the way to Joe, or we can knock you both out and let you sleep it off behind the bar while we look for him ourselves."

"I lead you to him and I lose my job. Or worse."

"Then point the way," Lucien said.

The man did so, jerking a thumb over his shoulder to a shadowy staircase at the back of the club.

"Thanks," Lucien said. He passed the second gun to Brak, and the Gor gradually lowered goon number one to the floor. Lucien kept his aim on both of them as he and Brak backed toward the stairs.

He needn't have bothered, both men turned and ran for the exit, probably thinking to get a head start on whatever retribution awaited them for failing their jobs. Lucien tried not to think too hard about that. He was on the other side of the law now; he couldn't afford to let his conscience get in the way. At least not yet.

They reached the back stairs and Lucien gestured to Brak, indicating he should hang back. Brak nodded once, and Lucien climbed carefully, watching for more guards as he reached the landing and turned to climb the next flight of stairs. There were two more guards in plain sight, standing beside a thick metal door at the top of the stairs. Both had their weapons drawn and aimed, having somehow seen him coming.

"One more step, and you're dead," one of the guards said.

Lucien raised his hands. "Hey, don't shoot," he said. "I'm just looking for the bathroom."

"With a gun?"

Lucien glanced at the slug thrower pistol in his hand, and flashed a grin. "It's a dangerous joint."

"Nice try," the guard said as he descended the stairs. "That gun is Coretti issue, and I ain't seen you before, meaning you stole it."

"I'm new," Lucien said.

"Drop the weapon."

Lucien let it clatter to the stairs.

A fan of blue light flickered out from a padlock dangling by a gold chain around the guard's neck. A hidden scanner. It flickered over Lucien's face and the guard snorted. "Lucien Ortane, Chief of security for Fallside. *Brutha,* you must have a death wish comin' around here. I should jus' shoot you right now. Get myself a nice promotion."

Lucien shrugged as if he really did have a death wish. That was when Brak made his move. Perfectly invisible but for the gun in his hand, he cold-cocked the guard still standing at the top of the stairs, and the man fell with a *thump* that blended perfectly with the sounds of the music below. What didn't blend was the metallic clatter of his gun jumping down the stairs.

"What the—" The guard standing in front of Lucien half-turned to see his partner lying in a heap on the landing.

Lucien kicked the man's hand, and the gun went flying. Then Brak reached him, and an invisible hand wrapped around the man's throat, hoisting him into the air.

"Be nice, Brak," Lucien said, just as the Gor de-cloaked and appeared as a naked gray wall of rippling muscle with even less claim to modesty than the dancers downstairs. Brak hissed in the guard's face, and the man's eyes bulged. He batted impotently at the vice around his throat.

"You're going to kill him like that," Lucien said. Brak brought the man down and put him in a choke hold, waiting until he sagged. Now safely unconscious, Brak set the guard down gently, and Lucien went to fetch the guard's pistol, tucking it into the right side of his belt. It was an upgrade from the slug thrower he'd stolen from the guard downstairs.

That done, he patted down the guard, searching for a key to open the door at the top of the stairs, but all he found was an illegally-modified communicator for off-the-grid comms. He activated the device.

"Joseph Coretti, it's Chief Ortane from Fallside. Remember me? I've got a business proposition for you. I'm waiting at the back door on level two of the Crack of Dawn."

Wordlessly, Brak cloaked himself again and waited. The door at the top of the stairs burst open a moment later, revealing no less than six armed guards. These guys were carrying automatic pulse rifles. A pair of them descended the stairs while the others kept their guns trained on Lucien. As soon as they reached him, they patted him down and confiscated his two pistols; then they scanned him for good measure.

"Satisfied?" Lucien asked.

"Come on," one of the men replied, as the two of them grabbed him by his arms and jerked him roughly up the stairs. The other four parted ranks and fanned out, making way for them to cross the threshold.

Lucien jerked his arms free of the men holding him. "What do you think I'm going to do without any weapons? It's six against one!"

"I wouldn't want to be you right now," one of the men walking beside Lucien said.

The door swung shut behind him with a heavy *boom,* and the group led him down a shadowy corridor to another door. Upon reaching it, one man pressed the button for an old-fashioned intercom, and said, "We got him, boss."

"Bring him in," a familiar voice replied.

Locking bolts slid aside and they pulled the door open.

Lucien got an eyeful of a private show being put on by three fully naked girls. He glanced away, looking down at his feet.

"What's the matter?" that same familiar voice asked. "Are you going soft on me, Lucy-lu?" The man snapped his fingers, and said, "Later, darlings." Bare feet padded on tiles as the girls departed, and Lucien looked up into the grinning face of none other than Joseph Coretti, eldest of the three Coretti brothers. His silver eyes were glazed, and it was easy to see—and *smell*—why: the air was thick and glittering with smoke from *glow* sticks. Several smoking butts were still smoldering in an ashtray on the table beside Coretti's throne-like chair. Glow sticks didn't just glow from the lit end, but all along their length.

Joseph grabbed one of the longer sticks from the ashtray and took a deep drag from it. His eyelids fluttered as he did so, and he blew out the smoke with a sigh. He turned the butt around and offered it to Lucien. "Want a taste? Our best batch yet, guaranteed."

Lucien shook his head. "I don't smoke. Sorry."

Joseph frowned and raised his eyebrows. He took another drag while leaning over the ashtray and staring sideways at Lucien. "Why the frek not?" he asked, letting out another stream of smoke. "You haven't lived until you've smoked glow. You officers must have a few kilos lying around that no one's going to miss. You should roll them up and see how the other side lives. It'll blow your mind, Lucy-lu."

"Thanks, but no thanks."

"Your loss," Joseph said, shrugging as he left his glow

stick smoking in the ashtray beside him. "You mentioned you have business to discuss?"

Lucien nodded. "I'd like to help you out."

Joseph arched an eyebrow at him and smirked. "Weren't you the guy who spent a year trying to help me out of my freedom? What are you going to help me out of now?"

Lucien explained, and pretty soon even Joe's witless goons were glancing at each other in shock. For his part, Joseph was leaning forward in his throne, looking equal parts intrigued and outraged. The glaze had left his eyes, and they were suddenly as sharp as Brak's teeth.

"Frekking aliens!" Joseph said. "You know how much product we lost in Fallside when they blew the place open?"

"I'm not sure I want to know," Lucien replied.

"So what are you doing here? You should be on your way to arrest Ellis and his alien buddies right now."

Lucien shook his head. "He's got control of the military and the government. But what's worse is he's got control of the Resurrection Center. If we try to go after him head-on, he could alter our memories and wipe away our suspicions, then all we'll get for our trouble is a bad case of amnesia."

"So you've come to me for help," Joseph said, nodding slowly and smiling. "Ironic, isn't it?"

"I do appreciate the irony, yes."

"What are you proposing?"

"I need a bomb. Something small enough and powerful enough to sneak into the Resurrection Center. I'm going to infiltrate the center with it and hold the place ransom while I find proof that the Faros have taken over *Astralis.*"

Joseph's eyebrows elevated slightly at that, and he sat back in his throne. "Not a bad plan, but what makes you think

I have a bomb?"

"Come on, Joe, you and I both know you do."

"All right, so what's in it for me?"

"You mean besides avoiding whatever fate the Faros have in mind for us—death at worst, slavery at best?"

"You don't know that. If they've gone to all this trouble to take over, they must want *Astralis* intact."

"Maybe, but whatever they're planning, I doubt it lines up with your goals for building a criminal empire. They might be planning to take us back to the Etherian Empire to gather intel for an invasion, in which case your little operation is going to get wrapped up real fast when Etherus is back in charge."

"True..." Joseph said. "Business has been booming ever since we left. All right, I'll help you, but on one condition—"

Lucien waited. *Here comes the catch...*

"I'm sending a team with you."

"A team?" Lucien wasn't expecting that.

Joseph spread his hands. "Sure. You can't hope to do this on your own, and it's in my best interests to make sure you succeed."

Lucien considered that, his brow knitted tightly enough to give him a headache. Or maybe it was the muted thumping from the music downstairs. "I don't want to be an accomplice to the murder of some unsuspecting desk clerk at the center."

"I'll make sure my boys stick to stun. Fair enough?"

Lucien still didn't like it. Joe was up to something. "Do I have a choice?"

"Not if you want my help, no. Thing is, I could pull this off without you, but you can't do it without me."

"Not true," Lucien countered. "You do this without me, and the operation will lose any possible claim to legitimacy. Your men will get arrested when it's over, and you'll be implicated in whatever they've been charged with."

"Not if we find the evidence you're looking for. We do that, and my boys will be heroes, and so will I. In fact, I might even decide to run for office after that." Joseph grinned and laced his hands over his stomach. "Yeah, I think I might just do that," he decided, nodding to himself.

"All right, fine. Your team comes with us, but I'm still in charge of the operation."

"Sure," Joseph said and stuck out a hand. "It's a deal."

"I'll take your word for it," Lucien said. "I don't know where that hand has been."

Joseph laughed. "You come here, begging for my help, and then you insult me like that? Must be hard dragging around those boulders you call balls. I've killed men for less."

"You want to state that for the record?"

Joseph smiled, but his silver eyes were cold as ice. "Maybe I *should* just kill you, Lucy-lu." He mimed a gun with one hand and fired it at Lucien's head.

"You do that, and my partner will kill you next." With that, the air behind Joseph shimmered, and Brak appeared, his skull-shaped face looming over the back of the chair.

"Boo," Brak growled.

"The frek!" Joseph jumped up and spun around, backing away quickly. His goons belatedly adjusted their aim. "Motherfreker!" Joe screeched.

The Gor bared his teeth, grinning at the crime boss.

Joseph looked from Brak to Lucien and back again. "Touche, Lucy-lu. Touche." Turning to his guards, he said,

"Who the frek let that monster in here?"

His men glanced at each other, redirecting the blame.

Brak hissed and straightened. "Who do you call a monster?"

Joseph waved his hand dismissively at the Gor. "It's all good, Skullman. Come on, Lucy, we're going bomb shopping."

CHAPTER 40

Astralis

—TWELVE HOURS LATER—

Tyra had a hard time finding a chance to meet with Lieutenant Commander Wheeler away from the bridge where Admiral Stavos and General Graves would be privy to their conversation. She ended up hanging out in the wardroom around lunch time under the guise of inviting officers to the charity dinner she was organizing.

Finally, at just after one o'clock, Lieutenant Commander Wheeler came in. Tyra tried not to watch too conspicuously as Wheeler made her way down the line-up at the fabricators, and then found a table with a group of other officers. Tyra wove around the room until she reached that table. She pulled out one of the empty chairs and sat down.

"Commander Wheeler," she said. "It's good to see you

again."

Wheeler's eyes darted up, but her head remained hovering over her plate of pasta to avoid spilling. Her eyebrows formed the question that her mouth was too busy to ask, and Tyra launched into an explanation about the charity dinner. She invited Wheeler, along with everyone else at the table, telling them to bring their friends and families.

"I hope you'll all be able to make it," Tyra finished.

Commander Wheeler nodded slowly and washed down another mouthful of pasta with a cup of juice. "I'll see what I can do." The others gave similarly noncommittal replies.

"Thanks for your time, officers," Tyra said as she got up to leave. "Oh, and Commander—I wonder if you would be able to help me put together a list of other officers that I could invite? Along with their contact information?"

"I'll get someone to send that to you."

Wheeler wasn't making this easy. Tyra needed to meet her in person. "Thank you... and if I could trouble you for one more thing..."

Commander Wheeler looked up, wearing what was left of her patience on her face. "Yes?"

"Would you mind meeting me in my office to go over the invitations I'm planning to send to those officers? I'd like them to be convincing, and I was hoping you could help me come up with some incentives to offer that might appeal to the ship's military personnel."

"That's easy. Free beer."

The other officers chuckled at that, and Wheeler smiled at her own joke.

"Well, we can't offer *free* anything, since the idea is to

raise money... but I'd really like to consult with you on this in more detail. Is there a time you could meet with me later today? I'd consider it a personal favor. There are a lot of families counting on the funds we'll raise from this dinner."

Wheeler sighed. "I'm off duty at eighteen hundred hours. I was planning to use that time to hit the rack, but..."

"It won't take long. I promise."

"All right."

Tyra flashed a grin. "Thank you, Commander."

"Sure."

Tyra breezed out of the wardroom just as Admiral Stavos was breezing in. She bumped into him in the entrance. "Sorry, sir," she said.

He caught her by the arm before she could leave. "Councilor? What are you doing here?"

She explained about the charity dinner.

"An excellent idea! I'll make sure attendance is mandatory for all non-essential crew."

"Thank you, sir," Tyra replied, bobbing her head and smiling gratefully.

He smiled back. "Glad I could be of service."

"Yes, sir. I look forward to seeing you there."

"Count on it."

"And General Graves?"

"He's the XO. Someone should be on the bridge..." The admiral scratched his chin absently through his beard. "I suppose we could leave LC Wheeler with the conn. I'll invite him for you."

"Thank you, sir."

"Of course."

Tyra nodded and hurried off, her feet buoyed on a

stream of adrenaline. Things were working out perfectly. Wheeler was going to be alone on the bridge. Convincing her to join their plot was more important than ever now.

* * *

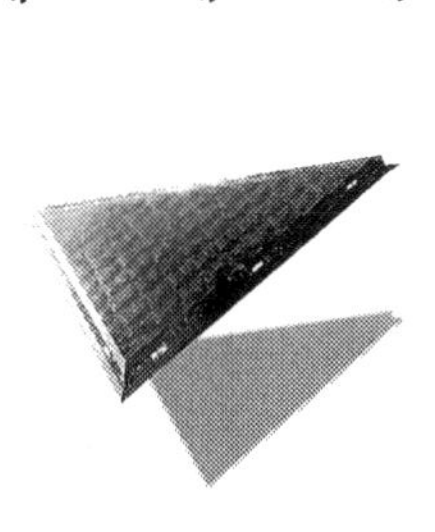

Astralis

Lucien and Brak were back at the Crack of Dawn for the second night in a row, going over infiltration plans with Joseph Coretti and three of his men.

"The ventilation shafts are the easiest way in, but while the fans are on, they're a death trap," Joe said, pointing to a holographic schematic of the Resurrection Center.

Lucien nodded. "We could cut the power."

"My thoughts exactly, but they'll send a maintenance crew to fix it within minutes, so we need to hack into their comms first. Then when we cut the power, their call to maintenance goes straight to us. Guntha here takes the call and goes in through the front door. From there he can shut down the security system in the ducts so he can get in to make repairs, and voila—the rest of our team will sneak in from outside with the bomb."

"That might work," Lucien said.

Joe just looked at him. *"Might?"* He thumped his chest.

"Come on, give me a little credit here."

"It's a good plan."

"It's a *great* plan. We came up with it years ago. Took six months to get our hands on the schematics and work out all the details."

"So why didn't you go through with it?"

Joe shrugged. "Too risky to hold the center ransom. It's a one-way ticket. Easy to get in, not so easy to get out."

"Once we find the evidence we're looking for, that won't be a problem."

"You better be right about that," Fizk Arak, the team's demolitions expert said.

Joseph patted him on the back. "No worries, Fizzy. Lucy-lu wouldn't risk going to corrections over this. He knows what happens to cops in prison—don't you, Lucy? We've got lots of old business associates on the inside waiting for you if you frek this one up." Joe grinned.

Lucien narrowed his eyes at that, and Brak hissed.

"Oh, don't worry, they'll be happy to see you, too, Skullman. So? When do we get the green light on this?"

"Four days from now, at seventeen hundred hours," Lucien said.

"Why so long? We've already figured out the details. We need to move!"

"My wife is setting up a charity banquet for Fallside."

"I don't give a fr—"

"It's a distraction," Lucien explained, holding up a hand to forestall Joe's expletive.

The gangster glowered darkly at having been shushed. "Fine. Four days."

"Seventeen hundred hours," Lucien repeated.

"Get here two hours early or we'll go without you."

Lucien nodded and glanced at Brak. "We'll be here. Till then, no more meetings."

"Fine by me," Joe said. "Having a cop prowling around here is bad for business." His goons nodded their agreement with that. None of them liked having to work with cops. Lucien wasn't thrilled about the setup, either. He glanced from Guntha, the hulking skinhead, to Fizk, the sneering, curly-haired demo guy, to the third and final member of the team, who had yet to be introduced. The man looked vaguely familiar: short dark hair, dark eyes, tall and trim with an almost military straightness to his posture. *Black ops? Ex-Paragon?* Lucien wondered. Where had he seen this guy before?

The man hadn't said a word, having spent the entire meeting in the shadows, leaning against the wall with his hands in his pockets and dark eyes gleaming. Those eyes tracked Lucien as he turned to leave, and he hesitated, staring right back. The man's face was an expressionless mask, and he didn't take his eyes off Lucien for so much as a second. Not even to blink. Something about the guy was just *off,* and it was more than the usual gangster vibe. His movements were too precise, his muscles too loose...

Suddenly Lucien had it. His mind flashed back to the stakeout he'd planned with Brak right before the Faros had invaded, the one where they'd seen the look-alike for Titarus Cleever, the late son of High Court Judge Cleever. This mystery guy had been there that night, too. Lucien was sure of it.

"Something wrong?" Joe asked.

"I have a policy about my partners in crime," Lucien

said slowly.

Joe snorted and elbowed Fizk in the ribs. "You hear that, Fizzy? The man's barely got his feet wet and he's already got a *policy.*"

Fizk snickered, his curly hair bobbing as air stuttered from his lips.

Lucien took the mocking in his stride, and nodded to the man in the shadows. "Who's he?"

Joe turned. "Him? He doesn't have a name."

"What do you mean *he doesn't have a name?*" Lucien demanded.

"He's a bot, an android. Frekking deadly. Our best fixer. Cost a damn fortune to build him off the books and splice in new code to get past all those pesky commercial bot laws about not injuring people."

"That's highly illegal," Lucien said.

"You aren't going nark on me, are you, Lucy?"

"No."

"Good. I wouldn't want Bob to have to fix *you.*"

"I thought you said he doesn't have a name."

"He doesn't. That's his human alias. He's got an ID and everything, don't you, Bobby boy?"

Bob nodded slowly, but said nothing.

Lucien grimaced and shook his head. "We'll see you in four days, Joe."

"It's a date, Lucy. Bob, why don't you see these boys out. Go strut your stuff for them."

The bot melted out of the shadows, but *bot* was the wrong term for him. He was an android. Creating androids was supposed to be illegal—an old law from the Etherian Empire that had yet to be overturned. AI, however, had been legalized soon after *Astralis* left, which explained how Bob could function.

Apparently Joe had grown tired of waiting for the laws regarding androids to catch up. As they walked downstairs and back through the club, Lucien found himself watching the girls on the stage and the waitresses sauntering through the room with their hovering trays and spotlights.

Maybe they were all androids, too. Androids wouldn't have the same inhibitions as people, and they presented none of the health or privacy concerns for clients that real humans did, which made them ideal sex workers.

One of the girls brushed Lucien's arm on his way out, her fingers grazing his. She must have felt his wedding ring, but she didn't even blink at that. "Leaving so soon?" she asked. "Stay, and I'll make it worth your while..." She whispered that last part in his ear, and Lucien felt his cheeks flush in spite of himself.

Bob shot the girl a look, and she paled. *An instinct for self-preservation?* Maybe these girls weren't androids, after all, but they obviously knew something about Bob. *Fixer slash pimp?* Lucien wondered.

Bob stopped at the entrance and held the door open for them. "Have a good night," he said.

Brak walked out without a word, but Lucien lingered in the entryway. "You, too," he said, and held out his hand to the alleged android. "Nice to meet you." The android eyed his hand, but made no move to shake it. "Are you going to leave me hanging? We're partners now."

Bob released the door—it smacked Lucien in the back, but he pretended not to notice—and took his hand. Lucien purposefully tested the man's grip by squeezing as hard as he could. Bob's hand resisted being crushed, and he showed no signs of discomfort. He didn't even exhibit the vengeful human response of squeezing Lucien's hand back.

Definitely a bot. "See you around," Lucien said.

Bob nodded. "See you."

Lucien caught up with Brak in the parking lot.

"I will never understand why your males visit places like this. Is it not frustrating to be enticed to mate yet not be able to do so? Are those males all... impotent?"

Lucien laughed. "Not likely, and I'm sure most of them don't stop at just being *enticed.*"

Brak snorted. "Growing up in the Etherian Empire I learned that humans were monogamous and mate for life. In the past eight years since leaving, I have seen much to support the opposite. Do your females not mind their mates visiting such places?"

"They can't mind what they don't know."

Brak hissed. "These men lie, too? They have no honor. My people would cast them out as exiles."

"Yeah, I think that's already happened, buddy. We're *all* exiles out here, and the irony is, we cast ourselves out."

"Yesss, I have thought this also. Perhaps we will have the sense to return home someday."

As they reached Lucien's car, he waved it open, and they climbed in the back. "Hubble Mountain, Winterside, 112 Evergreen Street," Lucien said as he buckled up.

"Right away, sir," the car replied. It pulled out of the parking lot and into the abandoned alley where the club was located. Down here in the sub-districts, hover cars all drove along the streets, since there wasn't technically any sky to fly up into. The streets themselves were really just one long tunnel after the next. Lucien was amazed people didn't get claustrophobic living down here.

The car took them straight up a *riser* street to the surface, and they popped out in the middle of a park filled with snow-covered evergreens. They soared high into the sky and joined a stream of traffic at five hundred meters heading for Hubble Mountain.

"Krak—" Lucien cursed, suddenly remembering. "—I forgot to stop at your place, Brak. You're welcome to stay the night with us if you want. You can help us keep an eye on Atara."

"That is fine," Brak said.

"Great. I'll take some steaks out of the freezer, for you."

Brak grimaced. "No, I buy fresh."

"Frozen's free."

"Tastes free, too."

Lucien laughed. "Suit yourself."

* * *

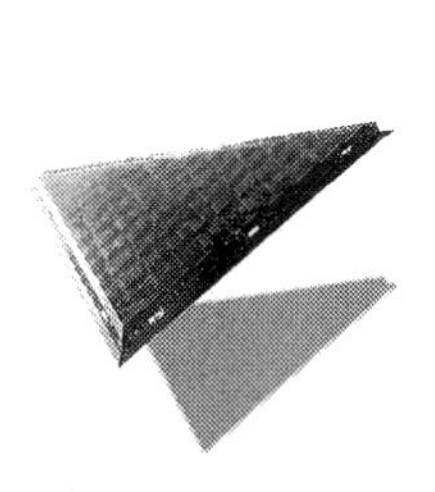

Astralis

"I have Lieutenant Commander Wheeler here to see you, ma'am."

"Send her in, please, Corita," Tyra replied via her

ARCs. "And make sure we're not disturbed."

"Yes, ma'am."

As soon as her secretary ended the comm connection, Tyra turned off her ARCs. A moment later, the door chimed and slid open, revealing Commander Wheeler. Her blond hair was tied up in a bun, tucked under a black navy hat, but frizzy strands leaked out at odd angles, giving her a frazzled look. Making matters worse, she wasn't wearing any makeup to conceal the dark circles under her eyes.

"Please, take a seat, Commander," Tyra said, and indicated one of the chairs in front of her desk.

Commander Wheeler sat down, looking both tired and wary. "You should have already received a list of officers from both the Navy and the Marines..."

Tyra nodded. "I did." As she said that, she indicated her eyes with two fingers, then pointed to Wheeler's still-glowing green eyes. She opened and closed her fist a few times fast.

Wheeler caught on, and the light disappeared from her eyes as she turned off her ARCs. She slumped in her chair, as if someone had just cut the strings that were holding her up, and relief flickered through her gaze. "You think they're watching us, too."

Tyra inclined her head to the other woman, surprised that Wheeler had begun figuring things out on her own. "Who's *they* to you, Commander?"

Some of the wariness returned to Wheeler's eyes. "The admiral, the XO, Chief Ellis... whoever else was touched by the Faros."

Tyra nodded slowly. "My daughter."

Wheeler's eyebrows shot up. "Your daughter?"

"Yes. She's been showing signs of strange behavior lately—*sociopathic* is the word that comes to mind."

"The admiral and the XO have been behaving strangely, too. They've been raving about Etherus with every other breath."

"Really?" Tyra asked.

"They make it sound like idle talk, but..." Wheeler shook her head. "Anyone who knew them, would know that they didn't join *Astralis's* mission because they were against Etherus or the way he was running things. They joined the mission because they're explorers at heart, and they wanted to know what's out there."

"So they've been displaying attitudes and behaviors that are out of character for them."

"Yes, ma'am. They've also been showing an unusual amount of solidarity. Graves and Stavos rarely agreed on anything, but lately it's like they're two halves of the same whole."

Usually the chief commanding officer of a ship would pick his or her own XO, but *Astralis's* mission protocol dictated that the senior officer of the Marines had to be the XO in order to balance power between the two branches of the military.

Wheeler went on, "Ever since the Faros got to them, they've changed. We must have missed something in their probe analyses. I keep thinking we should have them re-tested, but if they *are* somehow compromised, then how can I suggest they get tested without drawing attention to myself? I might wind up dead the next day, the victim of an apparent accident."

Tyra nodded. "Or they might just wipe your memory."

Wheeler's eyes sharpened. "They can do that?"

"I think they'd choose to wipe selective memories, such as the memory of your suspicions, but yes, I do. I signed the Emergency War Measures Act along with all the other councilors, and I *remember* signing it, but I know that it's not something that I or any of the other councilors would have signed."

"Then..."

"They have someone—or *several someones*—inside the Resurrection Center."

Wheeler blew out a breath. "How are we supposed to fight this?"

"My husband and I already have a plan, but we were hoping you might help us."

"What plan?"

Tyra explained what they were doing. When she was done, she added, "The dinner is in three days. You'll be alone on the bridge at the time, so you should be able to keep an eye on things for us, maybe even buy us some time."

Wheeler nodded slowly. "Risky, but if Stavos and Graves aren't there, I think I could manage to help you. You say your husband is working with the Corettis to pull this off?"

Tyra grimaced. "Yes."

"You realize they might have their own agenda for getting into the Res Center. They could hack some kind of back door into the network and then hold the ship's wealthiest and most connected people ransom using their own minds."

"Sounds like what the Faros are doing now."

"Maybe, but for different reasons. We could be trading

one devil for another."

"Better the devil you know," Tyra replied. "We can worry about re-securing the facility's databanks after we've got the affected people in custody."

Wheeler sighed. "I guess we don't have much choice, but I might have been able to get a bomb for you."

"Without someone noticing, or arousing suspicions? What business does a Navy officer have checking out munitions from storage? A Marine Sergeant might get away with that, but not you."

"I guess you have a point there."

"We can't go looking for a Marine to help us without exposing ourselves to additional risks of discovery. At least we know the Corettis haven't been compromised. What would be the point in Faros subverting them? They can't make any decisions on board this ship."

"Not important ones, anyway."

Tyra nodded. "So, can we count on you, Commander?"

"Timing will be crucial. How are we supposed to keep in contact without exposing ourselves to the ships' comm officers, or even simple eavesdropping?"

Tyra opened a drawer in her desk and pulled out a handful of small, transparent ear plugs with flexible arms for microphones. She placed them on the desk and waved a hand over them. With that gesture, the devices shimmered and vanished.

Wheeler leaned forward, peering at eye level with the desk and looking for some sign of the cloaked comm units, but there wasn't even a glimmer.

"Off-the-grid comms. How am I supposed to talk into one of these without the rest of the crew over-hearing?"

"They'll connect up with your ARCs for text-only comms."

Wheeler nodded and waved her hand over the devices. The air shimmered once more and they reappeared. "Where did you get these? The Corettis?"

"The Corettis," Tyra confirmed.

Wheeler took one of the comm units and placed it over her right ear. Having done that, she waved a hand past her ear and it vanished once more. Invisible accessories. Criminals used them all the time. Sophisticated scanners could still find them, but they got past all the more casual inspections.

"I'll send you a message a few hours before the dinner, at fifteen hundred hours," Tyra said.

"I'll be waiting," Wheeler replied.

Tyra breathed a sigh of relief. "It's good to have you with us on this."

Wheeler nodded. "I'm glad I'm not the only one who's been noticing things."

Tyra nodded. "Let's hope we can find the evidence we're looking for. If we fail, we'll likely all wake up in the Corrections Center with no idea of how we got there."

"Then you better make sure this works. Just whatever you do, don't *actually* blow up the center."

"The bomb is a bluff."

"But it is a real bomb?" Wheeler asked.

Tyra nodded. "My husband tells me it has to be, or the ship's sensors will reveal that it's a bluff."

"Exactly. I guess that's the Corettis' part in all this. Just make sure you keep an eye on them."

Tyra nodded. "I'll mention your concerns to my husband. One way or another, it's in their best interests to help us catch Ellis and the others."

"Sure, but after that..."

"All bets are off." Tyra nodded. "I'm with you there, Commander. We'll be careful."

"Good," Wheeler replied. "Let's hope that's enough."

CHAPTER 41

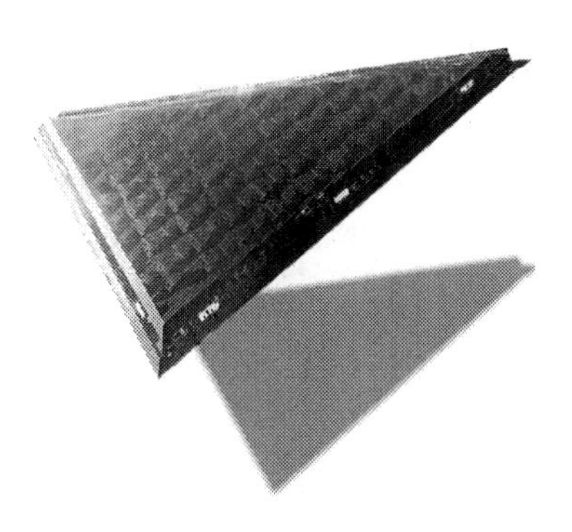

Astralis

Lucien sat with Tyra on the living room couch, her head leaning on his shoulder, his arm around hers. They watched the fire crackle in the hearth, mesmerized by the flickering flames, warming themselves by its light and each other's heat.

The kids were asleep—Atara in her room, and Theola in her crib in the master bedroom upstairs. They'd moved her crib now that they knew what they were dealing with.

Brak was out on the deck, enjoying the cold—he said it reminded him of *New Noctune,* the facet of New Earth that had been modeled after the world where his species had evolved.

That left him and Tyra alone together, enjoying a rare moment of intimacy that left Lucien feeling *whole* again for the first time in a very long time. They'd grown so far apart over the past few years that it was easy to forget how close they used to be. Lucien allowed his eyes to drift shut.

"I wish this could last forever," he mumbled.

"Mmmm?" Tyra asked.

Lucien repeated that sentiment, louder this time.

"I'd like that, too..." Tyra said, but trailed off as if she'd left something unsaid.

Lucien glanced down, seeking her gaze. "It *could* last. We could be like this again. All you have to do is resign from the council."

"And then? Do what?"

Lucien shrugged. "Whatever you want. So long as it's nine to five instead of nine to nine."

"We'd have to move. We won't be able to afford to live like this anymore. We might even have to leave the surface level."

"So? We get an apartment in the districts like everyone else. Is that so bad? We can still visit the surface, use the parks, go to the restaurants. All we'd miss is the view—" He gestured to the picture window beside them, the world beyond cloaked in the shadows of the night. "You're never here to appreciate that, anyway."

Tyra straightened, and her head left his shoulder; he removed his arm from around hers, and suddenly they were two mismatching halves again.

Lucien grimaced, angry at himself for ruining the moment by bringing up an old argument, and angry at Tyra for reacting the same way she always had.

The fire crackled in the hearth, and they watched the flames dance. After a while, Lucien glanced back at his wife. There were tears glistening on her cheeks.

"Tyra?" he asked, surprised to see that.

"Okay," she said.

"Okay...?"

"I'll resign."

Lucien blinked, not sure whether to trust his ears. He'd waited so long for her say those words that now he couldn't be sure he'd actually heard them. "You'll..."

Tyra turned to him, and nodded once. "I'll resign. We'll move to the districts, and then we'll be a family again."

Lucien pulled her into a fierce embrace, wrapping her up and cradling her to his chest. He breathed in the scent of her hair, reveling in the moment. His heart felt like it might explode.

"You've made me so happy," he whispered.

Tyra shook in his arms, crying. "I'm sorry it took me so long."

He withdrew to an arm's length to look her in the eye. "What changed your mind?"

She shook her head. "All of this. You, sending your clone to join the expeditionary forces. Atara, being turned into a..." Tyra trailed off for lack of words to describe what had happened to their daughter.

A faro? Lucien thought.

"Our family is falling apart, Lucien, and suddenly me being the councilor of a city that doesn't even exist anymore doesn't seem so important."

Lucien nodded. "We'll put the pieces back together as soon as this is over. I promise."

Tyra nodded hesitantly. "I talked to Wheeler today."

"And?"

"She's agreed to help us, but she doesn't trust Coretti,

Lucien. She thinks he's got his own agenda for getting into the Resurrection Center."

"I don't trust him either, and he probably *does* have his own agenda, but we need to deal with one threat at a time."

Tyra nodded. "That's what I told her. Just... be careful, okay? Make sure you go into this with both eyes open."

"I will." Lucien pulled Tyra close and kissed the top of her head.

"I wish I were going with you."

"We need you more at the banquet. You keep Stavos and Graves busy so Wheeler can do her part."

Tyra pushed him away, but he didn't have time to ask why, because she grabbed his shirt and pulled his lips down to hers for a real kiss.

With that, something snapped inside of Lucien and memories came flooding back, memories of all the good times, followed by visions of the bright future ahead. They were going to be a family again. Finally. Lucien couldn't think of anything he wanted more.

All they had to do was reverse whatever had been done to Atara and get *Astralis* back from the Faros.

After that, life would be just about perfect.

*   *   *

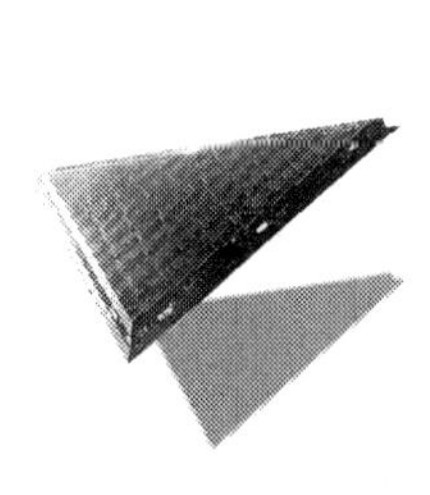

Atara sat in the dark on the landing at the bottom of the stairs. She'd been on her way up to see Theola. Poor, innocent little Theola. Atara smirked at the thought of her baby sister. One-year-olds were funny. They would put almost anything in their mouths.

Atara opened her fist, revealing a small, gleaming glass ball. She'd stolen it from a flower vase and had been on her way up to wake Theola and show her the pretty new toy.

But on her way up the stairs, Atara had overheard her parents talking in the living room, and she'd stopped to listen in. She knew they were suspicious of her, so she had to take advantage of moments like these to figure out what they were planning to do about it.

Most of their conversation was sappy and meaningless. Atara was just about to continue up the stairs when she overheard something interesting—

"I talked to Wheeler today."

"And?"

"She's agreed to help us, but she doesn't trust Coretti, Lucien. She thinks he's got his own agenda for getting into the Resurrection Center."

"I don't trust him either, and he probably *does* have his own agenda, but we need to deal with one threat at a time."

"That's what I told her. Just... be careful, okay? Make sure you go into this with both eyes open."

"I will."

"I wish I were going with you."

"We need you more at the banquet. You keep Stavos and Graves busy so Wheeler can do her part."

The mention of the Resurrection Center was interesting. Atara the five-year-old, knew nothing about the significance of her parents trying to get in there, but *Atara the Faro* knew plenty. It meant they weren't just suspicious of *her,* they were suspicious of the others, too, and they were trying to get proof.

There wasn't much Atara could do about it directly—five year-olds couldn't alert security and expect to be taken seriously—but Atara could do something better than that. She crept down the stairs and back down the hallway to her room. She opened the door carefully, and shut it quietly behind her.

Once she was back in bed, under the covers, she activated her ARCs and composed a message, text-only, to Chief Councilor Ellis.

She attached the audio log from her ARCs and told Ellis to listen to the last five minutes of it.

Chief Ellis answered a few moments later, thanking her for the information. He also told her not to draw any more attention to herself—that meant giving Theola the glass ball would have to wait. Atara wasn't happy about it, but she understood the importance of staying undercover, so she agreed to Ellis's orders. For now.

After the conversation ended, Atara lay awake in bed, dreaming up other kinds of mischief she could cause. The ideas she came up with weren't as much fun as slipping her sister a deadly new toy, but they would be amusing nonetheless.

Atara grew sleepy, and her hand relaxed. The glass ball fell from her hand and bounced noisily on the floor. Her eyes flew wide, and she watched the ball roll along the floor, gleaming in the dark. *Oops.*

A moment later, Atara heard footsteps in the hallway, and then the door to her room cracked open, and a bright wedge of light fanned out along the floor. She froze, listening to her parents whisper in the entryway.

"I told you she was asleep," Tyra said.

"I thought I heard something..."

"Maybe it was Brak?"

"Look." Lucien walked into view, and Atara shut her eyes to slits, watching him through a veil of eyelashes. He bent to pick up the glass ball and showed it to Tyra.

"What's that?" she asked.

Lucien straightened and held the ball up to the light. Tyra walked over to see.

"It's from my vase!" she said, her whispers suddenly sharp. "But that's up on the bar. How did she even reach that?"

"She must have stood on something," Lucien said.

Like a bar stool? Atara smirked.

Both her parents turned to look at her, and Atara froze, not even daring to breathe.

"Atara?" Tyra asked, not whispering anymore.

They don't know I'm awake. They can't!

"Her ARCs are on," Lucien said. "She's awake."

Oops. Atara noticed the subtle glow bouncing back off her eyelids.

"Atara..." Tyra pressed in a warning voice. "Stop pretending to be asleep."

She cracked her eyes open and stretched. "Mmmm?" she mumbled sleepily.

Her parents came to stand beside her bed. Tyra went down on her haunches, her brow pinched with suspicion.

"Why are you pretending to be asleep? And what are your ARCs doing on at this time?"

"I was watching cartoons, and I fell asleep. I wasn't pretending."

"So why didn't your ARCs turn off?"

Double oops. ARCs were designed to turn off automatically when the wearer fell asleep, unless they were specifically set to *always on*. "I don't know," Atara lied.

"Well turn them off, we'll look at the settings together in the morning,"

Atara nodded sleepily. "Okay..."

Tyra held up the glass ball. "Where did you get this?"

Atara shrugged. Her parents didn't know her plans for that bauble. "It looked pretty," she said.

"And you stood on a chair to reach the bar? You could have fallen and hit your head!"

You'd like that, wouldn't you?

"Don't do it again, do you understand me?" Tyra said.

Atara nodded. She'd do something else, instead.

"Turn off your ARCs."

Atara did so.

"Good. Now go to bed, honey." Tyra stood up and walked away.

"Okay..."

"Goodnight, Atty," Lucien said from the door.

"Goodnight, Daddy. Goodnight, Mommy. I love you."

"Love you, too," Tyra replied.

Lucien didn't say anything.

Still mad about the broken finger? Atara wondered, and smiled to herself. The door swung shut again, and Atara breathed out a sigh. *That was close....*

CHAPTER 42

Astralis

"You and I both know she wasn't watching cartoons," Lucien said.

Tyra gazed down on Theola, reticent to tear her eyes away from their youngest daughter. She and Lucien had come up to check on her right after leaving Atara's room. Thankfully she was fine. Slowly, Tyra turned to face her husband. "Then what was she doing?"

"I don't know, but I'm going to find out."

"How?"

Lucien smiled, then glanced around quickly, as if to make sure Atara hadn't somehow snuck in behind them. He walked up to the door and touched the keypad. Tyra heard the deadbolt slide into place.

"Lucien?" she prompted.

He turned back to her and answered in a whisper,

"Ever since Atara tripped me, I used the parental controls on her ARCs to enable monitoring. All I have to do now is check the history to see what she's been doing."

"What if she found out?"

Lucien shook his head. "If she knew I was monitoring her, then she wouldn't have been using her ARCs to do whatever she was doing. She would have known to be more careful."

"But if you use your ARCs to access hers, and someone in the Resurrection Center is monitoring *you,* then they'll know we're suspicious of her," Tyra said.

"We'll log in from our holoscreen," he said, nodding to the screen at the foot of their bed. The screen was innocuously disguised as a famous painting—*Passing the Torch*—that depicted one sun rising over a purple sea just as another one set.

Lucien waved the screen to life and the painting disappeared, replaced by a hub of available applications. He selected the browser application and summoned a holographic keypad to type in an address. The keypad was safer than using his ARCs right now. A login screen appeared with the title, *Monitoring for Atara Ortane,* and Tyra watched him type in his credentials. That done, an account summary with various tabs appeared. Lucien used his finger to move a floating cursor and select the tab titled *Activity Log*.

"Well, well..." he said, shaking his head. "Cartoons my ass. Look at this." He pointed to the most recent lines of the log.

Tyra walked over to look, and promptly gasped. "She sent a message to Chief Councilor Ellis?"

Lucien nodded slowly. "I guess that settles any doubts

we may have had about them. Let's see..." Lucien selected the message to see what Atara had sent.

"It's an audio log from her ARCs," Tyra said. "She told him to listen to it. What did she overhear?"

Lucien looked at her. "Us. Talking in the living room."

"But we weren't talking about anything..." Tyra trailed off, remembering.

"You mentioned Wheeler, and Coretti, and the Res Center, and I mentioned the banquet. We may as well have called Ellis and told him what we're planning." Lucien keyed the log for playback and dialed down the volume to make sure Atara didn't wake up. What they heard on the log only confirmed their fears. Atara had heard everything.

"It's over," Tyra said. "Ellis will have security officers here to arrest us by morning."

Lucien nodded slowly. "Probably. Or even tonight."

"Can't we use this to incriminate them? What would our daughter be doing talking to the Chief Councilor?"

"It's odd, I'll give you that, but Ellis could explain it easily enough. He could say he suspected we were planning some kind of terrorist plot and so he used our own daughter to spy on us."

"But why Ellis? Why not get the cops involved?"

"Because I'm a cop," Lucien said. "Ellis will say he didn't trust the ship's security forces to catch one of their own."

Tyra could feel her eyes drifting out of focus. Her heart thudded in her chest, and blood rushed in her ears. "What are we going to do?"

"We're going to break into the center now. Tonight."

"But the banquet—"

"Is no use to us now."

"What about the plan to get in with a maintenance worker? It's the middle of the night!"

"You've never heard of 24-hour repairmen?"

"Lucien—Wheeler won't be able to help you."

"You don't know that. Try and call her. If you can't reach her, then we'll just have to go in blind."

"And what am I supposed to do? Sit here and pray to Etherus that you pull this off?"

Lucien nodded. "Can't hurt."

"Lucien, I was being serious."

"So was I."

Tyra frowned.

"Stay here with Theola, and whatever you do, don't let Atara find out that Brak and I are gone."

"What if she gets up and goes to look in on Brak?"

"I'll lock his door before we leave, and if you lock yourself in here, too, then even if she starts wandering around in the middle of the night, she won't figure out we're missing until morning. Hopefully by then this will all be over."

Tyra frowned. "There has to be something else I can do."

"There isn't." Lucien went to her walk-in closet, and she followed him there. He dropped to his haunches in front of their safe and typed in the key-code. Locking bolts *thunked* as they slid aside, and Lucien opened the safe. He withdrew the three cloaking comm units that Coretti had provided. He fitted one over his ear and then waved a hand over it to make it disappear. Then he handed her another one, and pocketed the last for Brak. Tyra fitted hers to her ear as Lucien had done.

I'll let you know once we're in position, Lucien said via a text-only message. *If security arrives looking for us before then... stall them.*

Tyra nodded. That was the only useful thing she could do at this point. *I'll do my best. Be careful.*

I will. I love you, he replied, and kissed her quickly on the lips.

Love you, too, Tyra texted back. She followed him through their room and watched as he unlocked the door and left.

After a moment of staring at the shut door in shock, Tyra went and locked it via the keypad; then she composed another text message—

Commander Wheeler, come in!

She waited a few seconds, and then tried again. *Wheeler, this is Councilor Ortane, I need to speak with you urgently!*

But no reply came.

* * *

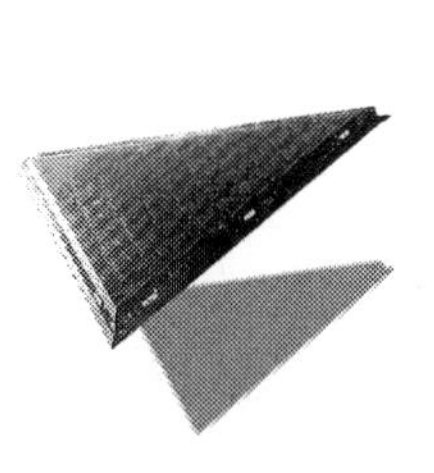

Astralis

Lucien and Brak went straight to the Crack of Dawn, hoping to find Joe Coretti there. They got lucky, but Joe wasn't amused about the change of plans.

"That little brat mentioned my name?"

"Technically my wife did."

Joe scowled. "Security will be swarming around here soon thanks to her. I wasn't planning to join you in the Res Center, but now I have to."

"You're coming with?" Lucien asked.

Joe nodded. "You think I'm going to stick around here waiting to get arrested as an accomplice in your plot? Frek that." He jumped up from his throne-shaped chair and snatched a still-smoldering glow stick from the ashtray beside him. He waved over his shoulder for them to follow. Bob the android waited for them to go first.

"What about the rest of the team?" Lucien asked.

"I'll get them to meet us along the way," Joe mumbled around his glow stick. He led them through a bedroom with rumpled sheets and holocorders sitting around on charging pads, to a big ornate walk-in closet with black, mirrored cabinets and gold trim. Joe walked straight to the back of the closet and opened one of those cabinets. Dozens of expensive suits hung inside, but Joe pushed them aside and waved his hand over the wall behind them. At that, a recessed door appeared and slid aside. Joe walked through and lights snapped on, revealing another type of closet, this one stocked with racks of weapons. Lucien and Brak followed him in, while Bob stayed to guard the entrance. The android was already wearing a pair of bulky pulse pistols.

"What's your preference?" Joe asked, standing in front of a rack of automatic rifles.

"We're infiltrating the center through ducts, so small is better."

"If you say so," Joe snorted, and grabbed one of the rifles for himself. He pointed to another rack filled with pistols, and Lucien walked over there.

Lucien was busy examining an automatic stun pistol when Joe came over and took it from him. "You planning to *stun* the Marine bots when they come for us?" Joe put the pistol back on the rack and removed a laser pistol and two spare charge packs.

Lucien accepted the weapon with a frown. Joe passed him a twin-holster gun harness, and Lucien belted it around his torso. "What about live personnel at the center? We can't kill them."

"Why not? They won't stay dead. It's just a longer-acting form of stun."

Lucien eyed Joe. "We're not killing anyone. We'll never get out of going to the corrections center if we leave a trail of bodies behind us."

"Fine," Joe said, and passed the automatic stun pistol back.

Lucien slipped it into the other holster. "If we do this right, we shouldn't have to use our guns at all."

"Sure, you keep thinking that," Joe said, and patted the rifle hanging off his shoulder.

Lucien turned to look for Brak and found him examining a rack of swords and knives.

"You like those?" Joe asked, strolling over to the Gor.

Brak picked a pair of razor-shielded swords from the rack and held them up to the light to examine the mirror-smooth blades.

"They aren't going to be much use without armor," Lucien said. "You'll never get close enough to use them."

Joe bent to retrieve a bulky belt and vest from a shelf below the melee weapons—a personal shield. He handed the pieces to Brak. "This should help."

Brak put down the swords and donned the pieces of the shield. The vest wouldn't close, but he cinched it shut with the belt.

"Does it work?" Lucien asked, eyeing the setup skeptically.

A loud *pop* sounded, and the air shimmered around Brak.

"Looks like it does," Joe said, and grabbed a matching vest and belt for himself. Lucien took another and tested the shield as Brak had done, activating it via his ARCs. His augmented reality contacts weren't connected to the ship's network, so he decided he could probably risk using them to make short-ranged connections with other devices.

"We'd better get out of here," Joe said. "We've taken too long as it is. Grab some grenades before you go."

Brak deactivated the shield and collected a pair of belts and scabbards for the razor swords he'd chosen. He strapped them crosswise across his back and went to get a stun pistol for his waist.

"We're ready," Lucien said, turning to Joe.

"If you say so," Joe replied, his nose wrinkling at their modest choice of weaponry. He led the way out, back through his clothes closet and bedroom, through his *throne room,* for lack of a better word, to an elevator beside the stairs. The elevator opened immediately and they piled in. Bob walked in last, and Joe selected P1 from the floors listed.

A split second later, they walked out into a parking garage filled with sporty-looking hover cars. Joe walked by all of them to a hover van marked with a generic utility company logo. He waved the doors open as they approached and they climbed in. Lucien and Brak sat facing Joe and his android, Bob. Joe gave directions to the driver program, indicating another night club—presumably where they were going to meet Fizk and Guntha.

The van's engines rumbled to life, and then it drove out of the parking lot, up a ramp, and through the public parking area behind the club. From there they joined the alley that Lucien and Brak had driven down all of half an hour ago.

Seedy bars and clubs flashed by the windows in a neon-colored blur.

"You look nervous, Lucy-lu."

Bob the android wore a blank expression, but Joe was smiling like he didn't have a care in the world. "And you look too calm for someone who's making an impromptu assault on the most secure facility on *Astralis*."

Joe shrugged and turned to look out the side window as the van rolled to stop outside a busy-looking bar. They hadn't even reached the end of the alley yet.

Two men were waiting on the curb. Joe waved the door open for them and they climbed inside. Guntha sat beside Lucien, elbowing him in the ribs to make him shove over, while Fizk, the demolitions expert, sat with a scowl beside Joe.

"What the frek, Joe?" Fizk said. "The op isn't supposed to be for another three days!"

Joe jerked his chin at Lucien. "Lucy's brat ratted us out."

"A narc just like her daddy," Fizk sneered.

Joe ordered the van to take them to the Res Center and

it raced down the alley once more.

"The Faros got to her," Lucien explained.

"Sure..." Fizk drawled.

Joe elbowed him in the ribs. "Shut up and listen. Skullman—" Brak hissed and bared his teeth. "—yeah, you," Joe said. "You're going to cut the power to the center's ventilation system."

"Why Brak?" Lucien asked.

"Because none of us can pull off that disappearing act of his. Now listen up, Skulls, it has to look like an overload, not sabotage, so you need to wire in a capacitor—we call it a *spike.* That will generate the power surge. The spike will dump its charge automatically after you hook it up. All you have to do is match the colors of the wires and splice them together. Don't let the wrong ones touch or you'll be the one who gets overloaded. You think you can do that, Skulls?" Brak hissed, and Joe looked to Lucien. "Is that a yes?"

Lucien smiled. "Close enough."

"All right. I'm going to get you close to the center, but you'll have to find your own way in." Joe produced a palm-sized holo projector and placed it on the floor of the van. He waved it to life and browsed through a list of files until he found the one he was looking for.

A *3D* schematic of the center appeared, and Joe zoomed in on the lowermost levels where the center's dedicated reactor lay. He selected a maintenance corridor and indicated a particular set of conduits. "These three conduits power the center's climate control system. You'll have to overload all three to take down the power to the ducts. Once you've done that, all those servers in the records room are going to start getting real hot, real fast. It'll trip an alert, and they'll call for a maintenance crew."

"What about hacking into the center's comms?" Lucien asked.

Joe waved his hand to dismiss that concern. "Already done."

"How?" Lucien demanded. "You only shared the plan with me earlier today. You're telling me you hacked in sometime in the past few hours?"

Joe just looked at him. "I'm a fast worker."

Lucien didn't buy that for a second. They either had someone working inside the Res Center or else they'd hacked into the center's comms a long time ago already. Either way, it implied that Coretti's plan to infiltrate the center wasn't an old, discarded idea, but a current one. Tyra was right: Joe definitely had his own agenda for getting into the center.

"Moving on..." Joe said as he zoomed the schematic back out. "The rest of us will be waiting in this alley here." He pointed to one side of the center. "As soon as Guntha gives us word that he's deactivated the security system in the vents, we'll sneak in and make our way to the records room."

"What about Brak?" Lucien asked.

"I'm sure Skulls can find his own way out."

"No, I mean, isn't he going to join us in the ducts?"

"I don't see how," Joe said, and eyed Brak speculatively. "He's too big to fit."

"If all I do is disable the power, then why do I bring weapons and a shield?" Brak demanded.

Joe shrugged. "Come back here and guard the getaway car."

"We won't need a getaway car," Lucien said. "Once we find what we're looking for, they'll realize why we had to break into the center, and we'll get to walk out the front doors—unless you're planning to commit some real crimes while we're there...?"

"I just like to know we've got our asses covered. You all clear on your jobs?"

Everyone nodded except for Fisk. "You have the bomb?"

Joe nodded over Lucien's shoulder. "It's in the back."

"Good."

Joe waved away the holographic schematic and pocketed the projector once more. That done, he withdrew a handful of glow sticks from another pocket and passed them out.

"For luck," he said, holding one out to Lucien.

"No thanks. I'll make my own."

Joe smirked and settled back against his seat. He squeezed the butt, and the stick lit itself, glowing blue-white all along its length and smoking from the tip.

Soon Lucien and Brak were choking on clouds of sweet-smelling smoke.

Ten minutes later, the van stopped, having arrived at its destination. Lucien waved the door open and scrambled out. His head was spinning so badly that he actually fell in the alley on his hands and knees.

Behind him, the gangsters all burst out laughing.

"What the frek is in those sticks?" Lucien asked.

"I told you it was a good batch," Joe replied, still chuckling. "Skullman, you're up. You wearing your comms...? Good. Guntha pass him the spike."

"Where is it?"

"Behind you. Reach around... there you go."

Lucien recovered to the point that he could climb to his feet without fear of falling again. He turned to see Brak getting out of the van. The Gor stepped on Joe's foot as he left, and the gangster cursed viciously and punched him on the thigh.

"Oops. Sorry," Brak said as he came to stand beside Lucien. He didn't appear affected by the glow smoke.

Joe scowled back at him. "Better leave your gear here, Skulls. You can come back for it later if you feel like having some fun."

Brak stripped naked and cloaked himself, but the *spike* remained visible, floating in one hand. Invisible fingers closed around it, and the device all but disappeared.

"Good enough," Joe said. "Let us know when you're done, and make sure you get the right conduits. They should be marked CC or CC-SYS. If you get lost, send me a message, and I'll try to guide you from the schematic."

Brak gave no reply, but Lucien heard a faint whisper of footsteps and felt the air stirring as Brak left.

"Skulls?" Joe asked.

Lucien nodded down to the end of the alley. "He's already gone."

"Frekking aliens," Joe muttered.

CHAPTER 43

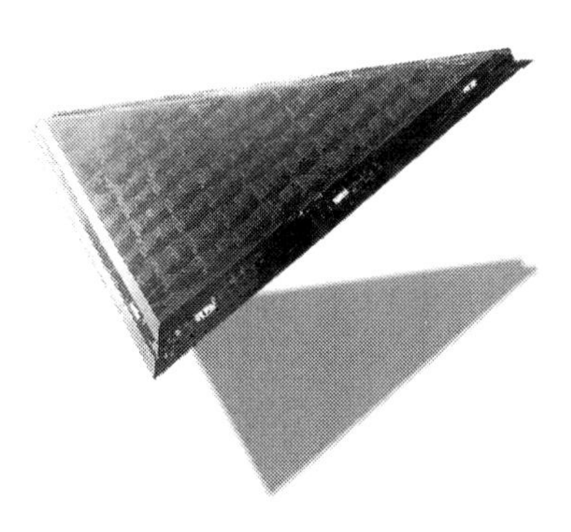

Astralis

Skulls? Joe asked via text message.

But there was no reply.

Brak? Lucien tried.

"Frek it!" Joe said. "Why doesn't he answer?"

Lucien shook his head. It had been over half an hour with no news from his partner.

"They must have been waiting for us," Joe said, looking around quickly, as if expecting to find a squad of security officers lurking in the shadows of the alley. He took two quick steps toward Lucien and grabbed him by his shield vest, as if to hoist him up onto tip-toes, but the difference in their heights made that impossible. "Is this some kind of sting?"

"You're joking, right?" Lucien asked.

Joe sneered and began nodding to himself as if he'd

suddenly figured it all out. "That bit about the Faros taking over *Astralis* was a load of krak, wasn't it? You're undercover, trying to pin something on us. Well it's not going to work. I tape everything that happens in the club. I've got a recording of you explaining how all this was your idea."

"This isn't a setup," Lucien growled, and jerked out of Joe's grasp.

"Then why's your partner gone dark on us?"

A telltale hiss sounded, and the air beside Joe shimmered. "Boo," Brak said as he appeared.

Joe almost jumped into Lucien's arms. "For frek's sake!" he roared and aimed his rifle at the Gor. "I should shoot you!"

Brak grinned and chuckled darkly. "Gors are hard to kill. You shoot me, I'll still have time to rip out your throat."

Joe scowled. "Why didn't you reply?"

Brak waved a hand over the comm link to make it de-cloak, too. "No signal on the reactor level," he explained.

"Did you overload the conduits?"

Before Brak could answer, Guntha called to them from where he sat inside the van. "We've got the call! I'm starting the clock. Twenty minutes."

"Everybody in!" Joe barked.

Lucien jumped in the back of the van and buckled up while Joe gave directions to the car. They turned around and went back up the alley to join the main street running by the entrance of the Resurrection Center. From there they drove by the entrance and pulled into the guest parking lot. Joe directed the van to park near the back, in the shadows. Guntha waved the door open and climbed out. He'd changed into a maintenance worker's coveralls while they'd waited for

Brak, so he was ready to go. Guntha walked around the back of the van and retrieved a tool box.

I'll let you know as soon as I've got the security disabled, Guntha texted via their comm links.

We'll be waiting, Joe replied. "Looks like you get to come along, after all, Skulls," Joe said aloud.

"Yesss..." Brak replied as he retrieved his equipment from where he'd left it littering the floor of the van. Before long he was dressed and ready for action again.

While they waited for Guntha to check in, Fizk popped open the briefcase in his lap to check on his bomb, and Lucien thought to check on his wife.

"Tyra, are you there?" he asked aloud.

"Finally!" she replied. "I was afraid to call and distract you at the wrong moment. Is everything okay?"

"We're about to go in. No word from Wheeler?"

"No, sorry. You're on your own."

Lucien nodded. "All right. I guess—"

Lucien, they're here... Tyra said, switching to text-only comms.

Who is? Ship security? Stall them. Ask to see their warrant.

Not security. Marines. Graves is with them.

A muffled *bang* sounded in Lucien's ear, followed by the sound of Theola crying and Tyra whispering reassurances in their daughter's ear. *They just broke down the front door, Lucien... they're coming up the stairs!*

Hide!

Another *bang* sounded, followed by Tyra saying, "Don't shoot! I have a baby!" Then came the muffled screech of weapons fire and a *thud.* Theola screamed. Another *screech* of weapons fire sounded, and then her cries cut off sharply.

"Tyra!" Lucien yelled.

No reply.

"Shhh!" Joe hissed. "Are you trying to get us caught?"

Lucien was shocked speechless. Graves had just shot his wife and his baby girl. His mind raced. He must have stunned them. He'd never get away with killing them. But still, if they hadn't adjusted the intensity of their weapons properly, they could have killed Theola by accident.

"Talk to me, Lucy-lu..." Joe said. "What's going on?"

Before Lucien could say anything, a gruff voice joined the conversation. "Hello." It was Graves, speaking to them over their comm links.

"I'll kill you!" Lucien roared.

"You can't kill me, Lucien," Graves replied. "Who else is on the line? Coretti?"

Joe's eyes widened, but he said nothing.

"Listen up. Security at the Resurrection Center has already been alerted, and in case you think you can get by them, the Marines are on their way. You're not going to get far, so I suggest you turn back now while you still can, and maybe we can all just forget that this happened."

"Frek you, Graves," Lucien said.

"I have your wife and daughter here. If you *do* somehow expose me, then I'll expose them—to space. What do you say? Fair trade?"

Lucien gritted his teeth. "If you touch a hair on their heads, I'll rip you apart!"

Graves laughed at that. "You're welcome to—"

Joe ripped the comm link from Lucien's ear.

"What are you doing?" Lucien demanded, swiping at Joe's hands to grab it back.

The gangster held it out of reach, and he removed the comm unit from his own ear and tossed it aside. "You don't need to listen to that krak. We need to move. It's now or never."

"He has my *family,*" Lucien said.

"Yeah, and if you give in to him now, he'll still have them—but he'll also have everyone else on board." Joe shook his head. "The faster we pull this off, the faster we can send the authorities after them."

Lucien shook his head. "I can't wait that long."

"Then don't, but we've got a ship to save—with or without you."

Lucien looked to Brak, feeling torn.

"I go after your family," he said. "You stay. Get what we came for."

"Good idea. Take the van," Joe added.

"Guntha reports that the security system in the ducts is down," Bob declared.

"We need to move," Joe said. "Let's go!"

Everyone piled out of the van except for Brak.

Lucien traded one last look with his partner. "Find them."

Brak nodded and bared his teeth. "Do not worry."

Joe waved the door shut and ran, taking Lucien by the arm and dragging him along as he went.

Lucien kept half an eye over his shoulder to watch as the hover van raced off with Brak inside. Lucien's mind railed at him. He should have been the one in that van racing off to save his family.

They came to a giant vent along the wall of the Resurrection Center. It should have been blasting waste heat into the garage, but it was dormant now thanks to Brak's work on the reactor level. The vent was at shoulder height, but Bob reached up and ripped it out of the wall, popping rivets as he did so. The android set the cover aside and then turned to help give Joe a boost up into the duct. Next he helped Fizk climb in with the briefcase bomb. Lucien ignored the android's attempts to help him up, and grabbed the rim of the open duct to pull himself up. As soon as he was inside, Bob climbed in behind him. Lucien glanced back to see the android pull the vent back up. A bright flash of crimson light illuminated the duct as Bob used one of his pulse pistols to solder the grate back into place.

"Please proceed," Bob said.

Lucien turned back to the fore and hurried after Joe. As they crawled through the ducts—turning right, left, climbing up, shimmying down—Lucien realized that he had no idea which way they were going, but Joe led the way without hesitation, always knowing exactly where to go. Maybe he was following his stolen schematic, or maybe he had the way memorized. Either way, Lucien was beginning to feel more like the accomplice than the mastermind of this plot.

How was it exactly that Joe already had the van packed with all their equipment just a few hours after they'd supposedly formulated their plan, and several days ahead of schedule?

It was almost like Joe had been planning to execute this plan for some time already when Lucien had come to him with the idea. Joe had admitted this was an old idea that he'd decided not to use, but what if that was a lie? What if he'd caught them in the act of breaking into the Res. Center for their own reasons?

No small coincidence there, but it was possible. If that was the case, then they were using him to add legitimacy to an actual crime.

But what? What could Joe Coretti stand to gain from breaking into the Resurrection Center?

A muffled siren came screaming through the ducts, interrupting Lucien's thoughts, and Joe called out, "Someone sounded the alarm! They must have figured out that Guntha's not the repairman they ordered. Let's pick up the pace, people!"

CHAPTER 44

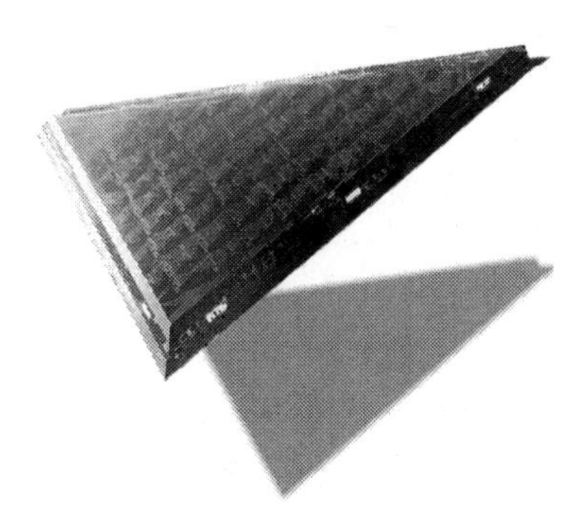

Astralis

Director Nora Helios awoke to the sound of her ARCs trilling with an incoming call. She blinked the sleep from her eyes and sat up.

"Hello?"

"The center has been compromised."

"Ellis? What's going on?"

"A group of insurgents have broken into the Resurrection Center. They're looking for evidence. Can they find any?"

Nora considered that. "If they know what to look for, yes. I covered my tracks, but an in-depth search from a terminal inside the records room will uncover us."

Ellis made an irritated noise in the back of his throat. "Then you'd better make sure they don't have the chance for an in-depth search."

"Have you alerted security? Who are the insurgents?"

"Just get to the center."

"Ellis?"

Connection Terminated flashed before Nora's eyes, and she jumped out of bed. "Lights!" she shouted, and spent a moment blinking spots from her eyes as she hurried to her closet and got dressed. It would take time to find evidence of who they were. Even if someone reached the records room, they'd have to crack the password to access any of the data.

There's still time, Nora assured herself.

* * *

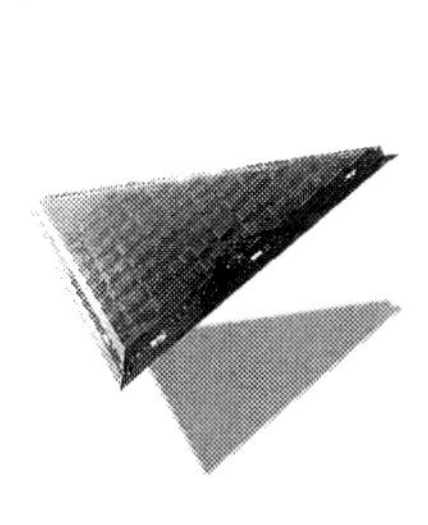

Astralis

"I'm reading multiple lifeforms in the room on the other side," Bob whispered to them as he gazed through the grille at the end of the duct where they were all waiting. According to Joe, this was it: on the other side of that flimsy metal plate was the records room.

"They're too late to stop us," Joe whispered back. "Bob, would you do the honors of announcing our arrival?"

"With pleasure." Bob shimmied forward and punched out the grate. It landed with a *bang,* and he jumped down on top of it with his hands already raised above his head.

Lucien scrambled back from the opening just as a tirade of reflexive laser fire flashed into the end of the duct.

"Stop where you are!" one guard boomed.

"I have stopped where I am," Bob declared.

"This is a restricted area!" a second guard said.

"It is?" Bob asked, sounding confused.

"I'm reading three more in the duct!" a third guard said.

"Come out with your hands up!" the first one ordered.

When none of them replied, another tirade of laser fire streaked into the end of the duct. This time the metal glowed red hot, and the air shimmered with the heat.

"Bob!" Joe yelled. "Enough frekking around!"

"You guards—get out, all of you," Bob demanded. "Shoo."

"What did you just say?"

Lucien snorted.

"We have a bomb," Bob explained. "And we will detonate it if you do not comply with our demands."

"It's a bluff," one guard said.

"It's not! Check the scans!" another said.

"What are your demands?" the first guard asked.

"That you leave the records room immediately. We'll communicate the rest of our demands via comms once you have done so."

Bob didn't get any more backtalk from the guards. There came a hurried shuffling of armored feet, followed by the sound of a door swishing open—then shut.

"That was easy," Joe said, and jumped down into the records room. Fizk handed his bomb down and then climbed down after his boss. Lucien went last. He looked around quickly to get his bearings.

"Bob, secure the entrance!" Joe ordered.

"Yes, boss."

"What now, Lucy-lu?" Joe asked.

The records room was mind-bogglingly large. It was like a maze, with aisles of data storage units extending for at least a kilometer in all directions. "There has to be an access terminal here somewhere..." Lucien said.

"That way," Joe pointed to a distant speck at the end of the aisle where they'd emerged from the ducts.

"How did you—"

"Schematics," Joe replied, cutting him off with a wave of his hand. "I'm going to get on the comms and make sure no one tries anything stupid."

Lucien nodded. "Should be safe to connect our ARCs to the network again." He started down the aisle to the data terminal, connecting his ARCs as he went. He was just in time to see the comms icon light up with a message on an open channel. Lucien played the message and heard Joe's voice echoing inside his head.

"People of *Astralis,* this is Joseph Coretti. I have infiltrated the Resurrection Center with a five kiloton bomb. It's wired to a dead-man's switch and it will go off if myself or any of my associates are either stunned or killed. If you try to remove us from the premises by force, we will also detonate the bomb. I have just one demand: I want a film crew from every holonews channel on *Astralis* to join us here in the records room of the Resurrection Center and bear witness to what we find. You will be shocked to learn that *Astralis* has been taken over from within, its leaders possessed by aliens."

Joe went on to explain more about their suspicions,

rattling off a list of people they suspected to be infected: Ellis, Stavos, Graves, Director Helios—even Lucien's five-year-old daughter, Atara.

"I await the arrival of the first film crew," Joe concluded.

Lucien reached the data terminal at the far end of the room and took a seat there to access the data. The terminal demanded a password to access the data. *Of course. Why didn't I think of that?* Dread stabbed Lucien's heart and panic swirled as he struggled to think of a way to get past the password. Fizk arrived and opened his briefcase on the edge of the terminal.

"What are you doing?" Lucien demanded, watching the bomb as if it were a snake about to bite him. Fragile glass cannisters of red and blue liquid explosives were packed inside the case and wired together with a simple pump. It was a binary explosive. If those cannisters broke...

"I'm fixing your problem," Fizk explained and withdrew a data wafer from a slot in the padding of the case. He inserted the wafer into a port in the side of the data terminal, and a split second later, the password prompt vanished.

"How did you do that?"

"You wanna sit here discussing the finer points of network security, or are you gonna find what you came for?" Fizk demanded.

Lucien frowned and shook his head, once again shocked by the amount of planning Joe had put into this.

"Well? What are you waitin' for?" Fizk prompted. "You better find some evidence before those film crews get here."

Lucien pushed his misgivings aside and set to work. He checked Chief Councilor Ellis's memories first, and selected the most recent records—uploaded just last night while Ellis slept. Drilling down deeper, he found specific memories and hunted through them. Most of them contained mundane details from his day-to-day life—the meal he'd eaten last night, the cloning bills sitting on his desk, council meetings...

But then things started to get interesting. Lucien found a seemingly innocuous memory from just a few days ago. Lucien watched as the terminal faithfully reproduced the view of an artificial sunset from the pool on the rooftop deck of the councilor's penthouse in Summerside. Ellis was busy sipping a cocktail and thinking to himself. His thoughts appeared in subtitles below the scene: *These humans can even rival us when it comes to luxury.* That sounded pretty bad by itself. Lucien flagged that memory, thinking it must contain even more incriminating thoughts—but just one memory wasn't enough. Ellis could claim they'd planted or altered it. Lucien skipped by it, choosing a more recent memory this time.

It was even more incriminating than the last. It depicted Ellis sitting in the dark, in a hotel room in District One, thinking about a power blackout he'd arranged. His thoughts identified him clearly as *Abaddon,* and the memory went on to reveal a message he'd sent to someone named Katawa via a Faro communicator that General Graves had stolen from one of the captured alien shuttles.

"Well, well..." Fizk said. "Looks like you were right."

Lucien nodded. "Yeah..." He was distracted, thinking about what he'd find if he searched Atara's records and looked into *her* recent memories, but he pushed those concerns aside. Saving his daughter would have to wait.

The comms icon on Lucien's ARCs flashed again, this time on a private channel.

"We've got company!" Joe said. "It's Director Helios with a whole lot of security bots. She's demanding we let her in."

"Don't let her!" Lucien said. "She's one of them. She'll probably gun us all down just to keep us quiet!"

"She'll blow the center if she does that!" Joe said.

"And erase all the evidence," Lucien said. "I don't think she cares."

"Frek... they're coming in," Joe said. "Bob! Hold them off!"

Laser fire sounded over the comms, and Lucien spun away from the data terminal, drawing both his pistols and scanning for targets. The aisles were clear, but the entrance wasn't visible from the terminal. Lucien ran to the nearest row of data storage units and took cover behind them. He waved to Fizk, and the curly-haired demolitions expert hurried over to crouch beside him.

"Where the frek are those film crews?" Fizk gritted out.

Lucien nodded to his briefcase bomb. "Is that thing really wired to a dead-man's switch?"

"Yes! Someone shoots one of us, and this whole place goes *boom*. Bob's the only one who's not tied to it."

"Can you disable it?" Lucien asked.

Fizk frowned. "If I do that, they'll just kill us."

"They're going to do that, anyway! At least if you disable it we won't *all* die if just one of us does."

"Right. Yeah, yeah, okay. Let me try. I'm going to need

some time."

"How long?"

"Five, ten minutes at least."

"I'll do what I can," Lucien said. He peeked around the data storage units to check that the way was clear. Fizk grabbed his arm to stop him before he could race out of cover.

"Where are you going?" Fizk demanded.

"To create a distraction!"

"You've gotta stay here and keep them off me while I do this. I can't shoot and defuse a bomb at the same time!"

Lucien looked around for a place that was less exposed. While hiding behind the storage units they could be flanked from either side, but the data terminal provided slightly better cover. Lucien nodded to it. "There. Behind the terminal."

"Nuh-uh. Not good enough."

"It'll have to be," Lucien said, peeking around the corner once more. He caught a glimpse of lasers flashing in the distance. "Call if you're in trouble," Lucien said.

"Frek you," Fizk replied.

Lucien ran out of cover, flicking off the safeties on both his pistols and dialed up the power on the stun pistol. Hopefully it would interrupt a bot's circuits for a second or two.

"Joe?" Lucien asked over their private comms channel. "Where are you?"

"Pinned down!" Joe replied. "Where the frek are *you?*"

"On my way."

"And Fizk?"

"Busy."

"If one of us goes down, it's game over, Lucy."

"Then let's make sure that doesn't happen."

"Like krak! We're outgunned ten to one at least, and more bots are still coming in."

Lucien's mind raced as he ran. Even if Fizk managed to disable the dead man's switch before a lucky shot turned them all into plasma, they didn't stand a chance against that many bots. "You need to tell people what's going on!"

"I tried! They're jamming us. No messages are getting out of this room."

Lucien blew out a breath. "Great."

Down at the end of the aisle a squad of bots came into view, marching in lockstep and firing their integrated laser cannons. Lucien snapped off a burst from his pulse pistol and a handful of stun bolts to draw their attention. Half the squad broke off and turned his way. Lucien ducked down the nearest aisle of storage units just in time to evade an answering stream of laser fire. Those lasers blew molten chunks out of the side of a storage unit, incinerating someone's cherished memories.

"Lucy-lu... where the frek are you!" Joe screamed over the comms.

Lucien peeked around the corner and popped off another burst of fire at the bots marching toward him. The bots fired back in the same instant, and two laser bolts hit Lucien's arm, drawing a hissing protest from his shield. Residual heat bled through the shield, scalding his arm. Lucien ducked back behind cover, gritting his teeth to hold back a scream. "I'm pinned down, too," he said.

CHAPTER 45

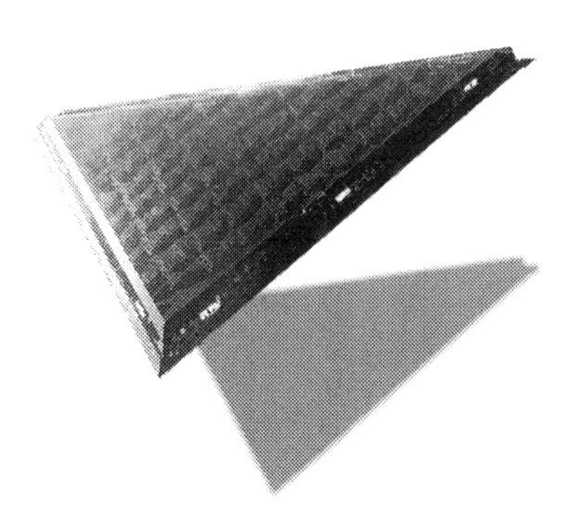

Astralis

"Weapons fire has been detected in the Res Center," Commander Wheeler announced as she leaned over the sensor operator's station. "Did you order the Marines to open fire?" she asked, rounding on Admiral Stavos.

He shook his head. "No, they haven't even arrived yet."

Wheeler scowled. "Well someone's firing! And we can't get anyone on the comms over there."

Stavos smirked. "Sounds like someone called their bluff."

"What if it's not a bluff?" Wheeler demanded. "Then what?"

Stavos arched a woolly white eyebrow at her. "You think they really went in there risking that they could die a permanent death?"

"We can't assume that they didn't," Wheeler replied.

"Admiral—Marines have just arrived at the center," the comms operator announced. "They've detected active comms jamming in the area."

Wheeler shook her head. "Someone's deliberately pushing them into a corner. If that bomb goes off..."

"The Marines are asking for orders," the comm operator said. "What should I tell them?"

"Tell them to hold where they are," Stavos replied.

Wheeler blinked in shock. "So we sent them there for no better reason than to hold a perimeter around the center?"

"You said it yourself—that bomb could go off at any second. I'm not sending people in just to get them killed in an explosion," Stavos replied.

"So send in the bots without their sergeants!"

"You're out of line," Stavos said.

Wheeler turned in a circle to address the rest of the bridge. General Graves was mysteriously absent, making her next in line for the conn after the admiral himself. "With all due respect to the admiral, he is one of the ones implicated in this alleged Faro conspiracy. How can we take orders from him under those circumstances?"

"You're talking mutiny, Lieutenant," Stavos growled. "I could have you court-martialed for what you just said."

"It's Lieutenant *Commander, sir,*" Wheeler corrected. "Guards—arrest the admiral!"

Stavos glanced at the pair of Marine sergeants and the half a dozen bots standing with them at the entrance of the bridge. The sergeants looked to each other before one of them took a hesitant step toward the admiral. "Stand down, Sergeant!" Stavos warned.

Wheeler scowled. This was taking too long. Before anyone could do or say anything else, she drew her sidearm and shot Stavos in the chest.

His eyes bulged as arcs of blue fire skittered over his body. He fell to his knees, teeth gritted, and muscles spasming. Wheeler shot him a second time, and he toppled to the deck and lay still.

A shocked silence hung in the air as Wheeler holstered her sidearm. "I have the conn," she declared. "Comms, tell our Marines to get in there and secure the records room *now*."

"Ma'am... you just shot the—"

"I'm well aware of what I did and of the consequences, Lieutenant," Wheeler said. "Now give the order before it's too late."

"Yes, ma'am..." the comms officer replied. The other officers on the bridge went on staring at Admiral Stavos's motionless body in shock, as if they couldn't believe what had just happened.

Wheeler could hardly believe it herself, but there was no going back now. If Councilor Ortane's husband and his gangster partners couldn't find the proof they were looking for, then Wheeler was headed straight for the corrections center.

She wished she knew why they'd bumped up the schedule for the operation without telling her, but they must have had their reasons.

"I've lost contact with the Marines," the comms operator reported. "They must be inside the center now, ma'am."

Wheeler nodded. "Let's hope they're not too late."

"Aye, Commander."

Several officers were still staring at Admiral Stavos's motionless body. "Eyes on your stations, people!" Wheeler snapped. "Guards, take the admiral to the brig."

"Aye," one of the sergeants replied as he hurried forward with a trio of bots.

"Sensors, get me whereabouts for the General and Chief Ellis."

"Yes, ma'am..." the sensor operator replied.

"Security, revoke all command privileges and authority for Admiral Stavos, General Graves, Chief Ellis, and Director Nora Helios."

"Revoking command privileges for ranking officers requires authorization from everyone on the bridge," the security officer replied. "That will make all of us complicit in this mutiny."

"And following my other orders won't?" Wheeler demanded.

The security officer stood up from his station, and one by one, all the other officers followed his lead. Only the comms and sensor operators remained seated.

"What is this? You can't mutiny against a mutiny!"

The second Marine sergeant from the entrance of the bridge walked up to her. "Ma'am, please come with me."

Unfortunately the sergeant who'd sided with her had already left with Stavos. Wheeler smiled ruefully at him. "Are you going to put me in a cell with the admiral?"

The sergeant shook his head. "By yourself. The admiral is coming back here as soon as he wakes up."

Wheeler's hand drifted to her sidearm, but the sergeant beat her to the draw. A paralyzing jolt of energy hit her, and she lost all control of her body. She fell to the floor with her muscles spasming violently, and then a second stun bolt swept her into oblivion.

CHAPTER 46

Astralis

Tyra awoke to the sound of Theola crying piteously. She blinked bleary eyes and fought against the thick fog swirling inside her head. Waking up from a stun blast was never a pleasant experience, but General Graves' Marine bots had shot her more than once, and that made it doubly unpleasant.

Tyra rolled over to find Theola crying and crawling in mindless circles, dribbling a trail of snot and drool on the carpet around the bed. Her heart leapt into her throat, and she struggled to reach Theola, but her legs were still numb. She ended up dragging herself along the floor until she could grab her daughter's legs. Theola struggled and cried louder, but Tyra flipped her onto her back and pulled her close, wrapping her body around her baby in a fetal position.

With the familiar warmth and smell of her mother,

Theola's cries subsided. She buried her face in Tyra's blouse and popped her thumb in her mouth. "There, you go... shhhh," Tyra whispered as she stroked Theola's hair and kissed her head.

She glanced around for some sign of the general or his marines. Graves was absent from the room, but a pair of bots stood by the broken door, quietly tracking her movements with their cold blue holoreceptors.

"What are you looking at?" she demanded.

Neither of the bots replied, but Tyra heard footsteps coming up the stairs. She clutched Theola tighter. A few second later, Graves walked in. Followed by Atara. Both of them were smiling. "You're awake! Good," Graves said.

"I'll frekking kill you! Do you hear me?"

Graves nodded reasonably and gave Atara a shove to push her in front of him. She glared at him, but he didn't seem to notice. "If you're going to kill someone you should start with her. After all, she's the one who alerted us to what you were planning."

Tyra stared at Graves in horror.

He drew his sidearm and sidled up to her, holding the weapon out butt-first. "Go on. Shoot her."

Tyra stared at the weapon, not trusting Graves, but unable to resist the chance. She snatched the gun, aimed it at Graves' chest, and pulled the trigger twice.

The weapon clicked uselessly, and both Graves and Atara laughed. The general drew a charge pack from his pocket and wagged it in Tyra's face. "It would help if the gun were loaded, wouldn't it?"

Tyra tossed the weapon aside, and it skittered along the floor. "What do you want from us?"

Graves' smile vanished. "Simple. If your husband succeeds in exposing us, then I'm going to kill you both, just as I told him I would. If he fails... then I'll stun you again and have Director Helios make some adjustments to your recollection of events."

Tyra glared hatefully at the general. She tried using her ARCs to call for help, but the familiar light of colored HUD icons in her periphery was gone. "You took my ARCs."

"Of course," Graves replied. He opened his mouth to say something else, but stopped himself and cocked his head, listening to something only he could hear. "Excuse me..." he turned his back to her and walked a few feet away. "What do you mean the admiral isn't responding?"

...

"A mutiny within a mutiny? That's got to be a first. If the loyalists have control, then what's the problem?"

...

"The Marines are *inside* the center? Who told them to go in?!"

...

"That seems premature. There's still time. And even if we fail, their bomb could still go off. If it does, we won't have anything to worry about. There won't be any evidence left."

...

"Very well. No, I understand. I'll let you know once I arrive at the stasis rooms."

General Graves turned back to Tyra, looking flustered.

"What's wrong?" she asked.

"Nothing you need to worry about." He flicked a glance at the bots standing guard by the door, then to Atara. "Watch them," he said, and handed her the charge pack for his sidearm. "I have an urgent matter to attend to." Turning to the bots, he said, "The girl is in charge until I return."

"Acknowledged," both bots replied in androgynous voices.

Graves left the room at a brisk pace, and Atara hurried over to collect his discarded sidearm.

"Atara..." Tyra said.

She loaded the weapon and aimed it at her mother. "Yes?" she replied in a dulcet tone.

"Think about what you're doing! I know you're in there somewhere. It's me, your mother!"

"You're right," Atara nodded agreeably, and her aim shifted to Theola. "Babies first."

"Atara, don't you dare!" Tyra wrapped herself more fully around Theola and twisted away, using her back as a shield.

Atara scowled and nodded to the bot standing closest to her. "Separate those two. I wouldn't want to miss and hit the wrong target."

"Yes, ma'am," the bot replied, as it stalked toward Tyra. She screamed as it laid cold metal hands on her. It pried her roughly away from Theola. The sudden absence of her mother's warmth provoked a dramatic frown from Theola. Her lips trembled, and she began to cry.

"It's okay, sweetheart!" Tyra managed, while struggling furiously against the machine holding her.

Theola didn't buy it. She started to scream.

"Let me *go!*" Tyra twisted and wrenched her arms with all of her strength. Warm blood trickled from her wrists and dripped between the bot's fingers.

"Please do not struggle," it said. "You are injuring

yourself."

"That... *monster* is going to shoot my baby!" Tyra screamed, trying to appeal to the bot's sense of logic as it dragged her away.

"The baby is a dangerous terrorist," Atara explained. "She must be eliminated."

"No..." Tyra whimpered.

"All threats must be neutralized to ensure the safety of the ship's passengers and crew," the bot replied in a reasonable tone. "Do not be afraid, ma'am."

Marine bots had human sergeants to command them for a reason. They were little more than walking guns waiting for someone to point them in the right direction.

Atara flicked a switch on the side of the general's pistol.

"Atty," Tyra tried, smiling through a veil of tears. "I know you're in there somewhere. Listen to me—if you do this, you'll never be able to forgive yourself."

Atara looked straight at her and grinned. "Oh, you're wrong about that. I've done far worse things and forgiven myself. The secret lies in knowing that there's no need for forgiveness, because there's no such thing as right and wrong. Judgment and guilt are lies from the pits of Etheria."

Tyra blinked in shock. No five year old talked like that. If there'd been any doubt before, there was none now. Atara was gone.

Taking the pistol in both hands, Atara aimed it at her sister's head.

"Atara! No!"

A deadly flash of crimson light shot out—

And *missed*, carving a chunk out of the wall behind

Theola.

The gun went flying from Atara's hand and skittered along the floor. She clutched her hand to her chest and screamed, casting about wildly, her eyes flashing with fury. "Shoot it! Shoot the Gor!"

Both bots looked around the room, their arms and integrated weapons tracking aimlessly. "No threats detected," one of them said just before its head popped off in a shower of sparks.

The other one watched as the headless body of its partner floated across the floor toward it.

"Shoot that bot!" Atara screamed, and scrambled to reach the general's sidearm.

The bot holding Tyra managed to spare an arm to fire on its partner. Crimson beams flashed out and sprayed molten chunks from the headless bot's armor. Then it fell to the floor, and the one holding Tyra lost its head, too. Both bots fell in a noisy clatter.

Tyra wasted no time gawking. She ran to intercept Atara, but she was too late.

Atara reached the general's sidearm and brought it up, one-handed to point it at her mother's chest.

She pulled the trigger.

A flash of crimson light blinded Tyra, and a blast of super-heated air hit her in the face. The sharp smell of ozone filled her nostrils, but the scalding stab of pain never came. Instead, Tyra heard chunks of castcrete debris pitter-pattering to the floor behind her.

She opened her eyes to see Atara trying to steady the pistol for another shot, this time with both hands, but her right hand was swollen and purpling with a bad bruise. No wonder she'd missed. She'd fired the gun one-handed. The recoil had been too much.

Before Atara could fire again, she was hoisted up by an invisible force, and held dangling by her arm. She kicked and screamed, cursing in a language that definitely wasn't Versal.

Then the air shimmered, and a wall of corpse-gray skin and rippling muscle appeared, hissing in Atara's face.

"Brak!" Tyra had never been more happy to see anyone in her entire life.

He wrenched the pistol from Atara's hand and flicked it back to stun.

"This isn't over," she said, smiling smugly.

Brak thrust the pistol into her chest and pulled the trigger. A flash of blue light rippled over Atara and her eyes rolled up in her head. Brak set her down gently with her muscles still spasming as arcs of blue fire leapt off her body.

The Gor turned to face Tyra. "Are you okay?"

She ran to pick up Theola before answering. "I am now," she said, while bouncing Theola on her hip to quiet her desperate cries.

"Where is Graves?" Brak asked.

"You didn't see him?"

Brak shook his head.

"He *just* left."

"I just arrive. I climb up to the window," Brak said, nodding to the en-suite bathroom.

Tyra let out a shaky sigh. "If you'd arrived just a second later..." she trailed off, shaking her head, unable to finish that thought.

Brak nodded. "Graves. Where is he?"

Tyra pointed to the open door of the bedroom. "He left.

I overheard him speaking to someone. It might have been Ellis. He mentioned something about going to the stasis chambers."

Brak hissed. "That is where the Faro prisoners are!"

"You think they're planning to break them out?"

"Maybe," Brak said. "Are there more bots inside the house?"

"If there are, they won't be a threat. They need a human to give them orders."

"Then make sure she does not wake up to do so," Brak replied, nodding to Atara's unconscious form. He passed her the general's pistol to her. "In case she does," he explained.

She took the weapon with a grimace and nodded, watching as Brak hurried for the door. "Where are you going?"

"To find Graves," he replied, and promptly vanished, the air shimmering around him as he cloaked once more.

As soon as Brak was gone, Tyra turned to Atara. She glared at her daughter, lying face down on the floor, her back rising and falling slowly. A paranoid thought skittered through Tyra's mind: Atara might only be pretending to be unconscious.

She almost stunned Atara again to be sure—the risks be damned—but a flash of guilt answered that thought. Atara was her daughter!

And yet she wasn't. Whatever this *thing* was, it only looked like her.

Tyra waved to the holoscreen at the foot of the bed, and selected the comms panel to place a call to emergency services.

The head and shoulders of the operator appeared on

the screen. She looked infuriatingly calm. "Emergency services, what is the nature of your emergency?"

"My daughter just tried to shoot her baby sister with a gun."

"Does she still have the weapon, ma'am?"

Tyra held the weapon up in front of the screen. "No. She's been stunned."

"Okay. The police are on their way. Does your daughter have a history of mental illness, or violent behavior toward family members?"

"No. Not until recently. She's five."

"I see..."

"Don't give me that look. She was touched by the aliens when they came aboard. They did something to her."

The operator's expression went from wary to suspicious. "Have you been watching the news, ma'am?"

"No, why?"

The operator frowned. "No reason, ma'am... the police will be there soon."

Tyra had an odd feeling that this woman didn't believe her. "I'd also like to report a break-in."

"Your daughter broke into her own home?"

"No. General Graves of the Marines did. He stunned us and held us hostage along with my daughter, but he left. You should send a squad to arrest him."

The operator's eyebrows beetled and her frown deepened. "I see... ma'am, have you taken anything recently?"

"Taken anything? Like what?"

"Pills, drugs, alcoholic beverages..."

"I'm not high!"

"Of course not," the operator said. "The police will be

there soon. Please try to remain calm."

"I'm already calm!" Tyra shouted, and hung up. She glanced at Atara again, but she was still out cold. It was too soon for the effects of the stun blast to be wearing off.

Tyra paced the floor while she waited for the police to arrive. Theola looked up at her with big eyes, sucking her thumb. The operator clearly hadn't believed even half of what she'd said. She probably thought Tyra was the crazy one, but she'd have to send the police either way.

Tyra's thoughts turned to Lucien while she waited, and something the operator had said clicked. *Have you been watching the news, ma'am?* She turned back to the holoscreen and tried using it to contact Lucien, but he was listed as *offline.*

Failing that, she set the screen to a local news channel to see what the operator had been talking about. A reporter appeared standing on a dark street in front of a bright holographic sign that read, *Resurrection Center.* Police patrol cars, fire trucks, and ambulances lined the street in the background, their lights all flashing blue and red. Glowing yellow police tape barred the entrance of the center.

The reporter on the screen was midway through her report. "...appears to be some kind of an armed confrontation in the records room between the center's security forces and the terrorists. As you saw just a moment ago, several squads of Marines have now gone in to join the fight. They declined to comment on their orders, but it seems they may have been sent to put a stop to the fighting before the bomb goes off."

The scene switched to show two more reporters sitting behind a desk back at the news station. The one reporting live from the center was reduced to a box in the bottom right of the screen.

They discussed the implications of everything that was happening amongst themselves, leading viewers to the unsettling conclusion that the center could blow at any second thanks to the dead-man's switch that the *terrorists* had wired to their bomb. Tyra's heart thundered in her chest. Things had gone badly awry at the center. Lucien was in the middle of a firefight. She imagined Coretti's bomb going off and Lucien being ripped apart in the explosion. If that happened, there'd be no bringing him back to life. With the center destroyed, he and anyone else who died in the explosion would be gone for good. *Get out of there, Lucien! Just get out!* But she knew he wouldn't. This was their only chance of saving Atara. Not to mention the rest of *Astralis*.

Sirens came screaming to Tyra's ears along with the idling rumble of hover car engines. The police had arrived. She waved the screen off and ran downstairs with Theola to meet the police.

Tyra reached the front door—what was left of it after Marine bots had blasted it open. Two policemen came running up the walkway, their stun pistols drawn. "Drop your weapon and put your hands above your head!" one of them yelled.

Tyra dropped the weapon, but raised only one hand. "I'm holding a baby!"

The officer who'd spoken stopped a few feet away. "Kick the gun toward us."

Tyra did so, and the policeman picked it up.

"I'm not the threat here!" Tyra said. "Look at the door! Do you think I could have done that much damage with that little gun? And why would I break into my own house?"

The policemen appeared to see the sense in what she

was saying.

"Who's inside, ma'am?"

"Just my eldest daughter. She's upstairs, stunned. She tried to shoot us with that gun."

"Wait outside, ma'am," the policeman said as he and his partner pushed by her.

Tyra watched them storm through her living room, their guns sweeping left to right, looking for hidden threats. Not encountering anything, they proceeded up the stairs, on their way to arrest Atara.

Tyra couldn't bring herself to feel anything but relief. A mother's love was supposed to be unconditional, but whatever Atara was, she wasn't her daughter anymore.

At this point all she could think about was Lucien and whether or not he was going to make it out of this alive.

Despite Tyra's utter lack of belief in Etherus, she found herself whispering a prayer to keep him safe. The true test of an agnostic was in facing death unafraid, but she was terrified.

CHAPTER 47

Astralis

Lucien fired another burst from his pulse pistol. This time it hit something vital and his target collapsed in a shower of sparks. "One down," Lucien muttered, as he ducked back into cover to avoid the bots' return fire.

"The dead man's switch is offline!" Fizk crowed over the comms.

"Finally!" Lucien replied. Feeling empowered by that news, he peeked out of cover again and fired a steady stream at the bots advancing on him.

He was gratified to see another bot fall, its head a molten ruin. Two of the four remaining bots broke off and went running down an aisle just ahead of the one where he was hiding, while the other two stopped where they were and returned fire. Lucien ducked back into cover just as one of their shots hit home, hissing off his failing shields. He checked the status of those shields via his ARCs and found they were down to just eleven percent. It wouldn't be enough to shield him from even one more shot.

Lasers pounded into the data stacks beside him, spraying bright orange globules of molten metal in all directions. Lucien cringed away from the super-heated shrapnel and waited for a lull in the bots' fire. This time they didn't let up, and with his shields almost depleted, Lucien couldn't risk peeking out for another shot. He glanced behind him, down to the end of the aisle, wondering if he could make a run for it.

An echoing *boom* sounded nearby, drawing his eyes up. He saw the two bots who'd broken off standing on top of the data storage units in the aisle just ahead of his. As he watched, their legs bent and they leapt across the aisle, landing with another *boom* on top of the stacks that Lucien was hiding behind.

He pressed himself flat against the storage units to avoid the bots' tracking weapons, and gripped his pistol tighter, waiting for them to jump down into the aisle with him. He wouldn't go down without a fight.

"Cease fire! Cease fire!" a booming voice said. "This is Marine Sergeant Garek Helios. Override, alpha, charlie, juliet, sixteen! Acknowledge!"

"Acknowledged," one of the bots replied, and lasers stopped slamming into the stacks.

The tension bled out of Lucien's muscles, leaving them trembling and weak. He belatedly recognized the sergeant's name and called out, "Garek! It's Lucien Ortane! Remember me? We signed up for the expeditionary forces together!"

"I remember," Garek replied in an amplified voice.

"Drop your weapons and come out with your hands up."

Lucien risked peeking around the corner, checking to make sure this wasn't some kind of trick. But the pair of security bots who'd been firing on him had dropped their arms and integrated weapons back to their sides, and they stood idly waiting for their next command.

Lucien dropped both his pistols and crept out of cover with his hands up. "I'm unarmed," he said.

"We'll be there in a minute. Where are the others?"

"Joe? Are you still there?" Lucien asked over an open comms channel.

"How do we know we can trust this guy?" Joe replied.

"Because I just saved your asses, that's why," Garek replied.

"Sorry, not good enough. Get the film crews in here like we asked or we'll blow this place. No more frekking around."

"They'll be here," Garek replied. "Where's Director Helios? I was told she came in with security."

Garek Helios, Director Helios... Lucien made the connection, but Joe was the first to mention it—

"She some kind of relative of yours?"

"That's none of your business," Garek replied.

"I'm here!" a woman said. "These people are dangerous. You can't trust them! You need to leave!"

"Where are you?" Garek asked.

"She's at the terminal with me," Fizk said. "And she's got a gun... I think she's going to try to erase the evidence."

"Stand down, Nora!" Garek said.

"Fizzy, you just gonna stand there and watch?" Joe demanded. "Do something!"

"Easy for you to say! You ain't the one with a gun in his face!"

Lucien turned and ran back down the aisle to the records terminal. He saw Director Helios there, one arm busy with a holographic keypad, the other aiming a gun at Fizk's head.

Lucien arrived at the terminal, breathless. "What do you think you're doing?" he demanded.

The director flashed a smile at him. "That's none of your concern."

Lucien took a quick step toward her, and her aim shifted to him. Fizk took his chance and lunged for her weapon, but she was too fast. She shot him in the chest just before he could grab her arm. Blue fire raced over him, and he collapsed in a pile of jittering limbs.

Lucien body-checked her, knocking the gun out of her hand before she could aim at him again. The director fell over backward with him on top of her. She kicked him in the groin, and Lucien squeezed both her wrists until he felt the bones grinding together. "Not smart," he gritted out.

The director screamed in pain and yelled, "Help!"

"Get off her, and put your hands behind your head!" Garek roared.

Lucien turned to three full squads of Marine bots running down the aisle toward them. He did as he was told. "She was trying to erase evidence from the terminal," he explained. "And she shot him," he added, jerking his chin to Fizk.

"So the dead man's switch was a lie," Garek said.

"No, we disabled it when we realized the director didn't care if the bomb went off and got us all killed."

Garek's gaze swept to her, watching as she climbed to her feet. His eyes were thoughtfully narrowed behind his helmet.

"There's no bomb," the director said, rubbing her wrists and wincing.

"Yes there is," Joe said. All eyes turned to see him and Bob approaching from the far side. Both the gangster and his android had their weapons drawn and raised.

Garek shifted his aim to them, as did the other sergeants and fully half of the Marines bots. "Drop your weapons!" he demanded.

"I don't think so. Get my film crews in here or I'll blow this place."

"You'd be killing yourself," Garek said.

"You sure about that? Seems a guy like me could benefit from having his own resurrection center tucked away somewhere."

"I don't see a bomb," Garek added.

"It's inside him," Joe said as they drew near. He nodded sideways to indicate Bob. "Show them, Bobby-boy."

The android lifted his shirt and dug his nails through his skin, revealing shiny metal. Then he opened a panel in his stomach and revealed three cylinders filled with red and blue compounds—another binary liquid explosive, just like the one Lucien had seen in the briefcase.

"That's not five kilotons," Garek said.

Joe shrugged. "It's still enough to decimate this place. You want to take the risk that *your* data gets atomized along with you?"

Lucien frowned. If Bob was carrying the bomb, then what had he seen in Fizk's briefcase?

Joe kept walking until he reached the records terminal.

"Get away from there!" Garek snapped.

"Relax, I'm just checking that Fizzy here is still breathing!" Joe bent down to check Fizk's pulse. But when he straightened again, he was holding the briefcase.

"Drop the case!" Garek said.

"You don't want me to do that," Joe said, and popped it open to reveal the bomb Lucien had seen earlier, with at least ten times the volume as the one inside of Bob.

The android sealed the compartment in his stomach and pulled his shirt back down.

"Oops. Looks like I have two bombs," Joe said, with his finger hovering over the detonator switch of the one inside the case. "Get the film crews in here like I asked."

"We don't negotiate with terrorists," Garek said.

"So make an exception. Don't you want to know if your wife here is really an alien in disguise?"

Garek glanced at Nora, and shook his head. "She's not my wife."

"Your daughter, then...?" Joe suggested. Garek said nothing to that, and Joe smiled. "Well? What's it gonna be?"

Garek turned to one of the other sergeants. "Send for the crews. Tell them the fighting is over and it's safe to come in."

"Safe?" Director Helios snorted. "They're threatening to detonate no less than *two* different bombs, and they're still armed!"

"Yes, sir," the sergeant that Garek had spoken to replied, ignoring the director's objections. He hurried off with his squad of bots running behind him.

"Big mistake," the director said.

Garek just looked at her. "What are you so afraid they'll find?"

She shook her head, saying nothing this time.

They waited for what felt like a lifetime before the sergeant who'd left came back. He marched down the aisle to the data terminal with a legion of reporters and hovering holocorders trailing behind him.

The news crews arrived and reporters all began speaking at once in front of hovering spotlights and holocorders.

Garek nodded to Lucien. "Show us what you found."

Lucien sat at the terminal and searched for Chief Ellis's records. He found the ones he'd flagged earlier and played them back with all the camera crews filming. Silence fell as they recorded Ellis's private memories and thoughts. Subtitles gave voice to his thoughts, revealing all the machinations he'd gone through with the help of Director Helios and General Graves to make contact with someone named Katawa. The actual conversation was confusing at best—something about a *lost fleet* and the *humans* they'd used to find it—but there was no confusing the way Ellis identified himself as *Abaddon.*

"Proof enough?" Lucien asked, turning to the film crews with eyebrows raised.

Before anyone could say anything, Director Helios lunged for the briefcase bomb.

Joe whirled it out of reach and Bob shot her in the face.

"Nora!" Garek roared.

She collapsed on the deck and Garek dropped to one knee beside her, checking her pulse.

"She's dead," he said, and glared up at Joe.

"She almost blew us all up!" Joe replied. "Besides, she's

not your daughter. At this point it should be clear what she really is."

Garek rose to his feet and aimed his rifle at Joe's chest, his fingers toying restlessly with the trigger.

Joe arched an eyebrow at him and clutched the briefcase bomb to his chest like a shield. "You shoot me, and the bomb goes off."

"Stand down, sir," one of the other sergeants said, with a hand on Garek's arm. "We'll bring Nora back when this is all over."

"Exactly," Joe said. He nodded to Lucien. "What about the others? The admiral and the general?"

Lucien nodded and pulled up their records next. Their thoughts proved to be equally incriminating. By this point they had more than enough evidence. Lucien heard the reporters summarizing the shocking news for viewers all over *Astralis*.

"We need to get those reporters out of here," Joe said.

"What's wrong?" Lucien asked.

"The comms are still being jammed. None of this has reached the public yet."

Garek nodded soberly. "And it isn't going to."

Before anyone could stop him, he raised his rifle to his shoulder and opened fire on the briefcase bomb.

CHAPTER 48

Astralis

Time seemed to freeze. A bright stream of crimson lasers stuttered out from Garek's pulse rifle.

A few shots went wide, and Joe flinched, his body shuddering as lasers burned through the open top of the briefcase and into his chest. His shield must have been depleted by the firefight.

Joe took the briefcase down with him as he fell, but somehow he managed to keep it from flying out of his hands. The news crews turned and ran away at top speed, as did one of the Marine sergeants, but the other one stayed and gunned Garek down. His shield overloaded with a loud *pop,* and he fell over with a dozen different holes in his armor.

A moment of ringing silence followed, then Lucien snapped out of it and went to check the bomb. At least half the canisters were shattered, with viscous blue and red fluids leaking inside the case and mixing freely.

Confusion swirled in Lucien's head. "How are we still alive?"

"Speak for yourself," Joe groaned.

The Marine sergeant who'd gunned down Garek came to examine the bomb. He shook his head and looked to Lucien. "Either we're the luckiest people in history, or this isn't really a bomb." The sergeant carefully moved the briefcase off Joe's chest, revealing glistening black holes where Garek's shots had punched through.

The stench of burned flesh choked the air. Lucien fought back a wave of nausea.

Joe smirked and then winced. "It is a binary explosive... enough to fool sensors..." he trailed off with a ragged gasp.

"But?" Lucien prompted.

"It's all X and no Y. Food coloring."

The Marine sergeant nodded, smiling. "So the threat *was* a bluff."

"We're going to get you out of here," Lucien said. "Come on."

"Don't bother." Joe whispered, sounding desperately short of air.

"His lung's collapsed," the sergeant said.

Lucien looked to him. "Can't you do something? Don't you have a medic in your squad?"

He shook his head. "It's easier to bring people back in new bodies than to save the old ones."

Joe's hands batted the air as if to fight off an unseen assailant, and his mouth opened and closed in airless gasps.

Bob appeared, gazing stoically down on his boss. Joe's eyes bulged and tears leaked from the corners of his eyes. His hands grabbed Lucien's shirt in white-knuckled fists. Lucien grabbed one of those hands and held on tight, weathering the gangster's death throes until he grew still.

"So dies an uncommon patriot," the sergeant said.

"He'll be back. They all will," Lucien replied, looking around at Garek and Director Helios.

"Let's go," the sergeant replied.

Lucien spotted Fizk, lying stunned behind the data terminal. "He's still alive. Help me get him out of here."

They carried him out between them with a dozen Marine bots clanking along to the fore and aft. Soon Lucien was panting from the exertion of carrying the demolitions expert, but the sergeant wasn't even winded thanks to the augmented strength of his exosuit.

As soon as they were outside the center, reporters and film crews descended on them, all shouting at the same time—

"Was the bomb a fake?"

"Did Sergeant Helios miss?"

"Is he dead?"

"Where is Joe Coretti?"

"Where is the bomb now?"

As those questions rolled over them, Lucien thought to ask a question of his own—"Where's Bob?" He stopped and turned to look behind them, but there was no sign of the android.

A rumbling roar came shivering through the ground, and an onrushing wall of light swelled behind the windows in the Resurrection Center.

"Get down!" Lucien said, dropping Fizk and himself at the same time.

The windows all exploded with a thunderous *boom,* and a deadly hail of shattered glass whipped through the crowd. Lucien heard shards of glass hissing off what was left of his shield. A gust of super-heated air rolled over him, and the shock wave roared like a furnace in his ears.

In an instant the noise was gone, and a dull ringing sound replaced the noise. A strong hand grabbed Lucien by the arm and pulled him to his feet. It was the Marine sergeant. His lips were moving behind his helmet, but Lucien couldn't hear. He stood swaying on his feet, surveying a scene of utter chaos. Flaming debris cluttered the street, bodies strewn between them. Some were dragging themselves through the wreckage and moaning—others weren't moving at all.

Just two reporters out of what had been nearly a dozen remained standing. They were cut and bleeding, but enduring their injuries to explain what had just happened for their viewers. Not that it needed any explaining.

Lucien turned back to look at the center. Fire gushed from open windows, a greedy inferno gobbling up three hundred million peoples' claims to immortality—as well as Atara's only hope of ever going back to normal. He stared in shock, struggling to comprehend what had just happened. The bomb was a fake, so how had it gone off? And why now?

Then Lucien remembered the second bomb inside of Bob, and suddenly everything made sense. The two parts of the binary explosive had been separated from the start. All of one compound had been inside the briefcase, while all of the other had been inside of Bob. There'd never been any risk of them mixing—by means of a detonator or a dead man's switch. Either Fizk had just been twiddling his thumbs and pretending to disable the switch, or he'd been equally oblivious to the deception.

Bob obviously had standing orders to follow, and he'd carried them out just as soon as he could, but in so doing he'd also killed his maker, Joe Coretti.

Why would Coretti want to kill himself?

Then Lucien remembered something Joe had said to Garek: *a guy like me could benefit from having his own resurrection center.*

"Motherfrekker!" Lucien roared, his voice sounding muffled to his ears.

"Are you okay, sir?" A pair of EMTs swept into view, looking him over.

Lucien turned to them in a daze. All of his suspicions came rushing back. Now he knew why Coretti's plan had been ready to go on such short notice. "They planned this all along..." Lucien muttered, sinking to his knees in the rubble. Learning about Ellis and the others had added another objective to Joe's operation, but as soon as he'd exposed them, he knew it was safe to execute his original plan—or rather, Bob did.

Taking his collapse as a sign of injury, the EMTs rushed in to steady him. They rattled off questions about where he was hurt and how bad the pain was.

But Lucien was too shocked to reply. *This was Joe's agenda from the start—blow the center and make us all mortals again. Except for Joe himself.* Somehow, some way, he was busy coming back to life in his own private resurrection center.

CHAPTER 49

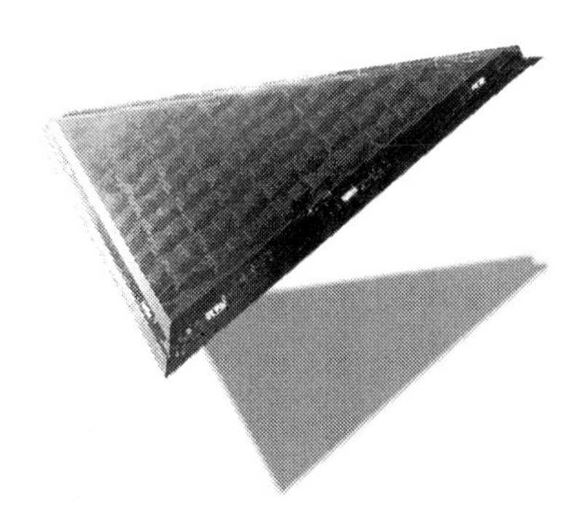

Astralis

Brak stood right behind General Graves, listening as he argued with the Marine sergeant guarding the stasis chambers.

"I can't open these doors, sir."

"You'll open them, and that's an order!" Graves bellowed.

"You're not yourself, sir."

"What the frek are you talking about?"

"It's all over the news. The records in the Res Center proved it. Stand down, General."

"Stun him!" Graves ordered, but the bots standing beside him made no move to obey that command. "Did you hear me?"

"You are under arrest, General," the sergeant said. "Your command privileges have been revoked. Raise your hands behind your head and—"

Graves launched himself at the sergeant and grabbed the man's rifle.

"Shoot him!" the sergeant yelled. All six bots opened fire, and flurry of crimson lasers converged on Graves from the front and back. It was over in an instant, and Graves fell with a *thud.* Thin black tendrils of smoke rose from his corpse.

The sergeant stared at the general's body in shock. Maybe he'd forgot to say *stun him* instead of *shoot him.* Bots were nothing if not literal-minded.

Whatever the case, Graves was no longer a threat. Brak turned and ran back the way he'd come. There were still two others to catch—Chief Ellis and Admiral Stavos.

Brak decided to go for Ellis first. The Marines on the bridge would take care of Stavos.

* * *

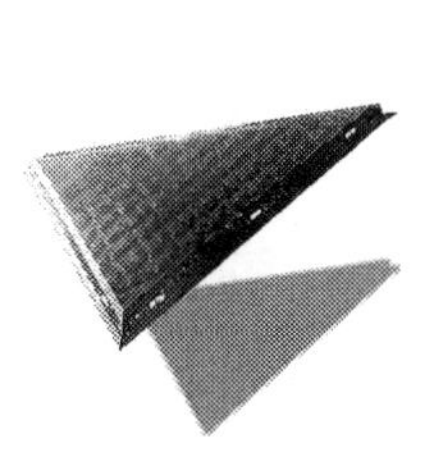

Astralis

Abaddon sat scowling in his living room as he watched the news. Both Garek and Nora had failed. It wouldn't be long before Marines or police came up to his penthouse to arrest their Chief Councilor.

Abaddon walked through his living room, up to

another holoscreen, this one displaying a painting. He removed it from the wall and set it aside, then he waved his hand over the wall behind the painting. The air shimmered, revealing a cloaked safe.

He typed in his combination and opened the safe; then he reached past a stack of worthless valuables and data wafers to retrieve an illegally modified pistol and the Faro comms unit he'd used to speak with Katawa.

Abaddon took both the pistol and the unit and sat down at the head of the dining room table, with a clear view of the hallway leading to the front door. He toggled the pistol's illegal *overload* setting and laid it carefully on the table beside him.

The Faro prisoners in the stasis rooms weren't much of a liability—they only had pieces of the overall plan, and their thoughts were all encoded in Faro, not Versal, but he and the other humans were another matter. A rigorous mind probe would reveal everything. He couldn't allow them to take him alive. Hopefully Stavos and Graves would take similar precautions.

Abaddon hurried to configure the comms unit to make contact with the Faro fleet that was shadowing *Astralis.*

Once contact was established, he spoke into the device—in Faro, not Versal, so that no would know what he'd said.

"This is Abaddon," he said. "Myself and my other instances have been discovered, but the lost fleet is on its way here. Do nothing until you detect its arrival. Acknowledge."

"Acknowledged," the reply came back a moment later.

Before Abaddon could say or do anything else, his front door burst open. He calmly lifted his pistol from the table and aimed it at his own head.

But no Marines or police came storming in. Abaddon frowned, hesitating with his finger on the trigger. *What are they waiting for?*

Then he felt the air beside him stir, and a cold hand grabbed his wrist, prying the pistol away from his head.

Abaddon turned and saw the air shimmering to reveal a familiar gray-skinned, skull-faced monster.

The Gor.

Abaddon wasn't strong enough to resist him in this pitiful human body, but he didn't technically need to aim the weapon while it was set to overload. "Goodbye," he said, and pulled the trigger.

The weapon exploded in his hand, and everything vanished in an agony of heat and light.

* * *

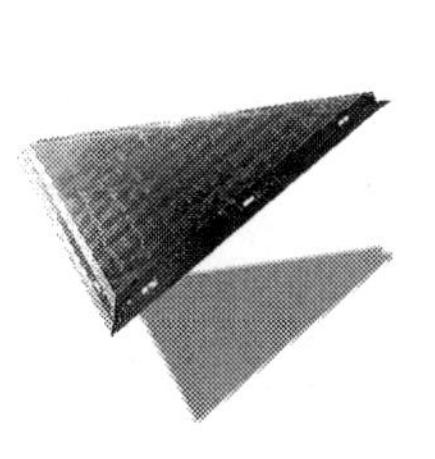

Astralis

Tyra bounced Theola on her knee while she filled out a report at the police station. The poor baby hadn't eaten anything for a long time.

Someone gasped and Tyra looked up. Everyone in the station had stopped what they were doing to watch the holoscreen on the far wall of the station. The headline read,

Terrorists Vindicated, and Leaders Exposed as Res. Center Explodes

It was Tyra's turn to gasp. *The bomb went off?*

Someone turned up the volume, and everyone watched as clips of Ellis's memories played, thoroughly incriminating him, followed by memories from Admiral Stavos and General Graves that exposed them, too.

They watched as first Director Helios and then her father, Marine Sergeant Garek Helios, tried to detonate Joe Coretti's bomb to cover up the evidence. The bomb turned out to be a fake—only to explode minutes later while reporters swarmed around Lucien and a Marine sergeant outside the center.

Tyra's heart froze in her chest and her blood ran cold, watching as Lucien dropped to the ground a spit second before the shock wave hit. It flattened the news crews, and the scene turned blurry with flying debris. As soon as the shock wave passed, the scene snapped back into focus, and Tyra saw her husband being pulled to his feet by the Marine who'd been standing beside him.

EMTs came rushing in from waiting ambulances to attend the wounded while firefighters jumped down from their trucks and ran out with hoses to put out the blaze. At least they'd been ready for this outcome.

But Tyra hadn't. She slowly shook her head, unable to put words to the horror bursting inside her. Even Theola's hungry cries had subsided.

Lucien was safe. Theola was safe. Their leaders had been exposed and were probably just about to be arrested. The crisis was over, but a new one had just begun: the

Resurrection Center was gone. That meant a lot of things, but right now it meant just one thing to Tyra: it meant that *Atara* was never coming back. It meant that her eldest daughter was dead.

CHAPTER 50

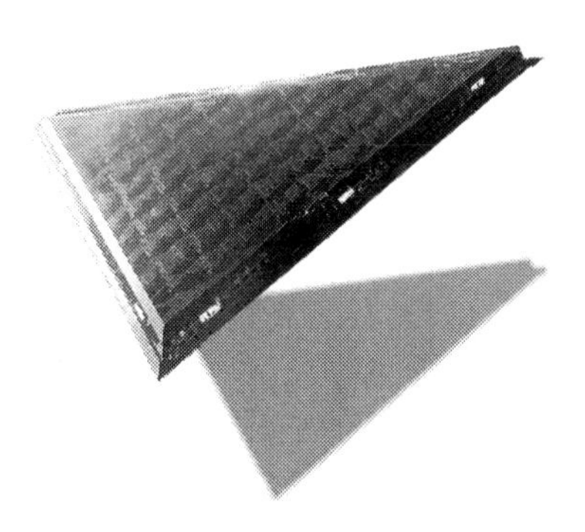

Astralis

Lieutenant Commander Wheeler paced up and down her cell in the brig, wondering what kind of trial she could hope to get with Faros in charge of *Astralis.*

Not a fair one. That's for sure.

She stopped at the door to her room and looked out the window into the hall. How long had she been in here? They'd taken away her ARCs, and she'd been stunned when she arrived, so there was no way to know.

As Wheeler was wondering about that, a Marine sergeant appeared and unlocked the door. She frowned at him as the door slid open.

"Time for my trial already? Or are we going to skip straight to the execution?"

"Neither, ma'am. You're being reinstated as the acting CMO."

Wheeler wondered if she'd heard correctly. "Say again, Sergeant?"

He launched into a quick summary of events in the center, then said, "We need you on the bridge, ma'am. There's some concern that the Faros know where we are and might already be on their way.

Wheeler nodded. "Let's go."

She followed the sergeant out and back through the brig. Noting all the empty cells, she asked, "What happened to the admiral and General Graves?"

"The admiral shot himself before he could be arrested. Graves was caught trying to reach the Faro prisoners in stasis and he was killed in the struggle."

"And Ellis?"

"Dead. Fired a sidearm on overload while a security officer attempted to arrest him."

Wheeler grimaced. "So we have no one to interrogate and no records to study in the center. We have no idea what they were planning!"

"No, ma'am."

They took an elevator up to sub level five hundred, and then spent another minute walking to the bridge itself. Wheeler endured routine scans at the entrance of the bridge and then breezed in.

"Commander on deck!" the sergeant who'd escorted her announced.

A female officer with bright golden eyes turned from the holo table on the upper deck of the bridge and saluted—Lieutenant Ruso, chief engineer. A pair of maintenance bots were on their hands and knees beside her, scrubbing a bright red bloodstain off the deck.

"Who has the conn?" Wheeler demanded.

"That would be me, ma'am," Ruso replied as Wheeler approached.

"At ease, Lieutenant. Give me a sitrep," Wheeler said.

"The bridge is secure, as is the rest of the ship—as far as we can tell. Marines and security forces are on high alert and on the lookout for more enemy agents. We've re-engaged outbound comms jamming—but not before a comms burst was detected going out from Chief Ellis's penthouse. We intercepted the message, but..." Ruso broke off, shaking her head. "We can't tell what it says. It's in the Faros' language."

"Probably calling in reinforcements," Wheeler said.

Ruso nodded. "We just plotted a jump to a nearby system. We've been waiting for you to arrive before we executed."

"Show me." Wheeler nodded to the holo table.

"Yes, ma'am." Ruso turned to the table and made a pinching motion with her thumb and forefinger. The display zoomed out until the green wedge of *Astralis* disappeared, and a glittering map of nearby stars took its place. One of them was highlighted with the yellow diamond of a nav waypoint.

Ruso selected that star and read the system summary. "Six planets, none habitable."

"Moons?"

"Fourteen that we've detected so far, but there's likely more that we can't see hiding behind the planets."

"Without a spectral analysis there's no way to be sure that they're not habitable," Wheeler mused.

Ruso nodded. "And if one of them is habitable, it could support a Faro colony."

"Habitable planets, or not, they could still be there with a self-contained facility or space station."

"Yes, ma'am."

"Which means we're not going to learn anything else from here. Execute the jump."

"Aye, ma'am—helm, execute jump!"

"Jumping..." the nav officer replied.

The bridge flashed white, dazzling Wheeler's eyes. Details of her surroundings gradually returned, and she barked out, "Sensors, report!"

"Clean sweep! No contacts!"

Wheeler let out a breath she hadn't realized she was holding. "Good. Helm, get ready to plot another jump."

"Aye, where to, ma'am?"

"Stand by..." Wheeler gestured to the holo table, zooming out and checking stars at random. She found one with just one planet and six moons at the edge of the galaxy where they were currently situated. The planet was too far from its star for it to be habitable. "System lima seven tango alpha mike november dash eleven," Wheeler replied.

"Aye, Commander... plotting jump," the helm replied.

"If this system is safe, why plot another jump?" Lieutenant Ruso asked.

"Just in case we're followed," Wheeler replied. She turned in a circle to survey the bridge—*her* bridge. As the ranking naval officer on board, this was now her command, but she couldn't help feeling like she'd stolen it. The admiral was dead, and with the Res Center gone, he wasn't coming back—nor were General Graves or Chief Councilor Ellis, or any of the others who'd died.

"Where's Councilor Ortane?" Wheeler asked, turning

back to Lieutenant Ruso.

The other woman shook her head. "I don't know."

"See if you can contact her for me. She's in charge of the executive branch now that Ellis is gone."

"Yes, ma'am," Ruso replied, and hurried from the holo table to the comms station.

"And someone get me my ARCs!" Wheeler demanded. She was starting to feel naked without them.

"Aye, Commander!"

Turning back to the holo table, she summoned a map of the system where they were now—L7RT-6. A system of six planets and their moons. Wheeler checked them one by one to find that they were all lifeless balls of rock, ice, and gas. The ice world might not be entirely lifeless, but close enough.

She grimaced and shook her head. If the Faros didn't show up, this system was going to be their home until they figured out what to do. Would the council decide to go back to their original mission of exploring the universe and risk more encounters with the Faros?

Wheeler frowned. Whatever people said about Etherus, his deity or lack thereof, one thing was certain: he'd kept everyone inside the Red Line safe from the Faros. If it were up to her, Wheeler would take them all back to the Etherian Empire and never leave again.

CHAPTER 51

Astralis

—TWO MONTHS LATER—

Acting Chief Councilor Tyra Ortane stared at the woman lying on the bed beside hers—a woman with dark hair, bright blue eyes, and an intimately familiar face. It was the same face she saw in the mirror each morning. The woman lying beside her was none other than Captain Tyra Forster. She'd never taken Lucien's surname, because she'd never married him. She was the captain of a ship that no longer existed, part of an expeditionary force that had been disbanded years ago.

The expeditionary forces had almost been reformed and redeployed thanks to Chief Councilor Ellis, but after everyone had learned who Ellis and the others really were, all of their decisions had been cast into doubt. No clones would be sent out to explore ahead of *Astralis,* and all the recent changes in legislation had been repealed—including the judiciary department's early ruling that Captain Forster and Councilor Tyra Ortane were distinct individuals and allowed to remain as such. The ruling was seen as a dangerous step toward whatever the Faros had been planning.

That was what brought both Tyra and Captain Forster to this probe room in Winterside General, waiting to be integrated. Of the two, Captain Forster was in better shape, so her body had been chosen to house both sets of their memories, a fact which made this whole process doubly unsettling for Tyra.

"It's going to be fine," Lucien said, squeezing her hand.

"Mama!" Theola declared and pointed to Captain Forster. The captain flashed a troubled smile. Lucien shook his head and redirected Theola's finger to point at Tyra. "No, that's Mama," he said.

"Not for long," Captain Forster added ruefully.

"You'll both still be you," Lucien insisted, glancing between them. "You'll just have a bunch of new memories that you never knew you had."

"I know," Tyra said, "but it's still unnerving."

"Tell me about it," Captain Forster said.

Lucien nodded and looked away. Councilor Tyra followed his gaze to watch as probe technicians scurried around, checking readouts on their equipment. Doctor Fushiwa came over and nodded to her. "We're ready to begin, Councilor."

"Are you sure this is safe?" Councilor Tyra asked.

He nodded, blinking his orange eyes and smiling. "Perfectly safe."

She regarded him dubiously. This was the same doctor who'd first performed the mind probe on Atara a few months back. Following the analysis of that probe, he'd subsequently cleared Atara of any suspicion. That didn't instill a lot of confidence now.

Tyra winced at the memory of what had happened to her eldest daughter. If Doctor Fushiwa had dug just a little deeper with that probe, Atara wouldn't be sitting in the hospital's psych ward right now. They would have been able to restore Atara immediately from her backups in the Resurrection Center—backups that no longer existed thanks to the late Joe Coretti.

Despite rigorous searches of the Coretti brothers' apartments, homes, and business establishments, Joseph Coretti was nowhere to be found. If he *had* somehow built his own resurrection center as Lucien believed, authorities had yet to find it—or Joe. So far it looked like he'd actually plotted to kill himself, or at least, that the bomb had gone off by accident, but Tyra agreed with Lucien. Joe was out there somewhere, probably with a new face and a completely different body, having just pulled off the perfect crime.

"Councilor?" Doctor Fushiwa prompted. "Do you need a moment?"

Tyra shook her head. "Let's get this over with."

The doctor nodded and turned to the other bed. "Captain?"

"What she said," Captain Forster replied.

A probe technician walked up beside Captain Forster's bed and injected a sedative into her arm. He injected Tyra next. She squeezed her husband's hand hard as the needle went in, and he smiled reassuringly at her. She took that smile with her as her eyes closed and darkness fell inside her mind.

The next thing she knew, she was waking up in another room, under a warming blanket, with Lucien sitting beside her and Theola running around the room giggling.

Tyra struggled to sit up. Memories swirled, pieces of a life she'd never lived. Her time on the *Inquisitor* felt real. All her memories leading up to that felt real. But the life on *Astralis* with her husband Lucien and her two daughters felt like something she'd watched in a holovid. The memories didn't feel like *hers.*

"Tyra?" Lucien asked, jumping up to stand beside her bed and grab her hand. "How do you feel?"

She frowned up at him. "I feel fine, Commander Ort—" She stopped herself there. "Sorry. I mean, Lucien."

His brow furrowed with concern. "You don't remember me."

"I do, but..." she trailed off, unable to express the confusion she was feeling.

The door to her room swished open and Theola stopped running around to watch as Doctor Fushiwa walked in.

"I see you're awake," he said, smiling as he approached.

Lucien turned and jerked a thumb at her. "That's not my wife."

"No?" The doctor turned to her. "You don't remember your life here, Councilor?"

"I do, but it doesn't *feel* like my life."

"Ah. I understand."

"So explain it to me," Lucien demanded.

"She's in a fugue state, not uncommon after this type of

procedure. A similar period of confusion follows resurrections. You surely remember something like it when you were resurrected, Mr. Ortane?"

"That was over eight years ago."

"Then perhaps you've forgotten how you felt. Don't worry, it's temporary. In just a few hours your wife should be her old self again—with the addition of some new memories from her time as captain of the *Inquisitor*."

Tyra listened to that exchange with her heart pounding and palms sweating. She tried to fight her rising panic, but failed. None of this was real! "Doctor..." she trailed off, as dark spots swam before her eyes.

The doctor leaned into view, took one look at her, and called, "Nurse!"

"What's wrong?" Lucien demanded. He sounded very far away.

"She's having a panic attack. Tyra, I want you to focus on taking deep, slow breaths. Slow. That's it... like that."

The dark spots fled, and Tyra's heart rate dropped, but every time she glanced at Lucien it sped up again, and her vision blurred once more.

"Deep breaths," Doctor Fushiwa urged. Turning to Lucien, he said, "Mr. Ortane, under the circumstances I believe you should leave. We'll call for you when your wife is able to receive visitors again."

He nodded slowly, his expression troubled. He left Tyra's field of view, saying, "Come on, Theola, let's go see Uncle Brak..."

* * *

Astralis

Lucien gazed into Brak's scarred face. His skin was shiny and off-color where it had been grafted in from other parts of his body. Where before Brak's face had been horrifying because of its bony, skull-shaped appearance, now it was horrifying for all its misshapen lumps and asymmetrical appearance.

It was the best that *Astralis's* surgeons could do on short notice. There would need to be subsequent reconstructive surgeries, but right now they didn't want to risk it.

Lucien pulled up a chair beside Brak's bed and listened to the beeping of a heart monitor and the sighing of the artificial lung that kept Brak breathing. Brak was in a coma, and had been for the past two months.

The doctors said he had extensive brain damage along with all his other injuries. They'd extracted what data they could, but even his AR implant had been damaged in the blast. A piece of shrapnel had scored an unlucky hit.

They wouldn't know how much of his memory or personality had been affected until they could grow a new body for him, and that would have to wait until the Resurrection Center was rebuilt.

Brak's old body was just about to be unplugged and

thrown in the incinerator. They'd kept him on life support, hoping he'd wake up so that could tell them some new detail about what had transpired in Ellis's final moments. Had he confessed to something? Had Brak overheard anything to shed light on the message Ellis had sent just before he'd killed himself?

The Faro prisoners had been impossibly little help. The Abaddons had all managed to kill themselves upon waking, and none of the others seemed to speak Versal, so they couldn't translate a thing. Mind probes helped by adding to their alien vocabulary, but contextual analysis and translation was frustratingly slow, even with hundreds of specialists on the job. They'd only managed to decipher about a dozen words so far.

Theola struggled in Lucien's arms, sliding down and making a break for the floor. She wanted to run around and explore, but Lucien pulled her back up. She batted him with her hands and started to cry.

"Shhh," he whispered and kissed her on the head. He couldn't let her run around in here. There was too much sensitive equipment. She'd probably unplug Brak and put him out of his misery before the doctors got around to it. When Theola's struggles and cries grew too insistent to ignore, Lucien stood up with a sigh. "Let's go, then." He cast a rueful glance at Brak. "See you later, buddy." He lingered a second longer, half-hoping to see Brak's eyelids flutter at the sound of his voice, but of course that was just a fantasy.

"Let's go check on your sister."

"Agaga!" Theola said.

Lucien smiled wanly. "That's right, Agaga."

They reached the psych ward and Atara's room just in

time to witness yet another mind probe. They were forced to wait outside in the observation area and watch while a police detective questioned his daughter under the influence of the probe.

"What are the Faros planning?"

"I don't know," Atara said.

"Why did they infiltrate *Astralis?*"

"I don't know."

"What is your name?"

"Atara."

"Your Faro name," the detective clarified.

"Abaddon."

That reply sent chills down Lucien's spine.

"And you don't know *your own* plans?"

"My transfer was interrupted."

"And that conveniently excluded all of your memories?"

"It was not necessary for me to have any of those memories. Only my personality was transferred."

"So you don't speak any Faro."

"A few words."

"What words?"

"Hello—*Sheeva*. Goodbye—*Heeva*."

"That's it?"

Atara just smiled.

Lucien scowled and turned to the security guard sitting at the desk in the observation area. "What's the point of this? They've asked all of these questions before."

The security guard shrugged. "They made some adjustments. This probe is supposed to go deeper than the others."

"Well it's getting all the same answers."

The guard gave no further comment. Lucien tapped his foot impatiently, waiting for the probe to end so he could go in with Theola. Atara continued stone-walling, casting the effectiveness of the probe into doubt, and Lucien's attention drifted to a holoscreen hanging above one corner of the security guard's desk.

A holonews story was playing about High Court Judge Cleever being taken into custody on suspicion of being a Faro spy. The screen was muted, but Lucien could read the subtitles clearly enough. Cleever had been identified as a potential Faro after being subjected to an AI-driven screening test. The test involved downloading and scanning every bit of data in a person's brain for suspicious thoughts or motives. Tyra and Captain Forster had both been tested and cleared, along with all the other councilors. Now the representatives of the house and the judges of the judiciary were being screened. Apparently Cleever was the first to be caught.

Unfortunately, the news report didn't mention anything about useful intel being uncovered in Cleever's thoughts, but that wasn't strange. Atara had also been identified as a Faro by the test, and she didn't seem to know anything useful, either.

Apparently, the Faros had infected different people to varying degrees, giving some of them memories and pieces of the overall plan, while others appeared to know nothing but their newfound allegiance to the Faros.

Apparently Judge Cleever fell into that category. Lucien wondered if that meant she and others like her could be brought back. The transfer of consciousness was obviously less comprehensive with them. Lucien glanced back at his daughter, Atara, and a small, desperate hope clawed inside his chest, even as a lump rose in his throat.

He looked away, back to the holoscreen, and watched as Judge Cleever was pushed into a waiting police hover car. Theola squirmed and wriggled in Lucien's arms, making a break for the floor so she could go explore. Lucien let her go this time, but kept half an eye on her to make sure she didn't do anything dangerous.

Cleever. The name rang a bell in Lucien's brain. Then he remembered why—he and Brak had seen a lookalike for her dead son, Titarus, on their stakeout at the Crack of Dawn. Lucien struggled to make a connection, but there wasn't one to be made. Even if that lookalike really was her son, somehow brought back illegally from the grave after being convicted of murder, why would the Faros bother to possess him? He was a ghost who couldn't show his face for fear of being discovered.

A ghost that might lead to Coretti? Lucien wondered. That was the connection his brain was searching for, a lead worth following. If Titarus was alive, finding him would lead straight to Joseph Coretti's illegal resurrection center, and then to Coretti himself.

"All right, you can go in now," the security guard announced, interrupting Lucien's thoughts.

Lucien cast about for Theola and found her sitting on the floor under the guard's desk, playing with a garbage can. He walked over and grabbed her by the hand to hoist her up. "Come on, Theebs." He tried to pick her up, but she insisted on walking by herself, holding his hand for support.

Lucien nodded to the security guard as they reached the entrance of Atara's room. The guard opened the door, and they walked in just as one of two probe technicians raised Atara's hover gurney to a sitting position. Her gaze found Theola, and she gave a chilling smile.

"Agaga!" Theola said, pointing to her sister as they drew near.

Lucien stopped walking before they could get within reach, but Theola tugged on his arm.

"Agaga!" she said again.

"Nice of you to visit me, *Dad,*" Atara said with a sarcastic smile.

"I don't care what you say, or how you say it, *Abaddon,* my daughter is still in there."

"I'm afraid not."

"Mind probes don't lie. They've found traces. Memories. *Thoughts.*"

"Even if you're correct," Atara said. "What makes you think I'm going to let her go? I'm in control. Not her. Your doctors already tried to bring her back. They failed. You think you can defeat me? You can't. You won't."

"You look pretty defeated from where I'm standing. Your stuck in the body of a child, locked up in the pysch ward of a hospital.

Atara laughed at that, and smiled smugly at him.

"You know something," Lucien said.

"Prove it."

The probe technicians traded glances with one another, and the detective who'd been asking Atara questions stepped forward. "You're talking like you know something." He glanced at each of the two probe technicians. "Could she be hiding something?"

They both shook their heads.

"Then what's she talking about?"

"It's a game to her," Lucien said. "She enjoys toying with us."

"Or maybe I know more about encoding memories and thoughts than you know about reading them."

This was the reason Atara had been subjected to a dozen mind probes in the past two months. She kept hinting at something she knew, some hidden knowledge that they somehow couldn't access inside her head, but each time they probed her it was the same old story.

The policeman in charge of the interrogation blew out an irritated sigh. "I still say we should beat it out of her."

Lucien turned to the man with a sharp look. "That's my daughter you're talking about. A child."

"Yeah? She doesn't sound like one to me."

Before they could argue any further, a call came in over Lucien's ARCs. It was from Tyra. He turned away to answer it.

"Tyra, how are you feeling?"

"Better, thanks. I'm on my way to the bridge."

"That's great—the bridge? They discharged you already?"

"They didn't have a choice. Duty calls."

"Right," Lucien said, frowning. In her new role as Acting Chief Councilor, Tyra had forgotten all about her promise to resign from office. She said it was just a delay, that she'd resign as soon as a new Chief was elected, but Lucien wasn't sure about that. Something occurred belatedly to him. "Why are you going to the bridge? Is something wrong?"

"No, quite the opposite. The rest of my crew is back. The survivors anyway, and they've brought a fleet of Etherian ships with them. You're one of the survivors, Lucien—you, Addy, Garek, and Brak. You might want to be there when we welcome them aboard."

Lucien shook his head slowly, his mind racing to catch up. "They brought a fleet with them?"

"About a thousand ships."

That sparked a connection in Lucien's brain. He remembered watching Chief Councilor Ellis's memories in the records room of the Res Center, hearing him talk to someone named Katawa about a lost fleet and how he was going to get it back.

"It's a trap..." Lucien whispered.

"What?" Tyra demanded. "What are you talking about?"

"The Etherian fleet. This is why Abaddon infiltrated *Astralis*. He wanted to get that fleet, and used *Astralis* as the bait!"

"How can you possibly know that?"

"Don't you remember the memories we uncovered in the records room? One of Ellis's memories was about exactly that!"

"If that's true, then there should be a Faro fleet descending on us right now, but there isn't."

No sooner had Tyra said that than emergency klaxons split the air, followed by an announcement over the ship's intercom: "Red alert! Red alert! All hands to battle stations! This is not a drill. I repeat this is not a drill. All hands to battle stations!"

"Tyra—"

"I heard it!" Tyra replied, sounding out of breath. "Get Theola someplace safe!"

Lucien glanced over his shoulder, back to Atara.

She was smiling broadly, her green eyes wide and bright with fervor. "They're here," she said.

THE STORY CONTINUES IN NOVEMBER WITH...

Dark Space Universe (Book 3)

Coming November 2017!

Get a digital copy of the book for FREE if you post an honest review of Book 2 on Amazon and send it to me by signing up here: http://files.jaspertscott.com/ds9.htm

Thank you in advance for your feedback!
I read every review and use your comments to improve my work.

KEEP IN TOUCH

SUBSCRIBE to my Mailing List and get two FREE Books!

http://files.jaspertscott.com/mailinglist.html

Follow me on Twitter:

@JasperTscott

Look me up on Facebook:

Jasper T. Scott

Check out my website:

www.JasperTscott.com

Or send me an e-mail:

JasperTscott@gmail.com

OTHER BOOKS BY JASPER SCOTT

Suggested reading order

New Frontiers Series

Excelsior (Book 1)
Mindscape (Book 2)
Exodus (Book 3)

Dark Space Series

Dark Space
Dark Space 2: The Invisible War
Dark Space 3: Origin
Dark Space 4: Revenge
Dark Space 5: Avilon
Dark Space 6: Armageddon

Dark Space Universe Series

Dark Space Universe (Book 1)
Dark Space Universe (Book 2)
Dark Space Universe (Book 3) -- *Coming November 2017*

Early Work

Escape
Mrythdom

ABOUT THE AUTHOR

Jasper Scott is a USA TODAY bestselling science fiction author, known for writing intricate plots with unexpected twists.

His books have been translated into Japanese and German and adapted for audio, with collectively over 500,000 copies purchased.

Jasper was born and raised in Canada by South African parents, with a British cultural heritage on his mother's side and German on his father's, to which he has now added Latin culture with his wonderful wife.

After spending years living as a starving artist, he finally quit his various jobs to become a full-time writer. In his spare time he enjoys reading, traveling, going to the gym, and spending time with his family.

Made in the USA
Lexington, KY
20 October 2017